She was late for w
there, but bad thin

A hand seized her right shoulder. She wrenched... ...tightened.

Fingernails dug into the hollow of her shoulder, broke through the skin. A searing sensation ripped through her flesh as a blast of hot air battered her neck. She swung her arm, whacking her attacker. But his other hand shot out, grabbed her. She spun around. His hand encircled her wrist in a vise like grip.

Pain mixed with fear. Fear she tasted in the hot, noxious bile bubbling in the back of her throat. It threatened to obstruct her windpipe. She swallowed, the fluid burning its way down to her stomach. Ducking her head, she twisted away, staggered, tripped. She was plummeting through the darkness.

He grabbed her arm, twisted, wrenched her upright. A paroxysm of pain shattered her wrist and her knees went weak. She tried to scream. Her breath froze. A strangled cry was all that came out.

His arm slid around her shoulder, pulled her backwards. She felt her feet being jerked out from under her. Powerful arms pressed her against a broad chest. She could smell the stale scent of his sweat. Her fists beat at him. His arms tightened, crushing her against him.

She opened her mouth to scream. Her cry was cut short as a damp cloth was slapped over her mouth. Her lips stung and a bitter smell made her gag. She couldn't breathe.

When she could finally open her mouth, she gasped for air and twisted violently. The cloth sucked into her mouth. A strong, sweet odor made her retch. The skin around her mouth burned. Within seconds a pleasant sensation filled her brain. Her struggling ceased.

It was several seconds before she took another breath and much longer before she moved. She didn't feel the hands that slid around her chest. She didn't feel her body being carried back through the trees. She didn't feel herself being thrown in the back of the van.

In fact, it was a long time before she felt anything.

KUDOS for *Without Consent*

Gripping terror and exploding suspense…a can't-put-it-down thriller. – *John Jeneroux…Crime Writers of Canada award winner*

A fine medical thriller. – *Lee Child, best-selling author*

When Claire is targeted by the serial killer, Gerry is determined to keep her safe. But of course, he can't. That would be too predictable. I found the story to be a fascinating, page-turning, thriller, which kept me reading long after I should have gone to bed. – *Taylor, Reviewer*

There are enough twists and turns that I had a real struggle putting the book down, even for important things like going to the bathroom. And as I said, the characterization is brilliant. A case in point is the part where the killer picks a victim on the kidney transplant list, fooled by her golden skin. He thinks it is a healthy tan, and it is really jaundice due to her shriveled kidneys. I love the way Irwin has the killer twist the situation in his mind until it is the victim's fault for being murdered. Without Consent has one of those complex plots that not only keeps you turning pages, but will make you want to read the book again and again to be sure you didn't miss anything. – *Regan, Reviewer*

She found the first victim…now she might be the next.

In South-Western Ontario a crafty, vicious psychopath is at work, excising the kidneys of the women he abducts. Doctor Claire Valincourt, recently jilted, finds his first victim and assists with the autopsy. But little does she know the killer has his sights on her, too.

Relationship-jaded Detective Gerry Rosko desperately searches for a serial killer who is on a quest of his own—the hunt for a perfect kidney for the terminally ill mother he tends. Will Rosko track him down before Claire becomes his next victim?

ACKNOWLEDGEMENTS

With every book there is a cast of characters that contribute to its making.

First to my ever-supportive writer's group, John Jeneroux, Kelley Armstrong, Pat (PA) Brown, and John Weiler. Your marked pages are always welcome. I know that a better book will come of it.

To DoctorsJane Gloor and Michael Rieder for their input on the drugs of choice.

To a great cast of readers Tina Gowing, Kim Stevens, Diana Lloyd, Sue Atchison, Karen Allen, Jackie Nestler, Karen Boyd, Erika Mirc, Nada Turudic, Claudette Foy. What amazing editing skills you have.

Wendy Olsen for her awesome design skills. She makes the best party invitations.

Brad McMillan for being a great computer go-to guy and for rescuing the manuscript when my computer got hungry and ate it.

Lee Child for his support over the years and for wonderfully endorsing my book.

Eileen Dryer for critiquing *WITHOUT CONSENT* in its early stages and her encouragement to finish it. Kelly and Kris, the PJ Parish team for their critiques of *MISSING CLAYTON* and *WITHOUT CONSENT*.

Michael Palmer for his encouragement and pitching tips.

There are many more to thank and acknowledge, but I will end with the great staff at Black Opal Books. Reyana, and Faith for being amazing editors. Jack, my great cover artist, who never objects to my requests to play with cover to get it just right. And lastly to the best editor a writer could have, Lauri.

Thank you everyone.

WITHOUT

CONSENT

Bev Irwin

A BLACK OPAL BOOKS PUBLICATION

GENRE: MYSTERY/SUSPENSE/THRILLER/ROMANTIC ELEMENTS

First Publication: JANUARY 2013

Published by Black Opal Books **http://www.blackopalbooks.com**

DEDICATION

To my brother, Doug, who passed too early. Miss you.

CHAPTER 1

The scalpel gripped securely between his fingers sent a delicious thrill up his arm. He laid the blade against her abdomen. The ease with which the razor-sharp edge sliced through the creamy white flesh triggered a response that was nearly orgasmic.

The woman's inert body jerked violently with the first slice, her face twisting into a grotesque mask of pain. He pressed on the stainless steel instrument and slid it across the taunt skin. She twitched several times, settled, then became still. The drug was working.

He inspected her naked form—so beautiful, so perfect, so calm. He studied the soft swell of her breasts. He saw no movement, but the flicker of the feather he'd taped to her mouth told him she was still breathing. He glanced at the empty syringe.

Maybe next time I'll use less.

He focused on her abdomen. Cherry bright blood oozed out of the incision. He picked a white cloth from the nearby table and wiped at the fluid. The fabric became saturated within seconds. He dropped the cloth. The smack of it hitting the cement floor ricocheted like a gunshot through the silent space.

Choosing a large towel, he draped it around the wound. Like long spider legs, blood scrambled along the towel tracing an intricate pattern on the white material. His hands trembled. Each beat of his accelerated heart rate hammered through his head.

He needed to hurry, he needed to finish before the blood stopped circulating, he needed to do this right. Sliding his hands into the incision, he felt a thrill as the heat from her body penetrated his gloves. How long would she stay warm once she'd taken her last breath?

A pool of blood filled the wound, obstructing his view. Damn. He needed to see. He pulled his hand out of the incision and used a dry corner of the towel to wipe away the fluid. The sight of so much blood sent a frigid wave sluicing down his vertebrae. He shuddered and reached for another towel. Within seconds it consumed the liquid gushing into the naked woman's abdomen.

He pitched the saturated towel over the table, grinning as it thudded on the cement floor. Dark fluid splattered in irregular shapes. He glanced at the family-sized ice filled cooler sitting a foot away. Droplets of blood showered the outer plastic and formed unique ink splat patterns. What would a psychologist make of them? His harsh laugh echoed through the room.

The ice inside the cooler glittered like a mountain of diamonds–pure and unspoiled. Expensive, but worth it, the cooler would preserve his treasure for hours. He could use it for beer later. But he couldn't think of that now. It was late, he needed to extract the organ and get it on ice before it spoiled. Then he could reward himself.

He swabbed the incision. So much blood. And the smell. He closed his eyes and inhaled letting the unique metallic odor fill him. His heart was racing so fast he could feel it pounding against his ribs. Suddenly lightheaded, he leaned into the table until the dizziness passed.

Hurry up. Get it out. Focus.

Willing his fingers to stop trembling, he forced himself to concentrate. He mopped at the pooling blood then inserted his gloved hand into the incision and probed her abdomen.

There it is. His fingers closed around the organ, so soft and slippery and warm. He lifted his hand. Resistance. Pausing, he let his fingers travel the edges of the kidney. *Gentle. You don't want to damage it.* He palpated the thin cord of vessel restraining the organ and encircled it with his index finger.

Careful. Don't be rough. You might bruise it. You know how important a good kidney is. You know what happens to the damaged ones. They can kill people, can't they?

Sweat trickled into his eyes and clouded his vision. Using the back of his hand, he wiped away the beads of perspiration coating his forehead.

A stainless steel table sheathed in a thin green towel stood beside the bed. On it, aligned in a neat row, lay several shining silver instruments. With one hand cradling his prize, he reached over and selected a fine–toothed clamp. He slid it into the incision and guided it around the organ. Snapping the tiny teeth over the vessel, he occluded the flow of blood.

He left the clamp in place and reached for the scalpel. Lifting the kidney a fraction of an inch at a time, he paused only when he felt tension on the vessel. He scrutinized the razor-sharp scalpel blade–a finely honed weapon. He had to be careful. It wouldn't do to slip and leave a trace of his own blood.

Inserting the scalpel into the gaping wound, he guided it beneath his hand. He felt the blade meet an impasse. With a swift slash he sliced through the tenuous strand. Blood spurted into the incision. Inhaling the scent, his heart skipped several beats and he became aware of the blood spurting through his own veins.

That was the artery, now for the vein.

He probed for the next vessel, clamping and cutting in a similar fashion. The cavity brimmed with blood and he couldn't see. But now, it didn't matter. He had what he wanted. He lifted his hand. He felt resistance. A thin tenuous cord stretched out of the wound. Another vein. Grasping the scalpel, he carved through the connective tissue and the organ came free. For several seconds he nestled the coveted organ as if holding a newborn robin in the palm of his hand. Its warmth seeped through his latex gloves. Below his hand, blood surged into the gaping wound.

He shot a glance at the woman's face. Mary Jane, her driver's license said. How plain. He'd call her Gabrielle. Yes, she was more beautiful than a Mary Jane. He smiled at the woman lying unconscious on the stainless steel table–her ashen cheeks exhausted of their normal rosy coloring, her lips and eyelids tinted a powder blue not derived by artificial means. Dark shadows ebbed into the fragile skin below her staring eyes. An irregular grunt of air erupted from between her lips. He had to hurry.

Should I take the time to stitch her up? Yes, finish the job properly.

Laying the organ on the bed of ice, he turned back to the woman. He ripped open a package of fine black sutures and deposited it on the sterile green towel. Attaching the suture to the needle driver, he threaded it through the mottled skin.

He worked quickly. Gabrielle wouldn't care what her scar looked like.

CHAPTER 2

Doctor Claire Valincourt's arms pumped in rhythm with the pounding of her feet. She glanced at her watch. Six-fifty-nine. Thirty-one minutes before she started her shift in the emergency room at Grace Memorial Hospital. Eight minutes to get through the park, she'd have lots of time to grab a coffee.

Running with a fierce determination, Claire kept to her usual path through Victoria Park. Today, she didn't admire the manicured gardens, the stately elms, or the soothing lines of the century homes bordering the park. Today, with her stomach wound in a series of macramé knots, she didn't give a damn about her surroundings.

Despite attempts to concentrate on the soothing thud of her runners on the pavement, fragments of her sister's conversation stuck on replay. "Well, you know you've been gone a long time…Michael got lonely…you couldn't expect him to wait forever…we didn't mean to fall in love."

Claire rounded a curve in the path. The screech of bike tires, accompanied by a tirade of curses, brought her to an abrupt halt.

"Watch where you're going, lady."

"Sorry," Claire mumbled.

She made a wide arc around the cyclist and continued along the path. The humiliation of betrayal raged through her and a tear slid down her cheek. How could he? She'd expect it from Paige, but Michael. Well, to hell with both of them. Claire used the sleeve of her cotton shirt to wipe at a tear. Where's your pride, Claire? Falling apart over a worthless man.

She saw a flash of red–a jogger. Turning her head to hide her tears, Claire focused on the flowering shrubs bordering the path. Something sticking out below a weigelia bush caught her attention, something pale and white. It looked like a foot.

I can't believe it. The park is a haven for lovers, but this is ridiculous. It's seven in the morning. Claire shook her head. You're just jealous. How long has it been?

When was the last time she'd seen Michael, or even talked to him? She'd been so busy at the hospital. Her residency finished, she'd taken extra shifts in the emergency room and the morgue to pay back her student loans. It had taken her two years, but now she could finally stop scrimping. Maybe it wasn't entirely Michael's fault, but damn him anyway. If he had to dump her, did it have to be for her sister?

Claire kept jogging. She expected to hear a chorus of giggles or intense moans. She heard neither. Not the slightest sound came from behind the branches. A chill ran down her spine and she experienced a strange sense of unease. She glanced back.

The foot was pale—pale and still. Despite the eighty plus temperatures, Claire felt as cold as if she'd walked through the doors of the hospital morgue. Hesitantly, she retraced her steps. Maybe the foot would retract into the bush, maybe she'd hear the rustle of fabric as bodies disentangled, maybe she'd hear the giggle of teenage voices. But the hammering of her heart was the only sound she heard. Reaching for the weigelia bush, she tentatively spread the fuchsia flowered boughs. Finally, another sound—a gasp, a gasp that slid hot and dry across her own lips. She stared at the ground.

A naked woman. Waxy. Pale. Still. Instinctively, Claire reached out her hand. But she knew before she touched the body what she wouldn't find—a pulse.

Still the stone cold firmness of the skin made her recoil. Claire closed her eyes. Another vision invaded her brain—her own body lying in the park behind the high school, bruised and bleeding. She'd repressed the memory, but now it was back punching her in the gut. Maybe it was a dream. A very bad dream. But when she opened her eyes, nothing had changed. The body lay on the grass like a fallen Roman statue.

Claire felt the vein at her neck twitching and felt a wave of nausea. Get hold of yourself. You're a doctor. You see dead bodies all the time. She pushed the old vision back into the recesses of her brain and forced herself to look at the body.

The woman was Caucasian, in her mid-twenties, brown hair, blue eyes. She lay on her back, her skin as pale as chalk, a bluish tinge invading the paleness. Her lips and fingertips, denied blood flow, were as white as the scales of a belly-up fish.

Claire's gaze traveled down the length of the woman's torso. A brown stain coated her skin and a fresh incision split the left side of her abdomen. Several inches in length, it had been crudely sutured together. She'd recently had surgery. Had she wandered unnoticed out of the hospital?

Claire fished her cell phone out of her backpack. Her fingers trembling, she pressed 911.

Her harsh breathing threatened to drown out the dispatcher's voice. The words tumbled out of her mouth. "I need the police, the coroner—there's a dead body."

Adrenaline raced through her body. She wanted to do something to help, but the woman was past anything Claire could do. Taking a deep breath, her professional side kicked in. She spoke calmly into the phone. "It's a woman—she's been dead a while. She's cold." Claire concentrated on the operator's question.

"Where?"

"The park. Victoria Park." The shrub-lined walkway was a blur of greens and black. What markers had she passed? She heard honking and saw ducks skimming across the surface of the man-made pond. "I'm by the pond. By the goose statue."

CHAPTER 3

The call came into the squad room at seven-twenty-three in the morning. Fifteen minutes later detective Gerry Rosko stood by the goose statue in Victoria Park. The strobe lights of police cars directed them to the site. Two officers were stretching yellow cordon tape across the entrance of the park. Others worked the crime scene—questioning bystanders, blocking the gate, controlling the spectators.

Rosko nodded to one of the uniforms. "Who was the first officer on the scene?"

"Thompson. He's over there." He pointed to a policeman standing by a clump of shrubs thirty feet from the entrance of the park. Just then, Jack Wilson, his partner, stepped over the yellow cordon tape.

Rosko grinned. "Hope I didn't disturb anything by calling you in early."

"Nothing that won't keep." Wilson winked. "What have we got?"

"A naked corpse." Rosko pointed to the bushes. "She's over there."

A mid-twenties officer stood over the body, his eyes glazed and staring. The black cover of his notebook stained from the dampness of his palm. Rosko knew it wasn't because he was sweating from the heat. It was more likely a result of finding his first body.

"You first on the scene?"

The officer jumped when Rosko spoke.

"Yes, Matt Thompson, sir." Thompson's head bobbed like a marionette.

Rosko held out a hand. "I'm Gerry Rosko, and this is Jack Wilson."

Thompson's handshake was rapid, damp, and went on too long. He took an awkward step back allowing the detectives an unobstructed view of the scene. Rosko was relieved the officer had resisted the usual first instinct to cover the body. It was bad enough what curious spectators did to a crime scene without some rookie officer contaminating it and destroying evidence.

Rosko approached the body. She lay partially hidden by the bush; face up, eyes open, staring skyward. Fear and pain etched in those sightless eyes as the last emotion endured. It was captured in the lenses like a frozen portrait—her cries for help unanswered.

Her body lay on a plastic sheet, the edges neatly tucked beneath her torso. Shoulder length brown hair, recently brushed, framed her pale face. Her intertwined hands rested in the middle of her chest as if in prayer. She almost looked as if she'd been prepped for a photo shoot. Had her body been positioned so that her right foot stuck out just far enough beyond the branches of the shrub to be visible?

His gaze moved down the body. A large brown stain coated her abdomen. In the center of the stain, its edges roughly aligned, was a recently sewn incision. He studied the stain. An attempt had been made to wipe away excess fluid before depositing her in her final resting spot.

"Hey, Wilson, doesn't that stain look like cleaning solution used in operating rooms to sterilize skin?"

Wilson nodded. "Looks like it." In a series of blinding flashes, his Polaroid captured the corpse. "She's pretty pale. The incision looks fresh, but there's not much blood. Looks like she died elsewhere then was dumped here."

Rosko scanned the area. The high temperatures of the past weeks had baked the ground too solid for a good set of footprints. Any hint of morning dew had burned off an hour ago. The blades of grass looked even and undisturbed—no matting, no evidence of dragged twigs, no broken brush. The road was thirty feet away. "Whoever did this had to be strong, strong enough to carry her a good distance," he said. "There's no drag marks."

"What type of person are we dealing with?" Wilson shook his head. "Wraps her in plastic, dumps her, then takes the time to pose her. Looks like he's folded her hands in prayer."

Rosko nodded in response to the gravely drawl of his partner. Was there some significance in the precise arrangement? He turned to Wilson. "Check with the guys at the gate. See if anyone saw something." He gestured toward Thompson standing five feet away. His shoulders stiff, his arms folded across his chest, he remained on guard. "I'll see what he's got."

The Crime Scene Unit arrived. Technicians in white overalls began working like a well-oiled machine, each one with a job to do. They took pictures, dusted for prints, collected samples of whatever the surrounding area had to offer.

Rosko crossed to Thompson. "Tell me about the person who found the body."

"A doctor from Grace Memorial." He looked at his notes. "Doctor Claire Valincourt." He glanced at the ground then back at Rosko. "Sorry sir, I couldn't make her stay. She insisted she had to be on duty. Said she didn't know anything. Just saw the body and called 911. She waited around for a bit. Said she'd answer any more questions at work."

"Did you see any ID?"

His shoulders relaxed as if a yoke had been lifted and his breath exhaled in an audible sigh. "I saw her hospital ID and her driver's license." His facial muscles relaxed apparently pleased he'd done something right. "I've got the numbers right here," he said, flipping through his notebook.

"I'll get them later. Go see what the hell's taking the coroner so long. I want to get the body out of here before the whole city shows up."

Thompson nodded and hurried away. It was early but the media was already gathering—crowding the yellow cordon tape, flashing cameras, pressing microphones into the faces of spectators thronging the park's entrance. Rosko noted the lanky form of Wilson bent toward one of the reporters—Sherry Simmons.

He wasn't surprised to see her—irritated, yes, but not surprised. Sherry worked for Channel 9 News. An elegant brunette who had come to Strathburn with a suitcase jam-packed with big dreams and bigger schemes. Rosko knew. He'd found out the hard way. Now he wanted her out of his life, professionally and personally.

Sherry looked his way and her hand raised in a wave. He turned back to the body. The technicians were still photographing the crime scene. One of them used tweezers to pick up minute samples from around the body. He placed each bit of evidence into a separate bag. Rosko watched them until his partner returned.

"Well," Rosko snapped. "What did you find out?"

Wilson raised an eyebrow at his partner's tone. "About the dead lady—or the gorgeous live one over there?" He gestured behind him.

Sherry waved again. With a curt nod, Rosko turned back to Wilson.

Wilson gave him a mock punch in the shoulder. "Why she carries a torch for you, I'll never know."

"Damn right you won't. And you should stay away from her, too, if you know what's good for you. That cat's got claws."

"Is that what happened? I thought I saw some incriminating marks on your back last time we played squash."

"Screw off, Wilson. Just keep her away from me." He shook his head. "Did you find anything out about the victim?"

"Nothing. Nobody saw anything. Nobody heard anything. Typical."

Footsteps sounded behind them. Coroner Kim Lee had arrived.

"Well, Lee, nice of you to finally join us." Rosko's words belied his tone.

"Your bodies aren't the only business I get."

Lee's face contorted into a crooked grin. It was rumored he'd been in an accident as a child that damaged the muscles on the right side of his face. His rotund cheeks remained in a perpetual frown. In his line of business, that might be a bonus. From his end of police work there wasn't much to smile at.

Lee set his battered leather medical bag beside the body. He bent, not touching, merely observing.

"Well, Lee, what do you think?" Rosko asked.

"I think we got a dead body, female."

"You don't say. And what might our body have died of?"

"From the look of her, I'd say shock, hemorrhagic shock, from blood loss."

"There's no blood on the body, even by the slash on her abdomen." Rosko glanced at the body, then back at the coroner. His brows raised in a question.

"Ah, yes." Lee grinned. The left side of his mouth curved upward, the right side remained immobile, creating a grotesque grimace. "The case of the bloodless body." The curve extended along the left side of his face and his eyes twinkled. "Always a Perry Mason fan."

"While you guys discuss the oldies, I'm going to see if the uniforms have turned up anything useful." Wilson headed toward the south entrance of the park.

Pulling on a pair of non-latex gloves, Lee began examining the victim. He checked her eyes, turned her head slightly to check both ears, probed her mouth. Starting at her neck and working his way down, Lee pressed his fingertips into various spots on her body. Rosko stood silently by. He turned away when the coroner checked her liver temperature. Lee jotted the numbers in a small black notebook.

Rosko didn't speak until Lee stood. "Well, what can you tell me?"

"Looks like traumatic shock from blood loss. Don't know where from yet."

Rosko pointed to her abdomen. 'Wouldn't it be from the wound?"

"Someone's done a hack up job on her, but the incision alone wouldn't account for the dramatic blood loss she's had. Have to wait for the autopsy." Lee grinned again. "But she didn't die here. And—" He paused. "Her blood drained out before she was dumped."

"What?" Thompson stood behind Rosko. His eyes brimmed with questions.

"We have an eager one here, do we?" Lee asked.

"He let her bleed out somewhere else. Then he dumped her," Rosko explained to Thompson.

Lee knelt beside the body and motioned Thompson to join him. He lifted the woman's underarm and pointed to the skin. "See the difference in color?"

Thompson stared at the area. "The skin closer to the ground looks darker than the skin at the top."

Lee nodded his head. "Good, good. He's smarter than he looks."

"How does that subtle change tell you the body was moved?" Thompson asked.

"When a person dies, the blood stops flowing, and gravity takes over. The blood drains to the lowest point and gets trapped in the vessels where it congeals. That produces the darker blush line you see on corpses. Now our lovely lady here doesn't have real distinctive lines. That's because most of her blood drained out before it had a chance to congeal."

"So the question is: where is her drained blood," Rosko stated.

"Where, is up to you to find out," Lee said. "You're the cop. I can only tell you she wasn't killed here. The technicians will check for occult blood on the ground, but I doubt they'll find much of anything. Now, wherever she was killed, that's where you'll find a mess of blood."

"Can you give us an idea of when our lady died?"

"From her temperature and the lividity of the body…" He reached down and pressed a finger into the woman's naked thigh. Rosko watched the skin around his fingertip. A depression remained when Lee took his hand away. "I'd say about one or two in the morning. I'll let you know more later."

"Any idea of what time later?" Rosko asked.

"The way you guys keep me running it should be a couple of weeks." The left side of Lee's mouth twitched as he grinned at Rosko's glaring face. He shrugged. "I'll get you a preliminary this afternoon, and a final one, hopefully by tomorrow. The boys are going to take her to Grace Memorial. Doctor MacFarlane will do the autopsy."

"Get us what you can as soon as possible. We don't have a clue who she is. We need to identify her and let the family know. Hate to have them find out on the six o'clock news."

Lee nodded. "As soon as I have anything, I'll let you know. But you could start looking for a van."

"A van?" Rosko asked.

"Your body has track marks down her butt."

Lee knelt beside the body and tipped her on her side. Rosko saw the distinct pattern of angled ridges traversing the woman's back and lower torso. A technician took the opportunity to snap several photos.

"A car mat?" Rosko asked.

"From the tread, I'd say a van mat. MacFarlane can make an impression when he does the autopsy."

Gesturing to the technicians that he was finished, Lee gathered up his leather satchel. He pushed past the reporters mobbing him and hurried to his black SUV.

Wilson had organized a search of the surrounding area. He jerked his thumb toward the retreating coroner. "How come he only talks to you?"

"Lee doesn't trust many people. Just says what he has to. Not like some people I know."

Wilson grinned. "Are you saying my chattering drives you around the bend?"

"There are times, Wilson. There are times."

The sound of rustling plastic drew his attention. Technicians were unfolding a large white sheet and laying it alongside the body. Two attendants waited with a stretcher. Together they slid the corpse into the body bag and onto the stretcher. The detectives followed as the trolley rattled away with its lifeless package. Rosko wasn't deeply religious, yet he said a silent prayer for the woman.

Technicians remained at the site collecting evidence where the corpse had lain. Others searched the surrounding area—more camera flashes, more evidence bags filled with clumps of earth, blades of grass, discarded gum wrappers, cigarette butts—anything that might give a clue to the identity of the woman, or her killer.

Rosko hoped they'd find a good set of fingerprints to match ones on file. Then they'd know who their killer was. If they were lucky, they might even have a current address. They could just drive over to the perp's house, pick him up, and have a signed confession by nightfall.

But Rosko suspected this one wasn't going to be quite so easy. The way the killer had positioned his victim spoke of someone who paid attention to detail. He wasn't likely to fold her arms just so across her chest, align her legs carefully with just one foot protruding beyond the cover of the bush, and then carelessly drop a gum wrapper or cigarette butt for the police to lift a print or DNA from.

No, this was going to be a tough case. Rosko could feel it in his gut.

CHAPTER 4

Claire pushed through the double glass doors of the emergency department of Grace Memorial Hospital. Her heart still pounded. What was wrong with her? She'd seen more grotesque things working in the emergency room—car accidents, traumas, beatings, stabbings, abuse. She'd seen it all, yet she couldn't let go of the image of the woman in the park. She told herself it was just another dead body.

But, it's not. You've never been personally involved before, never found a body, never been the one to call 911. The bodies always come to you.

She shook her head but another image flashed in front of her. She saw long brown hair, hair so much like her own, spread in a halo around a blood-drained face. Then the face became hers. A shudder went through her and she wiped a tear away.

Nurses gathered at the station for shift change, but afraid to trust her voice, Claire nodded and hurried past. The night physician, Doug Murphy, leaned against the office door. He glanced at his watch. Claire smiled apologetically. "Sorry I'm late." She swept past him into the physician's office. Focusing her attention on the patient information board, she listened while he gave a quick report of patients in the department. She felt his gaze on her.

"Are you okay, Claire? You look like hell."

"Thanks, Doug. You're such a charmer."

"Sorry, but you look like you didn't get any sleep last night." His eyebrows rose. "Did Michael come into town?

"Stay out of my private life."

Doug's head snapped back as if she'd slapped him in the face.

She sighed and tried to form her stiff lips into an apology. "Sorry. I didn't sleep well." She hesitated. "There was a woman murdered in the park."

"Sorry, Claire. Did you see her?"

She nodded. "I found her."

"Are you sure you're okay? It's not quite the same thing running into death on the streets as it is dealing with it here."

"I'll be fine. I just need to keep busy."

"Are you're sure?" He paused, his hand on his briefcase. When she nodded, he shrugged. "See you tomorrow morning then."

Claire reviewed the patient's charts then made her rounds. She checked Mr. Kelly's x-rays and sent him for an abdominal ultrasound. She checked the urinalysis on Mrs. Johnston and discharged her with a prescription for a bladder infection.

The humidity that had descended on the city in the past four days was creating havoc with people's breathing. At present, there were three patients in the department whose asthma was acting up. Claire examined them, ordering a Ventolin treatment for each.

For the next hour Claire kept busy dealing with the existing patients and several new ones. She'd just finished reinforcing a cast on a patient in the fracture room and was coming along the back corridor when she heard the whoosh of doors sliding open. Glancing toward the sound, Claire saw the covered stretcher rattling its way to the morgue. Her heart racing, she hurried back to the office and sipped her lukewarm coffee. When would the detectives come and question her? She didn't know anything. As if on cue, the phone's ringing interrupted her thoughts.

"Claire, there's a Detective Rosko here to see you," Betty Hammond the charge nurse informed her.

"I'll be right there." She took another sip of her coffee before leaving the office.

A man in a charcoal business suit leaned casually against the counter of the nurse's station talking to Betty. He was tall, at least six-foot-two. He turned at her approach. "Doctor Valincourt?" He extended his hand. "Detective Rosko."

With his tailored suit and gleaming leather shoes, Detective Rosko looked more like a drug salesman or a businessman than a policeman. She couldn't help noticing how nicely he filled out the fine linen suit. He smiled and Claire wondered if the lines around his eyes were from laughter or worry.

Intense blue eyes examined her. Was he gauging how she'd held up after her morning's discovery? The hand he offered was firm, the grasp solid. She released her hand but with the contact broken she felt a vague sense of loss. Something her father said came back to her, "You can tell a lot about a man by his shoes and his handshake." What would Dad say about this man?

The detective's voice interrupted her thoughts. "How are you doing?"

"Fine." Claire heard the shortness in her tone and saw an eyebrow rise as if he doubted her. "You have some questions for me?"

"I know you told the officer everything but I'd like to go over things in case there's something else you remember. Is there somewhere we can talk?"

"Page me if you need me," Claire told Betty before turning back to the detective. "We can go to the cafeteria, if that's okay with you. It's not busy now."

They took the elevator to the third floor. "Let's sit over there where we can talk without being interrupted, or overheard." He pointed to a corner table. "Coffee? I know I could drink a pot full."

"Please."

She sat at the table while the detective ordered their coffees and noted the breadth of his shoulders and the snug cut of the tailored suit. Someone had good taste. Was it him? Or did his wife buy his clothes? Claire bet on the second option. He was too attractive not to have someone in his life.

Claire looked out the window. What's wrong with you? You've just been dumped by Michael. How can you even think about men? Anger flared again at her sister's betrayal. Absorbed in her thoughts, Claire jumped when Rosko set their coffees on the table.

He sat across from her and placed a notebook and pen on the table. Running his fingers through his hair, he exposed several strands of gray previously concealed in the thick blackness.

"What happened to that woman?" Claire asked. "It looked like she'd had recent surgery but I don't know any doctor who'd do such a poor suturing job. And patients don't just walk out of the hospital naked."

"We don't know what happened." His faced tightened. "We don't even know who she is."

Claire thought of some poor family receiving this type of news and slumped in the chair.

"Tell me what you remember about this morning," Rosko said.

Claire listed what she remembered—finding the body, the cyclist she'd nearly run into, the jogger. "They were Caucasian, both in their late twenties or early thirties."

"Anything else?"

She shrugged a shoulder.

"What time were you in the park?"

"About five to seven. I remember looking at my watch and thinking I had half an hour before my shift started."

"Did you speak to anyone?"

"No." She paused. "Well, I said sorry to the guy on the bike. I wasn't watching, almost ran into him."

"Anything distinctive about the bike?"

Claire shook her head.

"Just try. Sometimes the littlest things are important." He spoke in a rich soothing baritone. "And sometimes, one detail leads to another." He laid his pen on the table, sat back in the chair, and sipped his coffee. He looked as if he had all the time in the world, not like a detective with a murder to solve.

Was he putting her at ease so she could recall more details? She thought of the baby shower game with a platter of objects you had a minute to memorize. She hated the game, but she closed her eyes and pictured the park. She saw the naked body, a flash of red, the jogger in red shorts and sleeveless top. She tried, but saw nothing more. Then the squeal of tires and the gleam of blue metal flashed in front of her.

"It was a mountain bike. Blue."

"What about the cyclist? Was he wearing a jacket?"

Claire closed her eyes again. "No. Blue jeans and a white T-shirt, the sleeves rolled up, and a package of cigarettes shoved in the fold."

"Good. Anything else?"

She tried to remember more details. "Brown hair. About six foot." Claire closed her eyes but nothing more came. When she opened her eyes again, he was nodding at her.

"Now, what about the jogger?"

Claire saw the flash of the jogger's red outfit. "He was wearing a suit, matching top and shorts. He looked fit."

"What color was his hair?"

"Brown, I think. I was looking away from him."

Rosko raised an eyebrow.

"I was upset. I didn't want anyone to notice." Claire shrugged and glanced out the window. But even with her face turned she felt the intensity of his gaze. "A family matter."

"That's good for now. If you remember something later, here's my card." He slid it across the table. "It has my number at the station and my pager. Call if you remember anything, no matter how insignificant."

Claire glanced at the card before sliding it into her pocket. Picking up her coffee, she took a sip. It was lukewarm and she pushed it away. "I should get back to work."

"I need you to come to the station to make a formal statement. Would tomorrow morning at ten-thirty be okay?"

"That's fine."

They walked to the elevator. At the first floor, he reminded her to call if she thought of anything. His gaze was direct and she found it difficult to look away. His brow wrinkled. "How are you doing?"

Could he see right through her? Claire shrugged, and forced a smile. "I'm okay. It's not the first dead body I've seen." She turned to go but his words stopped her.

"Just because you're a doctor doesn't make it easier. This senseless killing, the horror, it never gets easier. You just learn to hide it better."

The soft melodious tone of his voice surprised her as much as his words. Their eyes met and locked. "I thought I'd be able to handle it better, especially with everything I see here."

"It's different. Here you have immunity. The patients and their injuries are abstract. You treat their symptoms. It's not personal. What you saw today was. The sight of that woman will haunt you for a long time."

She shook her head, but she knew he was right. When patients came to the emergency room, you repaired their injuries, then sent them home or admitted them. Then there were the ones you fought to save—doing everything you could to resuscitate them, working for hours sometimes, eventually having to tell the family you'd been unsuccessful. Though emotionally draining at the time, you didn't know them long enough to develop a bond. You helped the families deal with their pain and suffering, then they, too, were gone from your life.

The young dark-haired woman's image flashed in front of her. The detective watched her as if he knew. He reached out a hand. Like an electric charge, his warmth and strength surged through her.

"Don't refuse to talk to a crisis counselor. One will be calling you. We can't be strong all the time."

Claire nodded. But today's body in the park wasn't the only vision that haunted her.

CHAPTER 5

Rosko and Wilson worked their way in a perimeter around Victoria Park. A troop of uniforms knocked on doors, talked to pedestrians, checked every garbage can and dumpster in the area.

They showed a picture of the victim. "Ever seen this woman? Did you see her last night? Did you see anything odd last night? Anything at all? A person who looked out of place? A car that looked odd? Circling the park, maybe? Idling by the curb? And what were you doing last night around two in the morning?"

Wilson had supervised the canvas while Rosko interviewed Doctor Valincourt. They gave the uniforms strict orders to call if they caught even a nibble of a lead. So far they hadn't gotten much. One citizen reported a suspicious person lurking in the park about eight in the evening, female, pushing a stroller with a crying baby. Another saw a couple of teenagers hanging around the washrooms.

"And that," Wilson told Rosko. "If you can believe it, is the best I've got. The uniforms haven't even turned up anyone who was awake at two a.m. let alone near the park after midnight."

"Anyone recognize the Polaroid? Rosko asked.

Wilson shook his head. "Surprise, surprise, nobody saw or heard anything. Let's hope the medical examiner can identify her. It would make our job easier. Did the doc have anything helpful?"

"Not really. She saw a guy on a bike, and a jogger. Both Caucasian, both brown hair, late twenties, or early thirties. Pretty nondescript. And they probably have nothing to do with the murder. She's coming to the station tomorrow to look at mug shots. Maybe—" Rosko's laugh was brittle. "—just maybe, we'll find our guy before then."

"Let's hope he's stuck to his own neighborhood," Wilson said.

They turned west on Gerrard Street, the border of the park farthest from where the body had been found. It divided the old section of town from the newer, more expensive homes at the north end of the park. The area had once been a thriving metropolis, but the convenience of shopping malls and super stores had left many of the family owned businesses to eke out a meager existence. No longer fashionable, the area had deteriorated as young people moved to better parts of town, leaving behind the aging, the poorly paid, and the unemployed. The proprietors had neither the ability, the money, nor the desire to keep up appearances.

Most of the businesses had walk-up apartments where the shopkeepers lived themselves or rented to tenants unable to afford the fancy new high rises. The smell of old wood, stale smoke, and decay permeated the area. Old bricks had faded, their mortar languidly flaking away. Wood surfaces forced to weather the elements had bleached to a dismal gray. Layers of paint, chipped and peeling, barely hid the signs of wood-rot.

The day was already simmering and Rosko felt the humidity seeping through his lightweight linen suit. Just what he needed—pounding the pavement on a street packed with two and three story walk-ups. He wiped his brow with a handkerchief. He could skip the gym today.

Wilson entered the first of the row of businesses. Rosko crossed the street. A variety store and an old butcher shop tried to hold up an air of respectability, but they were being squeezed out by scruffier establishments—a pawn shop, a tattoo parlor, a pool hall, and a couple of vacancies.

No one was happy to see Rosko. At the apartment above the Blue Dragon Tattoo Parlor an unshaven man in a grimy undershirt opened the door, caught a glimpse of Rosko's badge, and slammed the door. For good measure, he threw the deadbolt, but not before a cloud of marijuana billowed into the hall.

Rosko knocked again.

The man shouted through the door. "Go away."

"I'm investigating a murder," Rosko shouted back.

"Go away. You got no warrant."

"Look," Rosko said. "I'm not with narcotics. I don't care what you're doing in there, but you've got till the count of three to open this door and start answering my questions."

"And if I don't?"

"I kick your door down, arrest you for possession, obstructing justice, and resisting arrest."

"Oh, shit," the man muttered, but he opened the door.

Jonathan Delaware didn't recognize the photo, and Rosko learned nothing from questioning him.

"Sorry, man. I'd like to help you out here, but I passed out last night, like about one. And you know, I wasn't looking out my window anyway."

Three long nails held a navy wool blanket over the only window in the room. Rosko inched the blanket back. Only a narrow slit of the street below was visible. He let the curtain drop. The sweet smell of dope, and the stale smell of smoke, emanated from its lopsided folds. Rosko gave Delaware his card, as he had with everyone else he'd interviewed, and told him to call if he thought of anything that might help.

"You really not going to bust me?" Delaware asked.

"Not unless you murdered someone," Rosko said.

The next building, an empty storefront, wasn't empty after all. A Help Wanted sign hung on the door, and though the windows were smeared with soap, inside Rosko made out the shadowy shape of a man sitting behind a desk. Rosko tapped on the door and stuck his head in.

"You looking for work?"

"Afraid not." Rosko held up his badge. The man went deathly pale, but Rosko had been a cop long enough to know such reactions often meant nothing. All sorts of innocent people immediately started feeling guilty when confronted by a policeman. It was the civilians who showed guilt, not the criminals. Rosko ignored the response and gave his usual spiel.

Joe Duncan, an oversized Elton John, had broad shoulders, massive biceps, and deeply-tanned, hairy arms supporting the Darwin theory. His hair—an improbable orange-blond—had silver frosting combed through it. The beard he'd worked to a careful point matched the hair on his head. A white double-breasted suit jacket, with lapels as wide as wings, sat over an empty chair. But it was his glasses that suggested the Elton John comparison: oversized, with pink frames and lilac tinted lenses.

Elton was converting the empty storefront into a woman's clothing store.

"Bastard contractor hasn't shown up yet." He gestured at the bare walls and exposed wiring. "My business plan has me opening in two weeks. Can you frigging believe it?"

Rosko shook his head in sympathy and showed Elton the photo again. "You sure you've never seen her? Maybe walking past? Or maybe she applied for a job?"

Elton studied the picture. A tear glistened in his eye. "You say she was murdered?"

Rosko nodded.

"Wish I could help you," the man said. "I truly wish I could."

Rosko handed Elton his card and continued down the street.

The doorbell chimed as Rosko walked through the front door of the butcher shop. The dark-haired man behind the counter glanced up. Rosko didn't have to show his badge. The man knew he was a cop. It was hard for anybody in the vicinity not to know. The police had been canvassing the street all morning. Rosko nodded a greeting as he approached the counter.

The tall lanky man in his late twenties was cutting a large shank of ham with an electric slicer. Abruptly, he looked back at the machine and the large pile of meat accumulating on a stainless steel tray. Rosko wondered if the man's face had gone a few shades paler. And, was that a twitch in the muscles by his left eye? Nerves, or did he have something to hide?

There was only one customer in the store, an elderly lady who stood peering through the clouded glass display case. Despite the heat, she wore an ankle-length gingham housedress under a thick navy cardigan. She turned around. Birdlike eyes squinted at him. A quick measure taken, she turned her attention back to the slicing of her ham. This newcomer was obviously not a threat to her position in line.

Rosko waited. He had no problem seeing over her mop of tight silver curls. The butcher continued slicing the dwindling shank. Not until the ham was totally sliced did he flip off the machine. The blade whirred to a halt. Putting a piece of wax paper on the scale, he placed a few of the slices of ham on top.

"Oh Jefferson, that's not enough."

He added a couple of slices. "Will this be enough?"

"Oh, more than that."

He placed several more slices on the scale. "Is this enough, Mrs. Butterworth?"

"Way too much, Jefferson." Her voice was shrill. "Take some away. Your prices these days—rob a person blind."

Rosko saw the muscles in the butcher's face tense. His teeth clenched as if biting back a retort.

"I'll throw in the last few slices, Mrs. Butterworth."

"Thank you, Jefferson."

The butcher took the bill she handed him, and gave her change. His fingers shook as the till clanged shut. Rosko knew the butcher could feel his eyes on him and watched as the man slowly lifted his head.

Meeting his gaze, the butcher asked. "Can I help you, sir?"

"I'm Detective Rosko." There was a flash of a gold badge. "We're investigating a murder."

"Round here?"

"Oh, Jefferson, you must know about the woman they found in the park this morning." Mrs. Butterworth shook her head. "Some days, young man, I don't think you listen to a word anybody says." She turned on Rosko. "And you police. In my day it was safe to walk the streets. Never had to lock your doors. What's the world coming to?"

"Sorry, ma'am. We do try," Rosko said. "Did either of you see or hear anything about what happened in the park last night?"

"I certainly didn't. I was in my apartment, with my doors locked, and in bed by nine." Mrs. Butterworth stood to her full five-foot-one-inch height. Her eyes blazed. "And if the police did their job, things like this wouldn't happen." Clutching her purchase like a shield, she stormed out of the shop.

Jefferson rolled his eyes. "The old bat."

The men shared a grin as the door closed. Rosko took out his notebook.

"So, Jefferson, your last name would be?"

"Powalski. Like the sign says."

"Is this your shop?" Rosko asked.

"Yeah, family business. My father started it thirty years ago."

"Do you live around here?"

"Up there." Powalski used the tip of a butcher knife to indicate the apartments above the shop. "So, somebody got murdered in the park?"

"Yes." Rosko showed him the Polaroid. "Does she look familiar?"

"No." The muscle by his left eye twitched. "Can't say she does." The muscle twitched again yet he maintained eye contact.

"Do you go through the park?" Rosko asked.

"Sometimes."

"What about this morning?"

"Yeah, but I didn't see anything."

"And what time were you in the park?"

He shrugged his lean, broad shoulders. "About seven."

"Were you jogging, or riding a bike?"

"Just walking."

"Did you see anything?"

Powalski shrugged again. "Nothing out of the ordinary."

"Nothing?" Rosko asked.

"Nope."

"Here's my card. Just in case you remember something."

They locked eyes for several seconds. Powalski's hands were planted palm down on the counter. Rosko noticed a slight tremor. Lucky he wasn't using the meat slicer now, he might lose a finger or two.

"You'll let me know if you think of anything?"

"Sure."

Rosko stepped back onto the sidewalk just as Wilson was crossing the street. "Anything?" Wilson asked.

"Nothing."

The next few stores were the same. The woman in the B&E Variety spoke little English. From what they gathered from her shaking head, she hadn't seen anything either. The only thing they got out of The Sweet Shop was hunger pangs from the enticing aroma of freshly baked goods. Wilson and Rosko agreed they made the best cinnamon rolls in town. They were licking the last traces of the icing off their fingers when they reached the end of the block and the last two businesses, a pawnshop and a garage. Wilson took the pawnshop.

Lenny's had the typical poster board sign over its door, and an assortment of vehicles in various levels of disrepair sitting out front. A few of them had For Sale signs on the windshields. Advertisements for Pennzoil, and Michelin, because so much is riding on your tires, covered portions of a grime-laden front window.

A bell jangled as Rosko entered. A blast of hot air, heavy with the toxic stench of gasoline, oil, and sweat hit him and he almost took a step back. Beyond the office were three bays, each with cars parked in them. A mechanic in his late fifties looked up from under the hood of a silver Mustang.

Grease-coated hands set a wrench and screwdriver down on a vinyl tool blanket and their owner shuffled his short, pudgy body toward him. Lenny was stitched in large black script across the pocket of his oil-stained coveralls. He ran a hand through the remnants of graying hair combed in streaks across his glossy skull.

"You got a car you need looked at?"

Rosko flashed his badge.

"Hey, Lenny's is a clean shop. I don't want no trouble."

"We're investigating a murder."

"I know nothing about a murder."

"Have you seen this woman?" Rosko held the Polaroid in front of him.

"Nope. Like I said, I don't know nothing about anybody getting killed."

A clang echoed through the shop. Rosko turned to see another mechanic locking the side door of a white van parked a few feet beyond the open bay doors. The man glanced at them then strode back to the third bay where a brown Honda sat six feet in the air. He grabbed an air gun and popped lug nuts off the wheels.

Rosko took the photo and walked over. The tattooed mechanic kept his back to the detective, continuing to extract the lug nuts. He was tall, with a crop of scraggly, dark-brown hair. He wore similar coveralls, his sleeves rolled up to his armpits revealing biceps to make a weight lifter proud. A cobra, its eyes glowing like rubies, coiled up his left upper arm. Rosko saw his shoulders stiffen as he shoved the picture in the man's face.

Mark, or so his uniform said, gripped the air gun like a machine gun. He inched it to waist level, and turned toward the detective. Their eyes locked.

"Never seen her," he growled.

"Look at her picture." Rosko ordered.

"Never seen her!"

Rosko turned away. He was too tired for this shit. If this hoodlum had anything to do with their murder, he wouldn't be hard to convict. He probably had a record as long as his tattooed arm. He'd check him out as soon as he got back to the station.

"Thanks for your help, Mark." Rosko's sarcastic tone got lost in the pop, pop, pop of the air gun. On the street, he met up with Wilson. His luck had been no better.

Rosko hoped the uniforms had come up with something. The first twenty-four hours were critical. After that, memories became hazy, trace evidence got crushed into the ground, the trail grew cold. Interviewing had to be done as soon as possible. Maybe somebody besides Doctor Valincourt had seen something worth noting. Rosko sure hoped so.

Most murder cases solved themselves. Uniformed officers answered a "Shots Fired" to find the perpetrator standing over the victim with a smoking gun in his hand, babbling out excuses. Actual mysteries, who-done-its, were rare. And they usually more or less solved themselves. You just had to figure out who benefited from the murder and you had your perpetrator. Find out who had the best motive, or the most to lose. The tricky part was finding the evidence to prove it.

But this case looked different. The way the victim was left, displayed in a public park, made Rosko wonder about the killer. Maybe the murderer was trying to be clever, trying to make it look like some psychotic killer. Rosko wanted to know the motive, without that, the case became a whole lot harder to solve. And that's exactly what he would do, as soon as he found out who the victim was. If it turned out she left behind a big estate, he might have his reason right there.

In the meantime, they needed to canvass the neighborhood. Maybe, the park had some special significance for the killer. Maybe he was there every day feeding the pigeons or tending the public garden. Perhaps he lived in sight of the park or worked close by.

Sooner, or later, they'd identify their Jane Doe, and sooner or later, they'd catch her killer. Just let it be sooner.

CHAPTER 6

It was quiet when Claire got back to the emergency department, and she decided to do some investigating of her own. She rode the elevator to the basement and walked along to the end of the hall. The Authorized Personnel Only sign didn't stop her from pushing through the double metal doors. Doctor MacFarlane sat behind his desk looking through an open folder. His large body had once been firm and muscular from an obsession with bodybuilding. But several injuries curbed his weight-lifting activities. Over the years, the muscle had turned to a plumpness he carried with a rare sense of detachment. He glanced up as she entered.

"Hey, Claire. Heard you had a bit of excitement on your way to work today."

Mac's deep Scottish brogue hadn't diminished over the years. In fact, it intensified when he became angry or excited, which Claire was relieved to admit didn't happen often. She didn't think him typical of his heritage. His sense of humor belied the stereotype of the dour Scotsman. It was amazing that as a coroner he'd been able to maintain an optimistic outlook on life. He greeted her with a lopsided grin and Claire couldn't help smiling back.

"Definitely not how I thought my morning would start," Claire admitted. "I thought I'd at least get to work before I had to deal with dead bodies." She tried to laugh at her off-color humor, but her voice held a harsh shrillness.

"It's not quite the same when we have to deal with it outside of our detached environment." His face became serious. "How are you doing?"

"You know, Mac, it's bothering me more than I'd have thought. I keep seeing her lying there in the park. Like a bad dream."

He nodded. "It will hit you. Maybe later today, maybe tomorrow when you're home alone, or maybe next week when you're driving in your car. Don't feel too proud to find somebody to talk to. We aren't meant to find bodies in our normal lives."

"I'll keep that in mind," she promised. "Have you had a chance to look at her yet?"

"She's on table five."

Automatically, Claire's gaze went to the row of gleaming stainless steel stretchers. Number five was less than ten feet away. The white plastic shroud covering the form didn't prevent Claire from seeing the face below. A mirage of blood, seeping through the sheet and dripping onto the ceramic flooring, flashed in front of her. She reached for the back of a chair, her white knuckles clenching the wood. Mac's lilting brogue brought her back to reality.

"I've got a couple of jobs to finish off before I get to her. We're shorthanded this week. Probably won't be till three-thirty or four. Want to assist?"

Would it be better to put the whole thing out of her mind, or would it help her detach if she saw the girl as merely another patient who'd sustained a violent end? Mac raised a bushy eyebrow and Claire considered the wisdom of her choice. Before she realized it, she'd blurted out. "My shift is over at three-thirty. I'll see you then."

"Good. I'll have coffee on."

Claire wasn't sure how coffee would taste mixed with the overpowering scent of formaldehyde and antiseptic that permeated the room, but she needed to know what happened to the girl. Whether the girl had died out of hospital or not, she'd become one of her patients.

☙❧

The day dragged. Claire checked the clock every fifteen minutes. Finally, the hands made it to the three just as Doctor Evans walked into the department. She tasted blood and looked at her nails. She'd bitten them to the quick. Hadn't she'd gotten over that bad habit years ago?

A quick report to Evans then Claire headed down the winding hospital corridors to the morgue. Was she ready for this?

Not letting herself answer that question, she pushed through the double doors. Mac stood by table five. He'd removed his lab coat revealing operating room greens, with matching boots and cap. He glanced up as she came into the room.

"Hi, Claire. Want coffee now, or do the autopsy first?"

She glanced at the table. Her body trembled and her stomach lurched at the thought of coffee. Get hold of yourself. You're acting like this is the first autopsy you've seen. "Let's have the coffee after."

"Sure."

Claire leaned against the counter and gathered her strength. Thankfully, Mac was too busy setting up a tray of stainless steel instruments to notice. This isn't personal. Just because you were the one to find her, it shouldn't turn your brain to mush.

Maurice Kaufman, the morgue technician, handed her an operating room gown, boots, and cap. When she had the greens on, he opened up a pair of non-latex gloves and waited while she slid her hands into them. A pair of thick plastic safety glasses with face shield came next. Once her protective clothing was on, Claire crossed to stand beside Mac.

"I've already got her weight, taken swabs, blood, and done x-rays," Mac informed her. "I checked under her nails—nothing, no sign of struggle. She's got some redness by her mouth. Probably burn marks from being sedated with chloroform. She's got some blisters in her mouth substantiating that."

"Toxicology will show the chloroform?" Claire asked.

"Yup. We'll take some tissue specimens, too. Ready to get started?"

Claire nodded. She focused on the naked female lying on the metal gurney. The dark-brown hair lying loose around the woman's face added to the pallor of her skin. High wattage examination lights cast a harsh illumination. In death, the body was stark white, tinged with shaded layers of blue and purple. Bruises were visible on her arms, thighs, and around her neck. The eyes, closed postmortem, had eased open to reveal a glacial blueness. A shiver rippled down Claire's spine. In life, she'd been pretty, in death, she'd become a grotesque sight. Claire's gaze slid down to the woman's torso. There she could be detached and professional.

The torso could belong to anyone. It had none of the distinguishing features that made up one's character. Here there was no suggestion of what might have been an engaging smile or twinkling eyes—no sign of the personality ripped away with one brutal act. It was only a broad expanse of skin. Claire kept her focus on that stretch of skin while Mac made the first incision.

He slid the scalpel in a neat vertical line from the tip of the woman's sternum to her pubic bone. The blade sliced easily through the brown stain and through the incision. The pale skin eased apart. There was no sign of blood until the killer's incision was transected.

Only then did thick, dark fluid ooze out of the wound. Grabbing a handful of gauze, Claire wiped at the congealed liquid.

"What do you think, Claire?"

Claire glanced up at Mac. "About what?"

He kept her waiting while he reached for a pair of forceps on the instrument tray and used it to pick up one of the stitches that closed the abdominal wound. "The sutures. What type would you say?"

"I'd say Prolene." Claire looked at her colleague with raised eyebrows. "Probably 4.0."

"Right you are."

"Where would a lay person get sutures?"

Mac shrugged. "Could be a few places, a medical supply house, doctor's office, veterinarian's, or a hospital. That'll be something for the police to check out."

"Do you think whoever did this works at the hospital?"

He tugged at the stitch. It pulled easily away from the skin. "Don't think so." He grinned. "Unless he missed suturing 101."

Claire found herself grinning at Mac. Leave it to him to find humor in the darkest situations.

Mac put the forceps back on the tray and picked up the scalpel again. He transected the incision that had been roughly stitched sometime within the last twenty-four hours. It was slightly irregular and stretched from her umbilicus to her left flank. With quick snips, Mac cut through each stitch. The incision gaped farther and farther apart. A large pool of congealed blood occupied the cavity.

"Can you suction?"

Claire turned the dial on the suction machine, unwound the tubing, and slid the plastic straw-like instrument into the wound. Dark red fluid whooshed through the tubing and filled the wall mounted suction bottle. With the cavity cleared of blood, Mac used his gloved fingers to examine the layered edges of the wound.

"Look at this incision. Maybe a little rough, but whoever did it, I'm pretty sure they used a scalpel. See the line, fairly clean. If it wasn't a scalpel, then it was something damned sharp."

He excised part of the tissue and dropped it into a specimen bottle. Maurice labeled the specimen.

"Claire, pass me the retractors."

Mac slid the stainless steel instruments into the incision, stretching the cavity. He probed the abdomen for several moments. Claire's interest rose as Mac's eyebrows crept together.

"Well, well. Claire, look at this. I'll be damned. We seem to be missing an organ."

Claire jerked to attention. Blood obstructed her view. She suctioned again then peered into the incision. She ran through her anatomy. What should be there? Mentally, she listed the organs: liver, kidney, stomach, pancreas, spleen, and bowel. Liver was on the right side. The incision was on the left.

Sticking her hand inside, Claire felt for the organs. She palpated and identified each one, stomach, pancreas, spleen. They were all there. She reached behind the pancreas. There was an empty space. Something was missing. She probed again. Mac was right. One organ was definitely missing.

Mac dictated into the microphone pinned to his uniform shirt.

"Jane Doe, number 1153, age—approximately 24, Caucasian, female, weight 134 pounds, five feet, six inches. Time of death: sometime between 2400 and 0300, July 6, 2011. Primary cause of death: hemodynamic shock from blood loss. After a longitudinal dissection of her torso, heart and lungs appear normal. Abdomen full of congealed blood. Spleen and liver normal but the patient is missing her left kidney."

CHAPTER 7

Rosko answered on the first ring. "What you got, Mac?"

"So, laddie you got anybody up there having trouble taking a piss?"

"What?" Rosko heard Doctor MacFarlane's throaty chuckle on the other end of the phone. "Okay, Mac. Tell me what you've got."

"I asked if anybody up there is having trouble taking a whiz."

"Is this some joke?"

"Well, somebody is. Your killer's got himself an extra kidney."

Rosko held the phone away from his ear. He didn't need the medical examiner's hearty laughter bursting an eardrum. Shaking his head, he put the phone back to his ear. He was in no mood for Mac's weird sense of humor.

"Okay, would you like to explain what the hell you're talking about?"

"Well, laddie," he drew the words out in his Scottish brogue. "The autopsy is complete, except for the laboratory reports. Now, those will take a bit. You know how fast the system moves."

"Get to it," Rosko barked.

"I'm getting there, lad. Hold your horses."

"It'll be more than your horses I'll be holding if you don't hurry up."

"Idle threats, boy, idle threats."

Rosko closed his eyes as the medical examiner's laughter boomed through the lines. He'd met Mac when he'd started doing autopsies for the police seven years ago and had learned it was best to humor him if he wanted to get the job done quickly. Mac was one of the best, if you looked past his off-color humor. Rosko drummed his fingers on the table and waited.

"Well, after we snipped through the killer's suture job, and moved away the bowel and stomach, we found out our young lady is minus one organ."

Rosko played the game. It was quicker. "So Mac, what organ is she missing?"

The doctor chuckled softly. "Her kidney."

"He took her kidneys?"

"Nope. Just one. The left one."

"Holy shit." Rosko shook his head. "What type of crazy are we dealing with? Why the hell would somebody take one kidney?"

"Hey, that's your job. I just cut the bodies up."

"Could he sell it?" Rosko asked.

"Nope. To harvest a kidney you have to keep the vessels, the arteries, and the veins in perfect condition, and preserve the organ before it's transplanted. This guy didn't bother. He just sliced through everything then let her bleed to death."

Rosko took a fresh pad of paper and scrawled "'Jane Doe'" on the top. Below it he wrote in bold letters: missing left kidney. He drew several squiggles under the last line. Speaking into the receiver, his voice held none of the humor of his colleague. "Is the report done?"

"Being typed as we speak. I had the beautiful Doctor Valincourt assisting me. Too bad you missed it. She's one good looking lady."

Mac chuckled again. Rosko tried to recall the name. Was Doctor Valincourt a new coroner? Then the name registered—the doctor who'd found the body, the one he'd interviewed at the hospital. It must be time for a vacation. He couldn't remember names, let alone a beautiful face.

Mac's voice boomed across the phone lines. "You still there, Rosko?"

"Yeah, I'm here."

"Do you want the report now?"

"I'm on my way."

"I'll make sure it's ready. Then I get to start an autopsy on a seventy-five year old found dead at home. The postman noticed the smell. Want to assist?"

"Go to hell, Mac."

"Thought all these years on the job might have toughened you up."

Rosko slammed the phone down. He hoped Mac was still holding the receiver to his ear.

∽∾∽

Ten minutes later Rosko pushed through the morgue doors. Doctor MacFarlane sat behind his paper-cluttered desk. A long white laboratory coat, the pockets bulging with papers and pens, covered his stained operating room greens. He wore his thick, dark-rimmed glasses perched on the bridge of his nose. A wide smile spread across his weathered face as he recognized his visitor. He used two stubby fingers to shove his glasses into place.

"Okay, Mac, tell me exactly what you've got," Rosko demanded.

"Well, good day to you, too. Here I bust my ass to get your corpse done and all I get is 'give me the facts.'"

"Sorry Mac." Rosko shoulders sagged and he smiled apologetically. "It's been a long day and we still don't have a clue as to the identity of the victim, or the killer."

"Rest your weary butt while I tell you a story." Leaning his elbows on the table, Mac rested his head in his hands while Rosko settled his body in the only other chair in the room.

"It was a routine autopsy. Other than the burn marks around her mouth, probably from chloroform. Toxicology will tell us for sure. There's a bruise on her left arm where her vein was injected with something. Toxicology again will verify what. The brown stain on her abdomen was a skin antiseptic, Poviodine."

Rosko interrupted. "Where would he get it?"

"Poviodine's available at every corner drug store."

"Just my luck. Can you give me something I can use?"

"I can only give you what I got. But back to my story." Mac paused. "There was a lot of pooling of blood in the abdominal cavity. The bastard cut her kidney out while she was still alive. He severed the artery and the veins perfusing her left kidney. With the artery cut, she would have bled to death within five minutes. He didn't take anything else, just the kidney."

"So, do you have any theories?"

Mac laughed. "You asking for my help? You must be desperate."

Rosko grinned. "I'll take any help I can get, even yours."

"Well, since you asked…I think he used a cloth saturated with chloroform to render her unconscious. I didn't find much sign of a struggle. A few bruises. Nothing under her fingernails. There was a small puncture wound at her left elbow. It had some bruising around it. I think the bruising is from the killer trying to needle the vein and missing. I don't think it was self-inflicted. She has no signs of being a junkie. I think he drugged her so she wouldn't struggle while he removed her kidney."

"Anything to prove your story?" Rosko asked.

"Urine, blood, tissue samples, and stomach contents have gone to the Toxicology Lab. I'll know for sure when the results come back."

"Can we speed them up?" Rosko asked.

"You know the labs. They work on their own time schedule. You might want to try giving that cute little blonde number a call. The one that started a couple of months ago. I lost my edge when Sophia up and eloped. Knew I should have moved faster on that one."

Grief clouded Mac's weathered face and he shrugged his shoulders as if Sophia getting married was one of the great tragedies of his life.

"You old two-timer. What would Moira have to say about that?" Rosko asked.

"Well now, would we have to tell her?"

"She'd beat you silly."

Mac grinned. "She would, wouldn't she? Ah well, a man can dream, can't he? And what about you, my friend? Any good looking women tickling your fancy?"

Rosko shook his head. "Nope. Janice then Sherry. That was enough for me."

"Ah, yes. You do have a habit of picking the good ones."

Rosko diverted the conversation back to the victim. "Did you find anything else?"

"A few things. A few things."

"How long do I have to wait for you to tell me?"

"I'm coming to it."

Rosko raised an eyebrow. "Could it be tonight?"

"You know the design of a car mat was imprinted on her back."

Rosko nodded. "You made an impression?"

"Yep. It's already gone to the crime lab. Looks like a van. The guys should be able to match it to the manufacturer. That is, unless it's an after-market. Another thing, she had a ring on. Has a tan mark on her right ring finger. Plus a watch. They weren't on her list of belongings. But then, being found naked, you don't have much of a list do you?" Mac chuckled. "You don't happen to have them, do you?"

Rosko rolled his eyes. He wondered why they remained such good friends. "We've got nothing. You got her the way we found her, stark naked."

"I wonder if he'll pawn the jewelry, or keep them as trophies."

"Who knows? But it might give us a lead. We can check the pawnshops. Too bad we don't know what they looked like."

Mac grinned and shrugged his shoulders. "Sorry. All I know is she wore a watch and a ring."

"Anything else?"

"I've sent off dental impressions, and taken x-rays. She hasn't broken any bones. Maybe the dentals will give us an ID."

Rosko raised his eyebrows. "More?"

"Not for now. I'll let you know as soon as the reports come back. Now, when are you coming for dinner? Moira wants to know what's happening with your love life."

"It's nonexistent. And I plan on keeping it that way," Rosko said firmly.

Mac's hearty laughter followed him out the morgue doors. A blast of humid air hit him as he went outside. After the chilly atmosphere of the morgue, the warmth was momentarily refreshing. But by the time he crossed the parking lot, he cursed the continued heat wave. Slamming the door, he set the air to max and headed to his office. Hopefully Wilson's investigation had proved more helpful.

CHAPTER 8

Claire pushed through the double glass doors of the Strathburn Police Station. The foyer's terra cotta ceramic tiles harmonized with the interior brick walls. Live foliage, ornamental trees, figs, oleanders, and hibiscus were laid out in attractive groupings. A three-foot-high stone planter held smaller green leafy plants. Expensive paintings, donated by some of the city's major philanthropists, decorated the walls. It looked more like the lobby of a Hilton than a local police station.

Denning Enterprises constructed the new station in an election year keeping Mayor Jackson Denning in for another term. The local papers raved about his latest gift to the police station—a valuable Pratt to add to its collection of fine art.

Claire wondered about the timing. It seemed to coincide with his son's visit to the emergency department after a minor fender bender. A police officer came to the hospital to talk to the teenager, but somehow his blood alcohol specimen got lost and no charges were filed. Claire glanced at the Pratt. Would the painting constitute a bribe? Her heels clicked sharply on the tiled floor as she crossed to the information center tucked into a discreet corner of the foyer.

"Detective Rosko, please.

A uniformed woman made a call then directed Claire through electronic doors leading up to the second floor. Past the front lobby, the station looked like any typical office building, nondescript wall colors, linoleum floors, and narrow corridors. She heard ringing phones and muffled voices. Following along the hall, Claire took the elevator to the second floor. When the doors slid open, she followed the signs until she found the one stating, Detectives.

The positioning of several over-sized wooden desks divided the room into sections. Each boasted a black phone and a swivel chair upholstered in faded orange. Papers covered pen scribbled blotters. The far wall consisted of a row of paned windows. Glancing around the room, Claire saw Detective Rosko sitting at a desk in front of one of the windows. He was talking on the phone and waved her over. Claire sat in the chair across the desk and waited while he finished his call. "Thanks for coming in."

"Did I have a choice?" Claire tried to lighten her remark. "You've rescued me from two weeks' worth of laundry and the ordeal of restocking empty cupboards."

Rosko grinned. "Well, I won't take much of your time. Then you can get back to your day. Sounds like fun. Want to stock my fridge, too?"

"I'll pass on that, thanks."

Rosko handed her a form. "I've written a report from our conversation yesterday. Would you read it over and see if there's anything I missed, or if there's anything else you've remembered?"

Claire read the events of the previous day. It appeared to be in order. Even her name and address were accurate. She signed on the line indicated and handed it back.

"Thanks." He took the paper. "Would you look at pictures of known criminals in the area?"

"Sure."

"We've never had anyone murdered in Strathburn the way this woman was. I don't think we'll find the suspect's picture among our mug shots, but I'd like you to look. It may trigger something. You never know. Some killers like to hang around after the crime. It gives them a second high." His face was grim and he shook his head as if making a silent comment on the decline of social mores.

Claire spent the next hour staring at glossy black and white photos. None of them set off any triggers. They look so normal. Anyone of them could work alongside her, or be her neighbor. She might never know the dark secrets lurking beneath the surface.

Her eyes hurt from the glare of the fluorescent lights. She sighed when Rosko appeared at the door.

"See anything?"

Claire shook her head. "I can't believe how normal some of these people look."

Rosko shrugged. "Shows the old saying: You can't tell a book by its cover."

"Obviously not." She looked up from the photos. "Do you need me for anything else?"

"I'd like you to spend some time with our sketch artist? You saw a jogger and someone on a bike. They may have nothing to do with the murder, but you never know. It's better to get as much information as we can."

"I don't remember much, but I'll try."

Rosko picked up the phone, punched in some numbers, spoke briefly, then hung up. "Sue Taylor's our sketch artist. She has time right now. I'll take you to her office."

Claire followed Rosko to a small but tastefully decorated office. Several paintings hung on the walls, landscapes, and florals, each done in pastel shades. Claire noted the tiny Taylor scrawled in their corners. Obviously Sue's talents extended beyond the technical graphics of police sketching.

The next half-hour was certainly more pleasant than flipping through glossy black and white photos. Sue Taylor, about Claire's age, had an engaging smile and quickly put her at ease.

As they chatted, Sue's pencil flew across the page. She told Claire how her father, a retired detective, had brought her to the station as a child. He gave her paper and pencils to keep her busy while he did paper work. After graduating from basic drawing of animals and trees, she began drawing the people around her. Later, at police picnics, she would paint pictures of the officer's children.

The quality of her portraits attracted attention, and in high school, she'd received requests from officers to paint portraits of their family. Wanting to study art at university, she'd applied, and had been granted a police scholarship. Now, she was back doing a job she loved. It amazed Claire how quickly Sue put a few details on the paper and came up with a human face. Claire pointed to the wall. "Did you do these paintings?"

"Yes."

"You're quite talented."

"Thanks. Painting is my stress reliever."

"I always wanted to take art. But there were so many other courses I needed for med school. There just wasn't time."

Sue handed Claire the sketch. "Does he look familiar?"

Claire focused on the picture. "It looks like the jogger."

"Okay, let's work on the cyclist,"

When Sue finished, Claire stared at it. "It's hard. I only saw him for a couple of seconds. But yeah, I think it's him."

"I'll make copies. Someone will deliver them to you. Maybe later you'll remember something else. If you do, let me know and I'll adjust the sketches."

"Can you give me your number in case anything comes to me?"

Sue passed her an embossed business card. "Were you serious about wanting to take an art course?"

"Yeah, but I don't think I'd be any good at it."

"You don't have to be good, just do it for fun. There's an evening course on watercolors I'm planning on taking. It starts in a couple of weeks."

"Sounds like fun."

"Would you be really be interested in checking it out?" Sue asked.

"I've always wanted to," Claire told her.

"I'll give you the number." Sue flipped through a Rolodex, wrote a number on the back of her business card, and handed it to Claire.

Claire looked at the address. "I live on Alexander. I'm just a few blocks away."

"Maybe we could go together."

"Sounds great. I'll call you," Claire promised.

Rosko appeared at the doorway. "Is this a social event I can join?"

"Sure." Sue grinned. "Have you got your palette of paints ready?"

"Paints?" Rosko's eyebrows arched. "Is this a female only thing?"

The women exchanged conspiratorial grins but left him in the dark. Sue passed him the sketches.

"This one," he said, pointing to the sketch of the cyclist, "looks familiar. A bit like one of the shopkeepers nearby. He did say he was in the park yesterday morning but denied knowing anything about the murdered girl. The other one, I don't recognize." He handed the sketches back and asked, "Can you make copies?"

"No problem. I'll leave them on your desk."

"Thanks, Sue. Are you done with Doctor Valincourt?"

"Please, call me Claire."

"Claire it is. If Sue is done with you, I'll walk you out."

"I'm done." Sue stood and shook hands with Claire. "Nice to meet you. Let me know about the class."

"I will."

Rosko escorted Claire to the lobby and out to her car. "I'll give you the standard line. Don't leave the country and be available in case we need you for further questioning."

She grinned at him. "So I have to cancel my world tour?"

His laugh was hearty. She liked the way his smile lit up his eyes. He grinned roguishly. "No. I just like the line."

"Well, I don't have any travel plans."

Claire extended her hand. The hand grasping it was warm, the shake firm. If the handshake lasted longer than customary, neither of them seemed to notice. Claire drove away in a much lighter mood than when she'd arrived. There was something particularly nice about that man.

CHAPTER 9

Rosko returned to his office with a smile on his lips. It only lasted until he sat behind his desk and saw the open file. A stark white face stared up at him. Who was she? They'd checked missing persons, but nothing yet.

He reconstructed the scene and the investigation's progress since the previous morning. Wilson had stayed out supervising the streets while he'd come back to check on the computer searches. Officers continued to question residents, while others searched the park again. They'd widened the canvass, checking the surrounding streets in a grid formation. At the station, policemen had their wheels spinning full-tilt on paper chases and computer records.

After news of the murder aired on the radio and television, the police station received several calls, some crank, some with possible information, but nothing yet had led them to the victim's identity.

Dental impressions hadn't matched any missing person. Rosko hoped the toxicology report wouldn't take too long. It might give them something to go on. They were pretty sure the killer used something, probably chloroform, to subdue his victim then gave her an injection of an unknown drug. They knew her last meal, pasta. At least somewhere to start. Rosko opened the phone book and flipped to local restaurants.

He set a mug of hot coffee on his desk, his sixth of the day—so much for cutting back on caffeine. At least he'd given up cigarettes. One bad habit at a time.

He took a long sip then began to type his report. Jane Doe: Caucasian, age probably 22 to 28 years old, brown hair, blue eyes, no identification, no identifying birthmarks. Found naked in Victoria Park.

The only marks they'd found on the corpse were the brown stain on her abdomen and the track marks on her back. The pattern resembled a van mat. That narrowed the search, a little. But there were thousands of vans in the city. Was the killer even from this area? He might have been just passing through. Shit, they didn't even know if the victim came from Strathburn.

Rosko glanced at the computer screen and used the curser to scroll down the form. Cause of death. He filled in the section—preliminary cause of death: shock due to massive loss of blood—awaiting final report from coroner.

He tipped the mug to his lips. Lukewarm, but it was caffeine. Glancing at his notes, he filled out the rest of the form and sighed. Too much white, too many blank spaces, but he had no more answers. Her fingerprints, sent to AFIS, the Automated Fingerprint Identification System, matched nothing on record. Her clothes had to be somewhere. Was the killer keeping them as a souvenir? Hopefully, he'd left them in a dumpster or a garbage pail somewhere close by. Officers were searching the area, but how far would they have to go to find them?

A database search had been started for anyone who sliced up their victims. In all his years in Strathburn, Rosko had never seen anything like this. Shaking his head, he saved the file to his Unknown Persons folder then printed the report in triplicate. He attached the Polaroid pictures from the scene. He hated the unknowns. He wanted to be able to give them a name. Unknown was so cold and impersonal. At least the search engines were under way. He hoped it wouldn't be long before they identified the woman and gave her back her name. A sigh for all the anonymous souls escaped him.

He needed to get back out on the street and see how the investigation was going. Maybe they'd gotten lucky and found a witness who saw something. Picking up the coffee mug, Rosko took a sip. Cold. He slapped the mug back down on the desk, shoved the reports into the box labeled "'Current,'" and headed for the door.

"Hey, Rosko."

As he turned toward the sound of his name, a pain shot through his temple. He hadn't gotten into bed until after two and had been at the station before seven. The headache had started shortly after he arrived at the station, and now it felt like someone had a jackhammer to his skull. They were thirty-six hours post crime and still nothing to go on. Rosko didn't think this one was going to be solved within the critical forty-eight-hour period. He rubbed at his temples. It did nothing to ease the pain.

Jenkins from Missing Persons approached him. "I think we found your girl. We got a call about a woman who didn't show up for work today. Too early to make out a report—she hasn't been missing the required twenty-four hours—but we thought she fit the description of your victim." He glanced at the scrap of paper in his hand before handing it to Rosko. "Mary Jane Winters, twenty-four, brown hair, blue eyes, five feet, four inches, one hundred and thirty pounds. Could be her."

Rosko looked at the paper, then at Jenkins. He couldn't focus. The pain in his head now spread to his eyes. When he looked at the page, the lines blurred. "Anything else?"

"She's been an employee of Robertson's Travel for five years now. It's on Wellington Street. The owner knows her family. When she didn't show up for work today, and he couldn't get an answer at her home, Robertson called her mother. I guess Mary Jane's always been the dependable type." Jenkins paused. "Her mother went to her apartment. It looks like she hasn't been there for a while. Mary Jane has a couple of cats. Their food dishes were empty, and they were making quite a fuss."

"Do we have a picture?" Rosko asked.

"Her mother's bringing one."

"Call me when she arrives. No sense upsetting the woman if her daughter's not our victim."

"She'll be here shortly. She probably knows about the murder. The park isn't far from the travel agency. Mary Jane was the one to close up the office last night."

Rosko opened the middle drawer of his desk and took out a bottle of Tylenol Extra Strength. He swallowed a couple of tablets with the dregs of cold coffee. He stretched and twisted his neck. The muscles remained knotted. He looked up as Wilson entered the squad room. "Anything?"

"Nope. What about you?"

"The autopsy put her death between eleven p.m. and one a.m. She had pasta in her stomach."

"Did she cook it herself, or stop on the way home?" Wilson's asked.

"Doesn't look like she made it home. If she did, she forgot to feed her cats."

"You checking the local restaurants?"

Rosko nodded. "I've already got as far as the H's," he said. "Why don't you start at the R's."

They spent the next half hour flipping through the yellow pages and making occasional notes. The ringing of the phone interrupted them. Wilson waited, pen in midair while Rosko listened.

"We'll be right there." He slammed the phone down. "Looks like Mary Jane Winters is our victim. Her parents are here now. Jenkins hasn't told them anything yet. He's waiting for us."

"Let's go then."

Rosko knew there'd be no relief from the Tylenol now.

⌇⌇⌇

A middle-aged couple sat on a wooden bench outside the Department of Missing Persons. The man's balding head was stooped and his shoulders sagged. His attention was focused on the kaleidoscopic pattern of the linoleum floor. The woman's tightly curled gray head tipped, her attention concentrated on her lap. With the slightest movement in the hall, the gray head darted about like a tiny bird, peeking at the disturbance, then quickly retreating to the safety of her lap. The couple held hands stiffly, as if they had grown unaccustomed to displays of affection.

The pounding in Rosko's head intensified. Times like this made him wish he'd picked another profession. Could anyone ever get used to this part of the job? Maybe Wilson could tell them. He looked at his partner and saw a film of tears coating his eyes. Was he remembering being told his child had a brain tumor and had only months to live? Rosko couldn't ask him. It had been a year since his son died, but something like this brought the pain racing back. Rosko took a deep breath and pushed through the door.

The woman's gray head shot up at his approach. Instantly she read the look on his face and the grip on her husband's hand intensified. His head rose slowly, as if to postpone the ultimate horror. His eyes locked with Rosko's. No words were needed.

The body had been transferred to the police morgue after the autopsy. Rosko led them down to the basement. Mr. Winters's arm enveloped her shoulder as they walked like wooden puppets along the long hallway. At the door to the morgue, the footsteps halted. Mr. Winters' voice trembled. "Edna, I'll go."

"No. Walter." Her tear-filled eyes locked with his. "I need to know for myself."

They leaned into each other, walking as one. Rosko led them to the stretcher where a white plastic sheet covered the body. The morgue attendant pulled back a corner of the sheet.

Hours later Mrs. Winters' scream still echoed in Rosko's head.

CHAPTER 10

From a brief interview with her parents, Rosko found out Mary Jane had a boyfriend, Benjamin Harris, a nice young man. He couldn't have hurt her. They were sure there was no one in her life who might want to kill her. They'd interview the boyfriend right after they checked out her apartment.

Mary Jane lived in one of the new high-rise apartments on Mason Avenue. The building was clean and well maintained, the lobby professionally decorated in muted shades of blue and gray. Security cameras hid behind large potted plants. They'd have a look at the tapes. A coded entry ensured tenant safety. It hadn't helped Mary Jane.

Like the building's exterior, Mary Jane's apartment was neat and organized, decorated with contemporary furniture. Her taste ran to the brighter end of the color palette—red, green and gold patterned pillows adorned the green leather sofa. Scattered around the apartment were souvenirs of the places her job had allowed her to visit. Woven Mexican tapestries hung on the wall. The bookcase held wooden carvings from the Caribbean and Grecian artifacts. Travel magazines were methodically scattered on the coffee table. In the kitchen, the counters were clean and uncluttered—one plate, one coffee cup, and one spoon sat alone in the gleaming stainless steel sink.

Her three cats had been fed yet roamed the apartment like lost souls. As if they sensed their master's demise. Their high-pitched meows echoed through the lonely apartment. Wilson tried to comfort them. They hissed at him in return. Rosko hoped Mary Jane's family would be able to care for them.

Dogs were his preference. Another thing he'd lost with the divorce. Someday he'd get another dog. A big one, not a yippy, lap dog. Not that he hadn't liked Spike. It had surprised him how Janice's Bichon Frisse eventually won him over. When he'd opened his front door, Spike would be there to greet him, his tail wagging so fast his whole body shook. More than he could say for his ex. Too bad she'd taken the dog with her.

Rosko and Wilson searched Mary Jane's apartment—nothing appeared to be out of place. She'd left the apartment as neat and organized as the clothes hanging in color coordinated groups in her closet. Even her garbage was neatly organized.

Wilson pressed the flashing light on the answering machine. There were nine messages: four from a male voice pleading for her to call—probably the boyfriend—two from her boss, and the other three from her mother. No revelation as to why anyone would want to kill her. They gathered an assortment of paper—bills, receipts, banking statements, and letters. Someone would check through them at the station. They talked with the superintendent and the other tenants. No one had seen her Monday night. And no one had heard or seen anything out of the ordinary. Mary Jane was as quiet and polite as her apartment suggested—the perfect tenant and neighbor.

The boyfriend was next on their list. They'd asked Mr. and Mrs. Winters not to call him. They'd handle breaking the news. Ben Harris, a computer programmer for Ella Don, Strathburn's largest construction company, was in his office. After the receptionist announced them, a college cut young man in a navy tailored suit emerged from an inner office and greeted them. His smile was pleasant and his handshake firm, until they flashed their badges, and he realized they weren't there on company business.

Rosko watched Harris's face tense and saw the sudden stillness in his pale blue eyes. He knew a multitude of scenarios flashed through the man's mind. It happened to every upstanding citizen when the police came knocking. Harris rejected Wilson's suggestion to sit down. No matter how you tried you could never sugar coat the news. The color drained from his face and the smile he'd greeted them with seconds before dissolved. His head shook rapidly. "No! It can't be. I talked to her last night."

Rosko took a step forward. "I'm sorry, Mr. Harris."

"No. You have the wrong person. Nobody would hurt Mary Jane."

"I'm sorry. Her parents have identified her."

"Oh, my God." His body sagged like a slashed bag of rice. "What happened?"

"Please, sit down, Mr. Harris," Wilson said.

"Tell me what happened," Harris demanded.

Wilson gave him a brief summary.

He leaned on the desk for support, but his arms shook like willow branches. He stumbled backward and fell into the chair. Holding his head in his hands, he sobbed. "Oh, Mary Jane. My poor Mary Jane." Time stretched while they waited for his sobs to settle. When he looked up at the detectives and he could speak, his voice trembled. "I've been trying to call her all day. I thought she was still angry." He closed his eyes briefly. "We had a bit of a tiff yesterday. There was a show she wanted to see—then my friends got tickets for the game. Box seats." His voice quivered. "I told her we'd go to the movie tonight." He looked across at them, tears brimming. "If I hadn't gone to the game..." He wiped his tears on his sleeve. "Who did this?"

"We don't know at this point," Rosko said. "Can you think of anyone who might want to harm her?" Other than yourself.

"Everybody liked Mary Jane. She didn't have enemies." He choked. "We're getting married next summer." Anger flared in the pale blue eyes as he realized his proposed future had suddenly shattered. His fist hit the table with a resounding thud. "I should never have gone to that damned game."

His burst of anger short-lived, his shoulders sagged again. With a voice thick and unsteady, Harris reported his activities of the previous evening. After the game, he and his buddies had gone for a few drinks. There was no time unaccounted for. Harris's hands trembled as he wrote down their numbers.

Rosko and Wilson would check them out. Unless Harris was up for an Oscar, Rosko didn't think he was the violent murderer they were looking for. But he'd been wrong before.

೮೧೮೧

Todd Robertson, Mary Jane's boss, glanced up as Rosko and Wilson entered the travel agency. His customer smile vanished when they revealed their badges. He gripped the padded arms of his swivel chair, the color draining from his normally ruddy cheeks.

"I've known her since she was a baby." He waved his hand around the travel agency. His voice broke. "I never had kids. I planned to give her the agency when I retire next year."

Their clientele came mostly from the local neighborhood. He hadn't heard of anyone giving her a hassle. He didn't recall anyone hanging around or bothering Mary Jane. He didn't know anyone who might want to harm her.

Yes, he knew the boyfriend, and no, he didn't think Ben could kill her. "They were getting married next June. Honeymooning in Hawaii. My wedding present." He wiped his eyes with the handkerchief he pulled out of his suit pocket.

They found nothing unusual in a desk as neatly organized as her apartment. Robertson gave them a copy of her client list. Most of the addresses were close by. It was a long list and Rosko hoped they'd find the killer before they finished it.

"Did Mary Jane frequent any Italian restaurants in the area?" Wilson asked.

"She loved Belini's. It's over on Victoria Street."

"Is that the restaurant down the street from the park?" Rosko asked.

"Yeah, that's the one. She planned to meet Ben there for supper. Then he got tickets to the ball game and cancelled. She was quite annoyed. Said she was going anyway."

Robertson closed his eyes. Had it just hit him that Mary Jane's last meal had been at Belini's, and that she'd gone there on her way home from his business—shortly before she'd been killed. He escorted the detectives to the front door of the agency, promising to call if he thought of anything else. He put the closed sign in the window and walked slowly back to his desk.

Rosko and Wilson drove the couple of blocks to Belini's.

இ௦௧

Enticing aromas of herbs and garlic greeted them as they walked through the tinted glass doors of Belini's. The staff was gearing up for the evening rush and barely noticed them.

"You hungry?" Wilson asked.

"Famished. We missed lunch didn't we?"

"Unless you count coffee and donuts, we missed breakfast too."

"Want to eat here?" asked Rosko.

Wilson made a production of sniffing the air then nodded. "Smells good to me. My stomach's rumbling in anticipation."

A young hostess approached. Dressed in a long black skirt and white blouse, her gold plated nametag introduced her as Jackie. They let her seat them before taking out their badges and the picture of

Mary Jane. The one of her living was much easier on the eye than the photos taken postmortem. He handed Jackie the picture.

"Sure I know her. That's Mary Jane Winters. She works over at Robertson Travel. Ben and her eat here all the time."

"Was she here Monday night?" Rosko asked.

"Yeah. She came in about 8:30 p.m. She'd just closed up the agency. She was some ticked. Ben changed their plans at the last minute. Stood her up for a baseball game if you can believe it." Her laugh stopped suddenly and she squinted at the detectives. "Nothing happened to her, did it? Or Ben?"

"He's okay," Rosko told her.

Her head jerked back. "Oh my God. That wasn't Mary Jane they found in the park?"

"I'm afraid it was."

Jackie slumped into one of the empty chairs at the table. Her face went white. She looked from one detective to the other, verifying what they'd just told her.

"She was just here. She sat at the table over there." Jackie pointed to a table a few feet away. Her hand trembled. She quickly pulled it back and placed it over her stomach.

"Was anyone with her last night?"

"No." Jackie shook her head slowly as if mentally recalling Mary Jane's last meal.

"Did you notice if she talked to anyone? Did anyone bother her?"

Jackie's black eyebrows drew together. "I can't remember anyone other than the regulars last night. I was talking to her." She tipped her head. "Mary Jane's lived in this area since she was a kid. Always friendly." Jackie shook her head quickly, pausing before she continued. "The Walkers stopped to talk to her. They're an older couple, lived in the neighborhood for years. Other than them—I can't think of anyone."

"If you remember anything, here's my card."

Jackie shook her head again. "I still can't believe it. Poor Mary Jane."

The waitress serving them had also served Mary Jane. She couldn't remember anything unusual. Rosko took out Mary Jane's client list and circled the name Walker. He'd drop the list back at the station and have somebody start working on it. The rest of the day Rosko and Wilson spent interviewing Mary Jane's family and friends. It was emotionally exhausting, painfully unproductive, and a complete waste of precious time.

CHAPTER 11

Rosko glanced at the clock. One-fifteen. He should be home, not sitting at his desk rifling through papers he'd already been through a hundred times. The words blurred into thick horizontal lines. He rubbed his temple. He was past being efficient. He needed a break. He'd come back in the morning with a fresh perspective.

He and Wilson had spent the afternoon and evening contacting the names on Mary Jane's client list—nothing so far. A few, they hadn't been able to reach yet. They did a search on Mary Jane and Ben Harris, but neither of them had as much as a parking ticket. And nothing out of the ordinary came up with anyone in their circle of family and friends. Past the critical forty-eight-hour window, the trail was ice cold. Maybe after a few hours of sleep, he might see something he'd missed.

Rosko laid his hands on the desk and shoved his chair back. The desk vibrated and a heavy crystal paperweight rolled across the wood. His hand shot out and caught it just before it reached the edge. He felt its coolness against his palm as he stared into its multi-faceted surface. Shafts of light danced in and out of the globe's surface.

His grandmother had given it to him when he was eleven. She'd claimed it had magical powers. He heard her voice. "You only have to look deeply into its center and it will give you all the answers you need." He didn't believe it, but it was the only remembrance he had of her. He rubbed it for luck before placing it on top of the manila folder now marked M. J. Winters.

❧❧❧

"We need men at the church for the funeral." Chief Horace Richards addressed the group of detectives. "He may be too intelligent to leave us any clues, but he's got to be tempted to see the effect of his handiwork. He may have known the Winters girl. Sometimes killers are smart enough not to choose someone who lives in the area they live or work, but sometimes not." He looked at Rosko. "Have we gotten anywhere with the investigation?"

"Not really. We've interviewed her family, boyfriend, friends—no apparent motives there. We're keeping an eye on the boyfriend, Ben Harris. He's some sort of computer geek. So far he comes up clean. We're working through her client list. Still a few people we need to talk to. They're out of the country right now. We'll interview them as soon as they return. We're working on papers we found in her apartment. Nothing yet. Maybe something will turn up. Myers is checking out her computer."

"So, no motive and a gruesome killing. What have we got here?" Richards barked.

A sudden hush settled on the room. No one wanted to comment. The thought of what they might be dealing with was better left unspoken. They'd been around too many years not to know the difficulty of solving a random, vicious killing. Money, revenge, and anger were the main reasons people killed. You took them away, and there went your suspects along with any leads you might have, unless of course your killer was careless and left a few clues. Their guy hadn't been.

"Has there been anything like this before?" Richards asked.

"We've never seen this MO in Strathburn, and nothing like it in a three hundred-mile radius. The FBI denies anything similar, but they're still searching," Rosko said. "We initiated a VICAP search, but so far no matches have come up in the Violent Crimes database. Apparently there's not another criminal in North America drugging women and taking their kidneys, despite the urban legends."

"So you got nothing?" Richards barked.

Rosko paused before answering. Sometimes, the killer committed his crimes in one area, then moved to another area, and began again. The regional cops might be so glad he didn't repeat that they wouldn't think to input it into the database.

"There are some sickos out there using drugs to kill their victims, and some mutilating theirs, but none that matched this guy's exact MO. Or maybe there is, but the investigating officers haven't bothered to add the details to VICAP."

Richards shook his head and stomped back toward his office. Turning back to the men, he barked a command. "Get the hell out of here and cover the funeral. Take enough men to mingle in the church and the street. See if the pervert shows up." The chief's office door slammed behind him so hard the frosted glass panel shook. Only the rustling of material broke the silence as officers donned suit jackets and ties. Rosko straightened his own tie and slipped into a charcoal gray suit jacket.

He'd been reluctant to tell Chief Richards his fear that they had a serial killer on their hands. Rosko needed to go to church and say a prayer that he was wrong.

℮∕つℯ∕つ

The doors of Saint Justin's Church opened and the strains of organ music resonated out along with the heady scent of flowers. Men and women in somber gray or black suits began to file out, their heads bowed, their talk quiet, afraid that voices above a whisper would make the horror real.

Kleenex dabbed discreetly at moist eyes, swollen and red from the flow of recent tears, or blew noses congested from tears not yet shed. Furtive glances were exchanged as people hurried down the cement stairs. With the remnants of death still inside, the mourners were anxious to return to the world of the living.

Rosko watched as they trudged away. Some piled into cars; others, with lowered heads, fled down the street, past the stores and houses framing their sphere. Several people stood on the street shuffling their feet and watching as the gleaming oak coffin was borne down the steep flight of stairs and slid into the back of the waiting hearse.

Edna and Walter Winters stood at the curb, clinging to each other. The middle-aged woman's sobs were barely muffled in the jacket of her husband's dark suit. In the silent street the sealing click of the hearse door echoed like the blast of a shotgun. Mrs. Winters sagged into her husband. Relatives moved in. Supported on either side, the couple was guided to a waiting limousine.

Rosko held vigil as the mourners piled into cars and began the procession. Many of them, he and Wilson had interviewed over the past few days—family, friends, and neighbors of Mary Jane Winters—come to pay their last respects.

Was the killer here among them? Had he come to revel in his triumph while the family laid bare their pain?

CHAPTER 12

Rosko reviewed the list of Mary Jane Winters' clients. They still had a few people they hadn't been able to reach yet. He picked up the phone and started dialing. A Mr. and Mrs. Thurston had arrived home that morning from two weeks in Greece. They'd just learned about Mary Jane's murder. Yes, they had time to speak to the detectives. Another couple was due in from France in the afternoon. The Detectives would meet them at the airport. There were still three more names on the list but they weren't due back yet.

VICAP still hadn't come up with anyone who'd been excising kidneys. Strathburn definitely didn't know of anyone with that kind of history. But they were bringing in any felon with a history of violence—so far, nothing from that avenue either.

The phone rang. Rosko snatched it out of the cradle, listened. "I'll be right there."

Wilson looked up from his desk. "What's going on?"

"Mr. Winters collapsed after he left the cemetery. He's at the hospital now," Rosko told him. "I'm going to check on him."

"While you're there, I'll go talk to Mr. and Mrs. Thurston."

"Okay. I shouldn't be long. Then we can head out to the airport and talk to the Dominicks. They arrive at four, don't they?" Rosko asked.

"That's the time Robertson gave us."

Rosko grabbed his suit jacket. "I'll be back by then."

He parked his car in the fire zone and put the red dome light on the dash. There was a flurry of activity at the nurse's station and it took a moment before anyone acknowledged him.

"Is Mr. Winters here?"

"And who would you be?" a woman in a pale pink uniform asked.

Rosko flashed his badge.

"I thought he was at a funeral, not robbing a bank."

He ignored her attempt at humor. "Is Doctor Valincourt here?"

"She's in there." Pink Uniform pointed to a glassed in room down the hall. It was open, but a long striped curtain occluded his view. The nurse remained at the desk, looking through a patient's chart.

"Do you think you could tell her Detective Rosko's here?"

"Oh, sure." She dropped the chart on the desk and went behind the curtain.

When the curtain parted Rosko caught a glimpse of Mr. Winters semi-prone on a stretcher. His face was an unhealthy shade of blue-gray beyond the transparent green oxygen mask covering his mouth and nose. Two intravenous lines had been started, one in each forearm. Red-labeled IV bags hung from metal poles attached to the head of the bed. Some of the sparse white hairs sprinkling his shriveled chest had been shaved, and EKG leads pasted to his ashen flesh.

Rosko saw the monitor above the bed. Multicolored lines flashed across the screen. They meant nothing to him except that they weren't flat, and anything that wasn't flat meant Mr. Winters was still alive. The curtain fell back in place. The audible blip of the man's heart rate carried through the sea green material.

Pink Uniform reappeared with Doctor Valincourt behind her.

"Hello, Detective Rosko." Claire took the hand he offered. "You didn't need to come," she said. "I just thought you might want to know he was here."

"How's he doing?" Rosko asked. "The family doesn't need another tragedy."

"We thought he might be having a heart attack, but his electrocardiogram is okay. His pain is under control now. It's probably stress but we're going to observe him overnight."

"I'm glad he's okay. It probably wouldn't help if he saw me here."

Claire smiled. "No, I'm sure it wouldn't."

"I have copies of those sketches our artist did." He shrugged. "But I forgot them at the station. Can I bring them to you later?"

She glanced at her watch. "I'm heading home in about forty-five minutes. Would you be back before then?"

Rosko's didn't need to check his watch. "No. I have to get to the airport."

She raised an eyebrow and grinned. "You leaving town?"

He grinned back and could feel some of the tension easing out of his shoulders. "Nope. I'm stuck here. My partner and I have to meet someone. Can I drop the pictures by your place later?"

"Sure. I'll be home all evening." Claire said. "Do you want my address?"

"No. I have it on file."

Claire laughed. "Of course you do."

His grin extended. He knew she realized the police had her address, her phone number, and who knew what else on file.

"Claire," one of the nurses called from Mr. Winters' cubicle.

"Yes, Betty?"

"I need you back in here."

"Sorry, have to go," Claire said to Rosko.

"I'll drop the sketches by later."

Rosko watched as she slipped behind the curtain. He liked the way her ponytail bounced with each step. The hairstyle, childish on someone else, bestowed her with an innocent quality. Her figure wasn't bad either, even in hospital greens. He walked out of the hospital, the scent of her perfume lingering with him.

CHAPTER 13

Wilson interviewed Mr. and Mrs. Thurston. They had nothing to add to the investigation. The trip to the airport was uneventful except for the amount of traffic they had to deal with. They shouldn't have wasted their time. The Dominicks were shocked, but couldn't think of anyone who might want to harm Mary Jane.

When they got back to the office, Jimmy Dean Weaver had been brought in. He had a long rap sheet of assault and robbery. Ten years ago he'd stabbed his girlfriend twelve times in the abdomen, strewing her guts over the kitchen floor. Somehow he'd gotten parole three months ago. Rosko wondered if there'd been some sort of deal with the D.A. Uniforms had him in an interrogation room. Rosko and Wilson looked through the one-way glass.

Jimmy Dean sat at the table cleaning dirt-covered fingernails with his teeth. His greasy black hair was long and in need of washing. Maybe they didn't have showers where he was staying. It looked like his black muscle-shirt and faded blue jeans could benefit from some soap, too.

Wilson had been new on the force when they arrested Jimmy. "Prison hasn't been good to him. He was a weight lifter back then and had the body to match. Had lots of girls after him. Even if he did push them around. The ex-girlfriends we interviewed stuck by him. They didn't believe he killed Marci. Admitted he was a bit rough but swore up and down he'd never go that far. Looks like he's gained a couple more tattoos. That's where the guys picked him up—that tattoo parlor over by Victoria Park."

"Puts him in the neighborhood. Do you think he's capable of excising a kidney?" Rosko asked.

"Not unless he's finessed up a lot in the last ten years. What he did to poor Marci was butchery, not surgery."

Rosko noted the bitter tone in his partner's voice. "Did you know her?"

"Yeah. I was still a beat cop back then. Marci was a little lady of the night. She'd had it rough. Parents too boozed up and too busy fighting with each other to give a damn about her. Her dad started molesting her when she was eleven. Mother didn't give a shit. Marci left home at fourteen. At least the Johns didn't beat her up. That is, until Jimmy came along."

"Why'd he kill her?" Rosko asked.

"Denied he did. Said he found her that way."

"Did you believe him?"

"Hey, back then, Strathburn had never seen anything like it. His fingerprints were all over the knife and the apartment. He didn't have a clear-cut alibi. Yeah, I believed he did it." Wilson shrugged his shoulders. "And we haven't seen anything like it since."

Rosko nodded toward the door. "Let's go see what he has to say. I think he's ready for us."

Jimmy Dean leaned back in the wooden chair, examining his manicure. Sullen dark eyes glared up at the detectives. "I didn't do anything."

"Now, did we say you did?" Wilson asked Jimmy.

"Well, I don't think you brought me down here for a friendly chat." Jimmy examined his nails again. Apparently they needed more work.

They got nothing from Jimmy Dean, or JD, as he insisted they call him. He had an alibi. He'd gone to visit his sick mother in Detroit and hadn't gotten back until the day after Mary Jane's murder. They'd get the police in Detroit to check it out.

᎒᎒᎒

Claire picked up groceries on her way home. She added a bottle of wine to her cart just before going to the cash register. After putting the food away, she did a quick cleanup of the apartment, washed the morning's dishes, and ran a duster over the furniture. She told herself she was cleaning for herself, but the detective's impending visit might have had something to do with her attention to detail. Claire gave herself a mental shake. He was just dropping off photos. How could she even think of anything more? He was a cop investigating a murder. Besides, she'd sworn off men.

She caught herself checking the mirror. Was her forehead too high, her eyebrows too thick, her lips too thin? Picking up a tube of lipstick she traced the line of her mouth. Did she need blush? With a shake of her head, she hurried out of the bathroom. This wasn't a date.

Usually, when she came home from work, she got out of her scrubs, took a quick shower, and changed into something comfortable yet tonight she hesitated over what to wear. Get a grip girl. After what Michael did, how can you even think about men? Still, she took a discerning look in the mirror before finally leaving the bedroom.

She put on a pot of coffee and went into the living room. Relaxing back onto the sofa, she turned on the television. The news was on. Claire looked for the tuner to change the channel but heard a knock at the door.

Detective Rosko held a large manila envelope. "Here are the photos."

"Would you like a coffee while I look at them. I just put on a fresh pot."

"Sure."

She led him down the hallway and waved him to the living room area. "Have a seat. I'll be right back."

Rosko settled on the sofa as Claire crossed to the kitchen. In a moment she returned with a tray and two coffee mugs. She set it on the table in front of him.

They were adding milk and sugar when the sound of Sherry Simmons's voice came from the television. Claire glanced at the screen. The reporter stood by the south entrance of Victoria Park.

"The body of Mary Jane Winters was found Monday morning by a Doctor Claire Valincourt while on her way to work at Grace Memorial Hospital. The police still have no suspects in the murder investigation. If you have any information to aid the police in this matter please call the number on the screen."

Claire froze with the coffee mug half way to her mouth. She stared at the television. Her hand trembled as the mug clattered back onto the table. Coffee spattered over the rim. She turned to the detective. "How…"

Rosko's face was a tight mask, his lips a thin white line. He glared straight ahead. "Damn her." He turned to Claire. "I'm so sorry. I don't know how she got your name."

There was an uncomfortable silence as the news wrapped up. A sudden chill had enveloped Claire. Picking up her discarded coffee mug, she hoped some of its heat would penetrate her body. But the coffee was now lukewarm and she had no energy to replenish it. Instead, she reached for the manila envelope. Her hands trembled as she pulled out the sketches. She stared at them for several seconds before speaking. "I think they look like the men I saw…but it was so quick. I was jogging. I wasn't paying attention."

Rosko leaned over and looked at the sketches. "Is there anything that strikes you?"

Claire shook her head. "I wish I could say there was."

Rosko drained his coffee. "Keep the sketches. Maybe something will come to you later."

"Would you like another?" Claire asked.

"Never been one to refuse a good cup of coffee." He didn't add, especially with a beautiful woman.

"Want some apple pie with it. My neighbor, Mrs. Chegetto, loves to cook and I can't eat it all myself."

Rosko grinned. "In that case, how can I refuse?"

A Clint Eastwood movie started. He'd seen it before, one of his favorites. He relaxed into the sofa while he waited for Claire to return.

He devoured the slice of pie, gave his compliments to the chef, and accepted a second piece. It wasn't until near the end of the movie that his eyes would no longer stay open. He drifted in a space between sleep and dreams. He thought of the woman next to him on the couch, then memories of past relationships broke through.

Sherry had been fun, vivacious, and sweet, understood his erratic work schedule—the perfect girlfriend for a cop. That was until he found out she had a schedule for her career and didn't care who she used to get there. After she'd double crossed him not once, but three times, he'd finally let her know it was over. She wanted him back but hell would freeze over before he let that happen.

Yet Sherry was only a minor irritation compared to Janice. He was still hurting over that one. Janice, a fashion designer for Chaucer's, wanted kids and a career. So she said. Wedded bliss for four years, then the bomb fell. Their marriage ended the night he found her sleeping with his best friend.

Brian. Rosko never suspected him. They'd been friends since grade three. In fact, it was Brian who'd pushed him to ask Janice out in the first place. And Janice. No wonder she stopped complaining about the extra hours he worked.

Luckily for him, she'd been offered a promotion and a hefty pay increase to move to Chaucer's New York store. She jumped at the opportunity. The house belonged to his parents. He'd inherited it after they'd both died within six months of each other. The only good thing was Janice had totally redecorated it while they'd been married and now he could let it slide for a while.

His mother died of a stroke when she was seventy-four. That had been in April, by October his father joined her. It was as if he couldn't go on without her. Now that was the type of marriage Rosko wanted, and thought he'd had.

Janice had no remorse. She justified it with the time he spent at his job instead of at home. At least she hadn't tried to take the house. Now, with her and Brian in New York, he didn't have to worry about running into them. Rosko took pleasure in ripping up the Christmas and birthday cards she continued to send. Despite telling himself that part of his life was over, it still hurt.

What the hell's wrong with you, Rosko? Why can't you find a nice woman who thinks home and a career are equally important? Does that make you a chauvinist pig?

His eyes kept dropping. He'd just let them close for a second.

❧❦❧

Claire heard a soft snoring and glanced over at the detective. She couldn't help smiling. Should she wake him for the rest of the movie? In sleep, his features were relaxed and the lines around his eyes and mouth softer, making him look almost boyish. She'd just let him sleep for a few minutes. Her own eyelids felt heavy. The sound of a commercial woke her. The movie finished, it was after eleven.

"Detective Rosko." Claire placed a hand on his shoulder and shook gently. Instinctively his hand reached up and covered hers. It felt strong and warm. At least he hadn't reached for a gun. "Detective Rosko," she whispered softly.

His eyelids flickered open.

"You fell asleep." She laughed nervously. "Actually we both did…it's late…"

"Sorry."

"It's okay. Obviously, we're both exhausted."

Blinking his eyes, Rosko shifted on the sofa. He pushed himself to sit on the edge of the seat, shaking his head as if shaking himself awake. "I was dreaming. An angel stood over me." He fingered a loose tendril of brown hair that covered her cheek and smiled gently. "She looked just like you." He shook his head again. "Time to go home."

He rose as if every bone in his body ached. His cell phone chimed. Claire busied herself gathering their dishes. From his curt questions and the change in his tone Claire knew the call was not a social one.

She walked with him to the door. His hand brushed her face and Claire felt her cheeks burn. Was she blushing? She jerked and turned away in confusion.

With a deep sigh and a vague apology, he was gone.

CHAPTER 14

She was late. It was close to midnight and her shift started in less than fifteen minutes. Fred was really going to be pissed if she didn't show up on time. He'd probably can her. Why did she stay so long at Finnegan's? Damn Mark! Why couldn't he just walk her to work and then go home? No, not him. Had to stay with his buddies, have a few more beers. She was a big girl wasn't she? Tina didn't need him to hold her hand.

Damn this job. She'd seen that blonde slut checking him out. Could she trust Mark? Not likely. He'd turn out to be just like all the other losers she'd dated. But here she was walking through deserted streets just so she could have a couple more dances with him before getting her ass to work. "I'll bet five bucks he's dancing cheek-to-cheek with that slut right now. And from the looks of her, it'll be more than her cheeks he'll be getting close to."

Tina cursed Mark again. No way could she make it on time. No doubt Fred would smell the booze on her. She'd only had two beers, but he had the nose of a bloodhound. Maybe if she took a shortcut through the park she'd get there before midnight. Then she just had to keep downwind of him.

Smoke from the bar clung to her clothes. Maybe it would mask the alcohol. Fred would give her his lecture about smoking, but she knew how to tune him out, just like she'd done with her parents. "You're so bright. You can make something of yourself. Get out of this hole. You can do it. You have chances we never had."

Right. They had no idea how ostracized she'd been at school, laughed at for her hand-me-down clothes and Super Save haircuts. She couldn't remember how many times she'd repaired seams stretched to the bursting point.

At least that stopped when she sprouted boobs. Her dad made sure of that. "No daughter of mine is going around parading her wares." She'd upgraded to Walmart. Now, she spent most of her paycheck on clothes. More than she should, but she deserved it. So what if the landlord had to wait a week for the rent. He should be paying her to live in that hellhole.

The entrance to Gibbons Park was on her right. Lampposts lined the road at thirty-foot intervals. Like bright beacons, they illuminated the abandoned street. Tina glanced at her watch—nine minutes to twelve. She took a fleeting look at the sinister, tree-lined border of the park and its imposing ten-foot high metal gates.

It would take her fifteen minutes to walk the three blocks down Waterloo Street, across Stanley, and then back up Jarvis. She'd be late. But if she cut through the park, she could be there in five minutes and still have time to spare. Maybe, she could have another smoke before starting work.

She couldn't lose this job. She was running out of options. That's what she got for dropping out of school. Taking a last regretful look at the glow of the streetlights, Tina slipped through the iron gates and headed down the gloomy path. A shudder ran through her but she kept her feet moving at a brisk clip.

She'd barely walked fifty feet before any illumination from the street lamps vanished and darkness shrouded her. Like tentacles, the branches on the maple trees bordering the path seemed to reach out for her. She shivered. Any heat from the scorching day evaporated and Tina felt as if a cold chill permeated through to her bones.

Just a few minutes. Just a few minutes. Keep walking. Just a few more minutes.

Wind whistled through the maples. A strand of her long brown hair blew across her cheek. She thrust it out of the way. It was still in the nineties, but the breeze felt like a wave off a glacial lake. Electric shocks tracked between her shoulder blades. She heard her grandmother: "Someone's walking on your grave." Tina laughed at the thought, then shuddered.

Come on girl, you're almost through the park. Don't let your imagination run away with you. She glanced around. See? Nothing. Nothing to be afraid of, nothing but a bunch of trees. Tina forced herself to laugh. The sound was shrill. It reminded her of a witch's cackle. She looked up at the wispy sliver of moon. Yeah, a good night for witches. Well, get on your broom, girl, and fly. If you don't get to work soon Fred will be sweeping the floor with you.

Tina pictured her boss dressed as a witch—his food-stained T-shirt protruding beyond the edges of a silky black cape, his wild mass of Grecian Formula sticking out like cactus spines beyond a pointed black hat, and an ebony spiral on the tip of his size-thirteen runners. On the end of his bulbous nose, Tina painted a generous green wart. The comic image caused a throaty chuckle to erupt from deep inside her throat. Her fears almost vanished.

Through the trees, she saw the flickering lights from the lamp-posts on Jarvis Street. This isn't so bad. You'll get to work on time, girl. Tina glanced at the luminous hands of her watch. It had only taken three minutes so far. She'd be there in lots of time. She'd even have time to slip into the bathroom and use the mouthwash she'd stashed under the sink.

Tina sniffed, checking on the damage. Well, if she kept her face out of his direct line, he might miss the booze. She prayed for a slow night. Fred usually headed home by one if they weren't busy.

She hated nights, couldn't sleep worth a damn. She'd nailed a blanket over her window to keep the sun out, but it kept falling off. Gravol just made her drowsy. But most of all she hated leaving the party when everybody else was just starting to have fun.

If it was slow, she might get some sleep. Tom was the short order cook tonight. For a few sloppy kisses and a bit of a feel, he'd let her catch some shuteye when the place emptied out. That could be any time after two-thirty. When the bars closed people wanted a hit of caffeine to get them home in one piece. Sometimes they sobbed their life stories to you—that might make it three or later. About six, the early birds started coming in for their first coffee of the day. Maybe she could catch a nap in between.

Tina kicked at a branch lying on the path and sent it flying into the woods. She heard the smack as it hit a nearby tree. The sound gave her a sense of satisfaction. The light was getting brighter. Almost there!

A twig snapped behind her. Tina jumped, twisted around, stared into the darkness. Only the shadowy images of trees surrounded her. She waited. Nothing. Not even the whistle of wind winding through the branches. The lights were getting closer. She picked up her pace.

Crunch.

Every muscle in her body tensed. Her voice caught in her throat. Her words came out in a shattered whisper. "Who's there?"

Silence.

A chill traveled down her spine. She hugged her ribs and forced her feet to move faster. She focused on the phosphorus shimmer of the street lamp ahead. Just an animal. *It's okay. Keep going.* Only a few more yards.

Another crunch. Tina quickened her steps. Her heart raced and a series of icy fingers traced the outline of her spine. "Who's there?"

No response. Tina ran. A footfall sounded behind her. Then another, and another. She ran faster. The footsteps kept pace. Adrenaline surged through her veins. Her heart pounded so fast she felt dizzy. She swung her arms, propelling her body forward. She saw the black paved road less than fifteen feet away.

The drumming of footsteps grew louder. Something grazed the middle of her back. She flew forward. Her pulse pounded in her head. The street. *It's so close. I have to make it.* It was only a few feet. Tina sped toward it.

A hand seized her right shoulder. She wrenched away. The grip tightened.

Fingernails dug into the hollow of her shoulder, broke through the skin. A searing sensation ripped through her flesh as a blast of hot air battered her neck. Tina swung her arm, whacking her attacker. But his other hand shot out, grabbed her. Tina spun around. His hand encircled her wrist in a vise like grip.

Pain mixed with fear. Fear she tasted in the hot, noxious bile bubbling in the back of her throat. It threatened to obstruct her windpipe. She swallowed, the fluid burning its way down to her stomach. Ducking her head, Tina twisted away, staggered, tripped. She was plummeting through the darkness.

He grabbed her arm, twisted, wrenched her upright. A paroxysm of pain shattered her wrist and her knees went weak. She tried to scream. Her breath froze. A strangled cry was all that came out.

His arm slid around her shoulder, pulled her backwards. Tina felt her feet being jerked out from under her. Powerful arms pressed her against a broad chest. She could smell the stale scent of his sweat. Her fists beat at him. His arms tightened, crushing her against him.

Tina opened her mouth to scream. Her cry was cut short as a damp cloth was slapped over her mouth. Her lips stung and a bitter smell made her gag. She couldn't breathe.

When she could finally open her mouth, she gasped for air and twisted violently. The cloth sucked into her mouth. A strong, sweet odor made her retch. The skin around her mouth burned. Within seconds a pleasant sensation filled her brain. Her struggling ceased.

It was several seconds before Tina took another breath and much longer before she moved. She didn't feel the hands that slid around her chest. She didn't feel her body being carried back through the trees. She didn't feel herself being thrown in the back of the van.

In fact, it was a long time before Tina felt anything.

CHAPTER 15

Tina roused slowly. She felt as if she was awakening from the worst alcoholic binge ever. The pressure on the sides of her head was unbearable, like her skull was in a vice being tested for how much it could take before exploding into a million pieces. Tina lay still, hoping the pain would go away. It was definitely better when she didn't move.

Gradually, sensations from the rest of her body filtered through the haze. Her mouth was dry, her lips stung. She ran her tongue over her lips. It didn't help. Her tongue felt swollen and covered with a thick layer of fur. She swallowed. Her saliva tasted bitter. The effort of swallowing increased the pressure in her head. Had she been run over by a Mac Truck? It even hurt to think, yet she had a nagging feeling it was important that she did.

Had she been out drinking? Did she have the flu? She couldn't remember. Where was she? Something wasn't right. She twisted her neck and peered around her. Pain shot through her head.

The room was lit by the dull amber glow of a low wattage bulb somewhere beyond her line of vision. The ceiling was high and covered in gray stained tiles. She couldn't see the walls. The area must be large. It smelled damp, musty. There was an overpowering scent of antiseptic and old pennies.

Slowly her vision cleared. Tina concentrated on the objects closer to her. On her right was a large circular light fixture. It was off now, but it reminded her of being in Doctor Tam's office and the bright examination light focused on her private parts. She hated pelvic exams. Was that where she was now?

A small stainless steel table stood three feet away. Covered with a green paper sheet extending down both sides, it reminded her of when she'd had laser treatments to her cervix after some loser gave her genital warts. The green paper hid the doctor's instruments. Her body shuddered as she remembered the painful procedure. But she didn't have those warts back, did she? She strained to remember. She'd made sure Mark didn't have any before they'd…

Was this the doctor's office, or a hospital? She couldn't remember having an appointment. Had she been in an accident? She had to remember. Her mind was a muddle of blurred images. She tried to move. Her body protested and more pain shot through her head.

Despite the pain, Tina twisted around. She became aware of what she was lying on. The surface was hard, hard and cold as steel. A chill permeated through the thin sheet. Tina realized she was naked. Her body went rigid. The icy coldness penetrated deeper than her skin. What was happening?

Tina fought through the fog shrouding her brain. Her memories were a jumble of visions and emotions—trees, bushes, shrouded lights, darkness, and fear. She vaguely remembered something being held over her mouth. She had felt like she was being suffocated. Then she was spinning down a long dark tunnel into blackness.

Closing her eyes, she tried to make sense of the memories. Gradually images came into focus. Her hands started trembling, her heart raced, and a fine sweat broke over her body. Fear like an icy wave swept over her. She remembered the shadowed face of a man above her. Tina began to shake uncontrollably. She had to get away.

She struggled to sit up. She was so weak she could barely move. A wave of nausea assaulted her, and her head felt ready to explode. She managed to get up on one elbow then forced her torso to roll to the left. Her legs were dead weights. Finally, she got her left leg over her right one. She was moving…then to her side. Now if she could just get out of the bed—

A cloth covered her face and a familiar sweet scent tickled her nostrils. Her lips burned. The darkness came again.

CHAPTER 16

He liked the feel of the scalpel. The contour fit perfectly in his palm. It weighed almost nothing, but when held in his hand, it became a delicate, dangerous weapon. He took delight in the way the stainless steel gleamed when light hit it. And the blood—it cleaned off so easily. Hold it under a tap and the blood washed away, leaving the blade shiny as new again. So easy, just a little rinse and it was ready to be used again, and again.

He inhaled deeply letting the smells of the room fill him. The scent of copper made him think of old pennies, lots and lots of old pennies. He drew it deep inside him. Blood rushed to his brain and he felt a surge of power. He closed his eyes, relishing in the scent as he slowly inhaled and exhaled.

Tightening his grip, he placed the gleaming blade just above her taut abdomen. He felt omnipotent as he pressed the blade to the tanned skin and saw the first cleft in the epidermis, the first trickle of blood. He pressed harder. The trickle became a stream.

Then blood oozed out of the incision. He pressed the blade deeper. More blood. The longer the incision, the more blood. He wanted to extend it further, but he couldn't make it too big. He had to follow technique. He had to impress Sherry. She would tell the world how skilled he was.

It was too bad he'd had to poke her a couple of times before he'd found a vein. He needed more practice. But the ketamine was working well. Immobilized, she'd hardly flinched when he made the first cut. The drug gave him such control, and power. A thrill raced through him as he watched her. Her respirations were barely perceptible in the minute rise and fall of her naked chest.

He wiped the scalpel blade on the edge of a towel. Then holding the instrument under the bright surgical lamp, he tilted it back and forth and smiled. The stainless steel, now free of blood, glistened as light refracted off its surface. He pressed the scalpel deeper into the incision.

It sliced through the fascia, then the muscle, revealing layers of tender pink tissue. He pressed harder. He was in the peritoneum. Blood spurted from several tiny vessels. The gaping wound became dark. It was difficult to see. He flipped the switch on the portable suction machine and stuck the tip into the wound.

Blood swooshed up the plastic tubing. Mesmerized, he watched it fly up the clear hose and splatter in the bottom of the suction bottle. He shivered with excitement. Holding the instrument tip just above the incision, he waited. Blood poured into the abdomen. He let it fill the space before using the suction again.

He glanced at her face. The feather he'd taped by her mouth fluttered softly. He counted the seconds between each flutter. It was irregular. He stared at her chest. He couldn't see movement. Had the ketamine depressed her respirations too much? He checked her face again. Was there a slight blue tinge to her lips?

Shit. Had he given her too much? Damn. The last time he wasn't sure if he'd used enough, now maybe too much. How the hell was he supposed to know? He scrutinized the woman's face. Was she cyanotic? Was she getting enough oxygen? He put his face close to hers. He couldn't tell. He pointed the bright light at her face.

Her lips had a bluish tinge. He watched the feather. It was ten, then twelve seconds before he saw the barest flicker. He'd better hurry. It wouldn't do for her to die before he finished. He wanted to put her back right where he'd found her. Not quite the same though. Now she'd be minus one kidney.

CHAPTER 17

C laire laced up her runners and threw her backpack over her shoulders. Slamming the door, she turned the key in the lock. The door of the next apartment squeaked open.

"Is that you, Claire?"

Claire slid her key into the zippered pocket of her sweat pants. That would teach her. She should have known slamming the door would draw the attention of her nosy neighbor. But she'd been in a hurry to get to work, and it had taken her longer than usual to collect her keys, her stethoscope, and enough food to last the night.

"Hello, Mrs. Chegetto."

Her neighbor peeked through a crack in the door. Her tightly permed gray hair reminded Claire of a Brillo pad. Widowed for over ten years, Mrs. Chegetto was the neighborhood busybody. If you wanted to know what was happening in the building, you just said hello to Mrs. Chegetto. The challenge was getting away without offending her.

"You on the night shift, dear?"

"Yes." Claire grimaced. "My turn for the graveyard shift."

"Poor thing." Mrs. Chegetto opened the door several inches. Her diminutive form was cloaked in a long flowered housecoat. "My Giuseppe, how he hated the night shift. He—"

"I have to run. I'm on duty at eleven."

"Would you like me to make you breakfast? I could, you know. Some bacon and eggs. Don't sleep well anymore...you know...ever since...."

"I really have to go. Sorry, I have a breakfast meeting after work. Another time?"

Claire hoped her nose wouldn't grow with the lie. Each time she told the woman a fib in order to make a quick getaway, she thought of Pinocchio. She touched her nose just to make sure.

"Another time." Mrs. Chegetto sniffed. "You know I get so lonely without..."

Shaking her head, Claire raced down the stairs and out the front door of the apartment. Mrs. Chegetto sure knew how to ply on the guilt. She turned right toward the hospital, her feet keeping a quick pace. That was, until she neared the gates of Victoria Park, then her feet slowed, and she stumbled.

This had happened every day for the past two weeks—ever since she'd found the body. As soon as the park became visible, her body reacted. First her heart beat faster, then her breathing became labored. Every time she had to fight the urge to vomit. It took everything she had to force her feet to keep moving past the place where the young woman had lain.

Claire wanted to detour around the park, and she had for several days, but it took her another fifteen minutes to get to the hospital. She'd set her alarm earlier to compensate, but she was a nighthawk and couldn't get her body into bed before midnight. So she forced herself to jog through the park, increasing her pace until she passed the pond. But nothing could make her go there at night. Then, she didn't mind the extra distance required to detour the park. The streets were well lit and with the right number of people—few enough she didn't have to fight past them, but enough she didn't feel alone. Tonight the temperature remained in the nineties but the humidity had lifted and Claire needed the run to relieve the tension built-up over the past several days.

The entrance to Victoria Park was just ahead and, on cue, her heart rate increased in anticipation. She wiped the sweat off her palms. It wasn't like she'd even known the woman, but finding her brought back all the memories Claire had hidden away in a small chamber of her brain. She thought about her own attack, then she thought of the rape victims she'd treated. She had such empathy for them. She was a doctor, accustomed to trauma and crisis, yet she couldn't let it go. Maybe she should talk to someone. Detective Rosko had suggested seeing a counselor. Despite her denials, she knew she needed it.

The hospital had its own social workers, but that was too close. She wanted to keep her private life just that, private. Rumors ran rampant through the hospital grapevine, and she didn't plan on giving it any fodder.

A year ago, after the emergency department had a particularly bad run of traumas, the staff were required to talk to the hospital psychologist. Doctor Guttering, a skeleton of a man whose thick black-rimmed glasses seemed to weigh his head down and give him a permanent hunch, was the hospital's choice.

Her session went okay, at first. Doctor Guttering asked about the department, how the staff coped with tragedy, what they did to defuse personality clashes, what the lines of communication were. She'd told him about their debriefing sessions, time off, and staff parties. But prying into her personal life went too far. Finally, to evade his questions, Claire concocted a fantasy life. His cheeks turned crimson and he'd almost choked. That ended the session, and since then, he'd avoided eye contact.

The session was a waste of time. Would the police crisis counselor be more helpful? Maybe she'd call Detective Rosko and get the number. It couldn't hurt to talk to someone. Wasn't that the advice she always gave?

CHAPTER 18

Seven years on the same beat, and Matt Thompson wanted out. He was tired of the same old, same old. He needed a change, something more exciting. He'd been trying to get a transfer for a while now. It didn't help he couldn't please his asshole of a sergeant.

"Who the hell do you think you are? You been on the beat a lousy seven years and you think you're ready to move up," Jenkins snarled. "I was out there for twenty years before I got to be desk sergeant. Don't get too big for your britches, or you'll find yourself on nights for the rest of your career."

Appealing to the captain was no good either. That incident in his first year on the job hadn't helped. He'd been clean since. Why couldn't they let bygones be bygones? Jenkins kept bringing it up. Damn him. He had to find a way to get a transfer, somewhere far away from that bastard.

Thompson took his usual route through the gates of Gibbons Park and along the paved path from its north to the south end. His temper escalated as he thought about his stalled career. The continuing heat wave did nothing to soften his mood.

He was so busy blaming everyone else for the state of his life he almost missed the naked ankle sticking out from under the branches of a large lilac bush.

Rosko answered on the second ring.

"Hey, Boss. I think we've got another one."

Rosko recognized the gravelly voice of his partner, Jack Wilson. "What do you mean?" Automatically glancing at the digital clock by his bed, Rosko groaned. 3:31 a.m. Why the hell didn't people kill each other at a reasonable time of the day?

Wilson's drawl continued. "Well…there are similarities…"

"Cut the crap. What are the goddamn similarities?"

"Young, naked female, abdominal wound, but this one's on the right side."

Rosko switched the receiver to his other hand and forced his body to a sitting position. He hoped being upright would clear the fog around his brain—too many nights without proper sleep. Maybe it was time for a new job, or at least a vacation.

"Hey, Boss, you still awake?"

"Damn it. I'm awake. You think it's the same guy." Rosko heard Wilson's yawn through the phone lines. His body instinctively copied the gesture.

"Sounds like it. We'll know for sure when we see the body."

"Where is it?"

"Gibbons Park, by the southeast entrance. Meet you there in…say…twenty minutes."

Rosko glanced again at the bedside clock and swore. That would make it four o'clock, lovely time to start his day, especially since he'd just ended yesterday less than five hours before.

"I'll be there with bells on."

"Ho, ho, ho, we're full of humor this morning, aren't we?"

"Shut up, Jack."

Wilson's boisterous laugh echoed across the airwaves. Rosko's phone volume was stuck on maximum. He had to get around to buying a new phone with volume control. Maybe he'd get one with a mute button.

Slamming the phone down, he cut off Wilson's laughter. How the hell could the man be so chipper at this time of the morning? They were both putting in the same number of hours. He was dead tired. Did Wilson's vitality have anything to do with the new redhead he was dating? Maybe he needed a new woman in his life. An image of a bouncing brown ponytail and clear hazel eyes flashed through his mind but the thought of the work required to maintain a relationship squashed that idea. Rosko dragged himself out of bed. A quick shower should wake him up.

Riffling through his closet, Rosko grabbed the first clean dress shirt he found. That was one of the few things he missed about Janice. She'd been a stickler for appearances. She'd spent a shit load of his money on new suits and the exact shirt to match. Then she'd organized his closet so his shirts hung beside their coordinating suits, along with a choice of ties.

Lucky she wasn't around to see how he'd mixed them up. He would never hear the end of it. That was one of the good things about living on your own, nobody nattering at you, or criticizing you for wearing a jogging-suit to watch the football game. Unless he packed on the pounds, he was set for years in the clothing department. Now if he could just remember to pick his shirts up from the dry cleaners.

Out of habit, he held the blue striped shirt against the cobalt suit he'd planned to wear today. It looked okay. Did he really care what he looked like? He didn't have anyone in his life to notice.

Driving to the park, Rosko ran through his plans for the day. First, check out the body in Gibbon's Park. Would it be the same MO as Mary Jane Winters? He prayed it wasn't. That might mean they had a serial killer on their hands. What would the media have to say? The force was getting enough heat for not solving the first murder without having a second body.

Chief Richards would be waiting for him when he got back to the station. Rosko wondered how fast his Havana cigar would be twirling. He wasn't looking forward to the meeting, and he hadn't even seen the body yet.

Sometime this morning, he wanted to check on Mr. Winters. He tried to convince himself the man was his only reason for going to the hospital. The added chance of seeing Doctor Valincourt had nothing to do with the trip. But it wouldn't hurt to see if she'd remembered anything. She was on night shift this week and the park was only a couple of blocks away from the hospital. So if he dropped by after....

The pre-dawn streets were deserted and he made the drive in good time. He turned right onto Stanley Street and approached the park from the southeast entrance. The glowing phosphorus of the streetlights cast eerie shadows on the park. Several police cars were parked at the ground's entrance, their red lights flashing silently. Rosko pulled beside one of the cruisers. The digital readout on the dash said three-fifty-eight. A sweep of headlights blinded him briefly as Wilson's navy Monte Carlo pulled around the corner.

The heat wave showed no sign of letting up. The night temperature, down a couple of degrees from yesterday's record high, remained laden with moisture. Tempers were boiling over at the station, and now, another dead body. The last thing they needed was a scorching day to add fuel to the already simmering pot of personalities. He draped his suit jacket over the back of the car seat. There shouldn't be any brass showing up this time of night to worry about dress code. Rosko grabbed a large flashlight from under the seat and reluctantly left the comfort of the air-conditioned vehicle. Within seconds, he felt like a sticky shroud had enveloped him.

The press hadn't arrived yet, but he knew it wouldn't be long. The reporters would be their usual obnoxious selves—harassing them with questions—questions they didn't have answers to. Sherry was usually one of the first. Maybe they could get the body out of here before she arrived. Rosko joined up with Wilson and they headed toward the park entrance.

Metal gleamed as Rosko's flashlight's beam caught the chain used to deter vehicle access to the park. Now, it lay coiled on the pavement and a police car blocked the way. Two more police cars parked beside it, both unoccupied.

A gleaming black station wagon stood by the path. Rosko and Wilson nodded at the attendants leaning against its open back doors. The stretcher inside was empty. They were waiting for the coroner to release the body.

"Is Lee here?" Rosko asked.

"Not yet," one of the attendants said.

"Well let's hope we get the body out of here before the press arrives."

Wilson grinned at Rosko. "Is there any press person in particular you don't want to see?"

"Let it go, Wilson. I'm done with Sherry."

"She wants to get back with you."

Rosko growled. "Well, it isn't happening. And stay the hell out of my personal life."

"Okay. Okay."

Rosko strode ahead, leaving Wilson to follow. Gritting his teeth, Rosko headed toward a huddle of police officers. At least they'd found the body now instead of in the daylight when hundreds of feet would trample any possible clues. Maybe a clue would be preserved, that is, if any had been left.

A young policeman detached himself from the group and came toward him.

"Hello, sir," Thompson said. "This is my beat." He shook hands with both detectives.

Rosko recognized him as the officer at the scene of the Winters girl's murder. He'd heard a rumor that Thompson was on the wrong side of his sergeant. But he also knew Jenkins had a reputation of making life difficult for anyone he took a dislike to. Rosko had no use for Jenkins. The man had been a shit disturber for years.

"What have you got?" Wilson asked.

"A naked female, early twenties. The body looks similar to the one found in Victoria Park. She's got an incision across her abdomen. I recognize her. Tina something. She's one of the waitresses at Fred's Diner over on Horton."

Rosko nodded. He knew the greasy spoon Fred Spanzoli had run for the last twenty years. Best burgers this side of the city, guaranteed to raise your cholesterol fifty points after eating just one.

"She didn't show up for the night shift," Thompson reported. "I was at the diner just after one, doing my rounds. Fred was some pissed. Tina was supposed to be there at midnight. He thought she'd just taken the night off."

"She took it off the hard way," Wilson said. "Where is she?"

"Over there." Thompson pointed to clump of bushes several feet away where a couple of officers were setting up Klieg lights. "It looks like the same MO. And, it doesn't look like she's been dead long."

"So she probably died within the last four hours?" Rosko asked.

"That's what I'm thinking. Rigor hasn't started yet."

Rosko looked at the young officer in surprise. Most policemen weren't aware of the intricate time effects of rigor on a body.

Thompson noticed Rosko's raised eyebrows and grinned. "I'm taking courses. I want to make detective someday.

"Let's have a look at her."

They headed toward the body.

Like déjà vu, she was there, the glow of the Klieg lights casting eerie shadows on her flaccid body. Partially hidden behind a lilac bush, she lay posed just as Mary Jane had been, on her back, as if in final repose. Dark-brown hair haloed her pale face. Her blue eyes bulged grotesquely and her tongue, just beginning to bloat, protruded between swollen red lips.

Rosko knew the lip color was artificially attained. Any blood that might produce a modicum of coloring had already drained from her veins. His gaze slid down her naked form. Tina's hands were folded at her umbilicus, just below the dark incision line that spread across her abdomen.

Goddamn it. They had a serial killer on their hands.

Putting on a pair of gloves, Rosko knelt and touched Tina's face. Stone cold. He slid his fingers down to her neck, and then to her shoulder. Her jaw was stiff but her shoulder remained limp. Rigor mortis was just setting in. He would have to wait for the medical examiner, but he was confident from the extent of the rigor that, as Thompson said, she'd died sometime within the last four hours.

Rosko pulled a camera out of his pocket and took several pictures. He included shots of the pale face staring upward as if stargazing. But those big blue eyes would never again wish upon a star.

The squeal of rusty brakes echoed from the street. The Crime Scene Unit van pulled up beside his car, followed by the coroner's car. Kim Lee exited his vehicle, his weathered leather satchel clutched under his arm. The Crime Scene Unit technicians pulled a couple of large duffel bags out of the back of the van. Like a compact entourage, they advanced on the body. Chao Sugimoto was one of the technicians. Rosko slapped him on the shoulder.

"Good to see you, Chao. How's it going?"

He shrugged. "Can't complain. Nobody listens."

Chao, small in stature but big on optimism, didn't allow his job to get him down. Not belittling the repulsiveness meeting him every day on the job, yet nothing compared to the horrors he'd seen as a child. He didn't talk about it, but Rosko knew the story.

His whole family had been wiped out in a series of guerrilla attacks. Like other children, he'd survived by climbing into one of the tall palm trees surrounding his village. In the hollow crevice of a tree, Chao hid with his sister and watched villagers being slaughtered and their grass huts torched. The acrid smell of smoke stung his nostrils and the intense heat burned into his lungs, damaging them forever.

Chao, his sister, and a handful of other children hid in the trees for two days before fleeing to the forest. It was another week before friendly troops found them. Chao was taken to a hospital suffering from dehydration and smoke inhalation.

After spending weeks in the hospital, he was sent to a crowded orphanage, never to see his sister again. They told him she hadn't survived the ordeal. Eventually, he ended up in Saigon to be adopted by a childless couple from the United States. They enfolded him into their lives and tried to compensate for the terrors he'd experienced.

Grateful to be away from the fighting, and thankful for a safe home, Chao jumped at the chance of an education. Attempts to find his sister remained unsuccessful and eventually, he tucked the horrors away in some dark place. He refused to go back there despite being haunted by the screams of natives fleeing from the raider's guns.

Rosko often wondered why Chao picked a line of work where death surfaced daily, but he was the best technician they had and Rosko was always relieved to see him. There were no screw-ups or missed evidence when he took charge.

It had been after a vicious murder five years ago that they'd gone for a drink and gotten to know each other. Both were suffering from wounded relationships. Rosko was devastated by Janice taking off with his best friend, Chao from the death of his young wife after a car accident involving a drunk driver, leaving him to raise their two young children. The men drowned their sorrows over a few pints of beer. Five years later they were surviving, and so was the bond they developed that night.

"Is this our guy again?" Chao asked.

"Looks like it," Rosko answered. "Let's hope he left us something this time."

"I'll do my best to find you some evidence."

"I know you will."

Chao dragged equipment out of his duffel bag. A camera came first. He handed it to a technician who started shooting pictures of the body and the surrounding area. Evidence bags came next. Chao started filling them.

Rosko spoke to the coroner. "Anything you can tell me?"

"Don't think there's anything different. Same incision, same pose. Our guy likes brunettes." The left side of Lee's mouth twitched upward.

"By her temperature and the progression of rigor, I'd say she died somewhere between midnight and two. That redness by her mouth looks scalded, chemical probably, like chloroform. She's got fresh injection sites by her left elbow, looks like he jabbed her a few times before getting the vein. I'm sure we'll find ketamine in her system."

"Anything else?" Wilson asked.

"Look at this." The coroner pointed to several dark areas on Tina's upper left arm and the side of her cheek.

"Bruises?"

"That's right. They're in different stages of healing. These were done pre-mortem. This here." His gloved hand touched her upper left arm. "Looks like Tina's boyfriend plays rough."

Lee spanned his fingers to match one set of marks. Then he shifted his hand until it coincided with another set of small dark areas on her arm. Moving his hand to the left side of her face, he placed it over a barely visible yellow tinged area. The area matched the palm of his hand.

"Whoever gave her these bruises isn't a big man. He has small hands. Not much bigger than mine. He's probably got a little man syndrome and likes to push women around. He may be strong, but he's not tall. For these," he said, waving his hand over the bruises, "look for a man with small hands."

"Do you think he's the killer?" Rosko asked.

"Check him out. He may or may not be your killer. Whoever the killer is, he has to be strong enough to pick up and carry these women. He may drive part way into the park, but he's deposited them a long way from a road. I don't see any drag marks and there weren't any at the other scene."

"I agree. He's got to be strong. This one's got the same track marks on her back, so we know he transports them in some sort of van and then carries them to where he wants to plant them."

Lee and Wilson nodded in agreement.

"Don't know what you guys think…and I hope you don't mind my input," Chao said. "Our guy might be strong, but he's quiet, and a bit of a loner. The guy who gave her the bruises is a bully who likes to dominate women. The one who killed her dominates women on a more cerebral level. He uses brains more than brawn."

Rosko looked at Chao in surprise. "Our crime scene technician's becoming a profiler."

"Sounds reasonable to me," said Wilson. He slapped Chao on the back. "But it's four in the morning, just about anything sounds reasonable."

The men laughed. Even Rosko, usually serious, joined in. A lightening of the atmosphere was definitely needed. At this time of the night, or day, whichever way you wanted to look at it, they all felt over-tired, overworked, and underpaid.

Doctor Lee gathered his satchel under his arm. "Well, guys, much as I'd love to stay and shoot the breeze, my bed is calling. I'm done with the body, unless you guys need me for something. I think I can catch a couple of hours sleep before I'm due back at the office.
"

Rosko shook his head. "I'm finished."

"Then I'll tell the attendants to take her to the morgue. Mac can give you a report once he does the autopsy."

Rosko watched as the body was zippered into a white plastic bag and lifted onto the stretcher. The attendants wheeled the body away. They were just putting her into the back of the vehicle when the first of the press arrived.

It was four-forty a.m. and Sherry Simmons managed to look like she'd just stepped out of a fashion shoot.

"Gerry, Jack. How are you guys?" she asked, smiling brightly.

Wilson's greeting was cheery, Rosko's restrained.

"What happened? Is it the Kidney Slasher again?"

"No comment." Rosko's voice was terse and his face held no welcoming smile. While Wilson gave her a brief report, Rosko headed back to his car.

"Gerry."

Rosko jumped. He hadn't realized Sherry had come up behind him.

"Gerry. Please, can we talk?"

"There's nothing to say."

"I'm sorry. I didn't mean it to get out. It was an accident."

"I'm sorry, too, Sherry. But it's over."

"It was a mistake." Sherry's voice trembled. "Can't we…"

Sherry put her hand on his sleeve. The brightly manicured nails curled around his arm and her luminous violet eyes pleaded with him.

"No." Rosko wrenched his arm from her grasp and strode away. He ignored the pleas that followed him.

Wilson stood by his car, grinning from ear to ear. Slapping Rosko on the back, he chuckled. "Must be nice to have such a gorgeous woman chasing you."

"Shove it, Wilson."

Wilson made a gesture of using his hand to wipe the grin off his face. "Let's go check out the diner. It's close by."

"Will it be open?" Rosko asked.

"Fred will be getting ready for the breakfast crowd. Not only does Fred make a great burger, he also serves a mighty fine breakfast."

They had no trouble finding a parking spot. Most of the businesses didn't open till nine, and that was still hours away.

Rosko saw the reflection of lights through the windows, that is, what little light the dingy windows allowed through. Fred's Diner was a long way from earning stars for curb appeal. Hopefully the food would make up for it. He was starving, and he needed a good cup of coffee.

CHAPTER 19

Fred leaned against the counter chatting with one of his customers. His head jerked up when the door opened. He ran a hand through the few snowy hairs intersecting his gleaming head and nodded to them, his dark eyes narrowing slightly. He'd been around long enough to make them as cops. Mechanically, he wiped the counter top with a bleached-out washcloth, his pudgy hand making enlarging circles with each swipe. "What can I do for you, boys?"

Fred had a large round face, the type that makes it difficult to determine age. Thick, dark eyebrows overshadowed his ruddy cheeks. Combined with a veined bulbous nose, the total effect was of an oversized bloodhound. A once-white apron, now adorned with a multitude of ketchup, mustard and grease hung loosely over his protruding abdomen. It partially covered the slogan of his T-shirt. Rosko made out the SH and the T on the first line and a HAP…NS on the next line. He figured out the rest.

Rosko met his gaze. "We'd like to talk to you about Tina."

"Where is the bitch? She didn't show up for work. I had to stay all night. I've put up with enough of her shit, coming in late, smelling of booze. That's it, she's fired."

Fred's eyebrows drew together and he halted his tirade. "Hey, what do you guys want with Tina?"

"Somebody attacked her last night."

Wilson leaned on the counter and watched the man's reaction. Fred shook his head but continued to wipe the counter. "You're not surprised, Fred?"

"Not with the crowd she hangs with. Was it her boyfriend? Tell her if she straightens up and gets rid of him, I'll give her a second chance."

"She won't be needing another chance, Fred. She's dead."

"Oh shit. That bastard. I hope you get him."

"Who?" Rosko asked.

"The boyfriend, of course. He's a real jerk. I told her to get rid of him."

"We're not sure it was her boyfriend," Wilson said. "She was found in Gibbons Park. Looks like she cut through the park on her way to work."

"Ah shit," Fred shook his head. His hand halted mid-circle. "You mean she was on her way here when…"

"Looks that way. What can you tell us about the boyfriend?" Rosko asked.

"His name's Mark. Mark something. A real loser. I don't know what she sees in him. Comes in here all the time, expecting free food." He looked away and scrubbed at a spot on the counter. "She came to work a couple of times with bruises. Said she banged into a wall, but I knew better. Told her to drop him."

"Do you have an address for her? And her next of kin?" Rosko interrupted.

"Sure. Just give me a minute."

Fred rifled through an old shoebox. It looked like he needed to advertise for a waitress/secretary when he put up his next HELP WANTED sign. Rosko made a few notes while they waited. After a minute, Fred pulled out a crumpled piece of paper and handed it over. Rosko used his fingers to iron it out so could read it. He wrote down her address. He knew the street. Not one of the better areas of town. Her mother's first name was listed as next-of-kin, but no address. He wrote the information in his notebook.

"Do you know where her parents live?" Rosko asked.

"Sorry. She never said."

And you never took the time to ask, Rosko thought. Instead he asked, "Do you know where the boyfriend lives?"

"No idea. But he works over at Lenny's Garage. He's a mechanic there."

Wilson and Rosko exchanged glances. "Isn't that the garage over on Gerrard?" Wilson asked.

"Yeah, that's the one."

"We'll have a chat with Mark," Rosko assured him.

And this wouldn't be the first police chat with Mark Finnian. Were they finally getting a break on the case? Maybe they could even wrap it up before the news came on at eight. Wouldn't that be an ace up his sleeve?

Fred used a corner of his apron to wipe a tear away. "I hope you nail him good. Tina didn't deserve to die. She wasn't bad, just mixed up. Can I get you guys some breakfast? On the house, for Tina."

Rosko looked at his watch. It was just after five. Should they go and pick up Finnian, break down his door and drag him out of bed? Sounded tempting, but they'd better talk to him at a reasonable hour. All they needed was for him to slap a harassment suit on the department. They might as well get some food in their bellies before tackling the bastard. With their luck he'd have a solid alibi. But maybe not. Just maybe when they broke the news to Tina's parents they'd be able to tell them who murdered her. Letting them get another hour of sleep wasn't going to matter much in the long run. Rosko turned to Wilson.

"Shall we have a bite to eat while we formulate a plan to tackle our friend?"

Wilson nodded then rubbed the small pot at his belt line. "Sounds like a good idea. We don't want to go in guns blazing and screw it up." He turned to Fred. "I'll have the two egg special, sunny side up with bacon."

Fred nodded to Rosko.

"I'll have the hungry man special."

"Coming right up, boys. Have a seat over in one of them booths."

Within minutes Fred returned with two plates brimming with food. The scent of bacon had Rosko's mouth watering. He dug in, making short work of the meal. Sitting back with a sigh, he used a piece of toast to wipe the last of the egg drippings off his plate. "No wonder the truckers come here." He grinned at Wilson. "Let's go check out Tina's place."

At the counter, Fred refused to let them pay.

"That's for Tina. Just make sure you catch the bastard. She didn't deserve to die."

Rosko and Wilson left without telling Fred the details of Tina's death. He would hear them soon enough on the news.

෴

Tina Luciano's apartment building was a three-minute drive from the diner. They pounded on the door for several minutes before a disgruntled superintendent jerked it open. A flash of brass badges halted the barrage of curses mid-sentence. He mumbled an apology and, stepping into the hall, identified himself as Albert Gionelli.

His pores exuded the scent of three B's—booze, body odor, and bad teeth. A wrinkled muscle shirt with streaks of fresh and seasoned sweat strained to cover his huge paunch. Remnants of last night's pizza still clung to the material. He swiped a sweating palm and added to the mix.

Rosko avoided stepping on the pieces of food that abandoned Gionelli's shirt as he led them to the third floor walk-up. Musty reminders of stale beer, marijuana, mildew, and rotting garbage filled the narrow stairway and bright colored graffiti decorated the dingy, beige walls. Rosko didn't pause to inspect the obscene pictures or the invitations it boasted. He was too busy making sure he gave Gionelli a several-foot lead. His attempt to stay downwind wasn't successful. The sweat stains on the super's shirt extended with the effort of lumbering up the stairs.

The ascent was silent. Gionelli stopped at a poorly lit doorway. A series of mumbled curses accompanied his struggle with a large ring of keys. Rosko wondered if it would have been easier to find the proper one if he replaced the burnt out bulb.

Tina's apartment was small and sparsely furnished. Gionelli informed them it was rented by the month and came furnished. Tina had added little to it—empty beer bottles, pizza boxes and a few clothes, most of which were scattered on the unmade bed. Pulling gloves on, Wilson and Rosko searched the apartment. It didn't take long. They took away only a worn red address book.

After the super relocked the apartment door, the detectives stretched a length of yellow tape across the doorway. They were treated to more of Gionelli's colorful language as he read the "Crime Scene do not enter."

"When are you guys going to take that damn tape off so I can rent the room?

Wilson slapped another piece of tape across the doorway.

"Come on, guys, give me a break here."

The detectives hurried down the shadowed stairway without responding. Rosko was relieved to reach the street and take a breath of fresh air.

They found Tina's parent's phone number in the red address book. A quick computer search gave them the address. It was still early and they hoped they would find both parents at home. Rosko's worst nightmare was a parent finding out about their child's death on the news.

Wilson drove. Adderly was a small town outside of Strathburn. It took them less than an hour to get there. A gas station attendant gave them directions to the house. It was a small blue bungalow with a white picket fence and a porch stretching across the front of the house. An assortment of planters brimming with petunias and geraniums graced both sides of the path. Hanging pots of pink fuchsias adorned the porch. The house was freshly painted and had the charm of a secluded sanctuary. Too bad Tina left the shelter of its doors.

Many tears were shed, but they learned little. Reaching adolescence, Tina fought constantly with her father and his old fashioned ideals. She'd left home five years ago, and other than coming home for Christmas and birthdays, she'd kept them out of her life.

It was a few minutes before seven when they arrived back in Strathburn. Lenny's would open at eight o'clock. Rosko had Wilson drop him off at his car. They'd meet at the garage at 8:01 a.m.

The drive to Adderly had been fruitless. They had no more information than before they'd left. Maybe their visit with Mark Finnian would prove more productive.

CHAPTER 20

The night had flown by. Claire glanced at the circular clock. Less than an hour before her shift ended at seven. She sat at the nurse's station, unable to keep her head from bobbing. The wail of a child jolted her awake. A young blonde woman carried a screaming child through the automatic doors of the emergency department. His left forearm was swollen and distorted.

"Help! My son hurt his arm." Her tears flowed as quickly as those of her child. Between sobs, she recounted the injury. "He got out of bed—he fell." She paused to sob a breath. "He just hit the edge of the bed."

One of the nurses, Jan O'Sullivan, eased the boy out of his mother's arms and placed him on a stretcher. She slid a pillow under his injured arm. With his arm supported, the child settled. Claire attempted to calm the mother while she visually examined the arm. No point in touching it, the forked angle just above the wrist told her it was broken. She crossed to the bed. "What's your name, young man?"

"Tommy." He sniffed. "Tommy Alexander Davenport."

"That's quite a name. How old are you, Tommy?"

Tommy held up his right hand to show four fingers.

"Well Tommy, we'll get your arm fixed up and you'll be home in no time. First we're going to take a picture of it. It won't hurt," Claire told him. "Is that okay?"

Tommy sniffed again, his small head nodded rapidly.

She turned away from the child and spoke quietly to the mother. "I'm Doctor Valincourt. He'll be fine, but the arm is broken and will have to be reset. We can do that here in emergency."

While Jan distracted Tommy, Claire explained the procedure to his mother. "We'll start an intravenous, give him something for pain, and then confirm the fracture with an x-ray. After the x-ray, we'll decide how to repair his arm. Don't worry, we'll fix him up good as new," Claire reassured her. The woman, too upset for words, nodded her understanding.

Claire picked up the phone and paged the radiology department. She glanced at the clock—forty-five minutes to go before the end of her shift. Could they get the x-ray and have this child's arm repaired before then? The boy had settled and Claire didn't want him stressed by having to meet a whole new set of faces at shift change. Mrs. Davenport sat beside her son, stroking his hair.

Does Tommy have any allergies?" Claire asked.

"None that I know off."

"Good. When did he eat last?"

"About 6:30. I put him to bed at eight. He didn't eat anything after supper."

Claire glanced at the boy's chart. The information corresponded with what the mother had already told the nurse.

"So it's been over four hours?"

"Oh, yes," the mother said.

Claire quickly explained the procedure. "I'm going to give him ketamine. It will sedate him without making him unconscious and then I can fix his arm here in the emergency department. We don't need to go to the operating room and give him a full anesthetic."

Mrs. Davenport nodded. She stroked her son's hair. With his arm stable on the pillow, the pain had eased and Tommy dozed.

"So you can fix it here?" The mother asked.

"Should be no problem," Claire assured her. "We'll just get the x-ray first."

Claire went back to the nurse's station. She nodded toward the child. "Jan, I've paged radiology for an x-ray of his arm." "I'll go and get the fracture room set up. Can you start an intravenous on him and give him some morphine for the pain."

Having anticipated Claire's request, Jan held up the intravenous bag she was priming. She approached the child, and explained what she would be doing.

In the fracture room, Claire gathered the supplies. She placed three rolls of plaster and a ten-inch strip of white flannel padding on an over-bed table. Then she pulled a wheeled stand with two metal buckets over to the sink and filled one with lukewarm water. Crossing to the anesthetic cart in the trauma room, Claire opened the ketamine drawer. It was empty.

Damn. Why does the drawer have to be empty when I'm in a hurry? Why don't people replenish after they use the last one?

Claire recalled the hectic shift. She was sure she hadn't been the last one to use the ketamine. In fact, they hadn't used any all night. The department had been busy with ear infections, flu and chest pains, but nothing requiring ketamine. She was certain she'd seen Jan restocking the cart. Maybe she missed that drawer. Claire finished gathering the supplies and headed back to the desk.

At the child's bedside, the x-ray machine hummed. Jan, draped in a shoulder to thigh lead apron, held the child's arm while the radiology technician shot the films. Claire waited the required six feet back until she heard the blip indicating the x-ray was done. As the machine wheeled away, Claire approached Jan. "There's no ketamine in the trauma room."

Jan was busy repositioning the child's pillow under his broken arm and spoke without turning. "It's in the drawer."

"No, it isn't."

The child was crying again after the movement of his arm and Claire heard the frustration in Jan's voice. "It's there. I put a new vial in at the beginning of the shift. There was a half full bottle already there."

Claire walked away. "Well, it's gone now."

"I'll get it in a minute," Jan snapped then turned back to speak soothingly to Tommy. Gradually his cries settled and she came back to the nurse's station. She handed Claire an unopened vial of Ketamine.

Claire drew up a weight-appropriate dosage for the child, then she drew up a second syringe with midazolam, another sedation drug. The combination would put the child into just enough of a sleepy state that she could quickly fix the break. She put the syringes and a few alcohol swabs into the front pocket of her greens. As soon as she viewed the x-ray they could get started.

A moment later the x-ray technician returned and slid the film onto a viewing box. The arm was definitely broken. Jan put heart monitor leads on Tommy's chest, an oxygen monitor on his thumb, and a blood pressure cuff on his uninjured arm. The blip of his heart rate and his oxygen level flashed across the oscilloscope. Claire looked at the readings: blood pressure 105/62, heart rate 113, oxygen saturation 99%—everything normal.

She injected the medications into the intravenous lines and within seconds Tommy's eyelids began to twitch and he became still. Claire touched his broken arm. No response. The drugs were working. Jan checked his blood pressure again—still stable.

With a quick tug on Tommy's arm, Claire reduced the fracture. The boy barely moaned. She wrapped his arm in several layers of casting material then positioned it back on the pillow. His vital signs remained stable. The post reduction x-ray revealed good alignment. As soon as Tommy woke up, he could go home.

Claire glanced at the clock. Good timing. Two minutes before seven. She heard her bed calling. She hadn't been sleeping well lately. Memories of the body in the park haunted her dreams, waking her, and once awake, she had trouble getting back to sleep. Sometimes, there was time to lie down between patients, but not last night. She prayed she'd be too tired to dream today.

Her shift over, she headed out the hospital doors. Detective Rosko's car turned into the circular drive and pulled up beside her. The sight of him was reassuring. Something about him said trust, honesty, steadfastness. But then hadn't she thought the same about Michael. Obviously, she wasn't a good judge of character. It would be a long time before she'd trust a man again. The car window rolled down.

"Just finishing your shift?" Detective Rosko asked.

"Yes."

"Do you have time for a coffee? I wanted to see if you remembered anything else…and there's something I want to run past you."

"As long as the coffee's decaffeinated. I need to sleep before working again tonight."

"Are you driving?"

"No. I jogged to work, but the shift was so busy, I'll just be staggering home." She laughed. "No energy left."

"Well, hop in. I can drop you home after we have coffee."

Rosko leaned across the seat and opened the passenger door. They made idle chatter on the drive to a nearby café. Conflicting emotions ran through Claire's mind as she thought of their last encounter in her apartment. Was this meeting coincidence, or planned, purely professional? Would she be disappointed if it was?

Their arrival at the café quelled her rambling. She waited until they were seated in a booth before asking. "Have you found out who killed the woman in the park?"

"Not yet." Rosko added sugar to his coffee then looked up. "We're trying to get some sort of link between the women."

"Women? There was another one?"

"Last night. Looks like the same killer. From the autopsy on the first victim, the coroner thinks he used some sort of anesthetizing agent to render her powerless. We aren't sure yet what it was. We're waiting for the toxicology results. Mac thinks the guy used a chloroform saturated cloth to initially subdue her then injected her with something to sedate her before removing the kidney." He smiled. "But you probably already know that."

Claire nodded. "I was at the first autopsy. When is this one scheduled?"

"This morning." Rosko grimaced. "I guess I'll be there."

"Not one of your favorite things?"

"You can say that again."

"Not the nicest way to spend a morning."

"Mac's always harassing me about my weak stomach," Rosko confessed.

"Have you known him a long time?"

"For years. His wife, Moira, too."

Claire chuckled. "She's a nice lady. I don't know how she puts up with him."

"Moira knows his talk is harmless. They've stuck together though the proverbial 'in sickness and in health' and survived. It doesn't happen often."

Claire thought about Michael. It was time to change the conversation. "Do you have any clues about the killer? That is, if you can tell me."

Rosko shrugged. "There's not a lot to tell. We think he's a Caucasian male, between 25 and 35 years old, with at least college education, and fairly strong."

"How do you come up with details like that?" she asked.

Rosko grinned, taking a long draw on his coffee. Claire noticed how his face softened when he smiled. His boyish grin made him look like a man in his early thirties instead of pushing forty. "Just make them up to please the press."

Claire choked on a mouth full of coffee and banged her mug onto the table. It clattered against the wooden surface causing several people to look their way. She coughed several times before she could breathe properly. Rosko leaned across the table with a look of concern.

"Are you okay? I was just kidding."

Still unable to talk, Claire nodded. Right now, the quiet concern in his deep blue eyes affected her more than the misdirected coffee. His apologetic grin, intimate and disarming in the close confines of the cubicle, caused a tingle to radiate down her spine and she shivered.

He leaned across the table. "Are you cold?"

The softness of his tone sent another wave down her spine. She turned away from the intensity of his gaze and rubbed her arms. "No. I'm just tired."

"I'm on my way to an interview, I'll drive you home."

"That would be great." Claire smiled. "It was a long night, and I have another couple to work."

It wasn't until she was home in bed that she realized she hadn't asked him about talking to a crisis counselor. Maybe she'd call him later.

CHAPTER 21

Lenny glared at the detectives. "I told you boys I run a clean shop."

"We've got no problem with your place. We're looking for Finnian. Mark Finnian," Wilson said. "He does work here?"

"Yeah. Is he in some kind of trouble? I told you already. I don't want no trouble here."

"Can we talk to him?"

"Sure. He's over there."

Lenny pointed to a navy Cavalier in the second bay. Rosko and Wilson approached the car. Rosko checked out the work boots sticking out from under the vehicle. Were they size eight or nine? Small feet, small hands, how did the rest of it go?

"Hey," Wilson called out. "Mark Finnian. That you under there?"

The work-boots, along with a blue-uniformed coverall, rolled out from under the Cavalier. Their owner remained horizontal on the trolley.

"Yeah. I'm Finnian. Who wants to know?" He shaded his eyes against the change in light. "Oh, it's you guys. What do you want this time?"

Was his tone always surly, or was it just for their benefit? With his long greasy hair, pockmarked face, and sparse reddish-brown goatee, Rosko wondered what Tina had seen in him.

Wilson bent toward Finnian. His voice was quiet but harsh. "Look, you asshole, we can have a pleasant chat here, or we can take a nice long trip to the station. Your choice."

Finnian got to his feet and darted a gaze at his boss. "Look, I don't need any trouble." He waved grease-covered palms in front of him. "I'm not using anymore. I swear."

"We're not here about drugs," Rosko said. "Where were you last night?"

Finnian raised an eyebrow in question. "At Kelsey's."

"Till what time?"

"About two o'clock. I left at closing."

"Any witnesses?"

"Hey, what's this about? I had nothing to do with that fight. I swear I didn't."

"Who were you with?"

"I was with my girlfriend. Till she went to work."

"What time was that?"

"About eleven-thirty. She had to work at twelve. Hey, she didn't send you guys over here did she? I know she was pissed I didn't walk her to work…"

Rosko stared at Finnian. Was he for real, or a damned good liar?

"So who saw you after your girlfriend left?" Wilson asked.

"Everybody in the bar."

"Like anyone in particular?" Wilson asked.

"This girl I was dancing with."

Rosko raised an eyebrow. "Would you happen to know her name?"

"Kim."

"Kim who?"

"Kim Perry." His brow wrinkled. "What's this about?"

"You got an address for this Kim Perry?"

Finnian pulled a folded scrap of paper out of a frayed wallet. Rosko saw the impression of a condom in the vinyl. At least he was using them. Sure didn't want to deplete that gene field. Finnian handed the paper to Wilson and watched him write down the information.

"We'll be needing your home number, and address," Rosko said.

"Are you guys going to tell me what this is about?"

"Here, you might need this." Wilson waved the scrap of paper in front of Finnian and then pressed it to his chest. "Your girlfriend, Tina Luciano, was murdered last night."

At least Finnian had the grace to show a combination of shock, remorse, and guilt. But his baser instincts came to the forefront.

"Hey, you guys don't think I had anything to do with it, do you?"

Well so much for the loving concerned boyfriend. Rosko knew who was number one on Finnian's hit parade.

"What happened?" Finnian demanded.

"You'll hear about it on the news. Meanwhile we need to talk to your witness. Don't think about leaving town." Rosko glared at him. "Or calling her before we get there. We'll be talking to you again."

His hands were just about the right size for the bruises they'd found on Tina. Did this guy know how to use a scalpel?

ⒺⓈⒺⓈ

They'd obviously woken Kim Perry from a drunken haze. Her fine blonde hair hung in matted wisps around her face and her puffy eyes seemed to have trouble focusing on their badges. She rubbed at them lengthening the mascara smudges streaking her pale cheeks. The smell of cigarette smoke and stale beer emanated from her. When she opened her mouth, she displayed teeth stained from nicotine and poor dental hygiene.

Her speech was slurred, and from the medley of language it was evident she wasn't impressed with having her beauty sleep disturbed. And according to the dark circles under her eyes, she needed it.

They didn't keep her from her bed for long. She confirmed Finnian had been at Kelsey's. And yes, she'd been with him from eleven-thirty until the bar closed. He'd walked her home and left in the wee hours of the morning.

Too bad Finnian hadn't done Tina the courtesy of walking her to work.

CHAPTER 22

When Rosko arrived back in his office, Mary Jane Winters' autopsy report lay on top of his desk. Cause of death: hemorrhagic shock due to blood loss. It confirmed chloroform caused the irritation marks around her mouth. Two sites on her right arm showed evidence of needle punctures. Bruises were present around the sites. The killer obviously had trouble finding a vein.

The toxicology report showed traces of ketamine in the body. No other drugs were found. The trace of alcohol was presumably from a glass of wine at dinner. No sign of recent sexual activity. There was plenty of blood for DNA testing—too bad it was all hers. Time of death was sometime between eleven-thirty p.m. and three a.m.

Rosko put the report into Mary Jane's file. Other than giving a name to the drugs used, there was nothing new. So far, all they knew about their killer was that he was strong, he drove a van, and he had some medical knowledge.

The markings on Mary Jane's back had been positively identified as the tread of a van mat. It was an after-market one made by Goodyear and could be purchased anywhere. Similar indentations marred Tina Luciano's back.

At this point, they had no obvious link between Winters and Luciano. He doubted they ever would. Finnian had a rap sheet, for burglary and possession. Nobody had charged him with assault or rape, yet. None of the family or friends of Mary Jane Winters had anything other than parking tickets. But the police weren't finished investigating yet, and now, they had a whole new circle of people to look at. Would the investigation of their most recent victim be any more productive? Rosko hoped so.

He wasn't ready to dismiss Finnian as a suspect yet, despite his alibi. Alibis weren't concrete. If he was responsible for the bruises on Tina's body, he could stew for a good long time, at least until they found a better suspect.

What would someone capable of such mutilation look like? Rosko visualized a large man with greasy hair, disheveled and hanging around an unshaven face. The rest of him was just as unkempt—baggy jeans and large, stained T-shirt—a bully using his strength to dominate women. Finnian's face kept showing up in the picture, but Rosko knew he could be wrong. Their killer would probably end up being some meek and mild young man who, like a chameleon, slipped easily in and out of an unsuspecting society. Odds are he would be intelligent, clean cut, and rarely attract attention. He would be much more difficult to find than Rosko's imagined image of the killer.

No, this man would be an observer of society. He would stand on the fringes, watching, waiting for his opportunity. This type of bastard was hard to catch. They usually killed several times before they got sloppy and left any clues, or the police had enough victims they could find some pattern. Usually, by then he was reveling in the spotlight and becoming overconfident, taking risks. And that's when he usually got caught. Rosko prayed they caught him long before then.

He glanced up at the wall clock. He'd better get moving. He was due to meet Mac in half an hour. He slid the file into the desk drawer and headed out of the station.

❧❧❧

"Sorry I'm late, Mac."

Doctor MacFarlane shoved the last bit of a tuna sandwich into his mouth and wiped his lips with the back of his hand. "Well, she's not going anywhere." He grinned. "I'm ready to start. But I didn't want you to miss anything."

"Gee thanks. And I was hoping you'd be finished."

"No such luck. The experience is good for you. Builds character."

"I've got lots of character, thanks."

Mac crumpled the plastic wrap from his sandwich and pitched it at the garbage pail. It hit the rim and tipped inside. "Well, laddie, let's get started then."

Mac covered his green scrubs with a long green gown. Rosko exchanged his suit jacket for matching surgical garb and followed him into the adjoining room. Both men put on sterile gloves and masks before approaching the table.

A white plastic sheet covered the stainless steel table, silhouetting the figure below. Maurice stood nearby arranging instruments on a wheeled table. He covered the instruments with a sterile green towel and rolled the table beside the gurney. He flipped the switch on the surgical lamp and illuminated the room with a brilliant circle of light.

"You can uncover her now, Maurice," Mac said.

A tug on one end of the white plastic revealed the naked body. The sound of crinkling plastic filled the room as Maurice folded the long sheet. When he removed the green towel covering the instruments, Rosko saw the glint of the stainless steel and wondered what the hell he was doing here. Could he not just wait for the report?

But he knew it was better to get the information first hand. Whatever it took to catch the killer, he'd do. He just wished they had other leads so he could make his excuses to Mac. Unfortunately, they'd pretty well run into a brick wall with nowhere to turn.

Metal squealed as Mac pulled the instrument table closer. Rosko now had a full view of Tina Luciano's face. Strands of long brown hair trailed over the edge of the table. It was silky and unmatted, as if recently brushed. Her face resembled a marbled mask—the skin tinged a transparent gray-blue. Her lips were open slightly as if ready to speak. Had her final utterance been a scream for help, or had her drugged state prevented any response? Rosko glanced down the length of her body. Death had aged her beyond her twenty-three years.

In the interval since her death Tina's body had gone through a rainbow of colors—from the healthy pink hue of life, to the ashen paleness of recent death, to mottled cyanosis, and now, to its final gray cast. Bruises sustained in life were magnified. Shades of yellow, blue, and purple made bold splotches on the gray canvas.

Rosko examined the bruises on the sides of her neck. Had Finnian done that to her or were they from fighting off her killer? Were they one and the same?

Maurice pinned a microphone to Doctor MacFarlane's gown. Mac spoke into it.

"Tina Luciano, Caucasian female, age twenty-three."

Rosko stood a couple feet back trying to control the queasiness in his stomach. If Mac found something of interest he'd let him know. In fact, it took only a few seconds before he called him closer.

"See these marks?" Mac pointed to reddish marks around the woman's mouth. "We'll send blood and urine for toxicology, but I bet they're from chloroform. Same as the other one."

"Seems to be part of our killer's MO," Rosko said.

Mac nodded then spoke into the microphone again. "Pressure bruises around mouth. Body also has multiple bruises on torso and arms in varying stages of healing. All pre-mortem."

Rosko leaned close and examined the bruises. Damn the prick. Now she was dead, he couldn't get the bastard for assault but he sure as shit was going to do his best to get him for her murder.

"See this?" Mac pointed the exam light to an abrasion on the left side of her neck. It was barely visible. "It looks like a chain was pulled off. It may have been on purpose, or it may have come off in the struggle."

Mac traced his gloved hand along the middle of her neck. Then he used his thumb and forefinger to run the ridge of her trachea. "There's no sign of strangulation. The hyoid bone is intact, but there are these marks." He pointed to a series of small bruises on either sides of her neck. He placed his fingertips over the spots. They covered the purplish marks completely.

"He's got big hands. His glove size is probably about the same as mine, size eight."

"You're sure they're from the killer?" Rosko asked.

"Pretty sure. They're fresh. These ones," Mac said, pointing to a series of small yellow bruises on the arm closest to them, "were made earlier." He put his arm over the bruises. His hand obliterated them. "Maurice, can you come here?"

The morgue technician approached the bedside.

"What size glove do you wear, Maurice."

"Seven."

"Can you put your hand on her upper arm?" Maurice placed his hand as instructed. "Good, now slide it up a bit."

Rosko and Mac watched as Maurice's hand, like the piece of a jigsaw puzzle, became a perfect match to fit one set in a series of bruises on Tina's arm.

"What size gloves do you think the boyfriend would wear, laddie?"

"I'd say about the same size as Maurice's."

"Thanks, Maurice. I'll need you in a couple of minutes to help collect specimens."

"Everything's ready when you are, Mac," Maurice said.

MacFarlane nodded at his technician then continued with his external examination of the body. "Her rings are missing. She wore a lot of them, one on each finger. See the paler area where the tan marks end."

"So our killer is collecting trophies," Rosko said.

"Looks like it."

Mac worked his way down the victim, dictating his findings. Rosko's gaze followed his exam.

"Maurice, can you take some pictures before I open her up?"

Starting from the top, the camera captured every angle, not pausing until it had captured her entire body. When Maurice finished, Mac selected a scalpel from the tray and made the usual Y incision, intersecting the killer's slash. Then, with quick short slices, he snipped through the sutures.

After cutting through the third suture, Mac adjusted the overhead lamp to direct a beam directly into the incision. He selected a pair of forceps off the instrument tray and stroked them along the freshly exposed epidermis. Squeezing the ends of the forceps, he waved his hand in the air as if he'd just won a prize. Rosko stared at the forceps. A thin dark hair had been captured between the tiny teeth of the instrument.

"Well, well, look at this."

"It's a strand of hair, isn't it?"

"That's right."

"Is it the victim's?"

"Not the same as hers, different shade and texture. The victim has long auburn hair. This one is short, darker, and thicker."

"You think it belongs to the killer." Rosko knew his voice had risen in excitement but this might be a clue they could finally use.

"Well, it came from inside the victim. I'd say it's a safe assumption. We'll send it off for DNA."

Mac dropped the hair into the plastic container Maurice held open.

Rosko didn't want to get his hopes raised for nothing. "Could it be from someone at the scene?"

"Don't think so," Mac said. "It was stuck inside. Our killer probably wasn't wearing an operating room cap when he did his surgery."

Rosko crossed his fingers and waved them in the air. "Let's hope it's his, and we get some DNA. We need something on this bastard."

Mac turned his attention back to the incision, snipping quickly through the rest of the sutures until Tina's belly gaped like a crimson cavern. The slash across her right side had sliced neatly through the layers of skin, superficial fascia, and the muscle until it stretched into the peritoneal space. The cavity was filled with blood, some congealed, and some refusing to congeal. No longer contained, blood oozed out the edges of the incision, dripping onto the stainless steel table, splattering onto the floor.

Mac slid his gloved hand into the incision and examined the abdominal organs. He accounted for them all—all of them except her right kidney. "Look at this." He held up a thin tenuous strand in his gloved hands. "The bastard cut through the veins and the artery and let his victim just bleed to death."

"How long did it take for her to die?" Rosko asked.

"Once the artery was severed," Mac said, shrugging, "she'd only live about five minutes. The heart would keep pumping blood through the arteries into her abdomen until there was no blood left."

"So he doesn't have to wait long before he can dump his victims without them bleeding all over?"

"Well it looks like he might have suctioned some of the blood out, or drained it before he stitched her up. He made an attempt to clean her up."

"Gracious of him," Rosko retorted.

"Our killer's technique is improving. He did the same transverse cut across her abdomen as before, but look at how neat the line is. Our boy's learning to use his tools."

"Was the cut made with the same instrument?"

"Yup. He used a scalpel both times. The difference is the incision on the first victim was jagged. It was as if he hesitated when he made his cuts. Now, he's more confident. He's making sure, quick strokes." Mac looked up. "You better find this bastard before he passes himself off as a surgeon somewhere."

Rosko looked at the pathologist in disbelief.

MacFarlane shrugged. "Well, you know what they tell the surgical residents?"

Rosko shook his head.

"Observe one operation, assist with one, do one."

"You got to be kidding."

Mac chuckled. "Our guy wanted to be a surgeon. That might be a place to start. Somebody who couldn't get into a medical school, or got booted out."

"Let's hope he tried to get into med school around here. I'll start with the closest and radiate out. Do you think he used ketamine this time?"

"Probably. He'll stick with it as long as he gets the results he wants."

"Where do you think he's getting the drugs?"

"There's a few places. Hospitals, veterinarians, both use ketamine. He could be getting his supply from a pharmaceutical company, either stealing it, or buying if from someone who works there. Or he might be getting it off a dealer."

"Lee estimated time of death somewhere between midnight and three this morning. What do you think?"

"I think he was bang on." Mac answered. "Now, do you want to see the rest of this autopsy or not?"

"Well." Rosko looked at him hopefully. "If you don't think there's anything else relevant…I wouldn't mind going."

Mac's hearty laugh filled the room. "Sure, laddie. Never did have much of a stomach, did you? I'll call you if I find anything else."

Rosko couldn't make his feet move fast enough. At the door, he tore off the green scrub-gown and threw it at the open linen bag. The echo of Mac's laughter followed him through the double doors.

On the street, he finally took a breath without formaldehyde stinging his nostrils. He wanted to change his clothes but he needed to head back to the station. Mac had given him something to check on. How big of a radius should he cover, a hundred miles, five hundred? How many medical schools were there within a five-hundred mile radius? Would that be far enough? At least they had something to work with.

CHAPTER 23

Wilson was at his desk when Rosko got back to the station. He glanced up from shuffling papers and rolled his eyes toward the glass-enclosed office at the end of the room. "Chief wants to see us."

Rosko grimaced. "And I wonder what he wants?"

"Maybe the latest murder, you think?" Wilson's laugh was gruff. "Said he wanted to see us the minute you got back. He's had his morning coffee and donut so I hope his mood's improved."

"Another one of those days?" Rosko asked.

"Have we had any others lately?"

"Not since Alexis gave him the ultimatum. I thought wife number four might make him happier?"

"Guess not," Rosko said. "And this case isn't helping."

"I wish we'd get a lead we could work with." Wilson said.

"Well, we might have something." Rosko tilted his head and grinned. "Mac found a hair in the latest victim's incision. If he can get DNA off it, maybe it will match somebody in a database somewhere. Plus he thinks the killer might have wanted to be a surgeon. Let's go see what the chief's got to say, then we can get to work on some of the medical schools in the area. Did you read the autopsy report on the Winters girl?"

"Yeah," Wilson said. "I've started checking on possible sources of ketamine and chloroform. I'll show you my list when we get out of there." He nodded at the chief's office, then pushed back his chair, and followed Rosko.

Chief Horace Richards sat behind a large oak desk. He waved them into the room and tipped back the leather chair he filled to capacity until the hinges squeaked. Fleshy fingers twirled a Havana cigar the new smoking laws forbade him to light. The speed of the twirling mirrored his mood. Today was not good.

Rosko and Wilson stationed themselves at a point halfway between the door and the desk. The chairs were by invitation only.

Chief Richards gave none. The cigar paused in midair, the end squished into the flab of his fingers.

"I'm not hearing any good news."

"We've been working hard. So far there hasn't been anything to go on," Rosko admitted.

"And another murder last night," Richards barked. "Are they related?"

Rosko grimaced. "Afraid so. The MO for both murders seems the same."

The cigar made a circle. "Sure it's not a copycat?"

"Don't think so. We didn't release any details of the first killing."

"What do we know about the second victim?"

"She was a waitress at an all-night diner. Fred's over on Jarvis."

"Yeah. I know the place," Richards said. "Great burgers."

"Tina Luciano went through the park on her way to work."

"Anybody in her life want to mutilate her?"

"She had a boyfriend. Looks like he's pushed her around. She's got bruises." Rosko shrugged. "But would he cut her up like that? I'm not sure."

"We got two bodies. Do you think the killer tried to cover his tracks? Murdered the second one to throw us off, make us chase after an imaginary serial killer?" Richards asked.

"It's possible." Rosko shrugged. "But I don't think so." Rosko paused. "The MO's too intricate just to cover another murder."

"So Rosko, what exactly is this perp's MO?"

"He's takes their kidneys. Uses chloroform to subdue them, takes them somewhere, injects them with ketamine, then cuts out one of their kidneys. The sicko leaves the other one. Lets them bleed to death. According to Mac they'd die within minutes of the artery being sliced."

"Holy shit," Chief Richards snarled. "Is our perp a surgeon?"

"Not likely. He's not good enough. But he's got some medical knowledge. There's only one incision on each victim, and he doesn't go digging around. He knows where the kidney is and how to cut it out. And after, he stitches them up."

Richards shook his head. "Why bother stitching them up?"

"Who knows," Wilson said. "Following some sick regime."

"Maybe he flunked out of med school?"

"That's one possibility," Rosko said. "I'm going to check on lists of anyone who failed or dropped out of medical school in the last ten years anywhere within a hundred-mile radius. I'll get Myers checking on who's living locally and cross-reference for police records."

"Might be good to check any animal cruelty reports from the Humane Society," Wilson added.

Chief Richards nodded. "Serial killers often start their careers killing or mutilating animals. Too bad crimes against animals so often go unreported. And even the ones that get reported are often minimized."

Wilson snorted. "Maybe our perp is performing mock kidney transplants."

"You think he needs one for himself?" Richards asked.

"Who knows? The way he's operating, he's not getting a usable kidney. I'm pretty sure our perp is a man, serial killers generally are. He carries his victims some distance, so he's got to be strong, but his victims are women. Another thing—" Rosko paused. "He poses the bodies carefully with their arms crossed." Rosko demonstrated. "What's that pose remind you of?"

"Body in a casket," Richards replied.

"Right. I think the perp's obsessed with a woman who needs or needed a kidney." Rosko nodded. "That's my best theory so far."

"His wife?" Richards asked.

"Maybe, but most serial killers don't have the emotional wherewithal for marriage. More likely it is some girl he's obsessed with, worshiped from afar but never got up the guts to ask out, or even speak to. Maybe it's his mother, or some woman he worked with, or saw at the corner store every day. Maybe it's some woman he's stalked for ten years who suddenly up and died on him."

"You're really speculating now, aren't you?

Rosko nodded. "Yep. Pure bullshit. I haven't got a clue who he's obsessed with. But you can bet your pension she looks similar to his two victims. Mid-twenties, brown hair, blue eyes, about five-foot-three to five in height. I'll work on lists of women, aged twenty-five to thirty, who needed a kidney in the last four decades anywhere within a hundred miles."

Richards rocked in his chair. "Forty years? That's going to be a lot of names."

"Not really. Looks like it'll be a shorter list than the med school failures. We've got to go back a ways. The perp's psychosis could be rooted in some childhood trauma. I'll start by looking up the women here in Strathburn. I'll track down family members, ask to see photos. I'd like to find the woman who's our perp's original obsession."

"I assume you'll be interviewing the latest victim's family, co-workers, and so forth," the chief said. "See if anyone's been following either victim."

"Naturally, sir. We're working on finding a link between the victims, other than their looks. Our perp spotted his victims somewhere. Maybe they used the same health club or hair salon."

"Sounds like you're on top of it. Keep me up to speed."

"Uh, there is one thing, Chief."

"What?"

The rocking stopped and Rosko noted how the chief's thumb and forefinger clenched the end of his cigar.

"Our perp dumped both victims in the city's parks. Until we catch this guy, I'd like uniforms in every park from ten at night until seven in the morning."

"Every park! Are you nuts? Do you know how many parks we've got in this damn town?"

"Six, sir. Just six sizable ones. Plus twelve more that should be watched just in case. Riverside's the largest. It'll take six men to cover it adequately, but—"

"Six! For one damned park."

"Sir, it's our best chance of catching him."

"Get out there and find some evidence. We don't have the money or the manpower to patrol every park." The cigar circled the air. "You can have ten men. That's it. Just catch this bastard, okay? And do it before he kills someone else."

"I'm not a miracle worker. This kind of case, with no rational motive…" Rosko shrugged.

"I better hear something soon. I'm getting phone calls asking what the hell we're doing down here. The media's not helping either. You got any connection there, Rosko?"

"No!"

Why the hell couldn't people stay out of his private life? Was there anyone who didn't know about his relationship with Sherry? Obviously, the fact it was over hadn't yet made it all the way through the gossip mill. Richards glared at him. Would he reprimand him for his tone? No, his expression was enough.

Richards leaned back in his chair. His fingers compressed the end of the cigar until it was no longer visible.

"The FBI is sending over one of their profilers." He held a hand up in front of him. "Don't say a word. It's a done deal. He'll be here at ten. Make him welcome."

The chief turned his attention to the tip of his cigar. The meeting was over. Rosko clicked the door softly behind them. Neither man spoke until they'd returned to their respective desks.

"I guess we don't have a choice," Wilson said.

"Nope," Rosko agreed. "We'd better co-operate or the chief will be handing the whole case over to the FBI." Rosko pulled a manila file out of his desk. "Anything come in overnight?"

"A couple of calls about suspicious persons, and two about vans 'lurking' in the area. Myers is checking them out. He's also looking into a couple of Mary Jane Winters' clients who should be home from their vacation by now. He'll let us know if he comes up with anything. That okay with you? He looked like he needed something to keep him busy."

Rosko considered Phil Myers. The detective's recent split-up with his wife was affecting his concentration on the job. "Yeah. Get him looking into the medical and veterinarian schools in the area." Rosko opened the file to the autopsy report. "And let's get him to do a transplant list search for the past few years."

"Right." Wilson left the office, returning in a few minutes. "Wow. The guy's some kind of whiz. He's got four computers going with different searches on each one."

Rosko chuckled. "Lucky somebody around here likes the damned things."

They pulled out dog-eared telephone books and flipped through them. Rosko compiled lists of pharmaceutical suppliers and pharmacies, Wilson did the veterinarians and any clinic possibly using ketamine or chlorophyll. They had a few names in Tina Luciano's date book to check out, too.

At two minutes to ten the desk sergeant announced the arrival of the FBI profiler. Wilson didn't have much use for paper work, but he had even less for FBI profilers. "I'll just keep working the phones." He gave Rosko a wicked grin as his partner pushed away from his desk.

Rosko met Gerald Herd at the elevators. After shaking hands with the scarecrow thin profiler, he led him to a conference room that doubled as command center. A large city map occupied one wall. Positioned at the south end of Victoria Park was a red pushpin, a blue one in Gibbons Park. Other pushpins denoted Robertson

Travel, Bellini's' Restaurant, and the apartment building on Mason Avenue. On the adjoining wall, a large bulletin board displayed graphic pictures of Mary Jane Winters.

Rosko taped up glossy black and whites of Tina Luciano. Then he crossed to the map, pushed a pin onto Jarvis Street for Fred's diner, and one on Hamilton Road for Tina's apartment. Then he added another one for Lenny's Garage.

Glancing at the profiler, Rosko watched for his reaction to the pictures. Would it raise one of his sparse gray eyebrows? Rosko was disappointed. The man's demeanor remained as flat as a poker player's. Without a flinch, Herd requested the files on the victims and any other information they had compiled. He wanted an hour to review the data.

Exactly an hour later Rosko checked on the profiler. Herd thanked him for the coffee refill. Pictures of both women lay on the table in front of him. Rosko sat across from him and took a sip of his own coffee.

"Have you had enough time?"

"I can give you a brief synopsis. When I review the files in more detail, I'll be able to give you a longer report."

"So, what type of person should we be looking for?"

"He's probably Caucasian, in his late twenties, or early thirties, most likely a loner, with a high school, or college degree. He may even have attended university. Obviously, he's done his research. He has medical knowledge, but I don't think he's a doctor. His work is too heavy-handed for him to be a professional."

"Could he be a doctor, but doing a 'less than professional' job to avoid implicating himself?" Rosko asked.

"A surgeon is too arrogant to do such an amateurish job, even if attempting to disguise his work. But I must say, your killer knows his anatomy. Knows it well enough to go right for the kidney, and he knows how to slice through the vessels. And, from what I see from the autopsy report on Winters and then the preliminary on Luciano, his technique is improving."

"So," Rosko asked. "Where might we find him?"

"He could have a job in the medical field, maybe a nurse, a paramedic, or even a mortuary assistant. The scalpel gives him a feeling of omnipotence."

Herd paused and drank some coffee before continuing. "I would have to say there was some sort of trauma as a young child. Maybe a close family member died. He may have been abused by one of his parents or a sibling. Or, he may have been raised by a single parent, and suffered the trauma of a parent leaving him either by death, or after a bitter divorce. Maybe he's been an only child. I don't feel he's had a close, loving relationship with a parent." He looked at his notes. "The first murder was what, two weeks ago?"

"The first one we know about."

"Something must have triggered him recently. It could be the death of someone—a person who abused him, or deserted him. The death of a controlling family member allows the serial killer to finally live out their fantasies unhindered. Do we know of any similar murders?"

"None that have been reported," Rosko said. "We've checked your FBI data base. There's no match for this particular MO."

Rosko shifted in his chair then took a long sip of his coffee. He wondered how accurate Herd would be.

"Often serial killers have been in trouble as adolescents," Herd continued.

"What sort of trouble?"

"Aggressive behavior. They could be passive aggressive. They may have a history of bullying, fighting, damaging property, voyeurism, hurting animals. They may have even mutilated animals, practicing their fantasies."

"Anything else?"

"Not at this time. Can I take a copy of the files? I'll review them later…when I have more time to ruminate on it."

"Sure." You just ruminate as much as you want, Rosko thought. "I'll arrange for copies."

After escorting Herd to the station doors, Rosko returned to his desk to do some ruminating of his own.

CHAPTER 24

Rosko stepped over the pile of mail littering the floor. The hall was dim but he didn't bother with the light. Years of working nights with a wife who hated having her beauty sleep disturbed had accustomed him to maneuvering in the dark.

Gathering up the assortment of letters and junk mail, he dumped them on the antique sideboard. He had no patience to sort through a stack of flyers, let alone deal with bills that were multiplying as fast as the weeds in his garden. He walked through to the kitchen and flipped on the light.

He was past being tired. The case was taking up all his waking hours plus invading the few hours he regulated for sleep. Lately, he'd been leaving the house by six and not getting home until after eleven. But they had to catch the bastard. Two vicious murders committed within two weeks. People were becoming hysterical, afraid to be out after sunset, afraid to walk alone. City officials were breathing down the chief's neck, the heat passing down the line, to him, his detectives, and then on to the uniforms.

Usually he could snuff the flames before they hit his men but this fire was too big. The detectives were working at their limit, logging overtime, having vacations cancelled. They had their plates full without dealing with criticism from higher ups, not to mention the press saying they weren't doing their jobs. He had a good group of detectives, but tempers were smoldering.

Plus he had Phil Myers to worry about. His excessive drinking since the split with his wife a few months ago had been aggravated by the added stress. With all this shit going down, the department didn't need any bad press over a cop with a drinking problem. Maybe he should give him some time off. But that would just draw more attention to him, and it might not be the best thing for him. Rosko knew from experience it was better to keep working.

Right now, Myers was checking on medical and veterinarian schools, plus transplant lists. That shouldn't be too stressful. But he'd better get things under control soon, or he'd be taking enforced time off whether the case allowed for it or not. He'd talk to him tomorrow. Hopefully he wouldn't get his back up.

Rosko went to the fridge. All this heat, physical and emotional, had drained him and he just wanted to relax on his deck with a nice cold beer. His brief fantasy that someone had stocked his fridge vanished when he opened the door. A half-filled tub of margarine and a wilting head of lettuce occupied one shelf, three beers sat on another. Too bad the good looking Doctor Valincourt hadn't taken him up on his appeal to do his shopping along with her own.

He took out one of the beers then slammed the fridge door. He considered ordering a pizza, but he was too tired and hungry to wait for it to be delivered. One by one he opened the cupboard doors, half a jar of peanut butter and three cans of soup—two chicken noodle, one tomato. He grabbed the jar of peanut butter. At least there was a loaf of bread in the freezer. He knew better than to leave it in the breadbox. Mold and peanut butter didn't mix.

Cracking off four pieces of bread, he popped them into the toaster. He didn't remember having to eat frozen bread or cope with an empty fridge when Janice was around.

Rosko took his beer and sandwiches into the dining room. The map he'd tacked to a cork board leaned against the buffet. It matched the one in his office. Between bites he added pushpins for the latest victim. He stared at the map, two different women, two different lifestyles. Something had to link them together. How did their lives intersect the killer's? This map gave him no more clues than the one at the station.

He glanced at the clock, two-ten, and he was finally getting to bed. Too many coffees and he was flying high on a caffeine buzz. The beer did little to relax him as his mind continued to mull over the case. They had two bodies, two ragged incisions, and two vanished kidneys, yet no idea who the killer was. What were they missing? What was the killer doing with the kidneys? He couldn't sell them. They hadn't been harvested properly.

From what Mac and Doctor Valincourt told him the kidney needed to be perfused with blood until just before its removal. If blood stopped flowing through the organ the cells started dying, rendering it useless. A potential donor usually stayed on a ventilator to keep oxygenated blood flowing to the organ. Medications might be needed to maintain the blood pressure at a certain level. What did Mac say? The top number, the systolic, over a hundred, and the diastolic, the bottom number, over fifty? Plus, the donor should have an ounce of urine output every hour.

This butcher didn't give a shit about the victim's blood flow, or their urine output. He just cut out the kidney and let the victims bleed out. Rosko finally fell into a restless sleep. He dreamt of multi-colored kidney-shaped balloons floating above him. The balloons burst when the phone shattered his sleep at five-twenty-six.

CHAPTER 25

Virginia Gallingham looked at the clock. Fifteen minutes before eleven and the end of her shift. Shaking her brunette hair loose from its confining clip she grabbed a pile of charts and began to sign off her nursing notes. One by one she returned them to the chart rack. Finishing the last one, she threw her pen onto the desk and massaged away the carpal tunnel pain plaguing her right wrist. It was getting worse, but that was the least of her worries.

So much paperwork, everyday more forms, more records to fill in. Then you had to sign your name to everything. The hospital kept promising computerized charting. That'll be the day. With budget cuts and bed closures, administration wasn't about to spend money on more computers. Doing electronic nurse's notes would probably be even more work.

Virginia looked up as footsteps approached. "Hi, Marianne. Is your cold better?"

Marianne Cooper, the night nurse, sniffed loudly. "Damn summer cold," she said. "Spent my days off sick in bed. Walt and I were going to Sauble Beach."

"Well, you sound better than when you left."

"Not much. Working these damn nights doesn't help," Marianne complained.

"You got that right." Virginia hated nights and was glad she only worked days and evenings. "I can't sleep during the day."

"Well, talking about sleep, it's time you got your butt out of here and into a nice cozy bed." Marianne's voice lost its bantering tone. "How are you doing, girl? Heard anything from that doctor of yours?"

Virginia shrugged. "Not yet."

"Well, I hope he's got you on the priority list."

Virginia smiled. "He does, but these things take time."

"You going to call security to walk you out?"

"No. Pauline's off at eleven too. We'll go out together. The security guard's supposed to be in the parking lot between ten-thirty and eleven-thirty."

"Yeah, old Simon's there. But fat lot of good he'd be if something happened. Probably be so scared he'd piss his pants."

Virginia laughed. She wouldn't want to have to rely on Simon. Arthritis made his knees so stiff he could hardly make his rounds let alone chase somebody.

Pauline Phillips, a nurse from the orthopedic floor, poked her head out the elevator doors. "Hey, Ginny, you ready?"

"Give me a minute. Just have to give a quick report to Marianne. Do you want to grab a coffee? There's a fresh pot."

Pauline approached the nurse's desk. "Better pass. If I have coffee now I'll be up half the night."

After giving a quick report to Marianne, Virginia walked with Pauline to the elevator and then out to the dimly lit parking lot. In the glare of the florescent lights over the staff doors, Simon Wyshinski observed the safe passage of staff to and from their cars. Intermittently, he puffed on a roll-your-own, hacked violently, and spat out thick wads of yellow phlegm. Through the thick cloud of smoke surrounding him, he waved a gnarled hand at the nurses as they walked to their cars.

Virginia put her key in the ignition and prayed. The old Ford sputtered several times before springing to life. She should really take it in and get it checked but that was just another thing she was putting off. As long as it didn't stall on the way home. Maybe she'd get it checked out tomorrow.

Fifteen minutes later Virginia pulled into the parking lot of her apartment building. The drive had been short yet her head had kept bobbing and she'd almost nodded off a couple of times. The tiredness was getting worse but she couldn't take sick time for that. She hoped her doctor would call soon. Then she'd need all the sick time she'd accumulated and more.

She locked her car, crossed to the back door of the building, and cursed the landlord for the fifth time that week. The bulb had burned out two weeks ago and he still hadn't replaced it. First thing in the morning she'd call and complain again. She fumbled with her keys. Eventually finding the right one, she slid it into the lock. It didn't want to turn. Couldn't the landlord fix anything around this damn place?

A twig snapped. Virginia jumped. She looked at the bushes beside the parking lot. It was too dark. She couldn't see anything. Snap. A footfall. A second one.

Virginia forced the key to turn.

CHAPTER 26

He slipped the tourniquet around her right forearm and made a slip-knot. Still under the effect of the chloroform, she made only a weak attempt to pull away. Her hand looked like a tiny sparrow in his large palm. He held the slender fingers, examining the slight oval curve of nails manicured a deep shade of rose. "Such pretty hands. Just like mother's."

His right thumb stroked her fingertips while he waited for the veins in the back of her hand to fill. He'd been practicing. It didn't look hard when the nurses did it. Once the animals were dead, they didn't object. He didn't want bruises this time.

Within seconds the veins swelled until they were long, raised cords. Pulling a wheeled tray closer, he picked up an alcohol swab and ripped the foiled package open with his teeth. Some of the fluid leaked into his mouth. The bitter methyl alcohol merged with his saliva and he spat out the foul mix. He swabbed both of the blue lines radiating up her hand. If he missed the first vein, the other would be ready.

In the glare of the bright light, the girl's tan took on an artificial cast. There were no pale lines to mar the continuous stretch of color. Did she use tanning lotion or go to a tanning salon? Visible lines of excessive sun marred the outer edges of her gold-flecked eyes. The crow's feet made her look older than her twenty-five years. He reached out and combed his fingers through the rich brown waves, fanning them around her sallow face. Then he rearranged the wispy bangs on her forehead. She was so pretty. With a gloved fingertip, he stroked the line of her cheek.

The temperatures continued to be record breaking and he wiped the perspiration coating his brow. Sweat pooled in the tips of his gloved hands. He wanted to rip them off, but that would be foolish. He couldn't leave his prints, or his DNA.

Her veins bulged and he picked a syringe off the table. Bracing his hand on hers, he inserted the needle through the skin. He felt a pop as it slid into the vein. First time. This was getting easier. He taped the needle in place and yanked off the tourniquet. Pulling back on the syringe, he watched as her blood mixed with the clear liquid. He depressed the plunger and stared as the fluid disappeared into her vein. Removing the needle, he pressed an alcohol swab to the site. Now, all he had to do was wait. He had lots of time.

He pulled a stool beside the stainless steel table and sat. Taking her hand in his, he watched her face. In less than a minute he noted signs of the drug working—her eyelids flickered, her body went flaccid, the rise and fall of her chest became barely visible. In fact, her breathing appeared to have ceased.

It was time to start.

Adjusting the overhead light, he positioned a green towel on her abdomen then reached across to the stainless steel tray and chose one of the gleaming instruments. His fingers trembled as he poised the scalpel an inch above her darkly tanned abdomen. He felt the rush of blood surging through his veins. Taking a deep breath, he tightened his fingers around the curved steel handle. He pressed the weighted blade against the skin of her left flank and drew it swiftly across her abdomen, stopping two inches from her umbilicus. The pounding of his heart echoed in his ears as crimson fluid oozed from her pink flesh. Blood pooled in the incision. He inhaled deeply, his nostrils tingling with the scent of old pennies.

Inserting the scalpel into the wound, he sliced deeper, cutting through the layers of subcutaneous fat. The blood flowed faster. His excitement grew. He suctioned the fluid away and peered into the incision. He felt his own blood pumping, driving heat through his body, tingling his gloved fingertips, swelling his flaccid penis.

He returned the scalpel to the table. The retractors he'd stolen waited with their stainless steel edges shimmering under the bright light. He laid one on the green towel. When he picked up the second one, a rush of power surged through him.

Criminal how careless people were about equipment. They just left things lying around. He'd found the retractors in the soiled supply room. They were dirty, but soaking them in disinfectant for a few minutes removed the blood, and now they were good as new.

He glanced at the semi-conscious woman. Her eyes twitched occasionally, but otherwise she remained still. Only a few whimpers had crossed her lips before the ketamine took effect.

The last time he'd given too much. That was a mistake. This time he'd given less. He hoped it was enough. Her color looked okay. He counted the seconds until the feather at her mouth fluttered, ten. That put her breathing at six per minute. Was that too slow? He aimed the circular light at her face. Did her lips have a bluish tinge?

Damn. Would he ever get the dose right?

He needed to hurry. He needed to get the kidney out before she died. It had to be a living kidney. It just had to be.

He repositioned the light and slid the retractor into the incision. The second one clinked as he slid it into the wound beside the first one. He pulled carefully on both retractors, easing the skin back. He couldn't risk damaging the organ. Turning the suction on, he watched the blood whoosh up the clear tubing. He stared into her abdomen, yanked on the retractors, and stretched the incision line until the skin tore. With more of her abdominal cavity exposed, he watched the blood gush in to the area.

"Damn it."

There was too much blood. He jammed the plastic suction tip into the wound. A gush of red gurgled through the tubing and spattered into the plastic receptacle. The incision cleared. He stared into the cavity focusing on her left kidney.

The bean shaped object lay there, not red, glistening, and healthy, but withered and black. His excitement evaporated, replaced by rage. He jerked one of the retractors out of the incision and pitched it across the room. The clang of it hitting the cement floor echoed like a gun shot.

"Fuck. Fuck. Fuck."

All that time and effort. The bitch. She didn't look sick. He'd thought she just had a good tan. How the hell was he supposed to know she had a rotten kidney?

A voice spoke in his head. '*You can get the other one. You should have gone for that one in the first place.*'

"Shut the fuck up."

'*You could go for it now,*' the voice suggested.

"I don't want her kidneys. She's damaged goods."

He stared at the misshapen kidney and cursed, anger flaring like a red-hot poker. Grabbing the second retractor, he ripped it out of the incision and pitched it after the first one. His head felt like it was going to explode. He reached for the scalpel. His thumb grazed the razor sharp edge, slicing through the glove and across the tip of his thumb. Ignoring the pain, he rammed the scalpel into the incision, sliced through the vein and then the artery. He grabbed the withered kidney and pitched it across the room. It splattered in a dark, congealed mass on the cement floor.

"Bitch, you deserve to die."

A geyser of arterial spray spouted from the incision, blood flooded out of the wound, streamed down the woman's naked thigh, saturated the sheet below. It pooled on the stainless steel table then trickled to the floor, coagulating in a large, dark puddle.

He threw the blood-caked scalpel onto the tray. Snapping up a green towel, he tossed it over the incision then thrust the instrument table out of the way. It tipped, the contents crashing onto the floor. He screamed obscenities, the pain in his head increasing with each four letter word he uttered.

It felt like his throat had constricted to the size of a straw. He needed air. He grabbed his neck, sucked in. Air wheezed in. Not enough. He needed to get outside. Jerking away from the table, his foot caught the open cooler, its mountain of glistening ice waiting for its prize. The ice scattered in a wide arc across the room. He kicked the cooler, ignoring the pain that shot up his leg. The ice wouldn't be needed tonight.

He stormed out of the building gulping at the cool night air.

His body heaving, he leaned against the building, his hands clenching and unclenching. He felt the rapid rate of his heart as each beat pounded through his head. Sweat dripped down his face. He swiped at it with the back of his hand. When he could finally breathe normally, he fumbled with a cigarette package, rapping the box against his palm several times before his shaking fingers could knock one out. Then it took numerous flicks on the lighter before the tip glowed red.

He'd wanted to impress Sherry. She'd trashed him in front of the world. Her exact words hammered in his brain: "His work is that of an amateur. He sutures his victims after slashing out their kidneys. He is not a professional." He kicked the ground, sending a shower of gravel into the air. What would Sherry think of him now?

It was a long time before he reentered the building. The body was cold and rigor setting in. He stuffed the worthless organ into the incision, tore open a package of sutures, then yanking at the black silk thread, he pulled the edges of skin together. He'd been perfecting his technique, but tonight he didn't care what the incision looked like.

CHAPTER 27

Rosko picked up the phone on the second ring. Automatically he glanced at the digital readout on the clock radio. Five-twenty-six. It was never good news at this time of night.

There was no greeting, just a harsh voice. "We got another one. Same MO, different location."

"Where?"

"Fanshawe Park, not far from the pond," Wilson said

"I'll be there in fifteen." Rosko slammed the receiver back in its cradle. "Damn."

Wasn't it bad enough they already had two victims? Now another one on their hands. Hopefully the pervert left some clues this time.

His muscles protested but he forced his body out of the bed. A hot shower roused him and five minutes later he was pulling on suit pants and a shirt. He might as well get dressed for the day. By the time he finished at the scene it wouldn't be worth coming home for a few zzz's

He grabbed a coffee at a drive-through and was at the park within fifteen minutes. The scattering of police cars with lights flashing told him it was the right place. At least they don't have the sirens wailing. We'd have the whole neighborhood here. It's bad enough the media is starting to arrive.

Rosko eased his car behind one of the cruisers. Unwrapping a piece of spearmint gum, he popped it into his mouth and threw the empty wrapper on the dash. It had been four years since he'd had a cigarette, yet the urge to light up never left, especially at a time like this. Chewing gum was a poor substitute, but it kept the hounds at bay.

He put the rest of the gum package in his pocket and headed toward the crime scene. Purposely avoiding the CBR NEWS, he stepped over the yellow cordon tape and nodded to a group of police officers. Rosko hoped nothing else was happening in town—it looked like every cop on nightshift was here.

What were the odds it was one of the rookies who'd found the body? Would they have remembered the rules of crime scene protocol? They didn't need the scene contaminated. Yet even the most experienced beat cops got frazzled, ignored the cardinal rule—never, never, never touch anything.

Nothing could prepare a person for the first time they faced a murder scene. The "super cops" would look around before calling it in. Given a few minutes, they figured they could solve the case themselves. Then there were the others—they went into a state of shock and forgot to maintain the integrity of the scene. Both groups could do as much damage as a herd of elephants. Rosko drilled the new recruits on handling a homicide before they hit the streets. Some paid attention, some didn't. He hoped whoever found this body came from the first group.

Klieg lights illuminated the night sky and he had no trouble finding the technicians working by a cluster of tall trees. Someone had been over zealous, or bored, and a second circle of yellow cordon tape circled the body. After straddling the ribbon, he kept to the freshly trodden path in the grass. Lee knelt beside the body. Rosko headed toward him.

The victim lay spread-eagled, her legs protruding from behind a large oak tree. Her ashen form was a stark contrast to the lush green grass. Petite and brunette, the woman looked to be in her mid-twenties. Death had turned her tanned face into a grotesque mask.

Rosko's gaze slid to her torso. Crudely stitched together, the slash on the left side of her abdomen was red and swollen. Blood caked around the incision had attracted flies and the insects crawled between the sutures. Camera flashes captured the body from a multitude of angles. The coroner remained bent over the body taking his own photos. Chao collected samples of soil and vegetation. They looked up as Rosko approached.

"Is it the same guy?" Rosko asked.

"We got a killer who likes the knife."

"But is it the same guy?"

Lee grinned lopsidedly. "Pretty sure it's him. Suturing job looks rough, not as neat as usual. There's more blood, too. He didn't take the time to clean her up, or pose her this time, just dumped her. I've got to get her to the morgue. Can't tell if something is missing, but I'll bet she is minus one kidney."

Rosko looked at the naked girl. That was his bet too.

Her arms splayed away from her torso, not folded neatly on her abdomen. Her brown hair was disheveled, and partially covered her face. The abdominal wound was ragged, several black sutures partially holding the edges together. Lee was right. If this was the same killer, he hadn't taken his usual care arranging the body. Had he been in a hurry? Rosko hoped so. He hoped he'd been in such a hurry that he'd left a few clues behind.

Rosko sighed. "If you don't need me, I'll go see if the uniforms have come up with anything."

Lee nodded. "I won't be here much longer."

"Speak for yourself." Chao smirked. "I'm going to be here for hours."

"Cry me a river," Lee said with a chuckle. "I'm doing a quick report then back to my nice warm bed."

Rosko headed towards the officers. The group had dwindled. Maybe Strathburn had woken up and found something else for the police to do.

"Detective Rosko?"

Rosko nodded at the reporter then hurried on. The man trotted along beside him.

"Can you tell me what's going on? Did you find another body?"

Rosko stopped and faced him making sure the other reporters were close enough to hear. He wasn't repeating himself.

"A woman was found dead. That's all I have to say."

"Is it the Kidney Slasher?"

Sherry Simmons pushed past the other reporters and shoved her microphone close to his face. Her make-up was perfect, not a hair out of place. A pearl gray Gucci suit clung to her shapely curves. Even at this time of the day she dressed for a fashion show. Rosko knocked the microphone away from his face. "I don't know anything yet, other than there's a dead female back there."

"You saw the body. Has she been cut? Has her kidney been taken? Is that how she died?"

Rosko looked her in the eye. "I'm not saying anything else, not until the medical examiner is done with her and the body identified."

"You have to give us something."

Rosko glared at her. "No I don't."

Sherry recoiled at the anger in his tone. With the sudden weight shift, the heel of her shoe sank into the damp morning ground and she struggled to keep her balance. It took her a moment to collect herself, by then Rosko had pushed past her. Sherry hurried after him. Catching up, she grabbed his sleeve jacket. "Gerry…"

Rosko turned abruptly. Blue eyes, polished like sapphires, pleaded with him. But she'd burned him more than once and he'd promised himself it would never happen again. He kept walking.

"Please, Gerry…."

Her voice took on an uncharacteristic softness that sounded foreign to his ears. He couldn't look at her. He wouldn't let himself be hoodwinked by her again. He remembered her words: "I was just doing my job." Yeah, right. Just doing my job. He'd trusted her, told her things he shouldn't have, and she'd burned him, but good. He was done with her.

Rosko flung her arm away. The microphone flew out of her hand and she scrambled to catch it. He ignored her succession of pleas and curses.

Moments later she posed for the camera—as eloquent, beautiful, ambitious, and as always, composed–Sherry Simmons, ice queen of CBR NEWS.

"I'm here at Fanshawe Park, where, in the early hours of the night, police discovered another body. The woman is Caucasian, in her twenties. Police are not releasing any further information at this time. Has the 'Kidney Slasher' struck again? Police are being tight-lipped. We promise to keep you informed. As soon as we know anything, we'll pass it along."

The bitch. "Who's feeding her information?" Rosko asked Wilson. "I didn't give the woman's age, and I never said she was white."

CHAPTER 28

When Rosko arrived at the station, the door to Chief Richards' office stood ajar. The Chief waved him in and motioned for him to shut the door. Good news travels fast, bad news faster. Rosko felt sharp twinges in his stomach. Was this case giving him another ulcer?

Richards twirled a Havana cigar in his fleshy fingers. The fan was on and the blinds down. Rosko didn't think it was a good time to remind him he was violating the fire code. From the compressed end of the cigar the chief had been twirling it for a while. Not good. Rosko waited, the twinges in his stomach now razor-edged. He averted his eyes from the twirling cigar, and the circles of smoke making their way to the ceiling.

Instead, he focused on the photos of the chief's football days, decorating the walls. In his prime, he'd been a formidable figure, but time had stooped his stature, and years of living a political life had changed the former tight end to a corpulent sumo wrestler. Despite the aging process, Richards remained an imposing figure.

"How is it really going, Gerry?"

Richards' face was an indecipherable mask. He peered at Rosko over half glasses that sat on a misshapen nose—a trophy of his hard fight to the top. It hadn't been football though that had broken his nose. The nose was thanks to a violent narcotic bust. His part in breaking up the drug ring catapulted him up the ranks. He'd been police chief for six years now and held the reputation of running a tight ship with no mutinous behavior tolerated.

"Truth is, Chief, it's not going worth a shit. He's smart, this guy. Always wears gloves, covers his tracks. We know he's using a drug called ketamine. It's an anesthetic agent, but we don't know where he's getting it. He's got some medical knowledge. Not enough to make him a surgeon, but enough to know what he's going for, and how to get it. We did find a hair that might belong to the killer. We're waiting for the DNA report."

The chief ran a hand through the hair that, thanks to the miracles of medical technology, he'd regained. "Let's pray to God it matches someone in the data base."

Rosko continued. "Why he wants their kidneys, we don't know, but there has to be some explanation. Maybe he's on a transplant list, or knows somebody who is. But why ruin the kidneys by letting the person die?" Rosko shrugged. "We don't know where he kills them either. We're pretty sure he drives a van. There've been track marks on each victim's back. The technicians have identified the marks as coming from a van mat. We think he may work at a hospital or clinic. We've been checking them out, but don't have any clues yet." Rosko ran a hand through his own hair. "He's getting more confident with each kill, and his technique is improving. We have to stop him before he deludes himself into thinking he's a real surgeon."

"You're fucking right you'd better catch him. We're getting a shit load of heat on this one. The press is torching us. The TV keeps running the same clips. Every fucking channel." Richards examined the glowing tip of his cigar then took a long draw. Exhaling slowly, he concentrated on the smoke rings drifting in front of him. His voice was harsh. "I've had phone calls. Lots of them. Mayor Denning calls twice a day, and the District Attorney's Office—they're getting nasty, Rosko, suggesting we're not doing our job."

Rosko kept his mouth shut.

"The media's creating a panic—advising women not to go out alone, telling them to carry mace or pepper spray. Gun sales have skyrocketed. I don't want a bunch of hysterical women shooting any stranger within ten feet of them." He paused and examined the tip of his cigar. "With the pressure I'm getting from the mayor's office—" He shrugged. "I may have to put someone else on the job. This is an election year. If I don't look good—" He shrugged his massive shoulders again. "—you don't look good."

Rosko met Richards' gaze. "I'm doing the best I can. The guys are doing their best, working overtime, canceling vacations. But if you want to replace me, that's up to you."

Silence as heavy as the cloud of cigar smoke cloaked the room.

"Give me more time, Chief. I'm getting to know this bastard. He's going to make a mistake soon and I want to be there when he does. A change in command might jeopardize the investigation."

Several seconds passed before the chief spoke. His gravelly tone sounded like nails scraping across a blackboard. "There's a news conference at eleven. You don't need to take questions. Tell them we're investigating each case as separate. We're following all leads. And be damned sure you avoid any mention of a serial killer.

"Tell them you can't release anything for fear of jeopardizing the case. Keep it vague, and short. Promise we'll give them information as we can. Throw them a tidbit, maybe about the guy driving a van. That'll give them something for the news, and it'll give the community something to do. Feel like they're contributing."

Rosko hated conferences, hated the questions, the politics, the lies, the reporters badgering for information, insinuating police incompetence. He just wanted to do his job. Luckily, Richards loved the limelight. Maybe the press was right. Maybe they were bungling it. The guy had murdered three women so far. Maybe he should step down, see if a fresh face could see something he was missing. Closing the door to the chief's office, Rosko left the pungent odor of cigar smoke behind. Myers was at his desk.

"Nothing yet, boss. Western University has a list of dropouts from their medical program over the past few years. I'm picking it up this afternoon."

"Good, Myers. Keep me up to speed." Rosko paused. "Are you doing okay, Phil?"

Myers lowered his eyes. "Some days are better than others."

"If you need someone to talk to, or some time off, just let me know."

"But this case—I don't want to leave you short-handed."

"You do what's best for you. Let me know if you need the time."

"Thanks, boss."

When he got back to his desk, Wilson gave him a lopsided grin. "Well, how did it go?"

"Like shit," Rosko said. "You can go next time."

"Nope. I like the job, not the politics." Wilson's grin widened. "Got a surprise for you."

Rosko shook his head. He'd had enough surprises for one day.

"Gerald Herd is awaiting your arrival in the conference room."

"Damn."

Herd looked up as Rosko entered the room. "I've had a chance to go through the files, and make some additional notes." He took a sip of his coffee.

Rosko filled a mug from the coffeemaker in the corner, added an extra spoonful of sugar and sat opposite the FBI profiler. Herd glanced at a lined pad of paper.

"I hear he killed again last night."

Rosko nodded. "Another woman in her early twenties. Caucasian, brown hair—just like the others."

"I presume the MO was the same."

"Looks like it. But he didn't take as much care with this victim."

Herd's sparse eyebrows arched.

Rosko continued. "She wasn't cleaned up, or posed. And the suturing was rougher, more ragged. It was as if he didn't take his time with this one."

"Was he in a hurry? Or did something interrupt him? Autopsy done yet?"

"Doctor MacFarlane will be doing it shortly. Hopefully he'll uncover a clue or two, especially, if something got the guy rattled."

"I've been thinking a lot about him. I suspect he may be impotent with women. His sexual stimulation may come from having power over his victims. The act of cutting may be his arousal. The ritual he follows shows he's in control of the situation even if he needs the drugs to sedate the victims. On the other side of the coin, he's also controlled by his ritual."

"What if he's prevented from following it?" asked Rosko. "Say he's interrupted, can't complete this ritual?"

"It may leave him frustrated and angry. He may feel compelled to begin hunting for the next victim. So far, he's been careful and organized, hasn't left any clues behind."

"At least none that we've found," Rosko agreed.

"He may get careless. Then," Herd said, smiling, "you might have a chance of catching him."

"Let's hope he got careless last night."

"Only a couple of things to add. He has a job. It will be one requiring both intelligence and meticulousness. We've seen that he's a planner—brings what he needs, gloves, binding, chloroform. He has a sequence of events he follows, from subduing the victim to transporting her somewhere he can operate on her. It has to be an organized set up. Somewhere the surgery and the blood loss aren't out of place.

"Concentrate on where he's doing the surgery. He has a place to store his trophies, the jewelry he's collecting from his victims. He hides them, but keeps them handy enough that he can take them out and feast on them whenever he feels the need to relive his fantasy. I'm confident he lives alone, not married. He has anatomical knowledge and basic surgical skills. We could be dealing with some-one in the medical profession."

Rosko drained his coffee mug and glanced at the profiler. Mac had said the same thing. He wondered what Myers would come up with in that respect.

Herd shuffled his notes into a leather briefcase then rose and extended his hand. "Be ready. With this recent failure, he may strike again very soon."

Rosko offered to walk him out.

"I know the way." They shook hands. "Keep me informed of any new developments."

Rosko nodded then glanced at his watch. He had a date with Doctor MacFarlane.

CHAPTER 29

Her skin color is jaundiced. Yellowed from her kidney failure. Her blood work is consistent with chronic kidney problems, urea and nitrogen levels elevated." Mac paused and looked at Rosko. "The kidney filters out the bad stuff, the toxins. When the urea and nitrogen are elevated the body isn't eliminating uric acid and urea, the normal products of protein metabolism.

"I know I'm getting too technical here, but the bottom line is, her kidneys weren't functioning making the dose of ketamine more potent." Mac shrugged.

"So she would have had more of a reaction to the ketamine than the other women?"

Mac nodded. "Right."

Rosko spoke more to himself than to the coroner. "When he got in there and found a damaged kidney, he must have been really pissed off."

Mac's hearty chuckle shook his chest. "Hey, I thought the pissing jokes were mine."

"I have a sense of humor, too," Rosko retorted.

"You do indeed, just buried." Mac grinned at him and then continued. "From his sewing job, it looks like he was pretty angry. Pretty rough slash through the vessels, then he shoved it back inside and sutured her up. All the work he went to, and then found a damaged kidney." Mac shrugged again. "Hopefully, he got careless, left us a few clues."

"That would be nice. We've got a lot of nothing so far, just a mounting body count."

"I've sent all the routine bits and pieces. I got some scrapings from under her nail beds. Doesn't look like much, but we'll test them and see. Let's hope she got her claws into the guy."

"So you're sure it's the same guy?" Rosko asked.

"She's got the usual burns around her mouth—probably chloroform, and the injection site for the ketamine. Toxicology will confirm both tomorrow."

Rosko nodded. "We got those guys working faster, did we?"

"You bet. The heat's been migrating over their way, too."

"Anything different with this one?"

"Her stomach contents show she ate pizza within the six hours of death. So you can look for a restaurant that serves pizza, or delivers."

"The parks are within a few miles of each other. We're working a large radius around them, and we've been checking out the restaurants in the area. So far we've had Italian and Chinese as last meals, now pizza. I wonder if our guy is single and eats out. Maybe that's where he finds his victims."

"It's a possibility," Mac agreed.

Rosko picked up the phone and dialed Wilson. "Had lunch yet? Good, cause today we're checking out pizza joints." He turned back to Mac. "I'm going to lunch. Call me if you get anything."

"Sure will, laddie," Mac said and continued with the autopsy.

CHAPTER 30

Rosko and Wilson spent the afternoon checking out pizza parlors in the area. There were seven of them. Most of their business was delivery. No one recognized the victim. The detectives obtained a list of all deliveries from four o'clock yesterday afternoon until the shops closed. Most had gone to private homes, a few went to businesses. Three orders went to Grace Memorial Hospital. He'd drop by there later. Rosko wondered if Claire liked pizza.

His proposed visit to Grace Memorial became a reality when Virginia Gallingham failed to show up for her three o'clock tour of duty.

At three forty-five, concerned co-workers called the hospital administration. The nurses knew Virginia had kidney failure and had her name on the transplant list. The stress of her deteriorating health and her recent marriage breakup were taking a toll on her and she was increasingly tired at work. Fearing she might have collapsed, they decided to involve the police.

No one answered the door to her apartment, the superintendent let them in. With personal photos, the police identified the latest victim.

For the next two hours, Rosko and Wilson interviewed the nurses on the third floor. Several had worked with Virginia the previous evening. Some had known her since she started at the hospital five years before.

Trevor, her estranged husband, came to the hospital. When Rosko went to interview him, he was slumped in a chair in the nurses' lounge, his head in his hands, sobbing loudly. He and Virginia had been going to a marriage counselor and hoped to reconcile. As both their families lived in distant cities, he'd come to garner support from Virginia's co-workers. Marianne Cooper, the night nurse, had also come to the hospital. She sat with one arm around Trevor's shoulders, her tears running unchecked. Like family, the group clung together in their tragedy.

They couldn't think of anyone with a reason to harm Virginia. Trevor had last seen Virginia two days ago. They were going away this weekend and she had called him on her supper break last evening to check on their plans. No they hadn't argued. He had an alibi, had been at work till two in the morning. The police would confirm that.

Marianne had seen Virginia get on the elevator with Pauline Philips last night. She hadn't heard of any commotion in the parking lot. Simon Wyshinski's voice shook as he confirmed Virginia and Pauline made it safely to their respective cars.

"Waved to me as they left the parking lot." Wyshinski raised a trembling hand in demonstration.

On the fifth floor, they found a nurse at the desk attempting to transcribe orders. A wad of Kleenex curbed her tears from saturating the page in front of her. Pauline Phillips's voice cracked. "We walked out together last night. Virginia got into her car and drove out of the parking lot. She was alone." Tears streamed faster as she realized she was probably the last person to see Virginia alive.

ତ୬ତ

Claire saw Detective Rosko waiting by the nurse's station of the emergency room and felt a rush of pleasure. She had to force herself to concentrate on the discharge instructions she was giving to a patient. Self-consciously she brushed at a brown strand of hair that had come lose from her ponytail and crossed to greet him.

"Can I ask you a few questions?" Rosko asked.

"I'm pretty busy right now." Claire waved her hand toward the department.

Rosko's gaze followed her hand. Every stretcher was occupied.

"I'm off in twenty minutes, can it wait until then?" she asked.

"Sure. Can we get a coffee somewhere?" He grinned wryly. "Preferably not hospital grade, it's on a par with the police station's."

"I've had a busy day. A coffee away from the hospital sounds good. There's a restaurant across the street, the Saffron."

He glanced at his watch. "I have a few calls to make. I'll be there just after six."

Claire grabbed the next patient's chart. "I'll meet you there once I've given my report to the oncoming doctor."

She watched out of the corner of her eye as the dark-haired detective walked out the double doors of the emergency room. It was definitely a nice view. Her cheeks felt suddenly warm. *Stop it, Claire. This is professional. He just wants to talk to you about the case.*

It was six-ten by the time she'd finished up her charts and given report to the oncoming staff. She changed into street clothes, dabbed on a spattering of lipstick, and headed out. It was still hot and she was relieved the restaurant had air conditioning.

She dashed through the traffic and crossed to the Saffron Restaurant. The detective stood at the back using a pay phone. He pointed to a booth near the front of the restaurant. There were two coffee cups on the table, one half-full the other waiting to be filled.

The waitress noticed her and held up a glass coffeepot. Claire nodded then waited while her cup was filled. The detective, still on the phone, shrugged his shoulders in apology. She smiled and raised her coffee cup in a toast.

Claire sat back in the cushioned seat and took a long sip. Much better than hospital grade. Glancing out the window, she watched the activity at the doors of the hospital she'd just left. Her plans for the evening were simple—go home, take a long shower, put on the briefest pair of shorts she owned, and sink into a cozy chair with a good mystery novel.

Rosko waved at her and held up his index finger then pantomimed a cup to his mouth. Pretending not to understand, Claire mimicked him with the waving of her hands. He leered at her. She held her cup to her lips and made an exhibition of inhaling the aroma of the coffee but burst out laughing at the glare her performance produced. Cringing in mock fear, she caught the waitress's attention.

Their cups were being refilled as Rosko slid into the booth. He glared at her again before bursting into a hearty laugh. The sound was deep and warm. Claire couldn't help laughing with him. Their frivolity broke any tension left over from their encounter at her apartment a few days before, and Claire suddenly felt like her stomach was filled with a flock of butterflies.

What was going on? She was just here for a coffee and some questions. He was good looking, but she'd sworn off men for a long, long time. She took a gulp of coffee to drown the butterflies. They were good swimmers. She took another swallow. She was used to being in control, yet this man made her feel oddly shy, not to mention what he was doing to her hormones. The way he was looking at her didn't help matters in the least.

e/ɔe/ɔ

Released from the ponytail she wore for work, her nut-brown hair floated past her shoulders. When she gathered it together and let it drop down her back, Rosko caught a glimpse of delicately tanned skin. Something about the way her hair fell over her face and then was swept back behind her ears sent a chill down his back. It reminded him of something, but what? Why was the chill lingering? Realizing he was staring, he smiled and shook his head. "Sorry, I was thinking…"

"About what?"

Rosko shook his head again. "It's this case. It's driving me nuts. There has to be something we're missing."

He looked down at the wooden table top and, spreading his fingers on its surface, he examined them one by one. "Did you know there was another woman murdered?"

"The waitress?" Claire asked.

Rosko looked up. His eyes locked with hers. "No, another one last night. I wanted to tell you before you heard."

"Heard?"

"It was one of the nurses from the orthopedic floor, Virginia Gallingham."

"Oh my God."

"Did you know her?"

"Yes. Not well. She's come down to get a patient from the emergency department, or helped out when we've been busy. She was waiting for a kidney transplant. Oh, God"

He remained silent, letting her absorb the shock. The sound of voices distracted him. The television was on in the background. Someone turned the volume up, and Rosko gritted his teeth as he turned toward the familiar voice of Sherry Simmons.

"Last night, the Kidney Slasher struck again. This time, though, he went away without his usual prize. Virginia Gallingham, a nurse at Grace Memorial Hospital, died last night. An attempt was made to remove her kidney, but Virginia had kidney disease. The Slasher performed his barbaric surgery but left behind her damaged kidney. Her body was found in Fanshawe Park.

"Again we are asking anyone with information that might lead to the capture of this serial killer to come forward. We need to stop this butcher."

Rosko's shoulders slumped and he stared at his clenched fists. "Damn it."

"What?" Claire asked.

"I'd like to know who the hell is leaking information to her. We need to catch this guy. We don't need the town in a panic."

They finished their coffees in silence.

"Has the autopsy been done?"

"Yes. Doctor MacFarlane—but you know him…"

"Yes, I know Mac."

"Of course you do." He grinned. "Well, he did the autopsy this morning. We didn't know her identity then."

"I'd like to have been there."

Rosko calculated the psychological effect of seeing an autopsy done on someone you knew, plus being a civilian who found a body, plus being a doctor used to being in control. He knew finding the Winters woman had bothered her more than she wanted to admit. "Do you think that would have been wise?"

"It's a hell of a lot easier doing something to help catch the bastard than sitting around feeling victimized. It's getting personal now. Before he was an unknown, now he's entered my sphere." She glared at him defiantly. "And I don't like it."

He was surprised at the sudden force in her voice. He reached across the table and took her hands in his. He didn't speak, he just held her hands, running his fingertips lightly over the top of her hand. After a few minutes he said, "I'd better get back to work. See if I can find this guy. Can I check on you later?"

Claire couldn't speak but nodded her response.

Outside the restaurant, Rosko felt the chill return. Claire turned and a slight breeze blew brown strands of hair across her face. Three black and white glossy pictures flashed in front of him—head and shoulder shots of women with strands of brown hair arranged around their bloodless faces.

Rosko shook his head but the images refused to leave. The women were all young, all attractive, all had brown hair that streamed past dainty shoulders. A shudder ran down his spine as he realized Doctor Claire Valincourt also fit the killer's profile.

He had to catch the bastard. And soon.

CHAPTER 31

Dallas Parker leaned against the wall outside the Daisy Mart Variety. Her arches ached from the spike heels she'd put on that morning. Sliding her feet out of her shoes she curled her toes in relief. They weren't a good fit, but they were the only decent pair of shoes she'd been able to find at the Goodwill. Blisters had already developed on her heels and stung like hot pokers.

She heard her grandfather's booming voice advising her father. "Shoes make the man, Jack. You got to have good shoes when you go looking for a job."

Well, that advice hadn't helped her father. He'd never had a good job in his life. Fancy shoes weren't doing anything for her either. She was down to her last five dollars and so tired she could sit down and cry. She would have, too, except she suspected the cop across the street would pick her up for vagrancy and throw her in the slammer. At least they'd give her three meals and a bed without having to fight for it. The food couldn't be any worse than at the shelter.

Dallas was tired of shelters, tired of looking for a job, and tired of this damn town. Why had she ever left Huntsville? At least she had family there. She closed her eyes. The sharp edges of the bricks dug into her spine. Hard, cold and prickly—just like everything else in this shit hole of a town.

If only she didn't have to go back to the shelter. Bernice would be waiting for her, butting into her space. Dallas tried to keep upwind of her. The baby powder Bernice plastered into her fat rolls reminded her of rotting potatoes. And her voice—it was like nails scratching on a chalkboard. She remembered Bernice screeching at her this morning.

"You tart, that was my roll."

"Did it have your name on it?" she'd screamed back. "You old bitch, you've had more than your share."

She'd let Bernice have the damn roll all right, right in the face. But now, with her stomach growling, she regretted wasting the food. And she'd have to go back to the shelter tonight, unless some miracle came along. But with her luck, that wasn't going to happen.

Just a few minutes to ease the ache in her feet, then she'd get back to looking for a job. Too bad school had been such a drag. Maybe one of those courses Mrs. Lepinski bugged her to take might have come in handy. She sighed loudly. Maybe it wasn't too late. If she could just get a job, maybe she could take some of them courses, make something of herself. Without moving her body, she opened her eyes and looked across the street. At least the cop had moved on.

"Excuse me, Miss.?"

She jumped then turned toward the voice. The glare of the sun blinded her and she put a hand up to her eyes. He was tall, blonde, good looking, and wearing a police uniform. Just her luck. Dallas sagged into the brick wall. Just when she thought nothing worse could happen and here was the damn pig standing right beside her.

How'd he gotten here so quickly? He was kind of cute though. Too bad he was wearing a uniform. He'd probably think she was a prostitute. Dallas smiled up at him.

Matt Thompson tipped his hat.

"Hello." Dallas kept her voice controlled.

"Can I help you, ma'am?"

"I'm fine. Just resting my feet. I'm looking for a job. But with this heat and all..." Dallas fanned her face with the newspaper. Could he see it was open to the want-ad section, and that several ads had been circled?

"We don't allow any loitering here."

Dallas forced herself to keep smiling. "I'm looking for a job."

"This is a decent neighborhood. You'd better be moving along."

She stiffened, forgot the pain in her feet, her teeth clenched, and she barely held back an obscene retort. She didn't miss the contempt in his steel blue eyes. "I'm not a prostitute."

Standing with legs braced, he smacked a long nightstick in a rhythmic thud against the palm of his left hand.

"My feet are tired. I just needed a rest."

"I said move along."

Bastard. And to think I'd thought he was cute. Dallas scrambled to get her feet back into her shoes, wincing as the vinyl scraped the blisters. Seething with rage, she hobbled down the street. The way I'm teetering, he probably thinks I'm drunk. Damn him. Just like all the power hungry cops in Huntsville.

Suddenly, the thought of three square meals in a cell lost its appeal. Dallas didn't look back until she reached the corner. At least the cop hadn't followed her. She slowed her steps. It was then that she noticed the help wanted sign in the store window. Maybe it was going to be her lucky day after all.

CHAPTER 32

He was getting discouraged. The sign had been in the window for a week now and the only applicants were fat housewives or skinny old maids. Maybe it wasn't such a good idea after all.

The bell over the door jangled. He couldn't help staring at the woman walking nervously into the store. The sun reflecting through the window made the copper highlights in her shoulder length brown hair glisten.

"I saw the sign. Is the position still open?"

His breath caught in his throat and it took several seconds before he could speak. The hand that passed over the application shook slightly. Oh yes, the position was definitely still open.

"Do you have a pen?" she asked.

He took a ballpoint pen from beside the till and handed it over the counter. A small, delicate hand, the nails painted a bright red, accepted it. He watched her cross to the chairs provided for customers and sat down. Even after a couple of tugs, her short skirt still exposed a long length of tanned leg. It was a nice shade of brown, not too dark, just enough to show she liked the sun. No sign of jaundice, not like the other one. He felt the muscles in the back of his neck tighten. No, this one looked healthy.

Keeping busy wiping the display case and rearranging the stacks of meat, he feigned surprise when she returned the paperwork. He smiled broadly. "Done already?" He took the application and flipped through the pages.

He liked the new business software. It let him format a job application—two pages of questions about education, previous work experience, personal history. He could even add his own questions. Stupid girl. She'd looked only slightly surprised when she came to the medical part of the questionnaire, then filled it out without question, and handed it back along with his pen. An honest type, she probably wouldn't consider pilfering from the till.

He watched her out of the corner of his eye. She perched on the edge of the chair, her delicate hands combing through shoulder length hair, or adjusting the hem of her skirt. Her right leg jiggled as she darted glances at him.

Concentrating on the front page, he read the childish scrawl. Dallas Parker, twenty-four, single. He noted the address, 151 Dundas Street. Wasn't that the woman's shelter? He looked at the next few boxes. His fingers itched to turn the page, but he forced himself to spend at least two seconds on each box before moving to the next.

"Do you have a washroom?" Dallas asked.

Relieved to be able to review the application without her scrutiny, he pointed to the back of the store. His fingers tingled. They held the form so tightly he almost frayed a hole through the paper. It seemed to take an eternity for her to rise and make her way to the bathroom. As soon as he heard the lock click he flipped the page zooming in on the section that most interested him. The medical one—no allergies, no hypertension, no diabetes, no communicable diseases, no known problems. Her parents were both alive and well. Her health history looked good. His smiled broadened.

He hoped she'd answered truthfully. He didn't want to make any mistakes, not like the last time. Bile rose in his throat as he thought of that shriveled kidney. All that time and effort wasted. Well, not totally wasted, he'd been able to practice his technique. It improved each time.

Crossing to the shop's entrance he removed the "Help Wanted" sign from the front window and locked the door. Had anyone noticed her entering the store? Probably not. Would anyone notice if the "Closed" sign went up a few minutes early?

The street was a banquet of diversity. Each store offering a different service: Lee's Chinese Cuisine, The Sweet Shop, Harper's Clothier, Powalski's Fresh Meats, Sterling's Jewelry, Duncan's Dynamite Dresses, B&E Variety, The Blue Dragon Tattoo Parlor, and Lenny's Garage. Most of the businesses had been passed from one family member to another without renovations. The signs had faded with time as had the interiors of the stores. For some, the passage of time had been gracious. Others had not born up as well, their cracked and peeling paint exposing the wood rot beneath.

Like their clientele who'd succumbed to the rigors of a hard life, the stores showed their sagging forms and graying roots. Outside their weathered panes of glass, pedestrians hurried by, shoulders slumped, intent only on getting home and resting their feet after a long, hard day. No one noticing a young woman going into a store, no one noticing that she didn't come out.

Hearing the gush of water through the ancient pipes, he shoved the "Help Wanted" sign under the counter. A metallic click announced the opening of the lock. He flipped the application over and pretended to be reading the front page. The door creaked, Dallas Parker, victim number four, stepped out of the bathroom. He smiled at the emerging figure.

Her returning smile was shy, her soft brown eyes full of questions. Was she going to get the job? Would it pay enough to be able to leave the shelter? She averted her eyes from his direct gaze and walked self-consciously back to the counter. Taking a big breath she asked, "Can I have the job?"

"Yes, Dallas, I think you'll do quite nicely. Shall I show you around?"

CHAPTER 33

Dallas lay naked on the stainless-steel table. Thick beige straps bound her hands and feet. She struggled, pulling so hard the straps bit into her flesh. She winced with pain yet continued to wrench. He hid behind the doorway and watched.

The table stood in the middle of the room. A large circular fluorescent light centered its beam on the figure below. She was definitely a fighter. He let her thrash, the inside of her wrists becoming red and raw until a few drops of blood trickled onto the gleaming metal surface. Her right hand inched through the strap. He stepped out from his hiding spot. Her head twisted at the sound of his footsteps. He heard her muffled cries as her body convulsed violently against the shackles, he saw her eyes widen as her captor came into view.

Leaning over the table, he smiled down at her then slid his finger between her right wrist and the strap. Too loose. That wouldn't do. He shook his head as if reprimanding a naughty child. With a jerk, he tightened the buckle. She wrenched away. He yanked again. The buckle slid to the next hole.

"Please. Please don't. Let me go. I won't tell. I promise."

He gave another yank, his smile widening as the strap scraped the delicate skin of her wrist. The leather tore through the outer layer of skin and a trickle of blood oozed down her arm. Still she struggled.

"You're just making it worse."

Dallas screamed.

Should he give her more chloroform? He'd thought it would last longer. He hadn't wanted to tie her down, but he needed time to prepare, needed to wait for night to fall. Should he give her another whiff? No. He enjoyed watching her struggle.

Adrenaline surged through his body and his heart raced. She was totally in his control. His anticipation grew. Maybe he could start now.

He peeled back the plastic wrap of the sterile gloves and laid the paper insert onto the side table, then he unfolded the crisp layers. A thrill ran through him as he exposed the surgical gloves, and his fingers tingled as he slipped his hands inside. Milking one finger at a time, he worked the material until it molded with his skin. He held his palms in front of him and felt another surge of power. He could have been a surgeon. He could have.

Sure. All you needed was the time and the money. You could have done better at school. You could have worked for a scholarship. You didn't have to listen to Father. He never thought you were smart enough, but Mother did. She thought you could do anything. And now, you're doing this for her.

He turned to the small, wheeled table and arranged the instruments. He ignored her pleas. Should he tape her mouth? Nobody could hear her. No, she'd be quiet soon, very soon. Picking up a sterile green towel, he positioned it over the instruments and glanced at the clock, still too early. He forced himself to go back to the store, but he left the basement door open a crack. If he listened carefully, he could still hear her cries for help.

Finally, darkness came. She'd stopped struggling, but started again as he descended the stairs and crossed to the table. The terror in her eyes caused his heart to skip a beat. He smiled down at her but she just struggled more. Picking up a tourniquet, he tied it around her left forearm. Once the vein bulged, the needle slid in easily. He injected the full five milliliters of ketamine. Placing the empty syringe on the tray, he sat down on a chair beside her. He held her tiny hand in his and waited for it to go limp.

Bit by bit, her fighting lessened. By the time he'd unbuckled the straps, she'd ceased struggling, in fact, she stopped moving at all. A glaze coated her eyes, replacing the terror. She looked as if she'd stopped breathing, but from her color, he knew it was the medication. This part always scared him. Had he given enough, too much? The thrill of pushing it to the edge always made him dizzy.

He laid his right hand on her chest and counted. Several seconds elapsed before his hand rose slightly. He touched a finger to her eyelash and saw the barest flicker of a response. Good, she was ready.

Pulling the wheeled tray close to the table, he removed the sterile green towel. The surgical steel instruments gleamed in the glare of the overhead lamp. He picked up the bottle of Poviodine, washed her abdomen, then wiped the excess away with a sterile towel. Holding the scalpel an inch above her abdomen, his fingers trembled with anticipation.

He followed the procedure to the letter, his use of the scalpel quick and even. Within seconds of the initial cut, he sliced through tissue, muscle, mesentery. The suction purged away the blood surging into the wound. He inserted the retractors and spread the incision, sighing with relief when he saw the red, viable organ. Its excision precise, the suture job was neat and even.

Sherry would be proud of him. Too bad Dallas Parker wouldn't live to see the fruits of his labor.

He positioned the oblong organ on top of the ice then examined his handiwork. The edges of the ureter neatly sliced, revealing no ragged edges. He was pleased. His practice had paid off. Placing the lid over the cooler, he closed the latch.

He turned back to Dallas. Blood splattered her flaccid torso. He picked up a couple of fresh towels, a bar of apricot soap, and a bottle of herbal shampoo. Carrying them to the table, he began to work.

Such a creative idea, instead of searching for victims, they'd come to him. He still had several application forms.

CHAPTER 34

Leaning back in his chair, Rosko drained his fifth coffee of the day. He shoved the autopsy report across the desk as if it were a repugnant snake. The same as the others. Nothing new, nothing to furnish one damned lead. The only difference being this victim had renal failure and the killer hadn't bothered taking her diseased kidney. He thought about Herd's warning. Would the killer be so incensed he'd already be looking for his next victim?

The whole department was pulling double duty on this one. They'd interviewed family, friends, and co-workers of the victims. The best suspect, so far, was Mark Finnian, but they could only link him with the Luciano woman. He drove a souped-up old Mustang, not a van. Rosko thought of the white van parked at Lenny's Garage. Finnian would probably have no problem accessing it.

One of Mary Jane's high school classmates had an old rape charge, but apparently Winters hadn't seen him in years. There were no weapons or drugs involved in the rape. He had an alibi for the night of her murder, and he didn't drive a van. They were keeping their eye on him just in case.

The medical school connection wasn't leading anywhere either. Investigating everyone who'd left the medical schools, whether of their own volition or not, was proving fruitless. Phil Myers continued to work that angle, along with the transplant list.

Every lead they got wound up at a dead end. He kept asking himself the same question. What were they missing? Still no answer. And now, the latest victim, Virginia Gallingham was a nurse at Grace Memorial. She'd been found in a small park not a hundred feet from her apartment.

They were trying to police all the parks, and increase street patrols. It just wasn't enough. Strathburn didn't have the manpower. Rosko picked up the coroner's report on Gallingham. Like the others, she had a puncture site from an intravenous injection. Chloroform presumably knocked her out. The lab wouldn't find traces of it, but her lips and mouth had blisters similar to the other victims. The body, again, moved postmortem. The tissue and blood samples Mac sent to the lab would take several days for results. Bruises on her upper arms had been made within hours of her death, presumably from a struggle with her killer.

Rosko flipped through the papers in front of him: the Corpus Delecti, autopsy reports, and toxicology tests. He spread out the photos of the victims. Black and white glossies made death even grizzlier. Picking up the crystal paperweight, he gazed into its kaleidoscopic center. He might get more out of it than the leads they had so far. He closed his eyes and hoped when he opened them some clue would magically appear. It didn't.

It kept coming back to the same questions. What type of person was capable of such meticulous and malicious mutilation? He obviously knew anatomy. Where had he learned it? His dissection skills, though not of a surgeon, weren't of an amateur either. Why did he want their kidneys? A black market kidney could go for anywhere from ten to a hundred thousand, depending on the wealth of the client. But if his intention was to sell them he wasn't harvesting them properly. He sliced through the renal artery too close to the kidney. Surgeons needed the whole length of the artery to transplant it. He thought of his conversation with Mac.

"What else would you do with a kidney?" Rosko had asked Mac.

Mac's laugh was hearty. "Well it's sure not on my list of delicacies."

"That's gross. You suggesting we've got cannibals in Strathburn?"

"Maybe he's collecting them," Mac suggested. "Different sizes, different shapes."

Rosko flipped through the pages again. Collecting them? Why, in God's name, would anybody collect kidneys, and where was he keeping them? They weren't something you'd want to find when you opened your freezer, or if somebody else opened it.

Could that be a clue? Did he live alone so he wouldn't have to worry about anyone looking in his freezer? Or did he keep the kidneys somewhere else? Did he even keep them long enough to freeze them? Was he a cannibal? Rosko shuddered. Too many damn questions and no answers. He slid the papers back into the manila folder and glanced at the clock. Nine-thirty-eight. Time to get out of here. There was nothing more he could do tonight.

As he stood, the chair scraped on the tile, grating on one of his last nerves. He needed peace and quiet. He ached to be home listening to some soothing music. Something good Janice had done for him—introduced him to the classical stuff.

At first, when she'd played Mozart, Bach, or Vivaldi, he'd told her to turn the crap off and put on some good country music. She called him uncouth and refused to let him touch the record player. Gradually, the music grew on him. When she left with their music collection, he'd gone out and replaced most of the classical CD's. Was he finally couth? Maybe on the way home he'd pick up Sarah Brightman's latest. The trill of the phone interrupted his thoughts.

"Rosko here."

"How you doing, Gerry?" It was Mac's Scottish brogue.

"I'd be a hell of a lot better if you'd give me something to go on. I just finished reading your report. Nothing."

"Well, now. I might just have something."

Rosko pressed the phone to his ear. "And what might that be?"

"Maybe our guy got careless."

"What have you got, Mac?"

"Well, our guy might have left a trace of his blood on Virginia Gallingham. She was O positive and…" He paused.

"And what?" demanded Rosko.

"And the what is," he said, pausing again, "I found another blood type on our lady."

"Do you think it's his?" Rosko shouted into the phone.

"Could be."

"How long before you know?"

"I'm running tests now. I should know in an hour or so."

Rosko's hand went damp. He switched the phone to his other hand and wiped his palm on his trousers. "Call me as soon as you know. You got my cell number?"

"Sure I got it. Right next to my heart."

"There's nothing next to your heart, Mac."

Mac's belly laugh echoed through the phone. "Hey, buddy, you want this information or not?"

"There'll be a round for you at Kelsey's if it's good. Cause I've got to tell you, my ass is on the line. I've got to catch this bastard, and soon. The media is having a heyday and Richards is on my back."

Rosko picked up his pencil and thought back to his grade twelve-biology. What was the anagram of blood types? O, A, B and AB. Then there were the positives and the negatives.

"Moira always said you had a nice ass. Maybe it's worth saving. I'll call you soon as I know."

"Did she really say that about my ass?" Rosko heard the clunk at the other end of the line. Smiling, he dropped the receiver back in its cradle. He sat down again and, folding his arms behind his head, leaned back in the chair. A grin spread across his face at the thought of Mac's wife, Moira. A Scottish beauty who endeavored to keep Mac on the straight and narrow.

His eyes drifted shut and immediately his mind filled with visions of mangled glossy black and white bodies. His eyes flew open, his smile vanished. He slammed his fist onto the desk and made a silent promise to each of the victims.

Draining the dregs of the coffeepot into his mug, Rosko grabbed a couple of chocolate bars from the vending machine. Hopefully it would keep him awake until Mac called back. Brightman would have to wait, especially if Mac had something good.

He devoured the candy bars, washing them down with stale coffee. It didn't help. Within minutes his eyelids felt like lead and drifted shut. The ringing of the phone jolted him awake. His head jerked forward and his palms hit the desk. Where was he? What time was it?

Years of having to wake abruptly came to his rescue. He was still at the police station; the phone was ringing, and he needed to answer it. Glancing at the clock, he reached across the desk, his arm knocking a pile of papers to the floor. "Damn it."

"Well, glad to talk to you too."

"Sorry. I just knocked a pile of papers on the floor."

"Been napping on the job again." Mac chuckled. "What's wrong with you? Getting old? It's only eleven. You did say you wanted the results as soon as possible. I can call back in the morning."

"Just give me the goddamn results."

"Don't get bitchy, or you'll have to wait until tomorrow."

Rosko yawned. "Just give me the results, Mac."

"Our killer is AB positive."

"Now, if we test everybody who knew the victims, we might find the killer."

"Hey, you wanted something."

"I know, Mac. I'm looking for a miracle."

Rosko's other line flashed. He pressed the button.

CHAPTER 35

Fifteen minutes later Rosko arrived at the crime scene. The press was already there.

"Detective Rosko." Peter Jasper of the NCV News pushed a microphone close to his face. "What's going on? Have you found another body?"

Rosko glared at the reporter blocking his way. Jasper's frequent binges and a reliance on fast foods had done a number on the body that was once a quarter back for the Miami Dolphins.

"Out of the way, Jasper."

"Ah, Rosko, give me something."

Rosko pushed the microphone away, muttering under his breath. He kept walking toward the crime scene. "No comment."

The reporter hustled along beside him. "The public has a right to know."

Rosko turned so suddenly he almost knocked the reporter off his feet. "Look Jasper, I don't want to start a panic. I'll give you what I can, when I can. I don't want to jeopardize catching this guy."

"Just give me a tidbit, Rosko."

"Say there was a body found and the police are investigating. Don't add any details. The guy's probably getting off on all the news coverage."

"Do you have any leads?"

"No comment."

"Is it the same killer?"

"I don't know yet. Somebody's stopping me from getting to the scene."

"Damn it, Rosko, you have to give me something."

Rosko glared at the reporter. "I don't have to give you shit."

The reporter's shoulders sagged and Rosko regretted his burst of anger. He'd heard rumors. Jasper needed a good story. Sherry Simmons seemed to be getting all the good ones. It was like she had an inside track, and it wasn't him. Even when they'd dated he refused to give her special treatment. The relationship ended when she wouldn't stop pressuring him, tricking him into giving her information, and even sneaking into his files. The rumors she and Rosko were sleeping together started quickly, but its ending seemed to be taking longer to get around. But of all the reporters in town, Rosko knew he could trust Jasper not to leak the story. He'd dealt with him before. Jasper had supplied Rosko with information leading to the arrest of criminals, so why not let him get the story?

Rosko stopped and met his gaze. "Jasper, I'll make you a deal. If you hold off for a bit, I'll give you first crack when the story breaks."

"I can live with that. As long as you don't mind if I print that a woman's body was found here, and you're following up several leads."

"If you co-operate, I'll give you anything I can. But screw me and it will be the last you get from me."

"Sure, Rosko."

"But this is as far as you go. When I get back from checking the scene, I'll let you know if there's more."

Klieg lights were being set up in the park. Rosko stepped over the yellow cordon tape and headed toward them. The semi-circle of policemen parted, allowing Rosko to see the focus of their attention.

The woman's body lay sheltered by a copse of trees. But for raging teenage hormones, discovery might have taken a while. Hopefully the poor kids who found her would avoid the woods from now on. Their parents were on the way. Once Wilson arrived they'd interview the kids then let them get home.

Rosko knelt beside the body. She resembled the previous ones—early twenties, petite, Caucasian. Other than the body being hidden better, everything looked the same.

Footsteps announced the arrival of the Crime Scene Unit. Coroner Kim Lee led the way. Rosko rose, waiting until they'd crossed the ground between them. At least the uniforms hadn't trampled the area. The Crime Scene Unit just might be able to find something.

Rosko nodded then stood back while Lee got to work. He checked her liver temperature, then took a camera from his satchel, and snapped several pictures.

"I don't think she's been dead long," Rosko said. His comment was part question, part statement.

Lee glanced up. "You're right. It looks like the same killer. Same pose, same incision, and I'll bet she's missing a kidney."

Rosko grinned. "That's a bet I'm not taking."

"Smart decision, my friend."

Wilson had just pulled up to the park and jogged over to them.

"What took you so long?" Rosko demanded.

Wilson grinned and shrugged his shoulders. His semblance of apology didn't cut it.

"Damn women," Rosko muttered.

"Sorry, Boss. I knew you'd get here tout de suite and I didn't think a few minutes would matter. The body isn't going anywhere."

"Well, your body better get its ass here faster next time."

"You wouldn't be jealous would you, Rosko?"

"Screw off, Wilson. Get your mind back on your work."

"Sure thing, Boss."

Rosko glared at his partner. "And stop calling me boss."

"Sure thing, Boss. Who found the body?"

"A couple of teenagers looking for some action got more than they bargained for. Doused their hormones pretty quick."

"That'd do it," Wilson agreed

"We need to lecture them on the dangers of being in the park after dark. Think you can focus on that?" Rosko asked.

"Sure. Let's see if we can scare them even more than they already are." Wilson gave his partner a poke in the shoulder. "Can I give them my lecture on safe sex while I'm at it?"

"Their discovery tonight might be enough to scare them off sex for a while. We can leave the birds and bees to the parents."

"Damn, it would have been fun."

Rosko turned back to the coroner. "Have you got anything, Lee?"

Lee shook his head.

"See if you can find something. We've got to concentrate on the small things. That's the only way we're going to catch this bastard."

"I'll see what I can do."

"Do whatever you can. The intervals are getting closer."

Lee turned back to examining the body and Rosko crossed to the Crime Scene Unit. They were combing the area for clues. Nothing useful had shown up yet. He left the team to do their job. Finished with the body, Lee turned it over to the attendants waiting to transport her to the morgue. Rigor mortis had set in and they were having trouble getting her stiffened body into the white plastic bag. Despite their care, Rosko heard a dull thud as they slid her body onto the stretcher.

The gurney rolled across the uneven ground towards the waiting vehicle. Away from the Klieg lights, only a quarter moon and a few stars illuminated the park. Several times the attendants had to stop and lift the stretcher when it caught in a rut.

"We've got footprints," Chao Sugimoto called out.

Rosko hurried over to where Chao was crouched and saw the slight depression in the grass. He touched the ground several inches away from the print. It remained slightly boggy from the brief storm earlier.

"Can you get a print?"

"I should be able to get something," Chao said. "At least a shoe size, hopefully some idea of weight. And maybe, if we get lucky, we might be able to determine if our guy wears runners or army boots."

"That would be nice." Rosko grinned. "I haven't gotten lucky in a long time."

Chao laughed at Rosko's double entendre. "Hey, there's a good looking brunette over there who'd love to change that."

Rosko's gaze followed the direction Chao's finger pointed. Sherry Simmons stood talking to Jack Wilson. Shaking his head slightly, he turned back to Chao. "Getting involved with her again would be the worst bit of luck I could have. I'll go without thanks."

The men shared a conspiratorial chuckle. Chao was the only one privy to how Sherry had used her relationship with Rosko to further her career.

Rosko circled the perimeter of the crime scene. Leaves caught by the gusty winds of the storm lay strewn over the ground and he crossed to an accumulation by the base of a large maple tree. Crouching, he slid his fingers into a pair of gloves and sifted through the leaves examining the soft, damp ground below.

"Hey, guys, I think I found something." Taking an evidence bag out of his pocket, Rosko picked up the butt of a cigarette, dropped it into the plastic bag and zipped it up. With a flourish, he handed it to Chao. "Looks fresh. Let's hope it belongs to our killer."

With Chao's help, they pushed away more of the leaves and found another butt and an area of depressed ground. Chao traced the area with his fingers. "Looks like another print."

"Thank heavens for the rain yesterday. Do you think you can get a mold of this one, too?" Rosko asked.

"Maybe between the two of them, I'll get one good casting," Chao said.

"I'll leave you to it. I'm going to see if Wilson got anything. Call me when you know something, Chao."

"Will do."

Rosko headed toward Wilson where reporters jockeyed for a glimpse of the body being loaded into the transport van. As the back doors closed and the van drove away, the reporters rushed the detectives.

"Detective Rosko." Sherry Simmons pushed her microphone close to his face. "What can you tell us?"

Rosko noticed Peter Jasper behind Sherry. If he had anything, he'd rather give it to Jasper, but he couldn't push Sherry out of the way to speak to him privately. As a compromise, he spoke to the group. "There's been a body found, an unidentified female, cut with a sharp instrument. That's all I can tell you for now."

Rosko pushed past them, ignoring their demands for more. Catching up to Wilson, they got a progress report from the uniforms who'd been questioning residents in the surrounding area. Several people came forward. Three had seen a van parked on the street a few hours ago. Two of them said it was light blue, the other one said white. Great. Did that mean there were two vans? Witnesses' memories were so often inaccurate.

At least this time people came forward to report something. Wilson showed the Polaroid they'd taken of the victim, but no one recognized her. As soon as the sun came up they'd extend the canvas to the businesses near the park.

Rosko and Wilson crossed the park to an all-night diner. The uniform sitting by the door prevented the teenagers in the back booth from fleeing. Rosko noted the pale faces and darting glances that made them look younger than their stated sixteen years. The boy was dressed in a black T-shirt and cutoff jeans. The girl wore matching but skimpier jean shorts. Her tight black halter-top exposed mounds of firm flesh.

The detectives spoke to the officer leaving the teens to squirm a bit longer before they slid into the bench across from them. Wilson took out his notebook, set it on the table, then wrote down their names and addresses. They lived in the neighborhood, and had "just been taking a walk" when they came upon the body.

No, they hadn't touched anything. And no, they hadn't noticed anyone else nearby. The teenagers had nothing useful. Rosko gave them his cards and a short lecture on the dangers of loitering in parks at night.

A commotion at the restaurant's door announced the arrival of their parents. The teenagers, still visibly upset from their discovery, fidgeted even more. From the looks on their parents' faces, there would soon be more for them to squirm about.

Disappointed, Wilson left the sex education lecture to the parents.

҂ӘҫӘ

Officer Matt Thompson reported for the afternoon shift. He was the first to recognize the victim.

"That looks like a girl I saw on Gerrard Street yesterday. She was leaning against one of the buildings. Looking for a job, she said. I thought she was a hooker. Told her to get moving. I got distracted, when I turned around, she was gone. Didn't see her after that."

"Too bad you didn't give her a ticket for loitering. Then we'd have a name on her," Wilson said. "Remember anything about her? Hair color, height, weight, or what she was wearing?"

"Brown hair, about five-foot-three, thin. She had her shoes off. She had to put them back on when I told her to get moving. They were black, with spike heels."

"Anything else?"

"She wore a short skirt, black, I think. And a red patterned top. Tight. That's what made me think she was a hooker."

"We're checking the area in a three mile radius. So far no one's recognized her or knows anything," Wilson said.

"Did she look down on her luck?" Rosko asked.

"Could be." Thompson thought for a moment. "The way she walked on those heels of hers, wobbling a bit, I thought maybe she'd been drinking…I don't know…I wonder if the shoes weren't hers, hurt her feet. They didn't look new. Maybe we should check the YMCA's, or women's shelters."

Thompson joined Rosko and Wilson as they made the round of women's centers. It was at Sunnyside Women's Haven that Dallas Parker was identified.

CHAPTER 36

The trailer park had been there for years. Rusting vintage cars sat in front of compact rows of mobile homes whose aluminum roofs, tattered and torn, pitched sadly toward the ground. Screen doors hung at odd angles, litter scattered the sparse grassy area. A visible attempt had been made to camouflage the deterioration in a few of the homes. This was not the case at number thirteen Cedar Lane where Rosko and Wilson found Mrs. Parker.

A lawn chair sat on the wooden deck abutting the side of the trailer. Mrs. Parker's body squeezed its limits. She nursed a bottle of beer, obviously not her first of the day. Mr. Parker was no longer in residence, and the Mrs. showed neither surprise nor concern at the news about her daughter. Who took responsibility for funeral costs, her only concern.

They wasted little time consoling Mrs. Parker and less than an hour after setting out they were pushing through the double doors of the police station. Rosko headed straight for his office. Maybe, just maybe, a lead had come up while they were gone. But there was nothing new. His desktop remained as empty as when he'd left. While Wilson checked with Myers, he decided to research ketamine.

He stifled a yawn while he waited for the computer to boot up. Sliding the cursor to the search browser, he typed, Ketamine. Within seconds a list of sites flashed on the screen. He browsed several of them. He couldn't believe the information available, too much and too easily accessible to the wrong people. Rosko took notes.

> —short-acting anesthetic with hallucinogenic and painkilling qualities;
> —for treatment of severely injured patients, reduction of simple fractures;
> —effects within fifteen seconds, unconsciousness within one minute, patients remain unconscious for ten to fifteen minutes;

–known as Ket, Special K, Vitamin K or just K.

Rosko rubbed his eyes. Sleep deprivation was catching up with him. He looked down at the files scattered across his desk, four profiles and not one releasing a single clue.

They'd pulled records of anyone with a history of violence. Interviews with petty criminals led nowhere. Rosko shoved the files out of his way and uncovered the glossy black and white photos of the slain women. He stared at them. What piece did he need to unravel the puzzle?

He examined each picture in turn. Four of them, all in their twenties, all slim, attractive, brown-haired and Caucasian. Mary Jane Winters, travel agent; Tina Luciano, waitress at Fred's Diner; Virginia Gallingham, nurse at Grace Memorial Hospital; and now Dallas Parker, unemployed. Similar, yet different. The same hair color and body statures, but their lifestyles held no common thread. At least none they could discern.

His phone rang. Edna and Walter Winters were on their way up to see him.

"We want to know what the hell you're doing to find our daughter's killer," Mr. Winters demanded.

Rosko motioned them to sit.

"I don't want to sit. I just want to know what you're doing to find the bastard."

Mrs. Winters tugged the sleeve of her husband's suit jacket. "Please Walter, you're not supposed to get upset."

Rosko saw the despair in her eyes. She'd already lost her daughter and now she had to deal with her husband's anger and its potential risk to his health. "I want to assure you we're trying to find her killer," Rosko said quietly. "And, we won't stop until we do." He paused. "I know you've been through a lot, but I'd like to ask a couple more questions."

"Walter, they're only trying to help. Let them do their job. Maybe there's something we know that might help them."

Winters slumped into the chair on the other side of the desk. He reminded Rosko of a day-old balloon, not enough pressure left to explode but deflating with a long, low hiss. Mrs. Winters took the seat beside her husband, holding his hand as the fight sighed out of his worn body.

"Did you think of anyone unusual hanging around the neighborhood? Did Mary Jane mention anyone bothering her, say at work or on the way home, or someone hanging around? Think of any-thing. It doesn't matter how trivial it seems."

"She said something about a guy watching her on the bus one night. She didn't mention it happening again." Mrs. Winters met his gaze. "It happened a couple of weeks before…"

Mrs. Winters's eyes misted and she paused, unable to continue the sentence, unable to say the words, before her death.

Rosko pulled out Sue Taylor's composite. They'd been shown the picture shortly after their daughter's murder but then they were still in a state of shock. "I know you saw this before…but I'd like you to take another look." He handed the penciled drawing across the desk. They studied it wordlessly for several seconds, shared a glance, then shook their heads. Mrs. Winters handed it back.

"It still doesn't look like anyone we know."

They stumbled out of the office, sagging shoulders, sagging hearts, leaning into each other for support.

It was mid-morning and Rosko had already had enough for the day. He needed to get out of the office, needed to feel like he was doing something. He was on his way out the door when Myers stopped him. "Hey, Boss."

"How are you coming with the search?"

"Nothing yet. I want to expand the parameters," Myers said.

"To what?" Rosko asked.

"So far, I've checked the transplant lists in a hundred mile radi-us for the last twenty years. It included anyone who died getting a transplant. Then I expanded it to two hundred miles. I'd like to go back thirty years and I want to check if anyone died within a three or four month period of having a transplant, or had complications after surgery."

"Why so long?" Rosko asked.

"Sometimes people survive the initial transplant but die from complications."

"Do whatever you think, Phil. The computer's your baby."

"Thanks, Boss." Myers paused, "I appreciate your keeping me working. I'm doing better."

Rosko nodded. "I'm glad. You're a good man. Let me know if I can do anything else to help."

"How's it going on the streets?" Myers asked.

"We've got a blood type, but nobody to match it to. Sightings of a blue, or a white van, and an abuser with alibis."

"That means you got shit."

Rosko shrugged. Myers was right, all they had was a big pile of shit.

CHAPTER 37

Vials of medications sat on the top of the cart. Claire sorted through them, reading the name on each one. There were several vials of xylocaine in varying strengths, a couple of vials each of midazolam, Valium, and sterile saline. She couldn't find the ketamine. She rifled through the vials again. Where was it?

Had pharmacy changed the supplier again? They were forever finding a new, cheaper supplier. And different drug companies had different brand names. Claire searched again. No ketamine. Maybe it had slid behind something. She shifted the bottles of cleansing solutions and sterile water. There were no vials of the short acting anesthetic.

Claire called out to one of the nurses. "Liz, where's the ketamine?"

"It's there."

"I can't see it."

"It's on the top of the cart."

Liz Canning was at the other end of the room fitting a young man for crutches. She was an attractive, young, single redhead and Claire could tell by her flushed face that her patient was flirting with her and that she was enjoying it.

The man, probably six-foot-three, wore tan chinos and a monogrammed golf shirt. The muscular arms holding the crutches were tanned to a rich gold. Blues eyes twinkled in amusement as Liz tried to make him understand the complexities of crutch-walking. He had a contagious grin and was using it to full advantage.

It would do Liz good to have a man in her life again. She'd been getting kind of crusty lately. At five feet, nine inches, there weren't a lot of men Liz felt comfortable dating. She'd confided to Claire that in high school she'd been partnered in dance class with a boy a head shorter than her. He'd been more interested in finding ways to get his face between her breasts than learning the dance steps. Liz was the one sent to the office after she'd hauled off and decked him. Since then she'd never dated a man shorter than herself.

Claire tried not to eavesdrop on their conversation as she searched through the vials again. The drug wasn't on the top of the cart. She opened each drawer and rummaged through the contents. She hunted behind paper–wrapped syringes, shifted boxes of needles, moved alcohol wipes. There wasn't one vial of ketamine. Where was the damn drug? She didn't want to disturb Liz but a patient was waiting for his broken arm to be reset and she needed the medication.

"Liz, I can't find it."

Liz was readjusting the length of one of the crutches and spoke without turning around. "I put a couple unopened vials there just half an hour ago."

"Well, they're not here now."

Liz turned her head toward Claire and rolled her eyes.

"Sorry, Liz, but I need it now."

"I'll get it."

Claire's shoulders slumped as Liz handed the patient the instruction sheet for crutch-walking before leaving the room.

On impulse, Claire grabbed the instruction sheet from the patient and wrote Liz's name and phone number on it. Her reward was a conspiratorial grin as he hobbled out of the room.

Liz returned with the anesthetic and Claire fixed her patient's broken arm. She remained busy with patients for the rest of the night. It wasn't until her shift was over and she was home in bed that she realized that night wasn't the first time ketamine had gone missing.

CHAPTER 38

D etective Rosko. Can I help you?"

"It's Claire. Claire Valincourt, from Grace Memorial Hospital."

"Hi, Claire. How are you?"

Was it her imagination or had his voice softened? "I'm fine."

"What can I do for you, Claire?"

A warm flush swept through her as she pictured his intense blue eyes and engaging smile. For reasons she couldn't understand, she felt comfortable in his presence. There was something special about the man, a softness that suddenly surfaced when he smiled, the twinkle in his eyes when he let his professional side relax, the way he smoothed over the gory details. And the touch of his hand…

In the few times they'd been together they'd talked about the victims, the killer, their work, and even delved into each other's private lives. He had such a compassionate way about him that she'd ended up telling him even more than her closest friends knew about her. His wry sense of humor eased her fears and encouraged her to let her hair down. She remembered the wink he'd given her, when he'd left the emergency department the other night, that had sent electric shocks running through her body. Their gaze had locked and she'd had to force herself to look away. Yes, there was a lot he could do for her.

"Well," She hesitated. "It's just…I think we have a situation you should be aware of. It's not really my place…I've reported it…I know it's important…but the hospital wants to keep it quiet."

"Claire, what are you talking about?"

There was a long pause before she spoke again. "Well…"

"Can you tell me over the phone?" This time he paused. "Or do you want me to come to the hospital?"

"No." Claire held her breath. "I don't want to discuss it here. I may be out in left field, but I think you should be aware of what's happened. Can you meet me after work?"

"I'll be busy until after seven. Do you want me to meet you somewhere, or do you want me to drop by your apartment?"

Claire thought about the feelings he aroused in her. Maybe him coming to her apartment wasn't a good idea. Damn it, Claire, get hold of yourself, this is about a murderer. The words, "It's a date then," almost blurted out of her mouth but she stopped herself. "I'll see you this evening then." Putting the handset down she couldn't deny she wished it was a date.

Rosko replaced the receiver.

Wilson's voice broke into his thoughts. "What's got you smiling? Got a hot date tonight?"

"None of your damned business," Rosko snapped.

"Touchy, touchy."

"Stay out of my personal life, Wilson."

"Righto, Boss, just business."

Rosko drummed his fingers on the desk. "Why does he take the kidneys? And why leave them alive while he does it then let them bleed to death? There must be some significance for him. But what the hell is it?"

"Probably a mother complex." Wilson countered. "Isn't that what the books would say? And didn't the FBI profiler say it was probably related to a traumatic event in his childhood? Who better to screw up a kid up than his mother?"

"Or a father." Rosko shrugged one shoulder. He laid the photos of the victims in front of him and stared between them and the map of where their bodies had been found. Nothing jumped out at him. "We need answers, not theories." Rosko turned to Myers. "Have you come up with anything yet?"

"I'm still searching the data bases. We found a few women on dialysis waiting for a kidney when they died. We're checking out their families, but that's not leading anywhere."

"He's collecting kidneys for some reason. We need to find out what it is. What's driving him?" Rosko paused. "Can we expand our search for anybody on the list in the last, say, twenty years, dead or alive?"

"That will take time," Myers answered.

"Well, since we can't find any other fucking clues," Rosko said, pounding his fist on the desk, "we'll just have to spend the time, won't we?"

Myers's shoulders stiffened as he retreated to his desk and Rosko regretted his outburst. The guys were all working hard, including Myers. Rosko modulated his tone before addressing the detective again. "What about where our killer learned how to do his butchery?"

"The medical and veterinary schools have had a dozen or so questionable students, but we've checked them out and there's nothing to link them to our murders."

"What about where he's getting the ketamine?"

"We've checked both hospitals, and all the clinics in town. Nothing suspicious has been reported. The veterinary clinics have come up clean, too."

"Shit, guys. We've got to get something. Dig deeper."

"Well, Staples Animal Clinic was broken into a few months back."

"What was taken?"

"There's five veterinarians working there and they couldn't find anything missing." Myers shook his head. "Nothing, or so they said."

"Go back and talk to them. Maybe they lost some ketamine but were afraid to own up to it for fear of having their clinic closed. Some of these places aren't overly careful about locking up their drugs."

The phone on Rosko's desk rang. He hoped Doctor Valincourt wasn't calling back to tell him not to come by tonight. His polite greeting turned into barking monosyllables. He hung up and slammed his fist onto his desk scattering papers into the air, some of them sliding off onto the floor. "Another worthless lead."

"What?" Wilson paced in front of the desks.

"They got a casting that might belong to our perp. He wears size eleven runners. Reeboks. Know how many pairs of Reeboks are sold in a year?"

"A few thousand, I'd bet," Myers answered. "Too many to track, that's for sure."

"And, oh yeah, we got DNA off the cigarette butts. Must be a smoker's haven. Twelve different people smoked in that spot in the park over the last few days. Now if we had a God damned suspect to match one of them to…" Rosko bent and retrieved the papers from the floor.

Wilson stopped pacing long enough to pour himself a cup of coffee. "What about the report on the latest body? Is it back yet?"

"Medical examiner's office is faxing it over now," Rosko said.

"I'll get it." Myers hurried out of the room. He was trying hard to keep his nose clean and his lips away from the bottle.

Rosko crossed to the coffeepot and drained it. The liquid churned as he added powdered creamer and two packages of sugar. His thoughts were as murky as the swirling brown fluid.

"Here's the report, Boss."

Rosko grabbed the paper reading the white document's particulars aloud.

> "Dallas Parker, Caucasian, age: 22, occupation: unemployed
>
> "Time of death: between one and three a.m. on Aug 14, 2005
>
> "Cause of death: hemorrhagic shock.
>
> "Bruises to body on upper arms coincide with being grabbed. Some bruises post mortem, probably result of transport from site of death to site of discovery. Skin abrasions at wrists and ankles. A sharp object, possibly a scalpel, was used to make eight–inch slash on the left side of the abdomen. Her left kidney was extracted by the severing of the ureter, the renal vein, and the renal artery.
>
> "With the severing of the renal artery the victim probably exsanguinated within five minutes. There was redness around her mouth. Possibly from chloroform. There was a puncture site at the right antecubital space."

Rosko threw the paper on the top of his desk. Nothing new.

"Let's go pound the streets and interview anybody we find within a mile radius of the park. And Myers, you go visit that veterinary clinic. Put some pressure on them. Our perp has to be getting his ketamine somewhere."

"Will do."

Myers, stuck in the office with data base searches for days now seemed pleased to get away from the computer for a while. He grinned broadly. "I've extended the computer search for people with kidney disease. Maybe when I get back, just maybe, it might give us something."

Rosko closed the folder and slid it into the top drawer of his desk. Slamming the drawer, he rose and motioned to Wilson. "That's good, Myers. Let me know as soon as it spits anything out."

Wilson grabbed his jacket and followed Rosko and Myers out of the station. Dallas hadn't been at the shelter long and had no apparent enemies and no jealous boyfriends that anyone knew about. Rosko and Wilson worked through the homes and business between the shelter and the park but her only link to the other victims seemed to be her youth, hair color, and residency in Strathburn.

CHAPTER 39

It was seven-thirty when the apartment buzzer sounded. In deference to the continuing heat wave, Claire wore a pair of shorts and a loose-fitting T-shirt.

Rosko smiled, shrugged. "Sorry. I got tied up."

"That's okay. It's too hot to do much. I'm just vegging in front of the television. Would you like a coffee?" she asked. "Or something stronger?"

"I'm technically off duty, so, if you have a beer?"

"A cold one coming up." Claire motioned to the living room. "Make yourself comfortable. I'm just watching an old movie."

As he crossed to the sofa, Claire felt his gaze on her retreating figure. Her legs were long, tanned, and muscular, and she wondered if he could see the outline of the trim hips beneath the thin cotton of her shorts. Maybe she should have worn something less revealing. She heard him moving about the living room then a soft thud as he settled into the deep cushions of the sofa.

"Clint Eastwood. One of my favorites," he called out.

Claire, rustling around in the kitchen, replied. "Glad to hear that. It just started." She peeked around the corner. He had taken his suit jacket off and sat with his arm stretched out on the back of the sofa as if feeling very natural for him to be here. "Do you want a glass?" she asked.

"The bottle is fine."

"I'm having cheese and crackers. Want some?"

"I never refuse food. Need any help?"

"No. I'll just be a minute."

Claire emerged balancing a platter and two bottles of beer. She handed him one of the bottles and placed the crackers and mixed cheese slices on the coffee table in front of him. Taking her own beer, she curled up on the other end of the sofa.

She nodded at the plate. "Help yourself."

Rosko took a long draw on his beer and then attacked the food. He hadn't realized how hungry he was. They ate and watched the movie in quiet companionship. It wasn't until a commercial that Rosko seemed to remember the reason for his visit.

"There was something you wanted to tell me?"

Claire felt as if a lead balloon dropped into the pit of her stomach. She took her time before answering. "The hospital administrator doesn't think it's anything. But I think you should know. Maybe I'm making something out of nothing. Medications are misplaced all the time."

Rosko leaned forward.

"You know." Claire shrugged her shoulders. "There are so many drugs around, we can't lock everything up." She glanced up at him. "You'd spend your whole day looking for keys. But a couple of times lately…" She looked away for a second then met his gaze. "A couple of times its been missing."

Rosko was on the edge of the seat. Hospital. Drugs missing. One of the victims had worked at the hospital. Could this be the missing link? The hospital had assured them no drugs were missing.

Claire's hands worried the corner of a throw cushion. She was betraying her hospital, she could lose her job if they found out. She looked up at him and was startled by the intensity of his gaze. It gave her the courage to go on. "I don't know if anyone else has noticed. It's not something you pay a lot of attention to. The nurses stock the cart. Twice now I've gone to look for it, and it wasn't there, yet the nurses told me they'd recently restocked it."

"Claire. What's missing?"

She jumped at the sharpness of his tone then closed her eyes for a second and whispered, "Ketamine."

Rosko grabbed her hand and squeezed it. "This is important." He held her gaze. "Do you know how many inquiries we've put out to pharmaceutical companies, hospitals, and veterinary clinics for missing ketamine? Not one has admitted to missing any, your hospital included. They flatly denied having missing medications." He shook his head. "I'll be talking to them first thing in the morning."

"Can you do it without giving my name?" she asked.

"Yeah, sure." His eyes said, "Another citizen who won't get involved."

"It's just—" Claire couldn't face him anymore and turned away. "I went to the administrator and he fluffed me off. I don't want to lose my job."

There was an awkward silence. Claire thought of all the people who passed through the doors of the emergency department in a day, a week, doctors, nurses, ambulance attendants, orderlies, cleaning staff, many of whom she cared about and trusted. She couldn't imagine any one of them could be stealing drugs, let alone be the killer terrorizing Strathburn.

Faces of the victims flashed in front of her. Rosko wasn't the only one asking for her help. She'd lowered her eyes, but when she raised them, her hesitation was gone. She spoke with fierce determination. "I will help whatever way I can."

"Thanks, Claire. Maybe you don't have to come forward. I'll just do a 'routine' check of the hospital and the employees. If I find anything suspicious I'll run it by you before I do anything."

"That would be good." She looked at the emptied plate. "Are you in a hurry? I could refill the plate." She met his gaze but looked quickly away. "Mrs. Chegetto dropped by another pie." Claire raised her eyebrows. "Key lime. We could watch the rest of the movie?"

"There's nothing I can do tonight." He grinned at her. "If you're not anxious to kick me out. Key lime, eh?"

"Is it my company or the pie you're staying for?" She laughed but got up quickly before he answered, or saw the blush she felt painting her cheeks. "I'll be right back."

He put his hands behind his head and leaned back into the sofa. His boyish smile made him look years younger. Suddenly her heart raced erratically and the hands slicing the pie trembled.

They downed the refilled plate of cheese and crackers, two slices of pie each, and another bottle of beer. A companionable silence passed between them. He reached out and squeezed her hand. The space between them somehow shrank and her hand stayed in his. They were two people starting a journey of discovery.

It was Clint Eastwood night, and enjoying favorite lines and scenes made the evening pass quickly. At the end of the first movie, like two teenagers they scurried around Claire's small kitchen making popcorn before the next movie started. Earlier Rosko had removed his suit jacket, now he stripped off his tie and unbuttoned the top two buttons of his short-sleeved shirt. Claire tried to avoid staring at the matte of brown hair revealed at the V of his shirt. Doing that just made her heart skip a few too many beats.

This time, when they sat on the sofa, there was no visible space between them. At some point during the movie his arm slid around her shoulder. She didn't pull away, instead she let her head rest against his arm enjoying listening to the beating of his heart and inhaling the leathery scent of his cologne. It wasn't passion, not heated awareness, just a golden peace. She relaxed against him letting his peace enfold her, heal her.

It was sometime near the end of the second movie that she heard the soft nasal resonance of his breathing. Claire settled in, enjoying the safety of his arms even while he slept. It had been a long time since she'd been held like this.

She thought about Michael. They were in high school when they started dating. She'd been happy, or so she thought. Yet she'd never experienced the feeling of safety that she had right now, nor the stirrings of passion this man beside her roused. Suddenly she realized her relationship with Michael had never matured into something that would last through a lifetime of trouble and strife. Maybe this friendship wouldn't lead anywhere either, but she knew she was willing to take the risk.

The blare of the late-night news woke Rosko. Claire started to pull away, but his arm tightened, and he pulled her back against him. She tipped her head and was caught in the intensity of his blue eyes. She didn't want to look away. His fingertips stroked her chin and a shiver ran down her spine. His lips found hers. His kiss was tender and breathtaking at the same time.

Then he was pulling back. "I'm sorry. I shouldn't have done that." He shook his head, but his arm remained around her shoulder.

"It's okay."

Her words were soft. She hadn't minded the kiss at all. In fact, she'd enjoyed it more than she wanted to admit. Enjoyed it so much that if she stayed there any longer she'd be tempted for more than either of them was ready for. He didn't stop her when she slid out of his embrace. Her heart was racing and she felt a strange sense of loss as she slid away from him.

Like two teenagers caught in a guilty embrace, they leapt up. Rosko slid on his suit jacket, stuffing his tie into a pocket. Claire grabbed the tray of plates and beer bottles and carried it to the kitchen. By the time they met at the door of Claire's apartment they'd recovered their composure.

His fingertips brushed her cheek and the gentleness of his touch made her want more. He stared into her eyes

"I'm not sure about this," he whispered.

"I'm not either."

"We've both been hurt." He laughed softly and traced the line of her jaw. "Two wounded hearts thrown together by a serial killer."

His blues eyes turned cobalt with intensity, she couldn't look away. Was she imagining passion, need, lust? She tried to focus on the man and not the feelings he was evoking He had a quiet intelligence, strength, and intensity that burned just beneath the surface. She had to look away. Instead she focused on the curve of his lower lip but the hint of sensuality she saw made her feverish.

Where was the control she was supposed to be exercising? She wasn't a teenager with raging hormones, panting for her first encounter. Yet right now, that was how she felt, and it didn't help that his presence seemed to fill the doorway. An electric current ran down her spine. She wondered if he could hear the pounding of her heart.

Then their heads tipped. Their lips met. A gentle brush, as if testing the waters. The pressure increased. The kiss was long and hard.

When he finally pulled away, she couldn't move, and her lips were on fire. His lips brushed her earlobe, his breath warm. "Maybe when this is over…"

He left the rest unsaid. Claire, dizzy with the scent of his aftershave, could only nod.

After he'd gone, she leaned against the doorframe, her heart racing and a lump clogging her trachea, making it hard to catch a breath. What was that man doing to her? She closed her eyes—his face was there, along with the pressure of his lips on hers. She pushed away from the door.

What was the sense of being so confident in every other aspect of her life if she let herself be swayed by a man? Claire gave herself a mental kick and started cleaning up the living room. It didn't help that the scent of his cologne lingered long after his departure.

CHAPTER 40

Brianne Sears was pleased with her class. The students had been labeled slow learners, difficult to handle, losers. But over the past few weeks, they'd opened up and actually begun to learn. A couple of them had even approached her about taking other courses. And to think she'd been reluctant to teach the class.

Tom had wanted her to spend the summer at his parents' cottage. He would join her on weekends. The thought of spending the summer with her overbearing in-laws was the final impetus to take on the six-week course. That left only three weeks of dealing with his parents.

"Mrs. Sears?"

Brianne paused midway down the front steps of Medway High School. She turned to see Sean Murphy, one of her students, taking the stairs two at a time.

"Mrs. Sears. I wanted to ask you about a book you suggested."

"Yes, Sean. Which one?"

"The one by McPhee."

Brianne smiled. Sean had been labeled a loser. The notes on his file said high IQ, but unable to concentrate, attention deficit, resentful of authority, no ambition, dubious learning skills. He may have been some of those things at the beginning, but after four weeks, he was one of her best students.

"Yes, John McPhee. He's a great non-fiction writer."

"That's what I want to write. Until I took your course, well, I didn't think I could even try."

"You have a bright mind, Sean. Read some of his work and let me know what you think of it. If you want, you could write something and hand it in to me next class."

"Really, Mrs. Sears? That would be great."

Brianne continued down the steps and crossed the parking lot. She glanced at the left front tire. Thank heavens she'd had time before class to get it fixed. The last thing she needed was to come out this late at night to find a flat.

Her steps were light. That was the part of the job that made it all worthwhile, bringing a spark into a student's eyes, especially one whose hopes had been squashed.

Brianne was humming the tune, "This little light of mine" as she pulled out of the parking lot. She waved at Sean as she passed him on the street.

He was the last one to see her.

CHAPTER 41

The woman's flaccid body lay on the stainless steel table. He inserted the needle through the vial's rubber stopper, withdrew the remains of the liquid, and placed the empty vial on the table. The tourniquet on her right forearm caused the vein in her hand to bulge. He held her arm straight and slid the needle through the skin. Depressing the plunger, he watched the colorless liquid flow into her vein. He removed the needle and placed the empty syringe on the instrument tray.

A few drops of blood oozed from the site. With a gloved finger, he wiped it away. His heart rate accelerated as he put the finger to his mouth and sucked at the salty fluid. A smile came to his lips. It turned to a grin when he saw the terror in her eyes.

Her struggle was brief. He watched her pupils dilate, the slight flicker of pale eyelids before they closed. Her breasts heaved once then went still. Tonight, there was no need for physical restraints. A surge of power rushed through him.

The time spent on research had been worthwhile. So easy. The Internet was a wealth of information. Most sites were about using ketamine as a recreational drug, but he'd found another use for it.

Taking care, he slid a blade onto the handle of the scalpel. The stainless steel was cold in his palm. It felt so comfortable. Maybe he should become a doctor. His fingers tingled as they tightened around the handle.

The feather taped by her lips fluttered softly. He could barely see the rise and fall of her naked breasts. He laid the side of the scalpel against her nipple, flattened it into the mound of breast, then held the blade steady. It would be so easy to jerk his wrist and mutilate her beautiful body.

A small drop of blood appeared where the tip of the blade punctured her flesh. He smiled, for what he knew he could do, then released the pressure on the blade. With a flick of his wrist, he rotated the blade sideways and slid it downward, stroking her skin without penetrating the epidermis.

Her abdomen was firm and, at a spot just left of her belly button, he paused and turned the gleaming blade. Pressing his index finger on the handle, he caressed the blade through the taut skin. Blood began to ooze. Adrenaline surged through his veins.

Suddenly, her eyes flew open. Her body jerked. The scalpel blade veered downward creating an uneven slash that extended three inches diagonally across her abdomen. He yanked the scalpel out of the jagged incision. What the fuck was going on? How could she move? His hand clenched around the scalpel, and he could feel the sweat trickling down his back.

Was this one of those reflex movements he'd read about? *Look at my incision, bitch! Now what will Sherry say? That the Kidney Slasher can't even cut a straight line?* He stared at the woman. Her eyes closed and her body went flaccid again. He poked her. There was no response.

Was she ready? Should he wait? His fingers spasmodically tightened and released around the handle of the scalpel. Carefully, he placed the blade into the straight line of the incision, hesitating before he drew it across her left side.

She moaned. Her eyelids fluttered then flew open. Her body shifted violently. He jerked the scalpel away from the incision.

What the hell was happening? The drug wasn't working. Did she need more? The bottle of Ketamine was empty. He'd given her a full syringe. Why hadn't it worked? As he watched, he saw her breasts rise and her eyelids flicker rapidly.

He had to give her more.

Shit! Shit!

He didn't have any more here. The other vials were at the house. Sweat beaded on his forehead. He threw the scalpel onto the instrument tray. Without the stimulus of pain, the woman lay still. She was under the effect of the drugs, but not deeply enough for him to proceed. He had to get more ketamine into her before she woke up completely.

He pushed the table out of his way, raced out of the building, and headed for the house. He'd hidden the box of drugs under the floor of the kitchen pantry just in case someone came to look at the house. Now he cursed that precaution. She shouldn't come out of it for a few minutes. But she shouldn't have reacted at all. He had to hurry. Next time he wouldn't be so stupid. Next time he'd make sure he had extra drugs handy. And, next time he'd make sure he had the straps handy to tie the woman up. His head pounded and he heard the voice.

'You're getting too cocky. Too big for your britches.'

"Shut up!"

'You better be more careful. You're going to get caught.'

"Leave me alone." He covered his ears and tried to outrun the voices in his head.

He raced up the porch steps and pushed on the back door. It didn't budge.

The voice chanted at him. *'Silly boy, you should have been ready. You shouldn't have locked the door. Will you never learn?'*

He dug the keys out of his pocket. His hands were shaking and he had trouble finding the right one. The pounding in his head now was so bad it blurred his vision and he couldn't focus. And the voice, it wouldn't stop. Finally his fingers found the one he wanted and he jammed it into the lock. It took several tries before it slid into the cylinder and the tumbler turned. He shoved the door with such force it hit the inside wall and bounced back at him hitting his shoulder. He pushed it out of the way and ran to the pantry at the far end of the kitchen.

Yanking on the handle, he threw the door open. Boxes covered the floor. He kicked them out of the way and began prying up the floorboards. Splinters sliced through his gloves and imbedded in his fingertips. He ignored the pain they caused. An edge of a board finally lifted. He snapped it up and tossed the broken wood out of his way.

He snatched at the small, square metal box that lay in the shallow cavity. His gloves slipped on its metal surface. He couldn't get a grip. Tearing off his gloves, he seized the box with his bare hands and dug at its edges until the lid, finally free, clattered to the floor.

Three vials tumbled out and rolled through the open door into the kitchen. He grabbed the closest one. It was only a quarter full. Not enough. He needed a full bottle. Where were the other ones? He looked around the kitchen. From across the room, he saw the gleam of glass. An edge of a vial stuck out from under an antique buffet. He crossed the room, got down on his knees, and stretched his arm as far as he could. His fingers blindly searched the grime-covered floor.

He felt something hard. His fingers grabbed for it, grazing the vial, causing it to roll farther away. Cursing, he lay on the floor and stared under the buffet. There it was. He stretched until his hand hovered over it. He closed his fingers over the hard glass vial and pulled it out, along with a layer of dust. He wiped the vial against his pants. It was half full. With both vials clenched in his hand, he raced back to the shed.

By the time he ran the distance his lungs felt like they were going to explode. He grabbed the handle of the door. Had he left it partially open? He couldn't remember. He leaned on the door for a second until his breathing settled. It would be okay now. He had the drug. All he had to do was give her more and then he could finish the job. He was back in control. The smile returned to his lips. He opened the door wide and went into the building. It took a few seconds for his eyes to adjust from the evening sky to the bright interior. He took several steps toward the middle of the room, toward the stainless steel table before he realized something was different.

The table was empty!

He gaze darted around the room. Where the fuck was she? Maybe she'd slid off the table and was lying behind it. He raced over. Nothing. Nothing but a small pool of fresh, bright red blood. His gaze now searched the room. Where was she? She had to be here. He'd given her a full syringe of Ketamine. She couldn't be far.

Maybe she was hiding. He ran over to the row of large cupboards along the back wall. He jerked the first door open. Not there. He checked each one. They were all empty. Where could she be? What else was big enough to conceal a body? He looked at the long workbench along the sidewall. He raced over to it, bending to check its dark and cobwebbed shelves. They were strewn with old tools and junk. No room for a person. Maybe she was behind the old freezer. He checked. There wasn't room. He checked anyway. She wasn't there either.

Where the hell was she?

'*You'd better find her. You shouldn't lose your toys.*'

"Where the hell am I supposed to look?"

'*Follow the evidence.*'

"What evidence?"

'*The trail, stupid.*'

The trail. That was it. She was bleeding. There had to be a trail.

He ran back to the stainless steel table. By now the pool of blood had congealed on the cement. A few inches from the table he spotted a small dark spot, beyond it, another. And then another. He followed them. They were headed toward the door.

Could she have gone out the door? How? The amount of ketamine he'd given her should have rendered her incapable of any
movement let alone escaping. What had happened?

'*No time to think about that now, stupid. Find her.*'

He ran for the door, flung it open. Beyond the shed stood an
open space for about fifty feet. Empty. The area around the shed
was surrounded by trees. He concentrated on the trees and the slender spaces between them. Still no body. He needed a flashlight. She
couldn't have gone far. But which way did she go?

CHAPTER 42

Brianne ran. Stabbing pains shot through her abdomen yet she kept moving. Her legs were unsteady and her knees kept buckling. It was an effort to stay upright, let alone force her legs to keep moving and she stumbled frequently. Placing her hand on her abdomen, warm, sticky fluid oozed onto her palm. Despite the pain, Brianne kept her hand pressed over the wound. The oozing lessened. She kept moving.

A fog had settled on her brain. But she remembered pain...someone standing over her...more pain...bright lights. Her eyes wanted to close. She was so tired. She fought to keep going.

Another sensation hit her—cold. Her body felt as cold as if she'd been locked in a deep freeze. Images like flash cards kept assaulting her brain yet still she kept her legs moving. She remembered lying on something hard and cold and metal. Her brain fought to close her eyes. Sleep it told her. No! She forced her eyes to stay open. More images. Bright lights, a face. She'd tried to get up...terrible pain...blood on her hands.

What happened? Where was she going?

It was dark. Trees surrounded her. There'd been a building. She had to get far away from it. She stumbled into trees, tripped over the uneven ground, sharp twigs dug into her bare feet. Branches scratched her arms and cold damp foliage stuck to her ankles. Why was she naked? Recent memories flooded back as she kept her body in motion.

Lying on a cold table...rolling onto her side...more pain...gripping the edge of the table...forcing her body to roll...bare legs hitting cold cement... knees buckling... her body sliding into a crumpled heap...pain jolting her to a state of semi-alertness. She couldn't remember how she'd gotten here but she knew she had to get away.

The door. She'd tried to stand, get to her knees, she couldn't. She'd crawled to the door. Using the door handle, she pulled herself upright. She turned the knob. It wasn't locked. She'd leaned against the door and it slid open.

It had taken her eyes several seconds to adjust to the darkness. She saw trees. If she could get to them, she might be safe. She might be able to get away.

Half stumbling, half crawling, she'd made it to the trees. She hadn't stopped to rest until she was several feet into the woods. Holding a thick limb for support, Brianne looked behind. Only the bright light coming through the open door of the shed illuminated the area. No other human was visible. Maybe she was safe.

Her breathing came in ragged gasps. She wanted to lie down and sleep. Her mind was fuzzy but she knew she had to get away. She caught her breath then forced her feet to move again. Sliding on the wet underbrush, branches clawing her arms, she scrambled through the trees.

Finally, she couldn't go any farther. She was so weak. Her feet refused to take another step. Brianne leaned against a tree and listened to the night sounds—a small rodent scurrying through the underbrush, leaves rustling softly, a dog barking.

Where was she? Was she near town? If she followed the sound of the barking dog, would it lead her to safety? She tried to determine where it was coming from, but before she could, the barking stopped.

Every tree looked the same. Was she getting farther away from that place or just going in circles? She'd never felt so lost and so alone. She could taste the fear welling inside her.

Which way should she go?

A twig snapped. It came from behind her—from the direction she'd just come. Another snap. Her legs felt like lead weights, but she forced them to move.

Suddenly, there was a flash of light through the trees. Brianne ran toward it.

CHAPTER 43

The distinctive ring of the ambulance phone jarred Claire awake. The doctor's sleep room was dark and all she could see was the florescent hands of the wall clock. One-forty-five. Still early in the shift. Claire had hoped to get a bit of sleep before the next patient needed her. It didn't sound like that was going to happen.

Most nights saw the patients trickle out until the morning brought a rush of patients who'd wakened with one ailment or another and decided they needed quick medical treatment before going to work. Some just wanted permission to stay home. But it was too early for them, and they didn't usually call an ambulance.

Should she get up now or wait for the nurses to come and get her? Maybe it was an obstetric emergency and would go right to the delivery room. She needed just a few more minutes of rest. It had been a non-stop barrage of patients since she'd started work at eleven last evening. Claire's eyelids drifted shut. When they opened again, the clock said one-forty-seven.

Usually she coped better with nights, but lately her sleep had been broken by nightmares of pale, young women with large gaping bloody holes in their abdomens. The bodies remained the same, but the faces changed. First she saw the face of the body she'd found, then one of the other victims. It might be Virginia Gallingham, or someone she'd never seen before. The worst though was seeing her own face staring back at her. Claire tried to get comfortable on the lumpy mattress. Maybe she could get a few more minutes of sleep before the nurses needed her.

The ambulance phone rang again. Were two patients coming, or was this an update to the first call? She turned toward the nurse's station. The walls were thin and she heard Betty Hammond speaking to ambulance dispatch. Claire forced herself to get up.

"Do you have a name?" Betty asked. The phone was pinned between her chin and shoulder. She was busy taking notes on a clipboard.

"What's her age? The extent of her injuries?" Betty looked up at the large circular clock across from the desk. "What's your ETA?" Her pen flew across the page. "We'll be ready. Fifteen minutes, right?" Betty hung up the phone and placed the clipboard on a hook on the front of the desk. She turned toward Claire. "Good, you're awake. Break's over."

Claire stretched her arms above her head. Every muscle protested. She rubbed at a numb spot on her right thigh. Her voice was raspy with sleep. "What are we getting?"

"Unidentified female, probably mid-twenties, stab wound to her abdomen, semi-conscious. The paramedics have a pressure dressing on her wound and an intravenous line in. They'll be here in fifteen. I'm putting in a page for the respiratory therapist. Sounds like we'll need him."

Liz Channing, one of the nurses on duty, arrived at the nurse's desk. Betty paged the respiratory therapist then gave Liz a quick report.

"I wonder what shape she'll be in by the time she gets here. What's your bet, domestic quarrel, a fight with a John, or drug related?" Liz asked.

"Tonight," Betty said, "I'll go for a domestic."

"I'll put my money on drugs." Liz countered.

Glancing at the clock, Claire shrugged. "I'll go for a fight with a John. What have we got? Just over ten minutes?"

"About that," Betty said.

Jan O'Sullivan, another nurse, poked her head out of the trauma room. She was getting the room ready for the incoming patient. "What does that leave me with?" she asked. "Okay, I'll go for unknown attacker. If I win, you guys buy the coffee and donuts for tonight's shift."

Picking up the phone on the first ring, Betty spoke into the receiver. "Hi, Pat. We've got a trauma coming in. Want to get your butt over here? They'll be here in ten to fifteen." Betty hung up the phone and turned to the staff. "Pat's on his way."

Liz asked Jan, "Do you need any help setting up?"

"No. I think we're ready to roll."

"The paramedics have one intravenous line already in. Can you set up another one with Ringers Lactate?" Betty asked.

"Already done. The room's ready and waiting. I'll get Tracy back from her break." Jan headed down the hall to the lounge.

"Good then. I'm going to grab a smoke before they come," Liz said. "I'll be out in the ambulance bay waiting for them."

Claire put her stethoscope on the desk and headed for the bathroom. She needed to wash the sleep out of her eyes. Looking in the mirror, a pale face with dark circled eyes stared back at her. She winced at the reflection, she still had another night to work. Night shift was bad enough on the body without the nightmares. Maybe she'd take something to help her sleep today.

She thought again about talking to someone. Detective Rosko, or Gerry, as he'd told her to call him, suggested she see a police crisis counselor. The hospital had its own social workers. But that was too close. Claire wanted her private life left private. Rumor ran rampant on the hospital grapevine, and she was damned if she would give it any fodder. Maybe she'd call Gerry and get the number of someone with no association to the hospital. It couldn't hurt to talk to someone. Wasn't that the advice she gave everyone else?

Glancing in the mirror again, Claire saw the pink hue spreading across her cheeks. Damn. Just thinking about that man made her blush. She sluiced cold water over her face. At least it made her feel a bit more awake. Taking her toothbrush out of the vanity, she scrubbed her teeth. With her brief toilet done, she hung her stethoscope around her neck and went outside to meet the incoming patient.

While they waited, Claire and Liz made small talk. Claire'd had asthma as a child and stayed discreetly upwind of the cigarette smoke. It was hard to avoid the second hand smoke around the hospital despite the anti-smoking laws. So much for hospital staff listening to the health warnings. But now wasn't the time to give Liz a lecture on the virtues of quitting.

Her recent separation and subsequent plummet into single parenthood had halted her efforts at quitting. Added with the pressure of a stressful job and Liz had more than enough to deal with. The tip of Liz's cigarette glowed red in the semi-darkness. A good nurse, she did her job well, but she had a stubborn streak. Maybe that had affected her marriage.

Claire thought about Michael. Had her own stubbornness in staying here to work ruined their relationship? Would it ruin any future relationship? Hopefully there would be someone in her future that could deal with her life as a doctor. Could a doctor and a detective have a successful relationship? Way too soon to have thoughts like that. Claire shook her head and concentrated on her surroundings.

In an attempt to improve the image of the aging building, the hospital had planted rows of dogwoods and hydrangeas along the drive leading to the entrance. The temperature had dropped and Claire shivered with the chill breeze rustling through the trees. She looked up at the night sky. A film of clouds covered the moon. Not a star was visible, only the bright lights of the ambulance bay to cast away the early morning shadows.

"So are we swearing off men for life?" Liz asked.

Claire grinned. "Swearing off two-timing men and back-stabbing sisters."

"Does that mean you're not joining me in dropping men from your vocabulary?" Liz took another drag on her cigarette. "Maybe you like that good-looking detective who's been coming around?"

"He's just been getting my opinion about the case."

"Yeah right! I've seen the way he watches you. Didn't he pick you up after your shift the other day?"

Claire turned her head to look up the driveway. "He just happened to be here and gave me a ride home."

"Your nose is growing, Claire."

"After Michael, I don't think I can trust a man."

"We're together on that one." Liz checked the driveway. "They're coming."

Claire listened. She heard the faint wail of the ambulance siren. Liz took one last long draw on her cigarette, then, stubbed the butt into the sand of the overflowing ashtray.

The night was shattered as the ambulance's siren wailed through the nearby streets. The noise reached a crescendo as the vehicle spun around the corner into the hospital's circular driveway. Red strobe lights glared angrily in the charcoal sky.

The ambulance's tires squealed on the warm asphalt as it pulled to a stop. Claire and Liz simultaneously pulled gloves from their uniform pockets and slipped them on. The siren whined to a halt, leaving behind an eerie silence. George Harper jumped out of the driver's seat. He ran to the back of the vehicle and flung open its double doors.

"How are you ladies tonight?"

"Just fine, George. What shape is she in?"

"Not good. Pressure's low. She's lost a lot of blood. And it's still pouring out of her." George pulled the stretcher out of the ambulance. "Her respirations are shallow. We've got oxygen going."

Harper's partner, Ray Rabideau, was at the head of the bed holding an oxygen mask to a stark white face. Claire noted the slight rise and fall of her chest. She was breathing on her own, at least for now.

Claire scanned the thin white sheet covering the patient. A circle of blood had seeped into it. "I thought dispatch said you guys had a pressure dressing on. It's not working." She was tempted to pull the sheet off to see what was happening below, but right now the priority was to get the patient into the trauma bay and stabilized.

The wheels of the stretcher snapped into place and the gurney raced through the double glass doors of the ambulance bay, down the hall, and into the emergency department. Rabideau continued his report. "We do have a pressure dressing on. Put it on as tight as we could, but it's already soaked through. We put a sixteen gauge intravenous into her left hand and we've run Ringers Lactate wide open. Her blood pressure was in the sixties. At least it's into the seventies now. The bleeding does seem to have calmed down a bit."

Claire rechecked the bloody stain on the white sheet. It expanded as she watched. She looked at Rabideau, her eyebrows raised. "You said the bleeding was slowing down?"

"It has slowed. You should have seen her when we got there. The blood was gushing like a geyser then. Pull the dressing off and see what happens. Once I had that baby on tight, I wasn't taking it off to check." He paused. "At first, I thought it was an artery. But if it was, she wouldn't be alive now."

"True. If an artery was severed she should have died within a few minutes."

"Where'd you find her?" Liz asked.

This time Ray answered. "Really weird. Some guy was driving down Placid Boulevard. He was honking like crazy at us. Says he found her running out of the woods. Nearly ran her over. She was naked and holding her belly. When he stopped, she jumped into his car, screaming for him to get her out of there. Says he didn't see the blood at first. But when he did, he just floored it into town, saw us, and here she is. We called the cops to talk to him. The poor guy was still bringing up his supper when we left him."

They swung the gurney into the trauma room. The bright florescent lights accentuated the paleness of the motionless body. Together, they lifted the young woman onto the hospital bed. Her only response was a low moan. Her body remained limp and unresponsive.

Betty transferred the intravenous bag from the ambulance stretcher to a pole at the head of the bed. She checked that it was flowing quickly. Liz stuck wire electrodes onto the patient's chest and attached them to the cardiac monitor above the bed. Instantly, the patient's heart rhythm flashed across the screen. With each blip on the monitor, a corresponding beep echoed off the sterile green walls. It was too quick to count. The digital readout showed 168. Her heart rate was too fast.

Liz wrapped an automatic blood pressure cuff around the patient's left upper arm. The machine whirred into action. Next she placed an ultra-violet probe on a finger. Her oxygen level flashed on the screen, ninety-one, too low.

The respiratory technician, Pat Cassidy, arrived and transferred the oxygen tubing from the ambulance's oxygen tank to the wall outlet. He turned the dial to its highest level. Rabideau let Cassidy take over holding the oxygen mask to the patient's face then pushed the empty stretcher out of the room. Jan stood at the counter, charting the events and the patient's vital signs.

Claire began a head to toe assessment of the patient. Her pupils were dilated and reacted sluggishly to light. One small part of her brain raced through the possible reasons for the dilated pupils while the rest moved on with the examination. She placed her stethoscope on the patient's chest and listened to the shallow ebb of air in and out of the woman's lungs.

Not great, but she was still breathing on her own. Looping the stethoscope around her neck, Claire listened to the audible beat of the woman's heart. The visual tracing did a quick two-step across the screen. One-hundred and fifty-two. Sinus tachycardia. Still fast, but it was coming down. The patient's breathing and circulation were stable for the moment. Now Claire needed to check the wound.

She pulled the white sheet back exposing a large dressing over the patient's abdominal area. A sanguineous pool coated the layers of white gauze.

"Blood pressure is 86/47." Betty reported the number from the digital readout on the blood pressure machine.

"Let's get a second intravenous going," Claire said. "See if she has any good veins. If not, I'll do a cut-down and put in a central line. Get the usual trauma blood work sent off. And, let the blood bank know we're going to need at least four units of blood on hand. Have them send us two stat."

"Her oxygen saturation is dropping," Cassidy called out. "She's down to eighty-nine. I've got one-hundred percent oxygen on her. It's not helping."

Claire got her stethoscope out and listened to the patient's lungs again. The breath sounds had decreased, especially on the right side where there was only a faint whisper of air exchange. She looked up at Cassidy. "We need to intubate her. Her breathing's too shallow."

Cassidy nodded in agreement. "What size of tube do you want?"

"She's not a big woman. Let's go with a six."

Cassidy opened the top drawer of a cabinet behind the bed. He took out a breathing tube, a laryngoscope, and some Elastoplast tape.

"I'm ready," he told Claire.

"Okay, let me have the laryngoscope."

Claire took the stainless steel instrument Cassidy held out and snapped it open. A bright light shone down the metal surface of the blade. She inserted the blade into the patient's mouth and pressed down on her tongue to expose her trachea. Taking the plastic tube in her other hand, Claire slid it along the metal blade.

Within seconds the breathing tube was in place. Holding the tube, Cassidy inflated the cuff, then wrapped Elastoplast tape around the tube, and secured it to the patient's face. After attaching the tube to an Ambu bag, Pat squeezed air into the woman's lungs. Claire listened to the patient's chest again. She heard the whoosh of the air Pat forced through the tube.

"Sounds good," Claire stated. "She's getting more air now." She glanced at the monitor and watched as the patient's oxygen saturation rose to ninety-five percent. Not perfect, but it would do for now.

Liz and Betty were checking the patient's right arm. With the tourniquet on her forearm, the nurses waited for the slow filling of her veins. Liz massaged the woman's hand to encourage the blood flow.

"Not a lot here, but I'll give it a try." She held up the woman's arm. "Look at these marks. She's got similar ones on the other wrist. Like she had thick bands on her wrists."

Claire examined the patient's forearms. "You might be right. Let's get the intravenous in. We can check that out later."

Betty held the patient's arm while Liz slid the needle into a vein on the top of her hand. The arm remained flaccid, not even twitching as the needle slid through the skin.

"I've got it." Liz said.

There was a flashback of blood into the needle. Attaching a syringe onto the end of the intravenous catheter, Liz withdrew blood and filled tubes for the laboratory. Next, she attached an intravenous line and ran Ringers Lactate into the site. Betty taped the intravenous catheter in place and then secured the patient's hand on an arm board.

"How fast do you want it running, Claire?"

Claire was tugging at the adhesive edges holding the dressing. She glanced up at the heart monitor. "Her heart's still going at a good clip, run it as fast as you can."

Liz held up a selection of various colored blood tubes. "I'm going to run these to the lab."

"Tell them to get those blood results back as soon as they can," Claire directed. "And get a couple of bags of blood down here now." She turned to Betty. "Have we got another blood pressure?"

"86/43."

"How fast is her intravenous running?"

"It's going wide open."

Betty checked the flow of the intravenous inserted by the ambulance attendants. It was already flowing quickly, but she pushed the pole up as far as it would go. "This one's going as fast as it can."

Claire looked at the rapid flow of fluid through the drip chamber. "She's already had one full bag of intravenous solution. Let's give her a couple more. But if her blood pressure doesn't come up soon, we'll have to get blood into her and start dopamine."

"I'll get a bag ready." Jan went to the shelving unit that covered a sidewall of the trauma room. Her fingers ran over the labels on a set of small, see-through drawers. She took a glass vial out of one drawer. The snap of the vial breaking open echoed through the room. She checked the dose with Claire. "Four-hundred micrograms?"

Claire nodded, and Jan inserted the measured dose into a small bag of dextrose and water. Slapping a red label on the plastic, she lay the bag on the counter. "Dopamine's ready."

As if on cue, the programmed blood pressure machine whined as it automatically inflated the cuff on the patient's arm. Every eye in the room focused on the digital readout. It shuffled through a series of numbers before finally coming to rest at 91/49.

Claire shrugged at the reading. Better, but not much. "Start the dopamine." She glanced at the clock. How long had the patient been here? Only six minutes. Her condition was improving, but Claire hadn't examined the wound yet.

With her gloved fingers, Claire peeled the edges of the bandage back. The dressing was completely saturated with blood and slid off easily. Using her foot to position a stainless steel bucket closer to the bed, Claire dropped the sopping gauze into it. The dressing made a dull thud when it landed in the bottom of the bucket.

"Betty, put a page in for surgery. Make it STAT."

Betty was already dialing a pager number. "I think Doctor James is on call tonight."

Liz returned from the laboratory. "They'll call the results as soon as they can. They're working on getting the blood ready."

Claire nodded.

"She's lost a lot of blood," Liz commented.

Their attention focused on the slash that stretched across the left side of the patient's abdomen and the jagged downward slice marring the first incision. Automatically Claire ran her gloved finger along one edge of the wound. It was long, perfectly smooth, deep. Beneath the gash the cavity was filled with blood. Even as they watched, blood trickled over the edge of the incision, over the edge of abdomen, and over the edge of the patient's side. It pooled briefly, then absorbed into the stark white sheet.

Jan shook her head. "Somebody must have been pretty angry to cut her up that bad."

Claire focused on the woman's abdomen. A razor-sharp carving knife, or a switchblade, could have made a wound like this, but it looked like the slice of a scalpel. And the woman exhibited symptoms of drug use. They'd already given her dopamine. How did it react with ketamine? No, Claire determined, dopamine and ketamine were all right. But, shit. Did the woman still have a kidney? "Suction!" she snapped.

Liz turned the wall unit on full and handed the suction tip to Claire. The blood swooshed through the tubing, and within seconds it filled the plastic bottle.

"Has she got a bleeder gushing in there?" Betty asked.

"Can't see anything yet," Claire said.

The phone trilled and Betty reached for it. "Claire, it's Doctor James." Betty stretched the cord and held the receiver to Claire's ear. The suction was loud making it difficult to hear. Claire lifted the suction tip out of the wound and gave the surgeon a quick report. Nodding to Betty, the nurse hung up the phone.

"He'll be here in fifteen minutes. He's calling the operating room now. They'll be ready. Betty, call Detective Rosko. I think we've got another victim of the Kidney Slasher." Claire stuck the suction tip back in the wound. More blood swooshed up the tubing. "In the meantime, I have to try and stop the bleeding. Open up a laparotomy tray."

Claire repositioned the circular operating room light above the bed. Using retractors, she opened the edges of the wound. A fine shower of blood shot out. She grabbed a small stainless steel instrument off the tray and clamped it over the small bleeder. The blood spray ceased. Claire searched for other small bleeders. She found three more. She put a snap on each one. Doctor James could remove the snaps in the operating room once he'd dealt with them. She'd at least done her part and arrested most of the bleeding.

With a loud wheeze, the automatic blood pressure cuff inflated, and then deflated. Claire watched for the results. 94/55. It was slowly improving. The shrill ring of the phone startled the medical team. The operating room was ready. Doctor James should be there any minute.

"Let's get her up there," Claire commanded.

Betty hooked the portable monitor onto the rail of the bed while Liz transferred the intravenous bags to the poles at the end of the bed. The audible blip of the patient's heart rate echoed through the room as Claire layered gauze over the wound. Blood soaked into the gauze as soon as she put it down. Were there more bleeders? They would have to deal with them in the operating room.

Claire glanced at the cardiac monitor. The patient's heart rate was still fast. Suddenly the widened complex of an ominous beat flit across the screen. A few seconds later, there was another one, and then another. The woman was in shock and her heart was showing the effect of it. They had to get her to the operating room and control the bleeding now.

"Okay, let's go. Pat, have you got the oxygen tank hooked up yet?"

Cassidy was bagging air into the patient's lungs. "Liz is changing to the portable oxygen."

Liz was under the stretcher, hooking a pale green tube onto a metal cylinder. She turned the key and adjusted the knob. Straightening up, she gave them the thumbs up sign.

Cassidy asked, "Is everybody ready?"

Pat switched the oxygen tubing from the wall outlet and connected it to the portable tank. Without missing a beat, he kept up his rhythmic squeezing of the vinyl bladder that filled the unconscious patient's lungs with air.

"Let's roll." He remained at the head of the bed, deflating the bag every five seconds. Claire and Betty, on either side of the bed, held the metal rails, directing the stretcher towards the elevator.

"Jan call for security to hold the elevator."

"Already done. They'll be waiting for you."

A nurse, scrubbed, masked, and gowned in surgical greens, stood beside the operating room table arranging stainless steel instruments. Claire and Betty assisted the second nurse in getting the patient onto the table.

At the head of the table, Doctor Liebling was setting up the anesthetic machine. He nodded at Claire, then taking over from Pat, he hooked a long set of corrugated tubing to the woman's endotracheal tube. He adjusted several dials on the anesthetic machine. Air whistled back and forth through the clear tubing.

"I'm ready to go, Claire," Doctor Liebling said.

"But Doctor James isn't here yet."

"She's loosing a lot of blood. We may not be able to wait."

Claire looked at the clock, then back at the patient's abdomen. She wasn't a surgeon, but she had done a year of surgical residency before deciding to work in emergency. What should she do? Wait or go ahead?

The rhythm of the patient's heartbeat reverberated through the room. A sudden run of widened beats made Claire's decision for her. The patient couldn't wait.

"Okay," Claire nodded. She turned to the circulating nurse. "Get me a gown."

She donned a green cap and mask then did a quick scrub of her hands at the sink outside the room. Coming back into the room, she donned a long sterile green gown then slid her hands into the pair of gloves the nurse held out for her.

Seeing Claire was ready, Doctor Ivor Liebling picked up a couple of syringes and injected their contents into the patient's intravenous line. He nodded. He was ready for the operation to begin.

Claire positioned the surgical lamp so that the bright circle of light centered on the woman's abdomen. Using a long pair of metal tweezers, she grasped the edge of the dressing and pulled it off. The snaps she'd put on the small bleeding vessels were still in place, but the cavity had again filled with blood. She must have more bleeders. Claire took the suction tip the circulating nurse handed her and cleared the blood from the cavity. She found another bleeder and clamped a snap over it. She explored the cavity and found two more. Again she stopped the flow of blood from the vessel with a snap. After several long seconds the bleeding eased.

"Give me a suture and I'll tie off these bleeders," Claire directed the scrub nurse.

Accepting the suture, Claire tied a series of tight knots around the end of each vessel. Then, making sure there was no further bleeding, she removed the snaps one by one. Though small, the instruments had blocked her vision. Now with the bleeding lessened and the snaps out of the way, it was easier to explore the cavity.

As the slash extended across the left side of the woman's abdomen, Claire probed that area first. She breathed a sigh of relief when she found the left kidney still intact. Her hands shifted to the right. Verbally she listed each of the abdominal organs her hands contacted: liver, spleen, stomach, ovaries, and yes, the right kidney was there. Everything present and accounted for.

Was the woman a victim of the Kidney Slasher who'd somehow gotten away? Or was some other weirdo terrorizing Strathburn?

"Claire," Leibling called out. "She's throwing more PVC's, I'm starting xylocaine."

Claire glanced at the monitor. She'd been so intent on tying off vessels and getting the bleeding stopped that she hadn't paid attention to the irregular beats flashing across the screen. She watched the anesthetist inject a clear fluid into the patient's intravenous. "How's her blood pressure?"

"Low. Dopamine's infusing. But it's doing piss all to raise her blood pressure. At least it's keeping it from dropping into her boots. I'm giving her a couple of more units of blood. Hopefully replacing the volume she's lost will help. Once you're done, she's going straight to the intensive care unit. I'm not even going to try to get her off the ventilator tonight."

"Let's hope she survives the night," Claire grimaced. "The bleeding appears to have stopped...but she's lost so much."

There was a commotion at the door. Doctor James poked his head into the room.

"Would you like some assistance, Claire?"

"About time you showed up."

"Looks like you're doing a fine job."

"Well, the bleeding is finally settled. She had a lot of little bleeders, that was all. I think somebody was after her kidney."

Doctor Barry James stood at the large scrub sink beyond the operating theatre washing his hands. He held the door open with his foot. His eyebrows rose. "Really?"

"The wound looks similar to the ones of the other victims. Someone found her running naked on the road."

"Have you notified the authorities?"

"Betty called Gerry...Detective Rosko. He should be here shortly."

"Would you two stitch her up so I can get her to the intensive care unit." Doctor Liebling spoke from his position at the head of the bed. He was busy adjusting dials on the anesthetic machine. "Dicker around much longer and we won't have a patient to worry about."

"Hold your horses. Let me have a look." James donned his operating room garb and crossed to stand beside Claire. He carefully examined the wound. "Looks good, Claire. If you ever want to become a surgeon, let me know."

The scrub nurse handed him a needle driver with a suture attached and handed Claire the scissors. Within a couple of minutes, the patient's wound was sutured and she was on her way to the Intensive Care Unit.

CHAPTER 44

Exhausted, but filled with the euphoria of a job well done, Claire whipped off the green operating room garb and accompanied the patient to the Intensive Care Unit. She and Doctor James watched from behind the glass enclosed doors while the nurses settled the patient.

He gave her a friendly slap on the shoulder. "Good job, Claire. Looks like you saved her life."

"Thanks, Barry, but I think I'll stick with emergency medicine."

"Once Ivor is finished settling our Jane Doe, I'm going home to get some sleep. I've got a full schedule of surgeries in the morning."

"She'll be in good hands with the Intensive Care nurses," Claire said. "They'll call me if they need anything."

Claire watched the nurses scurrying around the patient's bed, checking lines, writing vital signs, making sure none of her tubes were constricted. Attached to state-of-the-art monitoring devices, the patient resembled a disfigured China doll.

Only time would tell how she would fare. At least she'd made it through the surgery. A ventilator assisted her breathing. When, or if, her condition improved, they'd wean her off the machine and see if she could breathe on her own. Her blood pressure had stabilized, but remained on the low side. Dopamine was at least keeping it in the nineties.

Xylocaine was still infusing and, for the present, controlling the irregular heartbeats. The nurses would titrate the medication down if her heart rhythm remained stable.

"Do you think the combination of antibiotics we have her on will be enough to fight off infection?"

"Hopefully. Who knows the condition of the knife she was sliced with." James shrugged. "We've put her on the best we've got. I've ordered a Tetanus shot."

As they walked to the elevator, Doctor James commended Claire. "She's lucky to be alive. And lucky that you were on in the emergency department tonight. You did an excellent job stabilizing her."

"Thanks, Barry. For a while, I thought we were losing her."

"It was touch and go for a bit, wasn't it? She's one lucky lady. He did quite a job slashing through her abdomen. Lucky he didn't sever any arteries. He got pretty close to the kidney."

"I've seen his work before, I wonder what stopped him. Why he didn't take her kidney?" Claire turned to face him. "Do you think he saw the small cyst on her kidney? Would that have made him leave it?"

James shrugged his shoulders. He'd already stripped off the operating room garb, and donned a white lab coat over his green scrubs. "I have no idea what went on in his mind. I don't think he would have seen the cyst; it's pretty small." He yawned. "Well, if you don't need me, I'm going home to bed. I have a bowel resection starting in four hours and I think the patient would appreciate it if his surgeon got some sleep before cutting him up."

"I think we're okay for now." Claire smiled. "Thanks for coming in."

"No problem."

Claire waved goodbye and returned to the emergency department.

♋♋

While the patient was in the operating room, the police had been busy and thought they might have tracked down her identity. Brianne Sears never made it home from the night school class she taught at Medway High School. The police were bringing her husband to the hospital to see if their patient and the missing woman were one and the same.

The emergency department was quiet, so Claire went back to the Intensive Care Unit. She needed to know how the patient was doing. From outside the glass enclosure, she stared at the motionless form. The woman was small and pale, and in her unconscious state, the hospital bed engulfed her.

They'd given her several bags of intravenous fluid to replace the blood she'd lost and as a result her face was puffy, her eyelids swollen and translucent. Dark circles arced below her closed eyes.

Clare focused on her face. Did she have a tinge more color? Maybe it was wishful thinking.

Blips of electrical activity made their way across the cardiac monitor. Each beat in rhythm with the next. A sigh escaped Claire's tension filled body. Thank you, God. Finally her heart rhythm is regular. The arrhythmia that had threatened her life was now under control. One less battle the woman had to win in her struggle to survive.

It would still be touch and go for a while. The blood loss had been extensive and she remained in a state of shock. Her body had initially responded by dropping its blood pressure, then the arrhythmia had started. It took a couple of bolus doses of xylocaine and several bags of intravenous fluid before the potentially dangerous heartbeats had been successfully controlled. Now, the xylocaine was being weaned off.

Claire listened to the regular audible output of the cardiac monitor also hearing the other noises in the room. A tube protruded from the patient's trachea and was connected to a set of double corrugated hoses that extended to the machine beside the bed. Air whooshed in and out off the cylinders in a cyclic pattern. The same cyclic rhythm of the rise and fall of the patient's chest.

Her pager went off. Claire glanced at the number, the emergency department. She took the stairs back to the department. Betty was at the desk doing paperwork.

"What's up?" Claire asked.

"That nice looking detective is here. He has a distraught husband waiting to talk to you. Who do you want to see first? Or do you want to tackle them together?" Betty asked.

What were her choices? She was exhausted, but she didn't think the answer "neither" would be acceptable. Instead, she asked. "Where are they?"

"In the quiet room."

The quiet room was a small but comfortable space where the families of seriously ill or distressed patients could wait. There they were sheltered from the prying eyes of other emergency room patients or their visitors. The room had a couch and a couple of chairs, all upholstered in muted shades of mulberry that melted into the pastel pink of the walls. A phone and a box of Kleenex sat on a mahogany side table.

Claire knocked softly then entered the room. When she saw Detective Rosko sitting on one of the chairs, she felt a warmth creep up her face. She hoped it wasn't noticeable. She turned her attention to the young man slumped on the couch. His dark head jerked up and intense blue eyes focused on her. He looked to be in his late-twenties. Detective Rosko started to rise but Claire motioned him to sit.

"Doctor Valincourt, this is Mr. Sears. There's a chance your unidentified patient may be his wife."

Claire nodded. She saw the man's drawn cheeks and recognized the tormented look in his gray eyes.

His voice trembled and tears threatened his eyes. "She was supposed to be home by eleven. When she wasn't home by twelve. I called the police. I thought, maybe a car accident." He paused to collect himself and wipe a tear away from his eye. "The police told me a woman had been found on the road. She'd been attacked. The description sounds like my Brianne."

His eyes pleaded with Claire. Did he want affirmation that the woman was his wife, or would he rather hear that the police had been mistaken and that the woman fighting for her life in the Intensive Care Unit was no relation? Claire hated this part of the job.

"Do you have a picture of her?"

His fingers fumbled as he pulled a wallet out of his jean pocket. He flipped it open and showed her a picture of an attractive brunette with an engaging smile.

It was hard to imagine the woman in the photo had any connection to the patient she'd spent the past few hours trying to save. That was, unless you'd spent years patching up the wounded and knew the effects trauma had on the body, then added the effects of medical science trying to save the patient from the throws of death. Yes, with a stretch of imagination, Claire could see a resemblance. "This may be her."

She watched the man slump back into the chair. He blinked the tears away while his brain registered the information. Claire glanced at Rosko. "Before I say any more, Mr. Sears, I need to know what you've been told."

His voice was barely a whisper. "They said she'd been attacked by someone. That she'd been brought here and the doctors were working on her."

Claire reached out and touched his hand. It was cold. "We had to take her to the operating room to stop the bleeding. She has survived the surgery...but the next twenty-four hours are crucial. She's still under the effects of her attack and the surgery. She hasn't woken yet. Actually we're keeping her sedated. She's lost a lot of blood. Her body needs time to heal. We have her on a machine to help her breathe. We want to keep her on it at least overnight. The next few hours, well, we'll just have to wait and see how she does."

A single tear tracked down his left cheek. Claire stopped. There was no point in telling him that her kidney may have been damaged by the attack. They had done what they could, but only time would tell how it was going to function. He could hear all that later. Besides, a lot of people functioned quite well with one kidney. Right now, all they had to worry about was keeping her alive long enough to need her kidney.

"When," he said, the words stumbling out of his mouth, "will I be able to see her?"

"Can we take him to the Intensive Care Unit and find out if it is his wife?" Detective Rosko asked.

"Yes. I'll take you up there. Just let me tell my charge nurse where I'll be."

Claire went to the desk, spoke to Betty, then called the Intensive Care Unit. She informed them she was bringing someone up for a possible identification of their Jane Doe.

They took the elevator to the third floor. Claire had them wait on chairs outside the automatic doors to the unit while she checked on the patient. She wanted to make sure all was in order before she brought him in. If this was his wife, Claire wasn't sure how he'd deal with the shock.

The woman was in a private room across from the nurse's station. Glass walls and doors provided visibility to the nurses, while giving some degree of privacy and noise reduction for the patient. She lay on her back, the head of her bed elevated slightly. Her mouth was hidden by a double row of brown tape that secured the breathing tube. Air whooshing through the breathing tubes caused her chest to rise and fall. Intravenous bags hung on poles above her bed. A clear plastic tube coiled from beneath the bottom of the bed and led to a urinary catheter bag.

Claire checked the patient's vital signs. The oscilloscope above the bed monitored her battle against death. At least for now, they remained stable. She compared this woman to the confident image in the photo. It was a difficult stretch. How would he react to seeing his wife this way?

The woman had already won several battles. She'd fought off her attacker, fought to remain alive until someone found her, and now, she continued to fight death. Claire wondered who would win in the end.

She went back to the waiting room. Was the man clutching the arms of the chair the patient's husband? She hoped so. The hospital needed a name, but more importantly, the patient needed someone to help her make it through this crisis.

Claire pushed the metal button on the wall and the double doors swung open. In the silence of the deserted corridor, the grating sound was deafening. The ashen-faced man she led into the unit didn't notice. His gaze darted from bed to bed, searching for a familiar face. Claire led him to the bedside.

From his loud gasp, it was apparent their Jane Doe had been identified.

They left him by his wife's bedside. Rosko informed him he'd come back in the morning. Intent on willing his wife back among the living, Mr. Sears merely nodded. Rosko waited until they were out of the unit before speaking to Claire.

"How is she doing?"

"Well—" Claire paused. "She's doing a damn site better than when she came in. She'd lost a lot of blood. She must have a strong constitution to still be alive." She paused and tipped her head to the side. "Have a look at her wrists when you come to talk to her. It looks like her attacker might have bound her at some point."

Rosko left eyebrow rose. "Really?"

"She's got some scrapes. And some bruising."

A slight smile lifting the corners of his mouth. "Thanks for letting me know. I'll check them out."

Claire nodded then turned to walk toward the elevator. Rosko kept in step. He waited until the doors had closed behind them before speaking.

"I don't have any medical knowledge, but from the look of her, well, with all those tubes sticking out of her, it doesn't look good. What are her chances?"

"Right now?" Claire locked eyes with him. "I'd say fifty-fifty. If she makes it through the night and she doesn't bleed any more, then the odds go up a lot, in her favor."

"I wouldn't have taken you for a gambler."

Claire grinned. The twinkle in his eyes was contagious.

"Oh, just wanted to let you know, I talked to the powers that be in your hospital and discretely asked about any medications like ketamine or morphine being reported missing. They flatly denied it."

Claire's eyebrows rose.

Rosko put a hand up in defense. "Hey, I'm not saying I believe them. I'm just telling you what they said. But I'm not letting it drop there. We're still going to check."

"Thanks for letting me know."

When she left him at the hospital doors, his "Can I call you later" seemed as natural as her response, "That would be nice."

CHAPTER 45

The blackness cleared slowly. Easing up through shades of gray, Brianne saw a pale white light. She reached for it but the darkness came again.

It was a long time before she saw the light again. Then, it began to come and go more often, getting closer and brighter all the time. But still just beyond her reach. During one of the periods of light, Brianne clawed her way through the fog. She regained consciousness, despite the medications to keep her sedated and control her pain.

Air was pushing into her lungs, forcing them to expand. A hard object blocked her mouth suffocating her. She had to get it out. She tried to lift her hands to her mouth. Too difficult. She felt so weak. It took several minutes before she could gather the strength to reach her mouth. Her fingers slowly circled the tube. She yanked. It wouldn't move. Something held it there.

She didn't have enough strength.

She heard loud voices. Someone pulled her hands away from her mouth.

"No! Don't touch that," a female voice shouted.

Where was the voice coming from? Her world was still layered shades of gray. She twisted her head. The tube pulled. A whoosh of air pressed through the tube, she bit down. A high-pitched alarm screamed. The sound hurt her ears.

Hands grabbed at hers. They pulled hers from her face. She tried to fight, too weak. The alarm blared over the female voice screaming for help. Brianne struggled. She needed to get away. Her heart raced, her breathing quickened, fighting with the thrust of air through the tube. She tried to turn. More hands were on top of her. They pulled her arms down, forced them onto the bed. Someone lay across her, pinning her down.

"Get the restraints on. Somebody call Doctor Valincourt."

Brianne heard a male voice. "What's happening? Leave her alone."

The voice sounded so familiar yet she couldn't identify it. She continued to struggle. Her energy drained, like a punctured balloon, she shrank into the white sheets.

Rigid leather straps slid around her wrists. She tried to pull against them. They cut into the tender flesh of her wrists. Voices, female, not the man in her memory, soothed her. "You're okay. Just rest." Could she believe them? What little strength she had mustered, now drained. There was no fight left. Like a damp dishcloth she felt her body submerging into the grayness.

She was a prisoner again.

❧❦❧

Claire was trying to get some sleep when her pager went off. She looked at the numbers—5281—the Intensive Care Unit. She tried to focus. Why were they calling her? Then she remembered. The patient, the one she and Doctor James had taken to surgery must be in trouble. Suddenly, she was fully awake.

Grabbing her stethoscope, she ran for the stairs, the elevator would take too long. She barreled through the double doors of the intensive care unit. Several nurses and a couple of orderlies congregated around one of the glassed-in rooms. It was the same cubicle where, three hours earlier, she had wheeled the patient from the operating room.

Claire rushed to the bedside. "What's happening?"

One of the nurses turned toward her. "She woke up and was pulling at her endotracheal tube. We've restrained her. I think the effort tired her out, she's quiet now."

Claire looked at the pale figure in the bed. Motionless, Brianne Sears looked like a deserted oyster shell. Only the audible blip of the cardiac monitor gave a glimmer of reassurance that she remained among the living. She glanced at the screen. The heart rate accelerated from recent struggling. As Claire watched, the rate dawdled to a near normal rate. She sighed. Another crisis overcome.

Sitting beside the bed, Mr. Sears had only slightly more color than his wife. Shock evident in his pale gray eyes. He flinched at the hand she put on his shoulder. She pulled her hand away, conscious of the boundaries he set.

"We have to keep her sedated. She's not ready to come off the ventilator. If the tube came out now—" Claire paused. "We might have trouble getting it back in. That would further compromise her chances. We need to buy time to allow her body to heal."

He stared back at her but she wondered if her words registered at all. He remained silent and still. She left the room, spoke briefly with the nurses, then returned to the emergency department. For the present time, there was nothing more she could do.

                                    ❧❧❧

Before leaving work that morning, Claire made one final check on the patient. Mr. Sears slept in the chair beside the bed. Someone had given him a pillow and a flannel blanket. His neck would be stiff when he woke.

She picked up Brianne's chart and flipped through the pages. Her vital signs were beginning to show a slow, but steady, improvement. Her systolic blood pressure was now over one hundred and her heart rate had come down and sat in the low nineties. No irregular beats flashed across the oscilloscope.

Several intravenous bags infused through rate-controlling pumps. Claire turned the red medication labels to read them. The patient was still on xylocaine, but the dosage had been titrated down from the levels she'd required last night. It would soon be turned off. Gentamycin, an antibiotic, was infusing through a second intravenous site. Ancef would be the next antibiotic the nurses would hang. Hopefully, the combination of drugs would be enough to combat any wound infection.

Claire followed the intravenous lines to their insertion points in the patient's arm, one on the back of her hand and another at her wrist. There were bruises visible on the backs of her hands and at her elbows. Were they from the paramedics and nurses as they attempted to get intravenous access, or had her attacker caused them?

Suddenly Claire felt exhausted. It was time to go home. Brianne Sears was in capable hands. Modern medicine would do what it could. The rest was up to the patient, and destiny.

CHAPTER 46

It was late the next afternoon before the patient in the Intensive Care Unit roused again. They had kept her sedated so she wouldn't pull at the breathing tube. An hour earlier Doctor James had lightened her narcotic state to see if she would be able to breathe on her own. One of the nurses was adding antibiotics to her intravenous line when she heard the patient moan.

The nurse laid a hand on her upper arm. "It's okay, Mrs. Sears."

Brianne Sear's eyelids fluttered open, confusion and pain visible in her blue eyes. Her right hand, now loosely bound, went instinctively to the large white dressing on her abdomen.

"Bre. Bre, honey…"

Through a muted fog, Brianne heard the familiar voice, her husband. She tried to make sense of what was happening. If she was a prisoner, why was he here? His face hovered over hers. Where was she? What had happened to her?

"Brianne, I'm here."

Then there was another voice, a female one. "You're doing fine, Mrs. Sears," it said. "You're going to be okay."

Brianne put her hand to the tube at her mouth.

"Do you want that tube out?"

Brianne made out the image of a woman bending over her. She wore a pink uniform and had a stethoscope slung over her neck. A nurse?

"Do you want the tube out, dear?"

Brianne nodded. She felt someone squeezing her shoulder, she twisted her head slightly. The tube in her mouth stopped further movement but she saw Tom out of the corner of her vision. She blinked. He was still there.

"I'll undo the tapes," the nurse said. "Then you can pull the tube out."

Brianne felt the tape tug at the tiny hairs around her mouth. She winced. Then the tapes were gone and the tube shifted in her mouth. She gagged violently.

"Pull it out then," the nurse encouraged her.

Brianne's fingers circled around the plastic tube. She pulled. The tube moved several inches, then stopped. She gagged again. Then the nurse's hand was on top of hers. Together they yanked and the tube slithered out of her mouth. She was free again.

She tried to speak, but a coughing spasm halted her attempt.

"Just rest." The nurse reassured her. "It will be hard to talk for a bit."

Tom stroked her hair as he spoke softly into her ear. Brianne heard the tears mixed with his words.

The coughing finally settled. Brianne struggled to move up in the bed. She winced with pain. Her hand went to the left side of her abdomen. It felt as if someone shoved a red-hot poker into her. She stared at the bulky dressing under her fingers then looked from Tom to the nurse.

Her voice was weak and raspy. "What happened? A car accident?"

"Now, dear, I'll get the doctor. There's a policeman right here, too. I'll get him to come talk to you."

Brianne watched the nurse hurry out of the room. She heard her speaking in hushed tones. "Tom. What happened?"

Startled doe eyes pleaded with her husband. "You're okay, Bre. Don't get upset."

What was so bad that even the nurse was afraid to tell her?

Brianne demanded, "What am I doing here, Tom? Tell me what happened. Why are the police here?"

"The nurse is getting the doctor." Tom stroked strands of auburn hair away from her pale face with one hand. The other hand, clutching hers was coated with a layer of sweat. "You're okay now, honey." The tremble in his voice belied his reassuring words.

"Tell me what?" Brianne tried to pull herself up, but pain ripped through her body and she slumped back into the hard rubber mattress. Her hand shot out to her abdomen, coming to rest on thick layers of gauze. Her other had grasped at her husband's arm, her fingernails sinking into his flesh. "You have to tell me, now."

The nurse was back. "Settle down, Mrs. Sears." She eased Brianne's hand away from the husband's arm, taking care the patient's fingernails stayed out of reach of her own skin. "You're okay. The doctor's coming." Her voice softened. "Do you remember anything about yesterday?"

Brianne shook her head slowly as if trying to shake away layers of fog. Had she been in an accident? Why did she have a bandage on her abdomen? Had she had an operation? It must have been serious for her to have needed a breathing machine. Why wouldn't they tell her?

Closing her eyes, she struggled to remember. Her mind, shrouded with a collage of vague, shadowy images, felt like a jigsaw puzzle. A million tiny fragments, but someone had stolen the picture, and she had no idea how to piece them together. So many sensations came from her body. She had felt like this after she'd had a laparoscopy and woken up from the anesthesia. Then she'd felt drugged, and her abdomen had been sore. But now her whole body ached as if she'd been run over by a transport truck.

If they'd operated on her abdomen, that would account for the pain and the bandage. She fought to remember, but even that was painful. Was there someone else she should be worried about? If it had been an accident, had others been involved? She felt there was someone she needed to be concerned about. Slowly images of a dark-haired man crept up through the fog. She twisted in the bed. Pain tore through her body, though now it was mixed with fear.

A terrible sense of dread enfolded her. Her throat constricted, the trapped air suddenly a flaming poker burning the delicate tissue. Brianne, unable to breathe, unable to speak, her fingernails clawed at the mattress below her, snatching fistfuls of stark white sheets. The pre-set monitoring alarms shrieked in competition with the high-pitched blip of her accelerated heart rate. Nurses scurried into the room. The sedation worked quickly. Answers to Brianne's questions would have to wait until the next time she roused.

* споσ*

Brianne Sears's hospital room was at a secluded end of the unit. Matt Thompson kept vigil outside her door, his chair positioned to keep an observant eye on all the activity in the unit, the nurses' station, the doctor's area, and both entrances into the department. He diligently examined each photo identification and wrote their name on a clipboard before allowing them to enter Mrs. Sears's room.

Just shifting position to ease a cramped calf muscle, he jumped when one of the nurses poked her head out the door.

"Tell your boss the patient's waking up and to get down here right away."

Matt used the police band to call the station. He was just putting the unit back in his belt pocket when the nurse poked her head out the door again. "Officer, Mrs. Sears would like to talk to you."

"Detective Rosko is on his way."

"Mr. Sears wants someone in there now. His wife is getting herself into a state again and I don't want a hysterical patient on my hands. She wants answers. Doctor James is busy in the operating room and we can't wait."

Reluctantly, he rose and went to the bedside. "I'm Officer Thompson, Mrs. Sears How are you doing?"

Tears brimmed in her eyes and her voice trembled. "What happened to me?"

"Do you remember anything from last night?"

Brianne closed her eyes. Thoughts and visions jumbled together. Everything was still so hazy. A man's voice. Someone grabbing her. Screams. Her screams. A bad dream. But it wasn't just a dream.

She remembered being in class, walking to her car, talking to one of her students. She was driving home. She stopped the car. Why did she stop the car? A man.

Then her world went blank. Brianne looked up at the officer. She shook her head slowly.

"That's okay ma'am." Thompson reassured her. You can let us know later if you remember anything."

It was all too much. Suddenly Brianne didn't care what had happened to her. She was too tired. She needed to sleep. Her eyelids drifted to a close.

❧❧❧

Rosko and Wilson had been out all day. They'd talked to Medway High School and confirmed that Brianne Sears had taught her usual evening class last night. One of the teachers remembered seeing her talking to a student outside the school. She was pretty sure Brianne had been alone in her car when she'd passed her at the parking lot exit. No, she didn't see the student then. And no she didn't know the student's name.

Did one of her students attack her? Could he be the serial killer they were searching for?

The man who'd flagged down the ambulance had left the scene by the time the police arrived. The ambulance drivers gave them a description of the car, a 2005 silver BMW. They had a partial license number. Myers was checking with DMV. There couldn't be too many silver BMW's in town. Strathburn didn't attract too many affluent families.

They had the class list and were interviewing all the students. So far they hadn't found anyone who admitted to talking to Mrs. Sears after class. They were more than halfway through the list when Wilson's phone rang.

"Hey, Boss, they found the Sears car up on Highbury Street, just past the bridge."

"That area's pretty deserted in the evening, isn't it?" Rosko asked.

"Yeah. Not well lit either."

"Tell them we'll be right there. Get the Crime Scene Unit to meet us." Rosko rolled his eyes. "And make sure nobody touches the car until we get there."

Brianne Sear's blue Toyota stood on the side of the road, twenty feet west of the overpass, and three miles from the school. It looked like she was on her way home and had stopped for something, or someone.

There was no visible damage to the car and no sign of a break in. The driver's door was unlocked, Mrs. Sear's purse and briefcase still tucked neatly under the passenger seat. They left the Crime Scene Unit examining the car while they went back to the class list.

It was two o'clock before they found him. Sean Murphy admitted to having a conversation with the teacher after class. According to him, Mrs. Sears had been alone when he saw her walking toward the parking lot. He'd ridden off on his bike to meet some students at a local bar. Murphy seemed genuinely shocked at the news of his teacher's attack. The rest of the people on the class list revealed nothing of interest. Myers checked all the names for criminal records, just in case.

It took all day, but Myers had finally tracked down the man who'd stopped the ambulance. Anthony Zamplony was in his fifties and wore an expensively-tailored suit that strained to cover a basketball-sized paunch. A senior partner at Lerner and Lloyds Law Firm, he knew his rights. But after the detectives threatened to check his alibi with his wife, Zamplony admitted to a tryst with his secretary. His secretary and the discreet club they frequented substantiated his alibi.

He didn't add anything new to the story he'd given the paramedics the night before. He saw a woman running along the road and stopped to see if she needed help. At first he'd thought she was drunk.

"She was naked, weaving, and stumbling on the road. I gave her a blanket, one of those car ones, you know. She was hysterical. I let her in the car." His hands trembled. "Then I saw the blood." He ran a plump hand through a head of gray tempered waves. "She kept screaming at me to drive. I figured she'd had a fight with someone. I figured he might come after both of us if I didn't get the hell out of there." He started talking with his hands. "I called 911. Then I saw that ambulance."

Myers visited the tryst site and the secretary. Zamplony's story checked out, but at this point Rosko wasn't taking anybody off their suspect list.

The Crime Scene Unit and teams of uniforms went out to search the area where Zamplony said he'd found her. Martha, the 911 dispatcher, reported they'd received two calls eleven minutes apart about a woman having been attacked and bleeding from her abdomen. Both calls had been blocked. Both cut off before giving any useful information other than that the driver was on Highbury Ave. But Highbury ran for miles north and south of Strathburn. Thankfully it was a quiet night and she dispatched one ambulance heading north and one heading south. She prayed she wouldn't be in shit for sending them on a wild goose chase. Then Martha waited for another call to come in with more details. She sighed a sigh of relief when the north-bound one got waved down. Her job was still safe, at least for now.

Rosko had another question. Had Zamplony called twice, or had someone else seen the victim? Zamplony claimed he'd made only one 911 call and that he'd picked the woman up ten miles from where he'd met up with the ambulance. A trail of blood along the road verified his statement. The blood trail was twenty feet long. It went from where he'd picked her up, across the pavement, through the grass edging the road, then ended at the woods. The timeline of their checking out of the hotel, dropping off his secretary, and being at that spot, supported his story.

Had someone else dropped Brianne Sears where Zamplony found her? Her attacker? Had he felt remorse and called 911? Technicians were comparing the voices. How far could someone drive in eleven minutes? Rosko got units checking in a fifteen-mile stretch going north, the direction the blood drops indicated.

If this was their serial killer, how had Mrs. Sears managed to escape? More damned questions without answers.

Myers reported in. The students Sean Murphy claimed to have met after night school confirmed his story. They'd interviewed the last student on the list. So far, Sean Murphy was the last person to speak to Mrs. Sears.

Rosko's phone rang. The patient had woken up. On the way to the hospital, Wilson arranged for an officer to keep an eye on Sean Murphy.

———

When Rosko and Wilson arrived at the hospital, Thompson reported how Mrs. Sears's had woken briefly and demanded to know what happened. She hadn't remembered anything more than a jumble of images. She'd fallen back to sleep and hadn't roused since.

Rosko looked through the glass partition of the Intensive Care Unit. Mr. Sears sat beside his wife, his head resting on the pillow close to hers. His eyes were closed, but Rosko could see his mouth moving as he spoke softly to his wife.

He hated having to intrude at such an intimate time. It was one of the worst parts of the job, having to bother families while they were dealing with trauma. But at least this man's wife was alive. He needed to talk to her. She was the only surviving victim—she had to be able to give them something to go on.

Mr. Sears must have sensed his presence. He turned his head toward the window and nodded at the detective. The intimate moment broken, he slumped back into the chair. His hand maintained contact with his wife's, as if letting go would somehow loosen her tenuous hold on life. He glanced at the monitor to reassure himself she was still okay then turned his head away as if that would make the detective leave.

Rosko coughed slightly before walking through the glass doors. He stood at the end of the bed without speaking. He wished he didn't have to disturb the woman. She'd been through too much already.

"I'm sorry, Mr. Sears. Could you tell her we need to talk to her? It's extremely important. If there is anything she can tell us…"

"She needs to rest."

Rosko spoke softly yet kept his tone firm. "She might know something that could help us catch her attacker."

Mr. Sears glared at him but leaned close to his wife. "Bre, honey. There's someone here to talk to you."

When her eyelids drifted open, Rosko thought she resembled a startled fawn. Her husband whispered reassuringly to her. The fear slowly faded and she attempted to smile.

"This is Detective Rosko. He wants to know if you can remember what happened to you."

Her face twitched, her eyes squinted shut.

"You don't have to do this, honey."

"Mrs. Sears." Rosko approached the bed. "We need to talk to you. We need to find the person who did this to you."

There was a slight movement of her head but her eyes remained closed.

"We need to stop him before he hurts any more women."

Her eyes opened hesitantly. She tried to focus on the detective. When she did speak, her voice was barely a whisper. "I don't remember."

Rosko saw a tremor shake her body. Was it that she couldn't remember, or didn't want to? "Your husband said you were coming home from teaching a class. Is that right?"

She nodded.

"Did you see who attacked you?"

She closed her eyes.

"Was it someone you know?" Rosko asked.

Her eyes still closed, she shook her head.

"You were talking to one of your students. Was it him?"

An intense look of concentration came over her face. "No." Her eyes fluttered open. "I don't think so."

"Did you see the person? Can you tell me anything about him?"

Her forehead wrinkled and she shuddered again. The room was silent a long time before her lips moved.

"Tall. Dark hair. Tattoo." She shook her head. Her voice trembled and her eyes drifted shut. "Can't remember any more."

"Tattoo? Did you say he had a tattoo?"

Her head moved imperceptibly.

Rosko's voice rose with excitement. "Can you remember what type of tattoo?"

"Long, on his arm."

"Can you remember which arm?"

Her eyes remained closed, her head shook once then went still.

"Please, leave her alone. Can't you see what this is doing to her?"

"I'm sorry. It's important. Mrs. Sears, can we come back later? Maybe you'll think of something when you've had more time to rest."

"Please!" Mr. Sears leapt out of the chair. His voice trembled with anger. "Leave now."

As Rosko turned to leave, he saw Mrs. Sears, her eyes still closed, squeeze her husband's hand. He was shocked at how pale and thin her hand was. Distended blue veins stood out on the back of her badly bruised hand. There were also bruises at her elbow and scratches on her upper arms. He assumed some of the bruises were from the nurses and doctors trying to insert intravenous lines but how many had come from the hand of her attacker? The scratches he was pretty sure were from her run through the woods. He just wished the trail hadn't stopped at the tree line.

Nodding to Mr. Sears, he quietly left the room. Mrs. Sears had already fallen back to sleep.

At least they finally had something. The perp had a tattoo. Rosko wished he could have pushed her. Maybe if they knew what type of tattoo. He hoped she'd remember more later.

ↄↄↄↄ

Rosko headed back to the office in high spirits. They finally had a usable clue. The attacker had a tattoo. That is, if Mrs. Sears's attacker and their killer were one and the same, and if her memory could be relied on. Maybe they were finally going to get lucky. He wondered if the Crime Scene technicians had found anything.

911 had checked back. There had definitely been two separate callers. They had two different numbers and two different voices. The second call matched Zamplony's cell phone but the phone number of the first caller didn't check out—one of those ten-dollar variety store cards that weren't traceable.

They needed to find the first 911 caller. Had he picked her up, and where? Why hadn't he told dispatch his location? What reasons did he have for not identifying himself?

CSI was still examining her car, but so far nothing. Myers work on the lists of transplant patients and medical schools wasn't showing anything. Nobody was getting back to him.

Rosko couldn't stand waiting around the office. He needed to do something. Medway High School wasn't far from Victoria and Gibbons Parks.

When Rosko returned to the hospital later that day Brianne Sears was awake. Her condition had been upgraded from critical to serious. There was more color in her cheeks and she was minus some of the paraphernalia since his last visit. She was down to one intravenous and the bag draining her urine had been removed. That must be a good sign. Rosko said a silent thank you that the woman had not joined the other victims.

Mr. Sears was not pleased to see him. He grimaced as Rosko entered the room. Mrs. Sears' smile was weak, but she waved him to a chair. He pulled it close to the bed ignoring the glare from her husband seated on the other side of the bed.

"I'm sorry to bother you again." Rosko said.

"It's okay."

"I don't want you upsetting her," Mr. Sears warned.

Rosko nodded. "Can you remember anything more about last night?"

Her voice was quiet and he had to lean forward to be able to hear her.

"I was driving home from class. It was dark. I heard a thud. I thought I'd hit an animal. When I got out to check, someone grabbed me. A tall, dark-haired man. He put a cloth over my mouth. It smelled sweet." She touched her lips. "It burned. Then everything went black."

Brianne closed her eyes and shuddered. Slowly her eyes opened again. "Sorry," she mumbled.

"It's okay," Rosko assured her. "Take your time."

"I don't remember anything else until I woke up in this room."

At first, Rosko thought she meant her hospital room. Then he saw her shudder again. She closed her eyes but continued to speak. He leaned closer.

"I was lying on something hard. Maybe metal. It was cold. Someone held my arm. There was a jab. Then everything went fuzzy. I heard him talking. But it was far away. I couldn't move. He was laughing, looking down at me. Something tight on my arm, a band, a tight band. I felt pain at my elbow. I tried to pull away. Then the room was spinning. I couldn't move."

Her body shook as if she might seizure. "He had a scalpel. He cut me." Her hand flew to her abdomen. It was almost the same color as the large dressing. Tears shone in her eyes and her voice quivered. "He cut my stomach!" Another tremor ran through her as her hand protectively held the white bandage in place.

"That's enough," Mr. Sears growled. "I told you not to upset her."

Rosko didn't move.

Brianne took a deep breath and closed her eyes. It was a long time before she opened them again.

"I remember trees. I was running. Running away, away from him. I felt pain, a terrible searing pain. Something warm ran down my abdomen. I knew it was blood. My blood!"

Brianne stiffened as if feeling the pain anew.

"I screamed. It hurt so much. He was yelling. Then…he was gone. I tried to move. I couldn't at first. Then…I don't know how long it took…I could move my arms…I got up…off the table…crawled to the door…I was bleeding…there were woods…I ran to the trees. I don't remember anything else."

She looked apologetically at him. Rosko sighed. He should be the one apologizing for putting her through this. She was lucky to be alive, and he was forcing her to relive the horror.

"Do you remember anything about the man?"

"Tall, about six-one or two, dark hair. Normal looking." She shuddered. "Didn't look like a killer." Her voice trailed off in unspoken thoughts. She stared blankly at the ceiling.

Her words echoed in Rosko's mind. '*Normal looking.*' Yes, just like any normal person. In this awful game, the killers didn't wear nametags. Rosko let her rest for a moment.

"Mrs. Sears, if you don't mind, I'd like to have a sketch artist come in later and ask you a few questions. I'm hoping you can remember a few details that will help her develop a composite of your attacker."

What little color the woman had drained away. She trembled under the white sheets.

"No. I can't let you do that," Mr. Sears said.

He sat beside his wife's bed, holding her hand. His dark blue suit was wrinkled as if he'd slept in it, which he probably had. Anger flushed under the dark growth of beard. He rose abruptly. "Don't you understand what my wife's been through?"

"Mr. Sears…"

"You can't expect her to do this."

"We need to catch this guy. No one else has been able to identify him. And yes, I have some idea what she's been through. Believe me, I wouldn't be asking if it weren't important."

"No." He dropped his wife's hand and clenched both fists. Both men had forgotten the woman in the bed and jumped when they heard her raspy voice.

"Tom. It's okay. I have to."

The anger drained from his face. Slumping back into the chair, he took her hand in both of his. Leaning toward her, his voice soft and full of tenderness, he whispered, "Bre honey, you don't have to do this. They can't make you." With his fingertips, he gently stroked the back of her wrist.

Her eyelids closed. She lay so still Rosko wondered if she'd fallen back asleep. The skin on her face was so pale that, if it weren't for the dark circles under her eyes and the tangled mass of auburn hair framing her face, she might have blended into the sheets. Both men watched her silently. The only sounds in the room were the blips of the cardiac monitor and the whispered clicks of the machine controlling the flow of her intravenous infusion.

Rosko was just about to leave when her eyelids fluttered open, her eyes shining like glazed blue marbles. She turned slowly toward her husband.

"Tom, I have to. What if he does this to someone else?" She sounded as if each syllable was being dragged out of her body. "I was lucky. I got away. Maybe I can help stop him."

Rosko noticed her labored breathing and the fine sweat that dotted her forehead. The beep of her heart rate seemed to have sped up. He glanced at the screen and saw the corresponding electrical blip on the monitor. He couldn't read the damn thing, but the constant blip, though faster, looked regular. He watched for several seconds. Soon, the audible blip came back down to a more normal rate.

He breathed a sigh of relief. He wished he could comply with her husband's wishes and not ask her any more questions. And he hated having to bring in the police sketch artist. It would just dredge up details she wanted to, and probably should, forget. He wished he didn't have to put her through all this. If only they had something else to go on. But they didn't. Not a damn thing. Her escape from the killer was the first real break they'd had.

Mrs. Sear's breathing settled and leaning towards her husband, Rosko asked, "Sir, could I speak to you outside?" He saw the instant refusal on his face. "Just for a moment."

With a glance at the monitor, then back at his wife, Mr. Sears slipped his hand away from his wife's. Silently he followed the detective out of the room.

Rosko nodded at the uniformed policeman seated outside his wife's private room, then lead Mr. Sears a few feet away. He needed her husband's co-operation. "I'm sorry we have to do this, but we need a description of the man. Nobody else has seen him."

Rosko didn't add that none of the other victims had lived to tell. He saw the look of fear cross Sears's face and knew that he understood.

"She needs to forget about it, not relive it." Sears protested. He shook his head as if he was trying to shake off his own images.

Rosko knew from experience the man was facing his own playback of what the attacker had done to his wife and berating himself for not being able to protect her. He knew it would be useless to tell him it wasn't his fault. It was small consolation that she hadn't been raped. His attitude would influence how well she coped.

"Sometimes it helps to talk about a traumatic experience. The hospital has psychologists, as does the police force. It would be good for both of you to continue with one for a while."

"We don't need your pity."

Rosko started to extend his hand. At this point, he wished he were a woman. They were so much better at reaching out. They could pat somebody on the arm, give them a hug, let them cry on their shoulder without anybody raising an eyebrow, all he could do was pretend he didn't see the tears welling in the man's eyes. So he shrugged and looked uncomfortable. His words came out more dispassionate than he intended. "Its not pity, sir. We just want to help."

"Yeah, right."

Mr. Sears watched his wife through the glass. Worry lines had cropped up overnight, aging him ten years. Out of his wife's vision, he didn't mask his concern. He knew the facts. He knew the physical recovery would be long. But how long would it take to get over the emotional trauma?

He punched one hand into the other. "Damn it! Why her? We were just getting our lives in order. Planning a family. What's going to happen now?"

There was nothing Rosko could say to ease the desperation in his tone. When he spoke, Sears turned as if surprised to see him still standing there.

"We'll let her rest today. I'll arrange to have the sketch artist come in tomorrow morning about ten. Will you be here then?"

"I'm not leaving."

"Do you need anything? We can arrange for someone to get toiletries or anything else you need."

Sears rubbed the dark growth of beard. Without answering, he walked back into the room.

❧❦❧

He hadn't been able to sleep. The previous evening haunted him. He'd opened the shop but couldn't concentrate. His body trembled with a rage that refused to be soothed. How had she gotten away? The dose he'd given her was the same as the others. It should have been enough. He'd given the whole dose, but she'd still been able to move. Why hadn't the ketamine worked? Was it a bad batch? Next time he'd make sure he had extra bottles, full ones. He couldn't let it happen again. He couldn't risk another one getting away.

He hadn't left her very long. How could she have gotten out of there so quickly? He could still see the trail of blood she'd left. He'd followed her into the woods, looked for her most of the night, but hadn't found her.

Until now. He turned up the volume on the television and concentrated on Sherry Simmon's voice.

"A woman was found running along Highbury Ave last evening. She was taken to Grace Memorial Hospital suffering from abdominal wounds. Is this the work of the Kidney Slasher?" The camera flashed to a close-up of Sherry standing in front of Grace Memorial.

The simmering rage boiled over. He pitched the tuner. It hit the corner of the television set then bounced off the wall shattering into several pieces. He crossed the room, put his foot over it and crushed it into a hundred pieces.

⟨⟩⟨⟩⟨⟩

Claire couldn't sleep. She kept thinking about Brianne Sears. How had the woman been able to get away?

She'd been given something to sedate her, probably ketamine. They already had the results back from the hospital's laboratory. The drugs they frequently saw were negative, no cannabis, no cocaine, no heroin, none of the common ones. They'd sent a blood sample to a special laboratory. It would take a few days for the results to come back, but when it did, Claire was sure it would confirm Brianne Sears had been given ketamine.

It hadn't been till nearly the end of her shift that she'd finally had a chance to get back to the Intensive Care Unit. Stopping at the nurse's station, she inquired about Mrs. Sears' progress. The report was good. The patient had been extubated and was breathing on her own. Her condition remained serious, but she'd been taken off critical list.

With the breathing tube out of her mouth, Mrs. Sears was able to talk and take clear fluids. They were keeping her in the unit to make sure she didn't develop any complications.

Claire glanced at the patient's chart. Her vital signs were stable. The medication to control her heart rhythm had been discontinued. Now the only drugs were massive doses of antibiotics and Morphine for pain. Claire thanked God for the miracle that had kept this woman alive.

She nodded to the policeman at the door, pausing to allow him to examine her ID, then stood outside the glassed wall.

Brianne Sears snored softly. Her sleep much more peaceful than the last time Claire had been here. Mr. Sears slept on a small cot beside her bed, refusing to leave his wife's side.

The oscilloscope above the patient's bed showed a normal heart rhythm. Her oxygen level was good and her blood pressure readings were stable. Thankfully technology had advanced to the point that patients didn't have to be woken every hour for vital signs. Once hooked to the monitors, patients could get the sleep their bodies so desperately needed.

Claire watched the even rise of the woman's chest. Color was returning to her cheeks and the swelling in her face was resolving. Mrs. Sears was beginning to resemble the woman in the photo she'd been shown last night. Leaning her head against the glass wall, she sighed, another life saved. This was what made all the years of hard work worthwhile, but right now she needed to go home and get some rest herself.

CHAPTER 47

The shadows were lengthening and Claire thought about taking a taxi, but she needed to get rid of the tension plaguing her body. A jog would relax her. At least the heat wave of the past month had finally lifted.

It would have been nice if the doctor scheduled for the evening shift hadn't phoned in sick at the last minute. At least they'd found someone to come in. There was no way she could have worked a double shift. She still had trouble sleeping. Not only did she see all the women who had died at the hands of the killer, now the woman who'd escaped his clutches and still fought for her life in a hospital bed, haunted her dreams.

At nine o'clock Doug Murphy had taken over from her. By nine-thirty she'd finished giving him report and could finally leave. If she jogged, she'd be home in fifteen minutes. It would be faster going through the park, but there was no way at this time of night. She glanced at the tree-lined park now shrouded in darkness and shivered.

Over a month had passed and she still got chills every time she came near the spot where she'd found the body. She forced herself during the day, but she wasn't going to push it with the sun setting and shadows lengthening.

A gentle breeze made the evening even more pleasant and a number of people were out enjoying the drop in temperatures. Claire kept to the outside of the side walk as she jogged past them. She was in no hurry, tonight the only thing calling was her bed.

Her heart skipped a beat as something snapped behind her. She kept jogging but twisted her head to look back. A plastic pop bottle rolled off the curb. She shook her head and kept going.

Just a few more feet to pass the wooded end of the park, then she could cross to the store-lined side of the street. She kept her feet moving. She had to stop letting fear control her life. Another sound.

The snap of a twig? She glanced over her shoulder. Still nothing. Claire picked up her pace. There must be an animal in the bushes.

She was crossing the street when the sudden sweep of headlights blinded her. A car advanced quickly. Claire leapt onto the sidewalk just as a light colored van flew around the corner. It seemed to be on a collision course with the curb, coming closer and closer. Then it jumped the curb. Brakes squealed. The van lurched to a stop.

Was the driver drunk? Had he had a stroke? That might account for his erratic driving. Claire tried to see past the windshield but twilight made visibility poor. Should she go and check? Then the driver's door flew open, a tall man vaulted out of the vehicle and ran toward her.

Claire froze for a second, then she ran, her feet flying along the sidewalk. Behind her came the thud of footsteps. She ran faster. Which way should she go? Ahead of her, the previously populated street was now deserted.

The footsteps kept coming. Like a deafening jack hammer Claire heard them pounding on the cement, coming closer and closer. She forced her legs to go faster. A hand grazed her shoulder. She kept running.

The footsteps were right behind her. Something smacked her in between the shoulder blades. Her body flew forward. Her feet left the ground. Then the cement rose up to meet her. Landing painfully, she lay on the hard surface unable to move.

He landed on top of her, the scent of his sweat overpowering her.

"I've got you now, Doctor Claire Valincourt."

Claire shuddered at the sound of his voice. She struggled to get free. His hand found her neck, his fingers straddled her throat. She tried to scream. His grip tightened. She couldn't scream, she couldn't breathe. A cloth covered her mouth, a sweet smell filled her nostrils. Desperately she tried to move, get away. Her lips burned. Darkness claimed her.

CHAPTER 48

A wave of nausea swept over her. Everything was foggy. She tried to open her eyes. The lids were too heavy.

Why did she have the sensation of motion? Her arms lay limp at her sides and her legs, they too were motionless. Was she on a boat? No, that didn't fit. Claire fought to clear her head.

Sound penetrated her darkness. The clatter of wheels. It came from somewhere close. She concentrated. It was coming from under her. It sounded like wheels rattling over a hard flat surface.

The fog clearing, Claire assessed her status. She was lying on her back, her arms and legs straight out. She tried to lift her arm. Something held it. She pulled again. A wide band pinned down her forearm. She felt pain in her upper hand, then pressure, someone's hand? She tried to pull away, she couldn't.

There were more bands, across her chest, across her upper arms. She tried to raise her legs. A band held them down. Claire knew she had to get away. But how? Wide straps stretched across her legs, above and below her knees. She tried to twist away, but the bands across her chest stopped her. Terror filled her as she realized flight was not an option.

A hand touched her arm. She jumped and tried to scream, but only a strangled cry escaped her throat. She heard voices, muffled slurred, distorted, like a foreign language, or listening to a tape on slow speed, vowels extended and sounds garbled.

Shades of gray penetrated the darkness. Claire forced her eyes open. She saw a blur of white. The nausea returned. It was better to keep her eyes closed. She strained to remember. Had she been at home or at work? She recalled running. Something stopped her. A voice? A noise?

"Claire."

Someone had called her name. She saw the blur of a speeding vehicle, someone running. Chasing her. Hands grabbing her. Fingers circling her neck, then pressure. She'd tried to pull the hands away.

She remembered digging her nails into his skin, feeling the coarse hairs on his arm. She could still feel his hands around her neck, tightening…She gasped for air. It was like breathing through a straw. The hands tightened. She was spinning down a dark tunnel. Around and around into blackness.

How long ago had that been? Had she been mugged…or raped? She couldn't remember. A wave of dizziness swept over her. She felt hot, like she was slipping into a steaming black pit. She had to fight it. Bile rose to the back of her mouth. She swallowed it. Opening her eyes, she saw white. Tiles, ceiling tiles, whooshed past her. Her stomach lurched. She closed her eyes again.

Voices droned above her. They came closer and louder. Gradually she made out some of the words.

"Okay, Doc…okay…fine now…roughed up….Okay…"

What was okay? Claire wanted to scream but the sound wouldn't come.

A bright light flashed in her eyes, they closed instinctively. The shape of the light was familiar, large, circular, metallic, like a surgical lamp. The motion halted with an abruptness that made the contents of her stomach pitch and reel and flounder. Hands pawed her. They dug into her back, her legs, her arms. Suddenly the bands were released. She could move. She struggled to get up. There were too many hands. They wouldn't let her get away.

Hands slid under her, lifted her into the air.

Afraid they would drop her, Claire stopped struggling. Then she was moving down, down, until she felt a hard cushioned surface beneath her. The hands slid away. The voices continued, some were vaguely familiar.

Claire forced one eye open. Bright lights, pale green walls and the odor of antiseptic, it was all familiar. She was in the emergency department of her own hospital. Faces she knew like a zoom lens came into focus. Betty and Jan stood beside the stretcher, demanding to know if she was okay.

Claire groaned. She tried to turn. Knife-like pains stabbed the back of her head. She closed her eyes briefly.

"Where do you hurt, Claire?"

"Everywhere," she whispered.

Her left arm and hip felt bruised. The ambulance straps gone, Claire reached up to the left side of her head. She winced as she touched a large swelling.

"What happened?"

"Somebody was chasing you," Rabideau told her. "He knocked you down. A woman in an apartment across from the park heard car tires squeal and saw you. She called 911."

Pain made it hard to think. The memory of being chased slowly returned. Terror filled her. She tried to sit up. It made her lightheaded. She lay back down. Betty rolled the back of the stretcher up to a forty-five degree angle and placed a pillow under Claire's head.

"Do you remember what happened?" Betty asked.

"A man was driving…it was a van. He was driving fast. He went up on the curb." Claire gasped for breath. "Then, he got out, started running. He chased me. Knocked me to the ground. He had his fingers on my neck." She hesitated. "I don't remember anything else."

Doug Murphy came into the room. "Well, well. What are you doing back so soon?"

"Maybe I should have stayed at work." Her voice was weak.

"Let's check you over and see if any damage was done."

"She has a swelling on the left side of her head and a couple of scrapes on her left elbow and hip," Betty reported. "Otherwise, just shaken. Her vital signs are stable."

Doctor Murphy checked her quickly. "You're one lucky lady. You seem fine, but I think you should stay here tonight for observation."

"No. I'm fine. I'm going home." She attempted a smirk. "But I think I'll take a cab this time."

Claire tried to sit up. Dizziness assailed her. She lay back down. Several minutes later, she tried again. Slowly this time, she swung her legs over the side of the stretcher. Ignoring the pain, she edged to the side of the bed. As her legs hit the floor, pins and needles shot up the bottoms of her feet. She tried to put her weight on them. With her first step, her legs collapsed and she grabbed at the bed rail. The dizziness came back. She leaned over the bed.

"Claire, are you okay?" Betty put her arm over Claire's shoulder. "Maybe you need to lie down for a while longer."

"I want to go home."

"Well, can you rest for a few minutes? That will give me time to call a taxi."

"I'm okay." Claire took a tentative step. She stumbled. Betty caught her and helped her back to bed.

"Just rest for a few minutes. And that's an order."

"Okay. Ten minutes. Then I want to go home."

Claire let her eyelids drift downward. Voices woke her, Betty coming back into the room. Someone followed her—Rosko.

"Look who I found." Betty grinned. "He was checking on Mrs. Sears. He's offered to drive you home."

"That is, if you don't mind?" Rosko said.

Betty looked knowingly at both of them then waved as she left the room. "I'll leave you in his capable hands."

Claire tried to sit up.

"Can I help?"

"I think I'll be fine."

Another wave of dizziness hit Claire. Rosko saw her body sway. Instantly he was beside her. He held her shoulders to keep her from falling back. "Shaken up more than you thought?"

"So it seems. I guess I do need your help."

"Do you want me to get a wheelchair?"

She glared at him. "I'll crawl out of here first."

"Maybe we could do a three legged walk."

She laughed. "That would be preferable to being wheeled out."

Rosko slid his arm under hers and helped her to stand. She leaned against him and took a few hesitant steps. She felt the heat of his breath on her neck and shivered.

"Are you cold?"

"No. No, I'm fine." But another shiver shot down her spine. She wrapped her arms around her body.

"Take my jacket?"

He slipped off his jacket before she could protest. She felt her face flush as he settled it around her shoulders. It was better to let him think she was cold than to know the real reason for her shivering.

Her legs were wobbly and it took several minutes to walk to his car. When they arrived at her building, she felt stronger, but accepted his offer to escort her to her apartment. She handed him her keys.

Just as Rosko pushed open her door, they heard another one open. A head of gray curls peeped around the doorway. "Oh, Claire, it's you. How are you, dear?" It was Mrs. Chegetto.

"I'm fine," Claire told her..

Mrs. Chegetto looked curiously at Detective Rosko. Claire knew there would be an inquisition until she found out who he was.

"Mrs. Chegetto, this is Detective Rosko."

"Hello there, young man. I hope you are going to do something about those kids running wild and playing their radios so loud."

"That's not his department, Mrs. Chegetto."

"Well somebody should do it!"

"Yes, someone should," Rosko agreed. "It was nice to meet you, Mrs. Chegetto."

Rosko extended his hand and shook hers briefly. With a quick nod he ushered Claire into her apartment. She started to apologize for her nosy neighbor but Rosko brushed it off. "No problem. It happens all the time."

He led her to the couch and made her sit. "How about I make you a coffee?"

She smiled gratefully up at him. "That would be nice."

Listening to him rustling about in the kitchen, she wanted to go and help, but couldn't muster the energy to move, let alone get up and walk. Still wearing his jacket, she sat, her arms wrapped around her body and shivered. His scent had permeated the material and she drew comfort from having it close.

Shutting her eyes brought back images of the man and the van. Instead, she stared at the arched doorway to the kitchen, not focusing on anything in particular until Rosko walked through the opening carrying a tray with two steaming mugs. He sat beside her on the couch, picked up one of the cups, and pressed it into her hands.

Claire took a sip. Her eyebrows shot up in surprise. The liquid's heat wasn't just from the coffee.

"I found some brandy in the cupboard. I thought it might help."

She took another shaky sip. The liquor trickled down her throat and begin to thaw her inside and out.

"Do you want some?"

He tipped his mug toward her. "I helped myself. I hope you don't mind. I'm off duty now."

Claire couldn't help the shudder that shot through her. Liquid in the mug spilled over the side as her hand trembled. Could he see the terror she felt?

Rosko took the mug and placed it back on the tray. He took her hands in his. "I'm off duty, that doesn't mean I'm going to leave you alone. I thought I'd stay here with you for a while. Unless you'd rather I didn't?" The muscles in his face tightened. "Claire." He paused for a few seconds while he decided what he was going to say.

"We have to assume the attack on you tonight could have been by the man we're looking for."

Claire instinctively pulled away. No! It couldn't be. It was someone else. A rapist. It couldn't be the madman killing women for their kidneys. It couldn't be. Not to her. Her right hand pulled away from his grasp and covered her abdomen. Her head shook back and forth in denial.

Rosko put his fingers to her chin, held it still, forced her to look him in the eyes. "Claire. I'm not saying it was him for sure, but the man fits the description, tall, dark, driving a light colored van, too many similarities."

He stopped before telling her how much she resembled the other victims. She'd seen the women's pictures, she already knew that.

She was used to being independent, but right now she felt as vulnerable as a child waking from a nightmare, except that this nightmare was all too real.

"Please, if you could stay for a little…" Her voice trailed off as she looked self-consciously away.

He squeezed her hands then handed the mug back to her. "Finish this. It will do you good."

She let the liquid slide down her throat. It warmed her in places that coffee couldn't reach. She wished she could ask him to hold her. He radiated strength, warmth and kindness.

As if he read her mind, Rosko placed his empty cup on the tray, slid his arm around her, and pulled her toward him. It felt natural to rest her head against his chest. They sat like that for a long time.

Claire was reluctant to move in case he decided to leave. She felt his heart thud through the thin material of his shirt. The heat of his body roused long dormant emotions. What was happening to her vow of not letting anyone get close to her? The feelings for this man intensified each time she encountered him.

"How are you doing?" He spoke softly. His warm breath against her ear sent a shiver down her spine. He must have thought she was cold because he pulled her closer and began to stroke her upper arm.

The hairs on her arms rose and her voice was barely audible as she went to pull away. "I'm better thanks."

"Don't." He pulled her even closer. He placed one hand under her chin and tipped her face toward him. His intense blue eyes softened as they looked into hers. His head tipped. A spark leapt between them. Claire accepted the invitation. Their lips met. The touch was soft, brief.

Raising his mouth from hers, he gazed into her eyes. A shiver of excitement ran through her. Their lips met again, no longer gentle, now demanding and hungry. His tongue traced the soft fullness of her lips, sending shivers of desire racing through her body.

He ignited a long buried passion in her and when he finally released her lips, they were sore yet craved for more. Her face felt hot and her heart pounded. Shifting, Claire wound her arms around him, snuggled against his chest, let her soft curves mold to his body. With her lips she caressed the pulse point at the nape of his neck.

His arms pulled her closer and his fingers stroked the back of her head. The gentleness of his touch stoked a smoldering fire. Claire lifted her face to his. He kissed her eyes, her cheeks, her lips. She felt the heat rising between them. His hands began to explore her body. Each area he touched exploded a new spark of electricity. Her body arched toward him. Taking his hand, she led him to the bedroom.

CHAPTER 49

Rosko should have felt exhausted but his night with Claire, despite their lack of sleep, had revived him. He tried to keep his mind on the case, tried to keep from thinking about their lovemaking, tried to keep from wondering how soon he would see her again. It wasn't working. He wanted to solve this case as soon as possible. Then he and Claire could spend time together that had nothing to do with work and murdered women. They could find out if the attraction between them was going to lead anywhere. Maybe it would end once the case was over.

He shuffled the papers on his desk. They needed to go back and see if anyone remembered the victim. And he wanted to remind Mark Finnian they hadn't forgotten him. He had a few tattoos, didn't he?

Rosko and Wilson spent the rest of the afternoon revisiting previous territory. They talked to Mary Jane Winters' fiancé. It was a reserved, sad eyed man who let them into his office. Grief had added five years. There was still nothing he could add to the investigation. Rosko empathized with his thinly veiled anger that they hadn't solved the crime and given him the closure he needed.

They went to Bertolini's for a quick bite. The same hostess was on duty. She recognized them, but had nothing new to tell them. At least the food was good. Rosko couldn't remember eating anything other than donuts and coffee all day.

Jonathan Delaware's apartment still reeked of marijuana. Rosko again assured the man he was just looking for information, not busting him for drug use. Delaware's lopsided grin revealed several missing teeth. The few still present were nicotine stained. Sorry he couldn't help. He didn't go out much, just to get beer, smokes, groceries, when his dole came in. He assured Rosko he'd call. Joe down the hall had a phone, if he heard anything.

Rosko noticed how Matilda danced when Delaware flexed his right arm muscles lifting the brown bottle to his lips. He couldn't imagine Delaware coming down from a high long enough to be able to cut a straight incision, let alone perform a complicated surgery.

The construction crew for Joe Duncan, alias Elton John look-a-like, had finally shown up. His dress shop was open and enjoying a brisk trade. Duncan offered the detectives a discount on something for your lady. He looked disappointed when Rosko denied having a lady to buy for.

Duncan took a long hard look at the photo of Mrs. Sears. "You know, she does look a little familiar, but then I get so many women in and out of here." He stared at the picture. "There is something about her."

The detectives watched the people passing on the street while Duncan went to the back of the shop. He returned a moment later sporting a huge grin and waving a piece of paper. "I knew I'd seen her."

He handed Rosko the paper, Wilson read over his shoulder. "What is it?"

"It's a bill for a dress she purchased. I remember because the only one I had in her size was in the window. Sexy red number, but very classy. She wanted it to wear for her husband's birthday dinner. She was in here browsing. Said she had some time to kill while she waited for her car to be fixed, had a soft tire." Delaware's face was lit up like a Christmas tree. "Nice lady. A teacher, right?"

"When was that?" Wilson asked.

"Oh, just yesterday. Sorry I didn't remember right away. So many people in and out. Dress is still here. Needed shortening." Sudden realization flashed across Duncan's face. "Hey, she's not dead is she? She'll be coming back for the dress, won't she?"

"No. She's not dead." Rosko reassured him. "Did she say where she was getting her car fixed?"

"Oh, probably Lenny's. It's just down the street."

Yes, Lenny's. Wilson and Rosko looked at each other. Lenny's, where Mark Finnian worked. Now they had even more reason to visit him.

"Well, you boys come on in here again." Duncan shook hands with both detectives, but looked directly at Rosko. "And you bring in your lady friend when you find one."

"Did you notice the tattoo?" Wilson asked.

"What, the Celtic armband?"

Wilson shrugged. "My kid went through a phase of wanting a tattoo. We said he could have one. We sort of bonded investigating them together."

"So what did he end up with?"

Wilson laughed. "By the time he spent a couple of months investigating them on the Internet he decided not to get one."

"Kids."

"You can say that again." Wilson shook his head. "Thank God mine are grown now. What do you think of Duncan as a suspect?"

Rosko shrugged. "He doesn't fit the profile, but at this point I don't want to rule anyone out. And he did admit to Mrs. Sears being there. Let's get Myers to do some checking on him."

Lenny's was busy. All three bays had cars in them. Lenny was in the first one, someone Rosko and Wilson didn't know was working on a vehicle in the second one. A car was up on the hoist in the third bay with Finian under it. Rosko and Wilson went to talk to Lenny. They'd let Finian stew a bit.

"You again." Lenny looked up from the car. "You guys got nothing better to do than harass honest citizens?"

Wilson shrugged. "We have to work through a lot of honest ones to find the guilty."

Lenny wasn't amused. He wiped the grease off his hands with a stained cloth and threw it onto the front fender. "What do you want?"

"Has this woman been here?" Rosko handed him the photo. Lenny took a quick glance and handed it back.

"Take another look," Wilson demanded.

Lenny took the photo back. "Looks like a lady who was in here yesterday. Hey, Mark, get over here."

There was a loud bang as Finian let a wrench fall to the ground. He sauntered over to bay one, his hands clenched into fists and a muscle in his left cheek twitched.

"What?"

"This woman," Lenny said, passing Finian the picture, "wasn't she in here yesterday?"

"Yeah. Had a tire with a nail in it."

"That's right. You fixed it and she picked it up just before we closed. Lenny turned to Rosko, did something happen to her?"

The detectives watched for a reaction. "She was attacked last night."

"Holy shit," Lenny said.

Finian's fists clenched and unclenched, his face tightened. He spat the words out, "Fuck you. I fixed her fucking car. That's all."

"What time was she here?" Wilson asked.

"Late afternoon. Brought her car in cause a tire was soft. I fixed it and she left. Never saw her again."

"How did you spend last evening?"

Finian glared at Wilson. "I was here till six, went home, then went to O'Reilly's. I was there until two."

"Any witnesses?"

"Yeah, the whole fucking bar."

"Anyone in particular?"

"My girlfriend, Kim Perry."

Rosko wondered how Tina would feel about being replaced so quickly? When they checked his alibi, would they notice any bruises on Miss Perry?

Mark Finian was as surly as ever, but they still had nothing concrete on him. They'd keep an eye on him. One false step and they'd pull him in. Too bad they couldn't do it just for attitude. They left him with the assurance they'd check his alibi.

They checked the rest of the stores. Maybe Brianne Sears had done some other business in the neighborhood. Robertson Travel had a curvaceous blonde at Mary Jane Winters' old desk. Mrs. Sears had not booked a trip or even inquired about one. The occupants of the other stores along the block didn't recall seeing the woman in the photo either.

In Powalski's Meat Store the butcher was cutting and wrapping cold cuts for an elderly customer. Rosko noticed the look of annoyance as the detectives entered the shop. It was quickly replaced by a friendly greeting.

"Well, gentlemen, nice to see you again. What can I do for you today? Roast beef's on special. But you guys can have a discount on anything you see."

"We're here on business," Wilson said.

His smile faded. "How can I help?"

Wilson showed him the photo of Mrs. Sears. The man looked at it for a long time. Rosko noticed a twitch at the right side of his mouth, as if he wanted to smile or frown but couldn't decide between the two.

He handed back the picture. "Looks like a lady who came in yesterday. Bought some meat, cheese, and a fresh roll. Just wanted enough to make a sandwich."

"Was anyone with her? Or anyone suspicious around her?"

"Not that I remember. The shop was kind of busy. I think she came in alone and left alone."

"Did she chat at all? Did she say why she was in the neighborhood or where she was going?"

There was that twitch again. "Nope. Just bought her purchases and left."

"So nothing else?"

"Nope. Not that I can think of."

Out on the street, Rosko asked Wilson, "Did you notice, he never asked why we were asking about the woman?"

"Sure. Was it because he already knew? Or because it was plastered all over the news this afternoon?"

Rosko said, "Let's add him to Myers's to do list."

The butcher had seemed charming, but something about him irked Rosko.

"Did you see the snake tattoo on his upper right arm? Wilson asked. "The Blue Dragon Tattoo Parlor is obviously a busy spot."

⌘⌘⌘

Rosko headed back to the station. He wondered what effect the woman escaping would have on the killer. Would it leave him angry, frustrated? Rosko feared the latter. They could soon be dealing with an increased frequency of attacks. The intervals were already getting shorter.

At first, it had been weeks between the killings, but the last attacks had been only days apart. What would happen now? Would he back off? He'd been careful so far. The profiler had claimed he was organized and intelligent, smart enough not to leave them any clues. All they had was the imprint of a van mat on some of the victims, but no idea what type of van. The killer was AB positive, but that wasn't much help. The DNA wasn't back.

And the tattoo. Maybe tomorrow Mrs. Sears might be able to tell them what type of tattoo.

Maybe the killer was getting careless.

CHAPTER 50

A fine sweat broke out on his forehead and his heart pounded so hard he thought his chest might explode. His brain spun with a powder keg of emotions—anger, anticipation, excitement, power, and fear. The television was already tuned to the CBR News. He pressed the volume control on the converter. He didn't want to miss a word.

He flopped into the LazyBoy. He hoped they'd have a lot of coverage, especially from Sherry. Part of him feared the woman would identify him, another part wanted full credit for his work. Well, maybe not for her. He'd let her get away. But alive, she could keep reliving the terror. The gift that keeps on giving.

His laugh held an edge of hysteria as he recalled the terror in her eyes and knowing he was the one responsible for it. His excitement grew, growing until it outweighed his fear. He felt a pleasurable sensation as his racing heart sent blood gushing to his groin. Her gift to him.

His mind kept going back to the same question. Why hadn't the drug worked? A bad batch? Expired? He should get more, get a fresh batch. He flipped the channel. There was nothing on the evening news. He'd had it on all day at the shop but it was so busy he hadn't been able to hear anything. And that Mrs. Butterworth. Stupid woman. Talked all the way through the twelve o'clock news. Couldn't decide what she wanted.

Was his victim still alive? Grace Memorial was the biggest hospital in the area. Maybe they'd taken her there. Would she still be there?

The voice of Russell Ward burst into the room. "Last night the Kidney Slasher struck again. The latest victim somehow escaped his clutches. She's in critical condition, but is expected to live. Police are not releasing her name and she remains under strict security at Grace Memorial Hospital."

So they had taken her there. He should never have let her get away. That was a big mistake. Could she identify him? Maybe tonight he'd try to find out. That was, if he could get close to her. Maybe Doctor Valincourt would be looking after her. He'd almost gotten her last night. But there would be more chances for the beautiful doctor.

Sounds from the television distracted him. The broadcaster had moved on to other news but it made him think of a particular reporter who might even be at the hospital.

He pictured Sherry standing outside of Grace Memorial Hospital with her red-lipped smile, the graceful curve of her breasts, and her long brunette hair waving across her face. He dressed her in a tight black silk skirt. The skirt's hem caught in the breeze, lifted the flimsy material, exposed portions of her long legs. She was talking about him, and everyone was listening.

Voices from the television interrupted his daydreams. He heard the male commentator's voice. He waited impatiently for her but Sherry didn't appear. Was it her night off? He hoped she wasn't on vacation. He hoped not. He had great plans for her. But, not quite yet.

He sat through the hour of local and national news, but there was nothing more. And Sherry wasn't even on tonight. What a waste of time. He leapt up and rammed his thumb into the power button. The TV rattled on its stand. What a piss off. No wonder the station's ratings were dropping. He slammed his fist on the top of the television set. It bounced on the stand and then settled.

He needed to see the woman tonight. The uniform got him into places normally off limits. Nobody paid attention to a floor cleaner.

He glanced at the clock, seven, too early to go there now, too many people around. Suddenly he was tired. He went to lie down.

He tossed and turned, unable to get into a deep sleep. When he finally dozed off, he dreamt of the woman. She was running and he was chasing her. They ran through the woods. It got darker and darker the farther they went. He kept running, but couldn't find her. Then lights from the road broke through the trees, he ran to the spot but all he saw was an empty road. Later he heard the sirens wailing in the distance.

When his alarm went off at ten, he hit the snooze button. His body stiff from unbridled tension, his muscles felt as if someone had set a match to them. It was as if the running dream had been real and he was exhausted from the effort.

He dragged himself out of bed and into the shower. Twenty minutes of letting the water sluice over him did nothing to ease the tension. His mind kept wandering back to the woman. He didn't even know her name. At least the dead ones got their names in the news. Maybe she would soon. A burst of Adrenaline rushed through him. Anxious to get to the hospital, he had trouble buttoning the uniform shirt.

He pulled into the parking lot at ten-forty-five and maneuvered his vehicle beside a silver Mazda Miata. The owner, the good looking doctor from the emergency department, Doctor Valincourt. Doctor Claire Valincourt, the one who'd found his first body. He wondered what time her shift was done.

The hospital buzzed, everyone talking about the woman who'd escaped the Kidney Slasher. The fact she'd been brought to Grace Memorial had even little Sandy in laundry talking to him. If only they knew the truth.

But there were too many damn people around—police, security, and media—just too damn many. Would he even be able to get on the same floor? He'd heard on the news that security had been increased. That excuse of a security guard, Simon Wyshinski, even stopped him at the parking lot to check out his pass and then again at the staff entrance. His stolen uniform and fake ID worked. Nobody doubted him. It didn't take much for him to find out that a policeman was posted outside her door and that her husband was with her around the clock. Tonight might not be a good night to get more ketamine but he needed to restock his cupboard. And somehow he needed to find out if she could identify him.

Lucky for him there was always somebody sick and casual staff filling in. Nobody questioned a new face. He'd been nervous the first time, after that it was a piece of cake. He just walked in. Wyshinski just glanced at his ID and waved him through. What a joke. A great lot of security he was for the nurses.

CHAPTER 51

Claire saw the anesthetic cart in the trauma bay. A large hand reached for a vial of ketamine. She tried to see the face behind the hand. It was shrouded in the darkness.

Her sheets were a tangled, damp mass when the alarm went off at five-thirty. She hit the snooze button several times. The thought of another night shift was not appealing. She hated nights. She'd never been able to sleep during the day and the events of the last few days weren't helping. If her mind wasn't occupied reliving the man in the van chasing her, or thinking about the dead women, it was thinking about Rosko and their night together. It had been amazing for her but she wasn't so sure about him. She sighed. What was she doing getting involved with anyone. It was the last thing she needed. But it had been so good.

The snooze button went off again and she dragged herself out of bed. Two hours and she had to start her night shift at the hospital. At five-fifty she finally dragged herself out of bed. She felt more tired than when she'd lain down and the looking glass in her bathroom told no lies. The dark circles under her eyes made her wince.

A brisk shower washed away most of her fatigue. She took extra care with her hair then put on a purple V-necked top and white pants. Digging her make-up out of the cabinet, she applied foundation and a coat of lipstick. A little better.

Claire glanced at the clock. Where had the time gone? She'd thought she had lots of time before getting in the shower and now she'd have to hurry to make it to the hospital by eight. She grabbed her bag and headed for her silver Mazda Miata. At exactly five minutes to eight, she pushed through the doors of the emergency department.

Dropping her bag on the office floor, she plunked down into the chair beside the doctor on duty. Doug Murphy.

"You look tired. Still not sleeping well?" Murphy inquired.

Claire shrugged. So much for her efforts at vanity. Doug had seen right through her cosmetic job. "Not really. Maybe I'll take something to help me sleep tomorrow."

"Good idea."

Murphy gave her a quick report on the department before heading home. Claire made rounds of all the emergency room patients. She checked test results recently back, ordered more tests on a couple of patients, and discharged some home. The flow of patients through the department remained constant and time passed quickly.

When the emergency department quieted down, Claire caught herself thinking about Mrs. Sears and decided to go to the floor and see how she was doing. She watched the sleeping patient from outside the glass windows. She could only imagine the horror when the woman had been given ketamine and realized she couldn't move. And then had to watch helplessly as some maniac held a scalpel over her abdomen. A shudder ran through Claire.

That was one of her worst nightmares, to have surgery without anesthetic. She'd heard the urban legends of people having operations while still fully awake. But that's all they were, legends, at least in this hemisphere.

A memory of the blue-tinged face of the girl from the park came back to haunt her. Black mascara smudged on her cheeks. It was as if she had been made up for some horror movie, the lines of black still running down her chalk white cheeks. Then her eyes moved and she whispered, "Help me, help me."

Claire squeezed her eyes shut. The vision remained. The eyes now bulging out of the woman's face. Her voice escalated, pleaded with her. Covering her ears, Claire tried to shut out the cries. She saw the corpse's arm move toward her abdomen. The abdomen, not yet stitched lay open, a large gaping cavity. Blood oozed from the incision and covered the pale hand. It trickled out of her body, ran in a small stream, congealing in a large puddle on the floor.

Claire trembled as she fought to escape the images. It was a long time before the woman's cries ceased and her body diminished into the night. A loud voice chased the image away.

"Hey, you can't go in there."

Claire's head jerked toward the policeman.

"I have to clean the floor."

"Not now, buddy. Nobody's allowed in there. Just the nurses and the doctors."

Claire saw the back of a dark head. The cleaner pushed a mop and bucket of soapy water toward the room.

"Just doing my job."

"Go do it somewhere else."

The mop sloshed noisily in the bucket, dispersing a fine spray of water into the air. A few splatters landed on the policeman's pant leg.

"Hey, get out of here." The policeman wiped at the wet spots on his trousers.

The bucket rattled down the hall. Claire glanced at the tall man pushing it. Did she know him? There were so many casual cleaners. Something about this one was familiar. Was he the casual cleaner who was always watching, or getting in the way in the emergency department? She caught a glance of a large hand pushing the bucket.

Something made a chill run down her spine. A large hand reaching out, grabbing—Claire gave her head a shake. Her imagination was getting out of hand.

CHAPTER 52

He watched from the van as people exited the front door of the television station. He knew Sherry would be one of the last to leave. She always was. She planned on going places. He had other plans for her. When she did emerge, he followed a couple of car lengths behind. She never even noticed. She parked on the street in front of the apartment building. They both knew she wouldn't be long. He looked at his watch. Just long enough to change. Would she wear something sexy?

He was enjoying this game of cat and mouse.

Parking his van, he stared at the end window on the third floor. Her bedroom. He knew because he'd broken into her apartment earlier that day. He remembered his excitement as he ran his fingers over her delicate undergarments. His erection had come quickly when he'd held them to his nose and inhaled her scent. He was so looking forward to tonight's meeting.

He pictured lying beside her on her queen-size bed. Naked, the silk sheets would feel cool against his skin, her voice a soft whisper in his ear. He imagined her manicured hands stroking his erection.

Then he remembered her latest newscast about him and went limp. He'd thought she was somebody special, she'd even reminded him of his mother. But she wasn't. He was going to enjoy teaching her how he operated.

He laughed at his own joke. Yes, it would be fun operating on her. Maybe he'd do something special for her. And he couldn't just dump her body in any old park. Her place would have to be special.

He watched as the bedroom light turned off, then the living room. He started the van and waited for her red Mercedes to pull out onto the street. He didn't have to follow her closely this time. He knew exactly where she was going.

❧❧❧

Sherry glanced at her watch. It was nine-thirty-five p.m. They weren't supposed to meet until ten. She had lots of time. She sat at a window table for two at Michaels On The Thames and watched the street.

She'd picked The Palace Restaurant as their meeting place. She's used it before for the same reasons as tonight. The Palace was a quiet family restaurant on a brightly lit street that was busy until late in the evening. The other advantage was that Michael's was directly across the street.

Michaels was her favorite restaurant. She loved pasta, and they made the best. A dinner of grilled chicken and Fettuccini Alfredo had been tonight's treat. After a busy day, she needed to relax. She leisurely sipped on a cup of their finely brewed coffee. It gave her time to think about her story outline. How much would he reveal?

The mini recorder was in place and ready to go. All she needed to do was press the red button, a movement she'd perfected, discreet and natural. Maybe it was against journalist ethics to record someone without their permission, but Sherry had her career to think of. She'd rationalized that the end justified the means a long time ago.

She thought about Gerry. Was the end of that relationship worth it? He couldn't understand her overwhelming need to be successful. So what if she hurt some feelings along the way?

The sheer curtains protected her from being seen by pedestrians and she felt safe peering outside. The street was relatively quiet this time of night. A few people strolled along the sidewalk. One elderly couple attempted to hold back a sleek greyhound. Another couple, young and obviously deep in the throws of lust, hurried down the street. They were probably concentrating on the closest site to scratch that yearning itch. It was quiet enough she shouldn't miss him.

Could one of them be the person she'd arranged to meet? They all looked normal and innocent. What would he be like? Ordinary, or a charming good-looker? Sherry was eager to finally find out. A group of noisy teenagers passed the window. Sherry focused on the other side of the street.

The Palace was winding down from the dinner rush. The table she'd reserved for ten o'clock was empty. She accepted another refill on her coffee then checked the street again. Would he be on time?

Sherry hoped she'd arrived first. He'd warned her he would only meet with her if she were alone.

Her watch read one minute before ten. There'd been no sign of anyone who looked like a killer. So much for her intention of checking him out first. Leaving a tip on the table, Sherry crossed the street.

Her reserved table was still empty. She took a seat facing the door and giving her a view of the street. It was quiet. The few people passing by the window looked unremarkable. Sherry wondered how long he would make her wait.

The service was not five star and Sherry had to wait several minutes for a waitress. She hated waiting and tapped her fingers on the table. Time to switch to decaffeinated. She wondered at the wisdom of her decision. Maybe she should have let someone know.

෴

He watched her cross the street. He liked the way her short red skirt clung to her hips. Then he recalled the six o'clock news and her voice echoed in his head. "He's unprofessional...starting to make mistakes...won't be long before he's caught." His hands clenched and unclenched. Just how humble would she be once he got his hands on her?

He walked swiftly through the dark shadows, hugging the alleyways, avoiding the streetlights that might illuminate a moving figure. The red Mercedes hadn't been hard to find. It was parked in front of Richmond's Dresses. Tonight the stars twinkled brightly in the indigo sky. There wasn't a cloud in sight. He slid into the shadowed alcove of the dress shop.

Too bad she wouldn't be able to report her own death.

CHAPTER 53

Wilson was waiting for him at the side of the road, the tip of his cigarette butt glowing in the darkness. Why wasn't he with the body, or questioning people? And what the hell was he doing smoking? Years ago he sworn he'd never pick one up again. Rosko was aware of Wilson watching him as he approached.

"Hey, Gerry. How you doing?"

"Tired as shit. How about you?"

"The same."

"What's going on?"

"Gerry—" Wilson paused then looked at the cigarette butt as if it offended him. He ground it into the loose gravel before facing his partner again. "It's Sherry."

What the hell was he talking about? And why wasn't he his usual jovial self? He'd been on the job a long time but he could always detach himself from the horrors they dealt with every day. Rosko forced himself to meet his gaze. "What about Sherry?"

"He got Sherry. He got her."

Rosko froze. He felt like he'd stepped in a frigid lake and his knees buckled. He stared at his partner, challenging him to say it was all a sick joke. He saw the depth of sadness in Wilson's eyes and knew it was no joke. He felt bile rise in his throat and he felt a deep pain in the middle of his gut as if he'd just been sucker-punched.

"God. Where is she?"

Wilson nodded at a treed area behind him. "In the woods over there. It's not pretty."

He paused as if thinking of the vibrant and beautiful woman Sherry had been. Wilson and Rosko had both known her since she'd come to Strathburn as a junior reporter. They'd watched her claw her way up the ladder to become the main on-scene newscaster. The good and bad sides, they'd known them both.

"He didn't follow his normal pattern." Wilson's voice was somber. "This was personal. Maybe he'd formed some weird attachment to her. She said some pretty nasty things about him. Maybe he took offense."

Rosko shook his head. He couldn't believe it. He didn't want to see her body, but knew he had to. He motioned Wilson to lead the way. "Let's get it over with."

The two walked toward an open area in the woods. Rosko saw the flash of lanterns and heard the subdued voices of policemen. They'd all known Sherry. Some, like him, had known her better than others.

"Is Lee here?"

"On his way."

Rosko heard the hum before they reached her body. Despite a police officer fanning them away, flies swarmed over her naked body. A thick black line ran across the left side of her abdomen. He realized the flies were clustering over the incision where once her kidney had been.

A sour tasting fluid rose in his throat. He had to walk away. It was several minutes before he managed to return. He stared at her body, shaking his head. He wanted to leave and let Wilson handle it. But he owed it to Sherry to find the bastard who'd done this to her.

Damn it. What type of person could snuff the life out of such a beautiful woman? What drove this madman?

Maybe they were looking in the wrong direction. They'd been concentrating on finding a connection between the women, someone they knew, or a mutual crossing ground. Maybe there wasn't one. What had made him pick Sherry? Rosko felt a fire in the pit of his stomach. He may have ended his involvement with her but he would never wish anything like this on her. Slowly he turned and walked away. The Crime Scene Unit and Wilson could handle it from here. He'd seen enough. He pushed past the media begging for answers. He'd let Wilson handle them too.

Rosko waited at the side of the road. The red tip of his cigarette cast an eerie glow in the darkness. He'd borrowed it from Wilson. Tomorrow, they'd promised each other, they'd quit again.

The weather had suddenly turned cold. Autumn leaves fluttered around him. He took a long draw. The cold he felt wasn't just due to the weather. He pulled his jacket around him. It protected him from the wind but nothing eased the chill encasing his heart. Poor Sherry.

The Captain would have his head on a platter. Mayor Denning was on his back, and the shit was following the usual course, right down to Rosko. Why couldn't they catch this guy? What was the connection between the victims? What the hell are we missing? He has to give us some clue, a trace of something.

Where the hell is Lee? It's damned cold out here.

Rosko thought of the body behind him in the woods. Didn't matter that she was stark naked, Sherry would never feel the cold again—she was long past feeling anything. By the look of her body, it must have happened within the last twenty-four hours. There was a loss of rigor, and the insects were at her. And the vultures hovering, human and feathered.

His throat was dry and it hurt to swallow. No matter how long a person was on the force, there were still things you never got used to, and decaying bodies was one of them, especially the decaying bodies of someone you knew. Once they were just bones, well, that made it a little easier. You could detach yourself from the bones, pretend they never really belonged to an actual person.

That was, until you had to tell the family. Then they became real. But something like this, with a naked body all cut up and the bugs crawling in and out, this was too real. And the smell. There was something about the smell of rotting flesh that worked its way inside you. Once you'd smelled it, you never forgot it.

He could have let one of the uniforms wait for Lee. Maybe he should have examined the scene some more. No. Wilson could do that. Rosko had seen enough of this killer to know his MO. Let the younger guys get used to the smell. He'd had enough. Where the hell is Lee? He'd better not have fallen back asleep.

Rosko was just pulling his cell phone out of his pocket when he saw the sweep of headlights coming up the deserted road. He snuffed out the cigarette with his heel. All he needed now was one of Lee's lectures on the hazards of smoking.

※※※

A flock of reporters waited for them at the precinct. They rushed the detectives as they climbed out of the car.

"Was it Sherry Simmons? Did he take her kidney too? Have you got a suspect?"

A dozen questions were hurled at them.

"No comment."

Rosko and Wilson pushed past them and hurried through the side door. The reporters tried to barge in but the desk sergeant was ready for them with a billy club clutched in his fist. At six-foot-four, two hundred and sixty-pounds, he formed an effective wall.

Rosko waved at the man. "Thanks, Charlie."

"No problem." His linebacker days for Ohio State had given him practice at intimidating angry mobs.

The television was on when Rosko walked into the office.

"It is with great sadness that we report the death of one of our own. Sherry Simmon's life was tragically cut short. Sherry, in the prime of her life and in the midst of a promising broadcast career, is no longer with us. Last night Sherry became the sixth victim of the vicious serial killer terrorizing Strathburn. It is ironic that the man she's been relentlessly warning the public about was responsible for ending her life.

"Sherry began working with us several years ago and quickly gained our respect and love. She will be sadly missed by her family in Trenton and by all of us here at CBR News. A memorial service will be held at St. Anthony's Church on Friday at two p.m. The family will have a private ceremony on Thursday. Following the ceremony, we will air a profile of Sherry's brief life."

Rosko's fist hit the desk so hard his aunt's crystal paperweight jumped off the table. The loud thud as it hit the ground made every detective in the room pause and turn. With their attention on him, Rosko picked up the crystal and slammed it back into place. The desk reverberated with the force. He bellowed into the room. "Damn it, we have to catch this bastard. There are absolutely no leaves and no vacations until he's caught. We need to go through every scrap of evidence again until we find something. Sherry was one of our own. He's made this personal."

Myers shook his head. "And we got the DNA back on that hair Doc MacFarlane found. Nothing. Not a match to anybody in the system."

Rosko slumped into his chair. "Shit. We need to catch a break here, guys."

"I'll go through all the lists of family and friends of each of the victims," Wilson said. "Have we got any more back from the medical schools?"

"Nothing relevant," Myers said. "But I'll go through it all again, Boss, and extend my search. I'll make more calls and put a nasty bug in the ear of people reluctant to give us information."

"Let's meet in the conference room in two hours and see what we've got. Anybody have suggestions, let me know. I've run dry."

CHAPTER 54

Claire tried to shake off the feeling that someone was watching her. It was probably nerves, and being overtired. She glanced behind her. There was no one there. No van. No man chasing after her. But yet a shiver ran down her spine. She glanced behind her again. There was still nothing there.

She was tired after her stint of nights. And now bruised and sore from being pushed down by the guy in the van. She'd slept most of the day away. At three she'd finally dragged herself out of bed, laundry first on her agenda, then shopping. She was down to her last couple of pairs of underwear, and two slices of bread.

Claire decided to walk. It meant she'd have to limit what she bought, but a good walk might clear her mind. It was still light and the streets were busy with pedestrians. Nobody would dare attack someone in broad daylight.

Sue Taylor, the police sketch artist, had enrolled them in an art class at Fanshawe College. Tonight was their first class and Claire was looking forward to it. She'd collected the basic art supplies she needed and even picked up a roomy black tote that doubled as a backpack. The brushes and a sketchpad were all neatly organized in their own pockets.

She glanced at her watch, a few minutes after six, just enough time to get home, have a quick bite to eat, and then pick Sue up for the class. She was pleased with her purchases and excited about learning to paint watercolors. It was one of those things she'd put on hold to become a doctor. She swung the bag over her shoulder and decided to cut through Victoria Park.

The park was busy yet she had no complaint about having to weave around groups of pedestrians and skateboarders, there was safety in numbers. Her feet still automatically sped up when she approached the spot where she'd found the body, but she couldn't avoid the area forever. She was just past the spot when she heard the snap of a twig behind her. She jumped, expecting the worst.

Fifteen feet away, a couple strolled hand in hand. A woman with a collie pulling excitedly at his lead was ten feet behind her. There was no one close by, no one that might prove a threat, yet silent panic plagued her. She tried to laugh at her fears. It was broad daylight, too early for ghosts and goblins and killers to be out.

But she couldn't shake the feeling of being watched, and her senses remained on high alert. She heard nothing else, but the uneasy feeling remained. Unconsciously, she picked up the pace and turned frequently to look behind her.

By the time she'd exited the park, the muscles in the back of her neck ached. She looked behind her one last time. No one. Was she going crazy?

She couldn't stand it. She started to jog.

დოდ

Three apartment buildings nestled on the cozy crescent, behind them was a small park with a swing set, tennis court, and enclosed pool. The front of the buildings had been landscaped to extend the feel of parkland. Tall trees, shrubs, and massive groupings of flowers lined the drive.

The beauty was lost on him. He had other things on his mind.

He eased the van around to the back of the apartment building and looked up. He knew which apartment was hers. He'd been here before, several times. Her apartment was still in darkness and he took care to find a spot at the far side of the lot. The trees of the park were only ten feet away.

The light above the back door was bright, and illuminated a path to the above-ground parking lot. Of course, she didn't park here. She had underground parking but he could still see her fancy silver car when she turned into the driveway.

He watched from the shelter of the trees. It had taken him a while to find the perfect spot but he was quite pleased with it. From here he could watch the path and both sides of the building. There was even an old maple with thick, low branches that he could shimmy up in an emergency. From there his range of visibility would be expanded and the densely leafed branches would make him virtually invisible. He leaned back against the tree and lit a cigarette.

Now all he had to do was wait.

He walked back toward the van and unlocked its back doors. He checked the interior and gave the plastic sheet another straightening tug. From the glove compartment he removed a small dark plastic bottle and a plaid handkerchief. He tucked them both into the back pocket of his jeans and returned to the shelter of the maple tree.

With autumn, the sun set earlier and the tip of his cigarette looked like a red sparkler. He played the childhood game of writing names in the darkness. He had several names that were all his now. He wrote them in the sky. Mary Jane, Tina, Debby, Sherry. His jaw clenched and he refused to write Virginia. Instead, he wrote and crossed out Brianne. He couldn't have her name yet. But soon he would have one more name to write.

He was on his fourth cigarette when the lights in her apartment came on. He hadn't seen her car. She must have walked. The thought of her alone in the apartment sent chills of excitement sprinting through his body.

Stubbing the butt on the sole of his Nike, he crushed the remnants into the ground and pulled a pair of latex gloves from his pocket. He surveyed the parking lot. No activity. What was taking her so long? He was getting impatient.

Footsteps clattered down the back stairs. He headed toward the door, his head tipped down so the baseball cap shadowed his face. His dark shirt and jeans were unremarkable. He fiddled with a set of keys. Reaching the building the precise moment a teenager hurried out the door, he caught the frame just before it slammed shut.

He started up the stairs, calmly, one step at a time. Her apartment was on the fifth floor. It would be easier to take the elevator, but the stairs decreased the possibility of being seen.

CHAPTER 55

The run home invigorated her. She took a quick shower then prepared a Greek salad and pork chops. Claire thought about the evening's art class.

Since coming to Strathburn she'd been so busy with work that she hadn't made many friends outside of the hospital. And until the last several months, when their relationship began to cool off, all her free weekends had been spent working or with Michael. Looking back, Claire couldn't really blame him. She'd never had a lot of time for him, and when he did come up, she was often too tired to do much of anything. What did it say about her feelings for him that she hadn't even noticed the dwindling of his visits? Maybe her sister was better suited for him. She wasn't ready to admit that to either one of them, though.

She really needed to get a social life. Heat rose in her cheeks as she thought of the night she'd spent in Gerry's arms. She tried to remember if Michael had ever aroused her to that extent. Maybe the scare had heightened their passion? Claire didn't want to think about him now. Relationships were too complicated. Maybe he had no intention of ever seeing her again.

Female friends, that was what she needed. Just to go out and enjoy herself. She was glad she'd met Sue Taylor. They'd gone for coffee a few times and the movies. Sue's dry sense of humor got Claire laughing more than she had in years. It was nice to find someone with some common interests other than work. Now, they were taking this art course. Maybe in time she'd let a man into her life again. Rosko's face popped into her thoughts.

Claire reached for the phone but her arm stopped midair. What was that? She thought she'd heard a thud. She waited. Nothing.

It must have been the television set. She dialed Sue's number. "I've got all my supplies. I'll pick you up in about fifteen minutes."

Putting down the phone, Claire headed for the bathroom. She dotted moisturizer on her face. A commercial came on the television and the suddenly raised voices made her jump. *Your imagination's in overdrive, first the park and now here.*

Claire reached for her mascara and raised the wand to her eyelash. A floorboard squeaked. Her hand jerked and she smeared a dark glob on her eyelid. Damn. She wiped at the spot with her finger, staying attuned for the slightest noise. Was that a soft whisper? It brought back memories of her sister sneaking up on her when she was sleeping. It sounded like her sister's feet on their bedroom carpet.

Claire froze, the mascara wand halfway to her face. The hairs on the back of her neck stood on end. She stared into the mirror. Behind her the reflection of the hallway remained empty. All that stared back was own face, drained of color. She held her breath and listened to the sounds of the apartment, weeding out the noise from the television. At first, she heard nothing. Then there was that soft whisper again, then another, and another.

Someone was in her apartment!

The footsteps were coming along the hall towards the bathroom. Claire slammed the bathroom door and twisted the lock. There was a loud thud. She watched the doorknob turn.

Her throat constricted and it was hard to breathe, the taste of fear crept into her mouth. Her gaze darted around the room. What could she use to protect herself? She wished she'd brought the portable phone with her. She heard a rattle, jumping as the doorknob turned.

She needed to make some noise. Maybe that would scare him off. Her first scream came out as a loud squawk. The doorknob rattled violently in response. She needed to do better. Her second scream went up several decibels. Would anyone hear her? She needed a weapon.

Claire pulled open the medicine chest. Nothing there could do much damage. She yanked open the vanity doors, and began pulling out objects, toilet paper, Q-tips, cotton balls. Great lot of good they would do. She pulled out the hairdryer.

"Open the door," a male voice ordered.

Maybe she could hit him over the head with the hairdryer. At least it was a bit sturdier than those cheap plastic jobs. She kept screaming while she dug deeper into the vanity. Her hand hit a large can of hairspray. That might work. She could hit him on the head or spray him in the face. Her fingers tightened around the cylinder.

"Open the door, Doctor Valincourt."

He knew who she was. This wasn't a random break-in. Who would want to do this to her? Was this the same man who had attacked her? Her heart raced at an alarming clip. Was he after her kidney? He pounded on the door. The door rattled on its frame. How much more would it take before the hinges let go?

The sound gave her an idea. Claire started pounding too, but she pounded on the wall of the next apartment. She prayed that Mrs. Chegetto would be home, prayed that the racket would upset her, prayed she would call the police.

Would she come through? She called the police for anything else that went on in the building, a late party, a noisy muffler, a dog barking. Or heavens above, if someone missed cleaning up after their pet in the back common, watch out. So far, Claire hadn't been the brunt of her complaints. How could she? She didn't have any pets, she was rarely home to play music too loud, and she no longer even had a boyfriend. Basically, she had no life.

She kept pounding. She prayed this wasn't one of the rare days Mrs. Chegetto abandoned her post as apartment warden?

The pounding on the bathroom door became louder. "Open the door, Claire. Or I'll huff, and I'll puff, and I'll blow the door down." The doorframe shuddered as his body hit it.

How long before it shattered into a million pieces?

Sweat beaded on her temple. She spotted a pair of disposable scissors from the hospital. It might not keep him from killing her, but she could leave him with a few good scars. She slid the scissors beside the can of hairspray and used her other hand to smash on the wall. Suddenly she heard a female voice, Mrs. Chegetto. "Now you stop that or I'll call the police."

"Help." Claire screamed. "Call the police."

"What is it dear? Are you hurt?"

"Call the police. Someone's in my apartment."

"I'm calling," Mrs. Chegetto yelled back. "I'm calling, dear. Tell him I have a gun. And I know how to use it."

The doorframe began to splinter. Claire fell back against the toilet. Scissors in one hand, aerosol can in the other, she took a deep breath. She extended her right arm, aimed carefully, then sent a stream of hairspray through the cracks in the door. She heard his scream mingle with her own. She kept her finger on the trigger while she waited for the door to crash in on her.

CHAPTER 56

When Claire finally stopped screaming, an eerie silence enveloped the apartment. Starring straight ahead, she waited for the splintered wood to give way, waited for the crack in the door to expose the intruder, waited for a large hand to push through. Unable to breathe, unable to move, she waited. It took almost a minute before Claire realized the onslaught on her bathroom had ceased. She sank back on the toilet, her body shaking, her heart racing but finally able to breathe. It was Mrs. Chegetto's shrill voice that finally penetrated her consciousness.

"Claire. Claire, are you okay, dear? He's gone. Open the door, dear."

"Mrs. Chegetto. What are you doing? He may still be here."

"No, dear. He's gone. Ran as fast as his long legs would take him."

The can of hairspray slid out of Claire's hand and clattered to the floor. Her legs were weak and she had to hold onto the wall for support. She saw the cracks in the wooden doorframe and her fingers shook as she pulled the door open. She fell into her neighbor's arms. In the distance, a siren wailed.

Mrs. Chegetto led her to the living room and Claire slumped onto the chesterfield. She smiled gratefully up at the woman. It was only then that she noticed the small gun in the woman's right hand.

Mrs. Chegetto saw the shocked look in Claire's eyes and grinned. "Oh, don't worry dear. It's not loaded. But he didn't know that."

"What?" Claire's mouth gaped open.

"I just told him to get the hell out of here or I'd shoot him. He took off pretty quick."

Claire shook her head. The tension eased out her body and she began to laugh hysterically. Mrs. Chegetto sat down beside her and giggled.

"Did you call the police?" Claire asked.

"Oh, yes, dear. They're on their way."

Claire grinned at her neighbor and pointed to the gun. "I suggest you put that away before they get up here."

"That's a good idea, dear. I'll be right back."

❧❧❧

Officer Matt Thompson was questioning her when they heard a commotion at the door. Claire looked up to see Sue Taylor with Rosko behind her. She tried to rise but collapsed back on the sofa. Sue rushed over and hugged her.

"Are you okay?"

Claire nodded. She'd been trying to minimize the situation so she could stay in control but Sue's sympathy dissolved her heroism. Tears welled and she began to tremble uncontrollably. Rosko took a seat on her other side. She grasped the hand he extended. Gradually the trembling settled, and she used the Kleenex Sue handed her to wipe the tears from the corners of her eyes.

She looked from Sue to Rosko and back again. "How did you guys know about this?"

"Oh, I told them," Mrs. Chegetto chirped. "I told your lady friend here."

Claire looked confused.

"The phone was ringing, you were in the bathroom, and that guy had gone, so I answered it. Told the lady your apartment had been broken into. Then I went to get you. In all the excitement, I forgot to tell you."

Claire looked at Rosko with raised eyebrows.

"I found out because I was at Sue's picking up the sketches she did with Mrs. Sears."

Claire shook her head in disbelief. She was just relieved to have all these people here for her. The clearing of someone's throat distracted her. Thompson still sat in one of the chairs positioned close to the sofa. Pen in hand, he had his black notebook open. Claire reluctantly dropped Rosko's hand.

"Do you want to take over the investigation?" Thompson asked Rosko.

"No. You carry on. I'm going to have a look around. The Crime Scene Unit guys are coming, so I'll just nose around with them. But, I do have a couple of questions for Claire."

No one showed surprise that he'd used her first name. "Do you think this was the same man who attacked you the other day?"

"I don't know. Maybe. He knew my name." She began to tremble again.

"I can tell you what he looks like," Mrs. Chegetto declared.

All eyes turned toward her.

"You saw him?" Rosko asked.

"Sure did. He's about five-foot-eleven, dark brown hair, tried to cover it with a baseball cap but it fell off when he was running away."

"Can you describe what he was wearing?"

"He was all dressed in black, jeans, T-shirt. I just saw the back of him." Her grey head bobbed up and down. "Can't tell you much more. I was reading a book before all this commotion started. Had my reading glasses on, not my bifocals. Can't see a durn thing at a distance without them."

Great, they had an eyewitness who couldn't tell them anything useful because she'd had on the wrong glasses. Rosko shook his head. "Why did he leave?"

"Oh, I told him he had better get out of here and fast 'cause I'd called the cops."

Rosko raised his eyebrows in amazement. "He ran 'cause you told him to?"

"Well..." She laughed. "He had a little persuasion."

Claire shook her head at the elderly lady. She didn't want the police to know she had a real live Annie Oakley living beside her. "Mrs. Chegetto, don't you think you should go warn Mr. Potter about the intruder? He should know."

"Oh, yes, good idea. You're in good hands." She winked at the detective as she left the apartment.

Rosko turned back to Claire and asked, "Do you think it might have anything to do with the missing drugs at the hospital?"

Claire jerked upright. She heard the intruder say, "Open the door, Doctor Valincourt." A cold knife scraped down her spine, touching each vertebra in turn. "He called me by name. He called me 'Doctor Valincourt.' Do you think it might be someone from the hospital?" She shuddered. "Someone I work with every day?"

Rosko shrugged. "Perhaps."

"Oh, God."

"I need to look around, first the apartment, then outside. I won't leave without talking to you. A locksmith is on his way. Sue and Matt will stay with you."

She wanted to ask him to stay. Instead, she nodded like a wooden puppet. Sue squeezed her hand yet all Claire could produce was a weak lifting of the corners of her mouth.

Rosko did a quick turn about the apartment then took the stairs to the first floor. Finding no trace of the intruder on the stairway, he followed the cement path around to the back of the building. It was edged with rows of petunias, their pinks and purples faded into the shadows by the time he reached the end of the building. The above-ground parking lot had only a few empty spaces in its back rows. The walkway from the parking lot to the back door was in darkness.

What had happened to the exterior light? Had it burned out naturally, or had it been tampered with? As he crossed to the back door, Wilson appeared, having followed the path from the other end of the building. He hadn't found anything either.

"Chao, can you come over here," Rosko called. "Shine your flashlight up there. The beam of light found the fixture just above the door. The bulb was in place. Rosko donned a pair of gloves and reached up to touch the socket with his fingertip. The bulb jiggled.

"Looks like someone tampered with it."

Rosko unscrewed the bulb from the socket. He was careful to not touch its neck. He didn't want to destroy any prints. Chao held open a plastic bag for the bulb.

"He must have waited here for her to come home. Let's check the area to see if he left anything else."

"Hey, Rosko. Look at this. I wonder if it belongs to our guy."

Wilson crouched a couple of feet away from a large maple. With gloved hands he carefully parted the brush at the tree's base.

Rosko leaned over his shoulder. "What have you got?"

"Some cigarette butts. And a partial foot print." Wilson looked up at Rosko and grinned. Chao joined them. He opened a separate specimen bag for each butt.

The Crime Scene Unit technician examined the hard baked clay. A five-inch oval of fresh earth had been exposed. Rosko could see ridges in it, as if someone had loosened the hard earth when stubbing out cigarette butts.

"If this is our guy, he's getting careless. Looks like he wears runners. We should be able to get a partial print and maybe his shoe size. We can compare it to the other one we've got. Don't know what else we'll do with it until we get the guy. If we find his runners we can do a match. And from the butt, well if he wasn't wearing gloves at the time, we might get a print."

"Anything else?" Rosko asked.

"What the hell you want, miracles?" Chao asked.

"We need a miracle to stop this guy."

"Well, get down on those knobby knees of yours and say a few prayers and just maybe we might get some saliva off the butt. We might be able to run a DNA match."

"If that's what it takes, I'll get down there right now."

"Wouldn't want to get your pretty suit dirty, Boss. Give me a couple of hours with it, and then I want to see you on your knees."

"You're on, Chao."

Chao called to one of the technicians, "Bring over the casting material."

The technicians collected earth from around the area. Rosko watched Chao carefully remove debris from a large circle around the footprint. Some of that dirt was collected in a specimen bag. Then the casting plaster was poured into the depression made by the runner.

Rosko looked towards the apartment building. Yes, this was a good spot for a stakeout. The light above the exit door left the comers and goers visible while the trees provided shelter for the watcher. Disabling the light fixture decreased the watcher's chances of being identified. He glanced up at the third floor. The lights in Claire's apartment were clearly visible. This was definitely not a random act.

"Well look at this." Rosko turned back to where Wilson was circling the big maple. "This isn't the first time our guy's been here. Hey, Chao, we've got more butts over here. Looks like the same brand."

Chao used his gloved hands and a pair of tweezers to pick up the other butts. "These ones aren't as fresh. Looks like they're a few days old."

"See if they match," Rosko ordered. "I'm going back upstairs to see if the technicians have found anything up there."

"I'll go with you," Wilson said. "We should start a canvas of the building. Someone might have noticed something."

The technicians were still dusting the apartment for prints. They'd collected dirt the intruder's sneakers had deposited on the hallway rug. Sue Taylor continued to sit on the sofa with Claire. They were trying to distract themselves by watching a sit-com. A locksmith was busy repairing the lock and installing a new deadbolt. The bathroom door could wait.

Mrs. Chegetto had returned to her apartment. She claimed all the commotion had tired her out but Claire suspected she wanted to get to a phone and start broadcasting the news. This was the most excitement their building had had since Mr. Dronyk in 511 set fire to the garbage chute.

Thompson had started interviewing the neighbors. It took them a couple of hours to canvas the rest of the building and the two adjacent ones. Most of the tenants were home. Somebody thought they saw a white van parked at the back of the lot. A dark haired guy had run to it then squealed rubber exiting the parking lot. No, the tenant didn't get the license number.

At least, if it *was* their guy, they had narrowed down the color of his van.

By ten-thirty they were winding down their initial investigation. The few tenants who weren't home would be questioned tomorrow.

"Hey, Boss," Wilson asked, "Do you remember where we saw a white van recently?"

Rosko furrowed for a few seconds, then snorted. "Well, I'll be damned. Lenny's Garage where our friend Finnian works."

"Right. Maybe I'll take a run by on my way home and see if it's there."

Sue offered to stay the night, but Claire refused. Her natural independence had returned. Police protection had been promised for the night. And, if she needed more help, she could pound on the wall for Annie Oakley. She smiled at the hidden talents of her next-door neighbor.

Rosko volunteered to cover for tonight. He chose to ignore his partner's raised eyebrows and Sue's quickly concealed smirk. Claire didn't protest.

Sue had driven over with Rosko. Wilson offered to drive her home. From the front door, he called to Rosko. "Boss, can I have a word?"

"Sure." Rosko followed him to the hallway. "What's up?"

"Just a gentle reminder. Make sure you don't get so involved that you forget your job. You know the rules. If the chief finds out that you're involved with a witness...But she is one hell of a look-er."

Rosko shook his head. Wilson was right. He should stay away from Claire. He didn't want to get involved with anyone, especially a witness. But it was too late for that.

CHAPTER 57

The apartment was warm yet Claire felt chilled to the bone. Now with everyone gone, she huddled on the sofa, her arms wrapped around her body. Tears ran down her face. She rocked back and forth. What was going on? Was this a series of unrelated events? Or was the killer after her? She couldn't take anymore.

Rosko came back from the door and, putting his hand on her shoulder, he squeezed gently. "You want coffee?"

Claire shook her head. He reached out and wiped her tears away. The gentleness of his touch made the tears flow faster. She found herself being pulled into his arms. Sobs racked her body. His arms tightened.

Finally cried out, and feeling foolish for her lack of control, she tried to move away but he drew her back against him and rocked her gently. Claire felt the roughness of his suit jacket against her cheek. No passion, no heated awareness this time, just a golden sanctuary. She stayed still for a long time, letting peace enfold her, letting it heal her. Finally, she raised her head. "I should let you go and get some sleep."

He stroked her hair back from her face. "I'm okay. You feeling better?"

She nodded. "Thank you for being here."

"Sometimes we just need a good release."

Only the soft hush of their breathing disturbed the silence. Claire relaxed against him. It wasn't long before her eye closed and she fell into a deep, exhausted sleep.

She woke to find the room in semi-darkness. Her hair was plastered to her face and her blouse soaked in sweat. What had woken her? The twist of a doorknob, the glass breaking, the tread of a footstep? She dared not move in case she missed any sounds of an intruder.

But the apartment was silent. Rosko slept, his arms encircling her. Claire laid her hand on his chest and felt its rhythmic rise and fall, and beneath, the beating of his heart. It was solid and regular and symbolized peace and safety. It was forever since she'd felt this way. Claire lay quietly, content to lie peacefully and let the night pass. She sighed deeply, drawing his scent deep into the core of her being.

Rosko startled, shifted his weight, then drew her back against him. His eyes opened, lazy with sleep. Claire met his gaze and smiled. His intense blue eyes radiated warmth, protection, and the hint of something more. Something she desperately wanted, but something that scared the hell out of her. She tried to look away, but his gaze held hers. The corners of his lips turned up in a tender smile. He had a vitality that drew her like a magnet and she couldn't prevent the responding smile that played at her mouth.

In the last few days she'd learned how vulnerable she was and that he was a man she could trust. Claire knew she should pull away, but she felt so safe in his arms. His gaze traveled over her face, pausing at her lips. A current tingled down her spine. His eyes questioned. The hairs on the back of her neck stood up and her heart accelerated. Before she knew what she was doing, her body arched toward his. The kiss was long, his arms tightened around her. His kiss became more intense. He pulled her even closer. Claire could hardly breathe. She didn't protest when he stood, drew her into his arms and led her to the bedroom.

☙❧

His arm cramped but he didn't want to move and wake her. He stroked the auburn hair spread across his shoulder. He wanted to stroke the head that rested on his shoulder then let it travel along the sensuous curves of her naked body. Instead, he let her sleep. There would be time enough for that in the future. Now, she needed rest.

It was early morning when she woke. She startled, but he held her gently and she relaxed. He smiled down at her, touching the base of her chin with his fingertips. "Feeling better?"

She nodded.

"I have to head to the office. We collected a few cigarette butts from behind the building. Maybe we'll get something from them."

Dressing quickly, he resisted the overwhelming urge to be inside her again. He leaned down and kissed her, long, intense, controlled. She slid out of the bed, wrapped the sheet around her still naked body. They walked silently to the door. As Rosko pulled it open, he said, "Make sure you lock up after I go. If you need me, don't hesitate to call. When you're ready to go to work, an officer will escort you."

"Okay."

Rosko's lips brushed hers. "I'll call you later."

Claire held on to the edge of the door as he went through it. Standing on the threshold, he realized how reluctant he was to leave. A sudden impulse overtook him. He leaned towards her and pressed his lips to hers then just as quickly pulled away. She gave him a smile that almost melted his resolve to leave, then grinned, and shut the door on him. He heard her turn the newly installed deadbolt and insert the chain in the second lock.

A mix of emotions raced through him as he went to speak to the officer due to take over his watch.

CHAPTER 58

Rosko was back at the office. He tried to concentrate on the files in front of him, but when he looked at the black and white glossy photos, he kept seeing another face, Claire's. Was that their killer who'd broken into her apartment? She did fit the profile, but the man had known her name. Was the killer someone from the hospital? He thought of the times they'd spent together and his growing feelings for her. Now he had even more reason to catch the bastard. He checked with Wilson about the white van.

"It was parked outside Lenny's parking lot. The engine was cold when I got there and the shop all locked up. I'll take a better look at it this morning and if I see anything suspicious I'll get a warrant and have Chao examine it with a fine-tooth-comb. I'll visit our friend there and see what he was up to last night."

"Sounds good," Rosko agreed. "I'll leave that to you then."

Rosko called Myers for an update. "How's the list of people with medical training coming?"

"Just got a report from the last one a few minutes ago. The medical school didn't think it was much of a priority. I threatened them with a warrant. That made them move. I also did a search for people with kidney disease who need transplants."

"How did that go?" Rosko asked.

"Well," Myers said. "Interesting. Years ago, many patients on the transplant list died before they got a kidney. And the ones who got a transplant often died of post-operative complications. Thankfully surgery has improved and the new anti-rejection drugs have reduced the number of deaths."

"Are you getting to a point, Myers?"

"I'm getting there."

"Well it would be nice if you did it sometime today."

Rosko was glad he'd assigned Myers to the gritty details of paper work. The man was a perfectionist and a computer whiz. When other guys complained about sitting in front of a monitor, Myers was in his element. His private life seemed to be improving and he'd lain off the sauce.

Myers continued. "I compared the names of anyone who died of kidney failure or after a transplant in the last twenty years, and then cross referenced anyone who had applied to medical schools."

"And." Rosko waved his hands in an attempt to speed up Myers' dissertation.

"There was a name that matched both lists. Powalski."

Rosko's forehead wrinkled. Why did that name ring a bell?

"I'm running a check on all Powalskis in the area," Myers said.

"Let me know as soon as you get something."

"Sure, Boss."

⁂

Wilson had the Crime Scene Unit going over Lenny's white van. Lenny was livid, claiming the van never left the parking lot last night. Finnian had an alibi and denied having keys for the van. Did Wilson believe him? No way. He'd wait for Chao's report. Maybe they could pick up Finnian and apply some gentle persuasion. Wilson wanted any excuse to get a search warrant for his apartment. So far his alibis checked out. They didn't have enough grounds, yet.

Myers was back within the hour. "Hey, Boss, got something interesting." He had a wide smirk plastered across his face. "There's several Powalski's in the Strathburn area, two couples in their seventies, another couple in their early thirties with four kids. Then there's a Jefferson and a Martin on the list," Myers said. They're both in their late twenties, single and live alone."

"That would put them in the FBI profile of the killer. Have you checked them out?"

"I've got a preliminary report. Martin lives on Maple Ave. Jefferson lives on Gerrard Street."

"That's near Victoria Park isn't it?"

"Just around the corner."

"Jefferson Powalski. That name rings a bell," Rosko said. "I think Wilson and I interviewed him. I'll check my notes."

"I've got a search going on the computer. Soon as their stats come up, I'll let you know.

Not fifteen minutes later Myers returned grinning and waving a piece of paper. "You're going to like this."

"It's about damn time I got some good news."

Myers let the report float onto the desk. Rosko lunged for it as it veered towards the floor. The paper crunched loudly as his fist closed around it. Laying it on top of his desk, he smoothed out the edges.

Now he smiled. "Let's tell the boys what you got."

Rosko leapt out of his chair and shouted over the clamor of voices. The hum of conversation ceased suddenly, replaced by a silence that hung like a pall of smoke. Everyone turned to look at Rosko.

Waving the report in the air, he swung his chair away from the desk and sat down dramatically. "Well, boys, I think we've finally got something." Enjoying his rapt audience, Rosko leaned back until the front of the chair lifted off the ground and folded his hands behind his head. A wide grin spread across his face.

"Okay, Rosko, what have you got?" Wilson asked.

"Weeellll." He drew out the word. "You know how Myers ran a search on patients with kidney transplants, and their families, blood types, ages, success of transplant, all sorts of parameters?" He nodded to his own question. "It looks like he finally got something."

"Give us the shit or I'll knock that damn smirk off your face," Wilson said. He raised his fist in mock threat.

Rosko let the chair drop to the floor with a loud thud. His expression challenged Wilson to make good his promise, but he couldn't keep the news to himself any longer. "Martha Powalski had polycystic kidney disease as a child. After she delivered a baby she developed kidney failure. She went on dialysis and stayed on it from 1978 to 1986. She was A positive. Her husband was B positive and not a match for a transplant. Neither was any of her family. So Martha went on the transplant list. Then, in June of 1986, they found a match and she got a donor kidney.

"Apparently she did well at first. But things were a lot riskier back then and she developed complications from the surgery, pneumonia and a blood clot. Then, she started rejecting the kidney. She remained in hospital for several months and had to go back on dialysis."

Rosko paused to make sure he still had their attention. "Her child was nine at the time. A boy named Jefferson. That would make him late twenties right now and if you do the equation, he's probably AB positive." He saw the wheels turning and let the information sink in. Were all of them thinking along the same vein?

Myers spoke first. "So if he's AB positive, he could be our killer."

"Right," Rosko said. "Sounds like he's got some weird idea of revenge. Taking women's kidneys and letting the women die like his mother did."

There was a brief silence.

"Sicko." Wilson shook his head. "Do you have anything else on him?"

"Guess what his father did for a living?" Rosko raised his eyebrows and waited.

"Okay, boss, enough with the dramatics, just goddamn tell us. What did the father do?"

Rosko let a chuckle explode into the room. "He was a butcher. A goddamn butcher!"

"And what about the son. What's his name? Jefferson. What does he do for a living?"

"Well, funny thing," Rosko added. "He's a butcher, too."

"Well, well. I'll be a monkey's uncle," Wilson said. "Would that be the guy in the meat market over on Gerrard Street?"

Rosko looked down at the report.

Jefferson Davis Powalski, born June 13, 1977,
Strathburn; Occupation: butcher
Address: 133 Gerrard Street, Strathburn

"Sounds like it." He leaned back in the chair and rocked it. "Myers did another search for medical schools. A Powalski's name came up as an applicant, but he didn't make the cut. Could be the same guy. Myers's still got searches running."

A secretary came into the room and handed Myers a piece of paper. "I just love the computer age." He smiled wickedly. "Hot off the fax."

"What the hell have you got, Myers?" Wilson demanded.

"Jefferson Davies Powalski, no criminal record, owner of Powalski Meat Market."

"Shit." Wilson exclaimed. "But how did he learn about this stuff? It's not like he has any medical training."

Rosko shrugged. "I'm sure as a butcher he's learned a lot about anatomy. Animals and humans aren't so different. And he was probably pretty keen on learning that stuff if he applied to medical school. I bet he did research on the internet about drugs."

Myers' brow wrinkled in thought. "Remember how the FBI profiler said a serial killer often begins by killing animals?" There were a few confirming nods in the room. "Well, I bet this guy got his jollies helping his father cut up animals. His dad probably thought he was a real keener, wanting to learn the business."

"But we still don't know where he's getting the drugs," Wilson stated. "Nobody admits to missing any ketamine."

Rosko thought about his conversation with Claire about the missing Ketamine and her question about her intruder working at the hospital. "I might have an idea on that score." He let the chair crash to the floor. "Let's pay Powalski another visit."

CHAPTER 59

Talk about getting a gift horse. All their work that had come to nothing and now out of the blue here was their "subject of interest" thrown into their hands. Before they'd had a chance to check Powalski out, here he was sitting in their interrogation room, thanks to Simon Wyshinski at Grace Memorial Hospital. The old guy had figured out Powalski was impersonating a hospital cleaner and had called the police. Wilson and Rosko watched through the one-way glass as their suspect fidgeted. Although the butcher was tall, his build reminded Rosko of a wrestler. He would definitely be strong enough to carry a body a good distance. His brown hair was short, its ends curling at the nape of his neck. It was clean, not shining, but obviously he took time with his grooming. His T-shirt was tucked into dress-casual khakis.

What had Gerald Herd said? A loner, careful, organized, intelligent, meticulous, a planner. Did Powalski fit the profile? There was nothing remarkable about him, but then, that was the problem. Serial killers didn't wear nametags.

Rosko looked at Powalski's runners. Reeboks, not new, yet not badly worn either. He tried to place the size. Could it be eleven? Wilson went in to interview him while Rosko watched through the one-way glass.

"Tell me where you were last Tuesday evening?" Wilson asked.

"I was working in my shop."

"Did anyone see you there?"

"No. I work alone."

"What were you doing at the hospital?"

"Nothing."

"Any reason you were wearing a cleaner's uniform?"

"It was a dare. Just a dare to see if anybody would notice."

"Who dared you?"

"Just one of my buddies."

"Does this buddy have a name?"

"Jonathan. Jonathan Delaware." Powalski peered out of the corner of his eye as if checking to see if they believed him.

Rosko snorted. Did Powalski pick Delaware because the man never came down from a high long enough to remember what he'd said that morning, let alone a few days ago?

"Will he testify to that?"

Powalski grinned. "Sure he will." His eyes dared them to question him. He knew how far they'd get.

Wilson paused before posing the next question. "Have you ever taken any drugs while you were at the hospital?"

Powalski shrugged nonchalantly. "Yeah."

Rosko leaned forward. Was he going to confess? After all their weeks of searching, was it going to be this easy?

"What did you take?"

"Well a few weeks ago I took some Aspirin for a headache?"

Rosko shook his head. This guy was either very stupid or very smart. Underneath the calm demeanor, Rosko suspected an extremely cunning mind.

"Then there was the time I was on Tylenol with Codeine. Pulled some muscles in my back."

Wilson pounded the table with his fist. "No, you ass. Did you ever steal any drugs from the hospital?"

"No. Somebody say I did?"

"There have been reports of some drugs missing lately. But you might already know about that?" Wilson raised one eyebrow. "Do you want to tell me about it?"

He shrugged. "I don't know anything about missing drugs."

Wilson leaned across the table. Powalski didn't even flinch when the detective's face came within inches of his own. "Are you sure?"

"That's what I said, isn't it."

What type of man were they dealing with? Rosko himself had involuntarily jumped at Wilson's quick movement, but Powalski hadn't even blinked. Did he have nerves of steel? Was that from years of living with an abusive parent? Maybe they should look into the relationship between the father and the son—a son growing up with no mother to soften the blows of an abusive father. That could do it.

If this was their killer, how the hell were they going to prove it? They couldn't hold him much longer without concrete evidence. The hospital might charge him for impersonating an employee but that wouldn't get him a jail cell. At least the interrogation was giving forensics time to look over his van.

They'd better be careful. If the guys found anything in a search that wasn't on the up and up, it wouldn't stand up in court. The DA's office would toss it out the window faster than it took for the ink to dry on an arrest warrant. It wouldn't matter that it linked this creep to the murders and got him off the street before he killed somebody else. No, he had "rights" and God forbid they be violated to save some innocent woman. Rosko's hands clenched at the challenge to his sense of justice.

Wilson leaned back in his chair, his foot tapping the floor. His fingers tapped out the same rhythm on the scarred wooden tabletop. He waited a minute before speaking. "Are you sure you don't have anything to tell me?"

Powalski's gaze met Wilson's. "Nope."

"Do you think the hospital might have something to say if I call them? They might want to charge you with trespassing and theft." Wilson leaned farther back, stretching one hand towards the phone on the wall behind him.

Only then did a flicker of emotion show in Powalski's pale fish eyes. It was gone before Rosko could identify whether it was fear, or irritation.

"Well," Powalski said. "I did hear that some drugs were missing out of the emergency room. But they leave those drugs lying around all the time. Anybody could walk in and help themselves. Not very smart if you ask me."

Wilson smiled broadly. "Well, I am asking you, Powalski. Did you take any drugs from the hospital?

"Like I said before. No!" Powalski crossed his arms and rocked on the back legs of the chair. The two men stared at each other, Wilson tired of the game first.

The legs of Powalski's chair thudded onto the tile floor and he leaned forward. "Well detective, if you don't have any more questions, I'd like to go home. Or do I need to make a call to my lawyer?"

"We'll be taking you home shortly," Wilson said. "No need to call a lawyer. I just have to go check with my partner to see if he has any more questions. I'll be back in a few minutes."

"So I've got to sit here and wait?"

"Afraid so, buddy."

"I need to take a piss, real bad. And if it's going to be long, I want a smoke. Know I should quit, especially with all the laws banning smoking in public buildings like this one, but you know…"

"I'll see what I can do." Wilson told him. "Oh, something else. Your father was a butcher, too?"

"Yeah. Why?"

"How did you get along with him?"

"What the fuck does that have to do with anything?"

"Just wondered," Wilson shrugged. "I'll get someone to take you to the can right away."

Wilson crossed to the door. When he looked back, Powalski was still grinning, but he thought he saw the glisten of sweat on his forehead. Maybe he'd better have somebody take him to the can. Nobody liked cleaning up accidents.

Rosko led the way back to the office. Wilson asked Myers to take Powalski to the washroom and then let him have a smoke in the inner courtyard.

"Well, Rosko, what do you think? Is he our man?" Wilson asked.

"Could be. He's smart, controlled. He didn't crack until you asked about his father, now that made him sweat. Think he has a thing about male authority figures?"

"Sounds like his father was abusive. Who knows what emotional scars he has in his psyche."

"Let's hope he goes out for his smoke. What size shoe do you think he wears?"

"Probably eleven or twelve."

"That's what I was thinking. I hope the ground isn't too dry. Maybe we can get a footprint. Did you ask Myers to note where he throws his cigarette butts?"

"Sure did," Wilson said. "That smoke he's so desperate for may end up being his kiss of death."

"Not if we can't get more on him, it won't."

Wilson booted up his computer. When the screen lit up, he began a two-finger type. He looked up at his partner, "How long do you think we should make him sweat it?"

"Let me call Chao and see how much longer he needs with the van."

⊱⊰

It was disappointing news. The van was fairly new, and Powalski kept it clean. Chao found minute traces of blood splattered on the back rubber matting. The bad news, it wasn't human. The only blood was of a bovine variety. He lifted some fingerprints just in case they found something else on him. He'd compare them with the ones they had for the killer. Maybe they'd match.

The good news was the rubber mat had the same type of tread as the marks on the backs of the victims. The bad news was that it was the same tread as thousands of other van mats. Chao took a cast of the tire tracks. They didn't match.

After returning Powalski to the interrogation room, Myers went back to the courtyard. He bagged a still warm cigarette butt and sent it to the lab. He also put a marker and a do not disturb sign around a footprint in the sand surrounding the tall metal ashtray.

CHAPTER 60

Chao cast the print. It matched the partial footprint from the murder scene. Powalski wore the same size and type of runner as the killer. But it wasn't enough. They were still waiting for the DNA match of the cigarette butt. Fingerprints lifted from his coffee cup were running through AFIS.

Thompson reported for duty. He asked Rosko, "Can we set up surveillance on him?"

"Yeah. But I don't want to scare him off. If he knows we're on to him, he might run. We'll put him under surveillance for a couple of days and see if we get anything back from the lab or AFIS. You and Wilson organize it."

Within thirty minutes Thompson pulled the surveillance van out of the parking lot and headed for Gerrard Street. Wilson and Rosko followed. There was a second and third floor above Powalski's Meat Market, each had two apartments. Powalski occupied one on the second floor. He'd parked his van in front of his shop.

Rosko indicated a spot more than halfway down the block. Thompson maneuvered the van between a Toyota and a Mustang and set up the long-range camera and infrared lights. Wilson took a discreet walk around the block. A narrow alley provided access to the stores. Some of the stores extended back to the paved lane while others had small garages. Powalski's had a garage.

Wilson peered through the dust-coated window of Powalski's garage. He made out shadows of furniture, a workbench, and cardboard boxes stacked by one wall. There was no room for a vehicle inside and only a small space on the outside. If Powalski parked back here, there'd be no room to turn around. He glanced up at Powalski's apartment. A light shone in one of the rooms he assumed to be a bedroom.

Wilson headed back to the van, Rosko had little to report. The closed sign had been put up in the shop window. Powalski hadn't left. His van remained parked in front of the building. Rosko got out the coffee and sandwiches. Wilson declined coffee but devoured a sandwich before settling himself into one of the van's reclining seats and closing his eyes. Years of working surveillance had taught him to sleep whenever he could. Thompson took the first shift monitoring the video cameras in the back of the van. It was a long evening. The lights remained on in Powalski's apartment and the van remained parked.

At eleven, Phil Myers stuck his head in through the back door of the van. "Anything?"

"Nothing. Bet he's up there glued to the news to see if he's on it. He probably knows we're here," said Rosko.

"Why don't you go home?" Myers said. "Thompson and I'll cover for the night." He winked at Thompson. "This will give you good training for when you move up to detective." He turned to Rosko. "We've got to get him sprung from that asshole Sergeant Jenkins. Matt's been doing a good job with our investigation. Maybe we can make his temporary assignment permanent?"

Rosko shook his head. "Let me see what I can do. You have been a great help on this case, Thompson, but no promises."

"Thanks, sir. I'd love to work with your team."

Rosko patted him on the back.

A television in the back of the van was tuned to the eleven o'clock news. As the anchor signed off for the night, they saw the lights go out in Powalski's apartment.

"Let's get the hell out of here and leave it to these guys," Wilson said to Rosko. "I've got a gorgeous redhead waiting for me. Myers and Thompson can handle this just fine."

Much as Rosko hated to admit it, Wilson was right. They didn't need all four of them watching a dark apartment. He wondered if he could drop by the hospital. Claire was on the night shift. Did he really want her theory on Powalski as their killer, or did he just want an excuse to see her? His car seemed to swing up to the Emergency Department of Grace Memorial Hospital of its own accord.

He didn't have long to wait before Claire was able to take a short break. They headed across the street to the all-night diner. The street was dark except for the sulfurous glow of an occasional streetlamp. Several feet ahead of the bright lights of the restaurant Rosko pulled Claire into his arms and before she could object, his lips found hers. He knew from her response his kiss was not unwelcome.

Hand in hand they entered the restaurant and found a quiet table. The aroma of freshly brewed coffee filled the room and Rosko reconsidered his resolution to cut back. He let the waitress fill his cup before he spoke. "Claire, I want to ask you about a suspect we have."

"Sure.

"He's a butcher. Would that give him the knowledge to remove kidneys the way the killer has?"

"Well the anatomy is not exactly the same, yet close enough to be possible."

"What access would a hospital cleaner have to drugs?"

Claire was shocked at the question and shook her head adamantly. "None."

Rosko said nothing but his eyebrows rose in question. He watched her intently as she considered the possibility. Her head became still and she met his gaze.

"Why?"

Rosko shrugged. "We have a suspect who's a butcher. He got caught impersonating a cleaner at the hospital."

"You think the killer's been at the hospital stealing drugs?" Claire's voice shook.

"He said he did it as a dare from a friend." Rosko shrugged. "But I don't believe him. He could have been there to steal drugs, or trying to see Mrs. Sears.

Her voice rose. "He tried to see Mrs. Sears?"

"Don't worry. Nobody has gotten near her."

Claire sank back in the booth unable to speak. A memory slowly formed. Being outside Brianne Sears's room, one of the cleaners trying to go in to mop the floor, the policeman telling him leave. She tried to recall his face, but he was one of the multitudes of nameless people who formed the support staff of the hospital. She described the incident to Rosko.

"Tell me more about the cleaners?"

"Don's our regular cleaner, but on his days off, housekeeping just sends casual workers to fill in. Sometimes I recognize them, sometimes I don't."

"Do you recall any suspicious behavior? You did say ketamine was missing on more than one occasion."

Claire's eyebrows drew together as her mind worked. "One night, I found one of the substitutes cleaning the anesthetic cart. It's not his job. The nurses do that. The cart has a lot of drugs on it. I reported him. His boss said he'd talk to him, and that he wouldn't say who the complaint came from. But you know about that."

"Did you hear back from him?"

"Yeah. He said he questioned the cleaner assigned to the department that night and he denied ever being near the anesthetic cart."

"Maybe he didn't question the right guy," Rosko said.

"What do you mean?"

"I think the guy you saw wasn't the one assigned to be working there."

Claire stared at him. "You think it was the killer?"

"Do you remember what he looked like?"

Her head shook slowly. "Tall, brown hair, nothing remarkable. I told him it wasn't his job to clean the cart. He just smirked and left."

"Had you seen him before, or since?'

He watched the wrinkles on her forehead deepen. "It might have been him trying to go in Mrs. Sears's room. And I think I saw him a couple of days ago. In fact, if it was the same guy, he was friendly, using my first name." Her fingers combed nervously through the auburn ends of her ponytail. "I remember feeling uncomfortable with the way he looked at me."

"Well, I don't say I blame him for watching you. You are a pretty good-looking woman."

Claire's cheeks flushed. Did it have something to do with the twinkle in his eyes, or the night they'd spent together? He tried to keep his mind on the case. "Do you think it could have been him in the van, or at your apartment?'

Her eyes widened. "Do you really think it was the cleaner?"

Rosko wondered how much he could or should tell her. He didn't want to scare her, but she needed to be cautious. He reached across the table and took her hands. His eyes had lost their twinkle. "Claire, you stock ketamine on that anesthetic cart, don't you?"

It took a second for her to catch the meaning of his words. He saw realization dawn only to be replaced by terror. He tightened his grip as she tried to jerk away physically and mentally. He pictured the thoughts running rampant through her brain.

"I want you to be very careful until we catch this bastard."

Rosko kept his arm around Claire when he walked her back to the hospital. Despite the warmth of the August evening, he felt the spasmodic shivers that plagued her body. Apparently his reassurance that the suspect was under twenty-four-hour surveillance didn't help.

The emergency room had filled up in the short time they'd been gone. He saw Claire's posture change as she picked a chart from the rack and went to access the patient. She'd slipped back into her roll as physician and thrust the one of victim into some dark closet.

CHAPTER 61

Have we got enough evidence for a search warrant?" Wilson asked.

"Not yet. Keep digging. I want this bastard. How's the surveillance going?"

"Powalski opened up the shop. Looks like business as usual."

Myers walked into the office. "I've got something you guys are going to like. You know the search we did on Lenny's van?"

Rosko nodded.

"Well, my computer kept working, and guess what?"

"I'm not in the mood for games, Myers."

"This game you'll like. Young Powalski sold his dad's van, a 1992 white Ford, to Lenny."

"Bloody hell," Rosko exclaimed. "He probably kept a set of keys. Just takes it off Lenny's parking lot whenever he wants."

"Crafty son of a bitch," Wilson said.

"That gives us enough for a warrant. Maybe only for the van, but for now, that will do." Rosko picked up the phone and called the D.A. He was beaming when he dropped the phone back into its cradle. "Let's go pick up the paperwork."

&∽&∽&

Lenny exhibited his usual joyful expression as Rosko and Wilson walked through the raised garage doors. He reined in the flow of expletives and tossed them the keys. "It's over there. But this is it. I'm calling my lawyer. I'm trying to run a clean business. I've had enough of your harassment. I'm losing business." Lenny pressed a number. Obviously his lawyer's number was on speed dial. Rosko wondered how often he needed to use it.

Chao started on the van. He dusted the cab with a feather duster lifting several sets of prints, some clear, others smudged. He left nothing unturned, sending even the smudged ones for partials. All of them would be run through AFIS. He lived up to his reputation of being a meticulous mother hen. Despite the ribbings he got, Chao knew he was the one the cops turned to when they needed to lock down a difficult case.

He bagged and labeled the overt evidence of garbage, hair fibers, cigarette butts, and papers. Then he sprayed the interior of the van with luminal. The carpet lining the back of the van turned blue in several places. Some of the stains were older than others. He took several fibers from each site and bagged them separately. A technician rushed them to the lab to determine if they were human or bovine. Next Chao ran an infrared light over the entire area, searching for more prints. He found the first one on the inside edge of the back door frame. The second was by the back window. He lifted both.

Shutting the back door, he put on a pair of thick goggles and shone an ultra-violet light over the dark interior and waited for the fluorescence process. Within seconds the blue light exposed several hairs and fibers previously invisible to the naked eye. He bagged each one. At the laboratory, he'd see which ones had a legitimate reason for being in the van and which ones didn't.

The ultra-violet light exposed more stains on the carpet, body fluids. Chao took more fibers from the stained area. The lab would be able to analyze them as human or animal. With his gloves, he smoothed out the carpet. In case the killer decided to use the van again, he wanted no trace that he'd ever been here.

Chao delivered the rest of the specimens to various departments of the Crime Scene Unit Laboratory. The fingerprints he scanned into the computer then imported them into the Automated Fingerprint Identification System. He grabbed a coffee and waited while the computer hummed away.

The computer screen flashed. He slid the cursor to the print icon. The ink was still wet when he dialed the phone.

"Rosko here."

"You owe me a coffee," Chao said.

"If you got something good, I'll buy you lunch."

"You're on."

"So what do I get?" Rosko asked.

"How about a fingerprint match?"

"What's the name?"

"It belongs to one Jefferson Davies Powalski."

Rosko's balloon deflated. "But we knew his prints would be there. He sold the van to Lenny after his father died."

"But they shouldn't be on the new steering wheel cover," Chao said triumphantly. "And they shouldn't match prints from the crime scene."

"Well, damn." A wide grin split Rosko's face. Things were starting to fall into place. Finally the puzzle pieces were fitting together. Rosko felt his excitement rise. He cautioned himself—it was early yet. He needed to get the warrant extended to cover Powalski's home and business. Rosko picked up the phone.

Within the hour, the district attorney had a search warrant granting access to Powalski's building. It included the butcher shop, his apartment, and the basement. If they found anything, they could dig deeper. The plan was to bring Powalski in for questioning again. While he was at the station, they'd search his apartment.

Surveillance continued. Powalski hadn't left the building since he closed the shop the previous afternoon. The killer was used to being in control. How would he act when he was the vulnerable one? Rosko took two units for backup and advised the men to exert extreme caution. They donned Kevlar vests and notified the S.W.A.T. just in case things went bad.

Wilson parked down the street from the butcher shop, the other units parked close by. Rosko checked with surveillance. Powalski had been in the shop as usual that morning. At noon he put the closed sign in the window, presumably closing for lunch, and went out in his van. So far he hadn't returned. Myers was following in an unmarked cruiser. Rosko sent two officers to the back alley in case Powalski returned that way. Two other officers joined Wilson and Rosko in front of the store.

The store should be open for business by now but the "Closed" sign remained in the window and the inside of the shop in shadows. Rosko glanced at his watch, one-fifteen. A call came in from Myers. He'd lost him. Where was he? Had he slipped back into the building? Rosko had checked with city planning and knew the building had been converted into four apartments in the early 1930s. Jefferson Powalski still lived in the one his parents had moved into when they bought the building and opened the store. The other three were rented. The basement ran the length of the building. It housed the furnace, a laundry area, and storage cells. An old coal cellar was closed off years ago when the furnace was replaced. They would check the basement later.

Releasing the leather strap securing his service revolver, Rosko headed toward the building. A door to the right of the store led to the apartments. He directed his men towards it. With guns drawn and ready, the officers filed up the narrow staircase. It smelled of wood rot, mold, and closed spaces. Wilson thumped on Powalski's door.

Silence.

After several seconds, Wilson banged again. "Powalski, open the door."

Still no sound from inside the apartment.

"This is the police. Open the door."

They heard footsteps. Suddenly the door across the hall opened and a gray haired lady appeared.

"Ma'am, stay inside," Rosko advised.

"What's going on?" The woman asked. Her voice was sharp and she planted her size four feet in the doorway.

"Ma'am, we need you to stay inside your apartment."

"The name is Mrs. Jensen and if you're looking for Jefferson, he's not there. Came up at lunchtime and then went out. Don't know what's become of him. Ever since his dad died this spring he's been acting strange. Coming and going at all times of the night. Closing the store whenever he feels like it. His father worked hard. Never closed the store, except on Sunday. Scrimped and saved his money. That boy's just being more irresponsible all the time. The shop should be open now, and where is he? I need to get meat for my supper." She peered at the detectives over her half glasses. "What trouble has that boy got himself into?"

"We just want to talk to him," Rosko said.

"Well he isn't home."

"Just go back into your apartment ma'am."

She stood her ground, assessing each officer in turn.

"Ma'am," Rosko nodded toward her apartment. "You need to go inside."

The woman muttered something as she stepped back into her apartment and swung the door closed. Rosko nodded to one of the officers to open Powalski's door. The officer was assessing the lock when Mrs. Jensen's door open again. She peaked out. "Do you boys have a warrant?"

"Yes, ma'am. We do."

"Leave the lock alone. I have the key. Jefferson doesn't know. But his mother, poor thing, gave it to me years ago. Back then Jefferson was a good kid. Between her getting sick and that father of his. Mean sort he was."

"You have the key?" Rosko asked. "It would save us from breaking the door down."

"Just a minute."

Mrs. Jensen, true to her word, returned bearing a gold colored key. Rosko hoped Powalski hadn't changed the locks. He hadn't. The key turned easily in the lock and Rosko slid the door open. They called Powalski's name. No answer.

Cautiously, the officers entered the apartment. There was the possibility Powalski was inside and refusing to answer. No one jumped out at them. Wilson shut the apartment door against Mrs. Jensen's prying eyes.

They checked each room in the apartment. It was empty. Rosko radioed the officers at the back of the building to be on the alert for Powalski's return. He sent the surveillance officers back to the van and had them put an APB out on Powalski. While he and Wilson searched the apartment, he had the two other officers search the basement.

The decor in the apartment dated back to the early seventies, brown and gold with big flowers, heavy wood furniture and dated green appliances. The only new item seemed to be the forty inch television perched on a cheap entertainment unit. Across from the television was a worn green vinyl recliner with a small table beside it. The table held a large ceramic ashtray overflowing with butts. Powalski had smoked the same brand at the station. Rosko placed a couple of butts into an evidence bag.

There were two bedrooms. One had an old veneered dresser set covered with a layer of dust. The yellow chenille bedspread had a long, narrow imprint. Someone had lain on it recently. A large rural landscape print hung above the bed. The smaller bedroom contained a single bed. On a desk by the window, a screen saver flashed across a seventeen-inch computer monitor. A five-drawer dresser beside the bed had dime-store toiletries on it. Rosko let his gaze wander around the room. He stopped at a framed snapshot of a young family. A man stood stiffly beside a dark-haired woman and child. From the clothing Rosko gathered it had been taken in the late seventies. Powalski with his parents? He noted the resemblance of the woman with the victims, young, attractive, brown hair.

Rosko put on gloves and began searching the room. He started with the dresser drawers then moved to the closet. Nothing here. Wilson checked the other bedroom.

The detectives met in the living room. Newspapers littered the dining room table. The Strathburn Chronicle and The Examiner, nothing out of the ordinary except that several articles had been cut out. Most of the missing pieces were from the front pages of the newspapers. Right where reports of the Kidney Slasher had been.

Rosko went into the kitchen and started opening drawers. He dumped one overflowing with papers onto the counter. Crumpled receipts, take-out menus, coupons, maps, pens scattered across the Arborite. He rifled through the objects. Opening up the city map he found circles around each of the nearby parks, parks where the bodies had been found. He flipped through the telephone book. There were more circles around some of the restaurants in the area, Bertolini's, pizza places, and Robertson Travel. He looked up Fred's Diner. There was a circle around it, too. Would Chief Richards think this enough evidence to press charges?

Rosko kept searching the room. There had to be more.

"Hey, Rosko," Wilson called. "You need to come here."

Wilson stood by the door of the bathroom. They had briefly checked the room earlier, found it empty and moved on to the rest of the apartment. Rosko raised his eyebrows. "What you got?"

Wilson pointed to the interior of the bathroom. Rosko stepped over the threshold, glanced around the room. Then he saw it. Another door, partially open. Another bedroom. The room was dimly lit, the curtains drawn against the sun. He drew his gun and pushed at the door with the toe of his shoe. He quickly surveyed the room. Someone lay in the bed, a layer of blankets covering a tiny form. Too small for Powalski. His eyes adjusted to the dimness. He tiptoed into the room. A grey-haired woman snored softly. He noticed the yellow cast to her skin, noticed the emaciated arms resting on top of the blanket, noticed the dialysis machine beside the bed. Mrs. Powalski! The Mrs. Powalski who'd had a kidney transplant years ago and then rejected the kidney. Now he could see some twisted, sick motive.

He tiptoed back out of the room. Shaking his head, he didn't speak until he'd reached the hall. "Holy crap. And we thought she'd died."

"Should we wake her, let her know we're here?"

Rosko shook his head. "Let's just check the son's bedroom. See what we find there. No sense waking her and getting her all worked up. She doesn't look like she's in great shape. I sure don't want to have her death on my hands."

They headed down the hall to the larger bedroom. Wilson had pulled several boxes off the top shelf of the closet and laid them on the bed. He pulled a manila envelope out from underneath a large photo album. With his gloved hand, he extracted several pieces of newsprint. Wilson sorted through the pages. His face lit up with a broad grin and he waved the pages. "I think we got the missing pieces from the newspapers."

"What else is in the closet?" Rosko asked.

"I've just pulled out these boxes out so far."

Rosko went to the closet and ran his hand along the floorboards. It was in the back corner behind an old suitcase that he found the loose board. He pulled a Swiss Army Knife out of his pocket and used it to pry up the board. He slid his hand into the cavity below. His fingers closed around a metal box. It was an antique, but its lock was new. He used the pliers attachment of the knife to cut the bolt. He held his breath and lifted the lid.

Folds of burgundy velvet padded the interior. Another layer of the same material was folded carefully inside. Rosko peeled back the fabric and saw the glitter of gold. A thin gold chain. Had it belonged to Mary Jane Winters?

He peeled back another layer. Several more pieces of jewelry lay in the velvet folds. He picked them out one by one. By the time he'd finished, he had an assortment of rings, watches, chains and pendants. There were several cheap rings, probably belonged to Dallas Parker, one for each of her fingers. And there was a wedding band he bet belonged to Virginia Gallingham.

His souvenirs. He probably got a perverse thrill every time he took the jewelry out and touched it. Maybe that was the only way he could satisfy himself. None of the victims had been raped.

One of the pieces was an antique gold locket on a heavy filigree chain. He examined the delicate pattern of roses embossed in the gold. Although not real gold, Rosko knew it was an expensive piece of jewelry not produced in the last twenty years. It was handcrafted and probably an heirloom passed down from mother to daughter or to the wife of the first-born son. It wasn't on the list of missing jewelry. He slid his thumbnail into the small indentation between the locket's two halves and gently pried it open.

He found himself starring at the portrait of a beautiful young woman. Brown hair hung in soft waves around a pale oval face. She wore a high-collared, long white dress trimmed with layers of lace. A wedding dress? The hairstyle and the high lace collar were dated. Not that he knew much about fashion, but Rosko would have put the style from the sixties.

The face was a younger version of the woman in the snapshot by Powalski's bed. It also vaguely resembled each woman who'd been attacked. He tried to deny any resemblance to Claire.

He placed each piece of jewelry into separate specimen bags. The fingerprint lab should be able to get something off at least one of them. He hoped their suspect had enjoyed fondling the jewelry without the confines of rubber gloves. Once they caught him, they had to be able to hold him.

They left the apartment in the same state they'd found it, its lone occupant still sleeping and unaware of their visit. Within minutes Jefferson Powalski's description was in the hands of every policeman in the city and surrounding areas.

CHAPTER 62

Claire shifted her weight. Her eyelids felt heavy, and her mind foggy. The mattress beneath her, lumpy and uncomfortable. She lifted her head. She saw nothing in the dark, damp space. The mustiness mixed with other odors, ones that were vaguely familiar yet the haze encasing her mind made it difficult to separate them.

This grogginess reminded her of a time she'd taken Ativan to help her sleep after working a string of night shifts. Had she taken it again? She couldn't remember. The fog engulfing her was too dense to allow clear thinking. Slowly memories of leaving the hospital drifted back. She'd walked to her car, heard her name called. Someone grabbed her. A cloth was shoved over her face. A sickening sweet smell. Her lips burned and then she was spinning down a long black tunnel.

Claire tried to turn. She couldn't. Something stopped her. She struggled. Her arms and legs would barely budge. Terror seized her and her heart rate took off till it hammered in her chest. She was bound! She yanked her arms. Thin bands cut through her wrists. She kicked wildly and pain assaulted her ankles. Perspiration beaded her forehead. She twisted from side to side. The bands cut deeper. Warm sticky fluid oozed from her wounds. Her blood.

Her head pounded. She closed her eyes and waited. It took several minutes for the pain to recede. With her eyes closed, Claire's other senses began to work. Over the damp mustiness she recognized the distinct scents of disinfectant, sulfur, and perspiration.

Her sweat or...

Was someone here? She concentrated, listening to the silence. Then she heard a sound. A thud. Was it a footstep? Another thud. Someone was coming this way.

Claire twisted her head toward the sound. The mattress shifted. Her body tipped sideways. Someone called her name. She'd heard that voice before, in her apartment, at the hospital. The floor cleaner. She blinked as a harsh light illuminated the room. When she opened her eyes again, she saw a face and a pair of pale blue eyes, flat and lifeless as a shark.

"So." The voice whispered. "The brilliant Dr. Claire Valincourt is finally awake."

His words dried up every bead of sweat on her forehead. Fear obliterated her pain and her heart rate slowed to a lethal level. She arched her body as far away from him as she could. "Who are you?"

"Don't you recognize me, Claire.?"

She stared. The brown hair, the angular face, the blue eyes. There was something familiar about him. The voice. Yes, it was the man at her apartment. Was he the same man impersonating a hospital employee?

"No. You wouldn't know me." His laugh was harsh.

Recognition must have shown on her face.

"You've seen me at your work and don't even recognize me."

"You don't work at the hospital," Claire challenged.

"No. But sometimes I put on a cleaner's uniform and come in and push a mop around." He snorted. "And sometimes I just help myself to a few drugs."

"You've been stealing ketamine."

He shrugged. "Got to get it somewhere."

"Where am I?"

His grin widened but it didn't change the flat affect in his eyes. "I've been watching you. Every chance I get. I follow you. I look at your schedule at work, I watch you come to work, and then follow you home. I've almost gotten you a couple of times."

She hadn't been imagining things. She'd been followed. The van careening towards her and the man in her apartment hadn't been random events. This man was behind it all. Claire thrashed her arms and legs. The bindings cut deeper. Pain seared through her body.

"Claire, don't struggle. You'll only hurt yourself."

"Why?"

"For my mother."

Claire recognized the glint of insanity flicker in his eyes. Panic hit her like a battering ram. He was crazy and she was his prisoner. She had to keep him talking until she could escape, or someone found her. Did anyone even know she was missing? Claire swallowed her fear and focused on distracting him. "For your mother?"

"She needed a kidney."

"Does she have kidney disease?"

His smile faded. "She did."

"Is she on the transplant list?"

"No." He shook his head rapidly. "No more questions." A muscle in his left cheek twitched.

"Why Mary Jane Winters?" Claire asked.

He seemed deep in thought. "The first time I saw her, I thought it was my mother. She was so like her, the same brown hair, the same small frame. Just like you."

"What about the others?"

"I had to learn to do it right. I didn't want damaged kidneys. They wouldn't be any good. So I practiced. I practiced on cattle and pigs. Their anatomy is quite similar you know."

Claire fought to keep her voice quiet despite her fear. Remaining calm might be her only way to survive. "Wasn't one kidney enough?"

"I needed to find the perfect one." He smiled down at her. "You know how important it is to have a perfect match."

Claire forced herself to smile up at him. "Yes, compatibility is extremely important."

Virginia Gallingham's jaundiced skin resembled a tan but would have looked similar to his mother's when her kidneys failed. Elevated toxins trapped in the cells caused the body to turn sallow or jaundiced. Did he know all that? She took a deep breath, "What happened with Virginia Gallingham?"

"Her. Her kidney was no good." His voice grated and Claire saw the muscles in his face twitch. "I opened her up. The kidney was small, dried up like a little black bean. It was no good at all. I got rid of her, dumped her in the park. Maybe she could have used one of the other ones."

Confused, Claire asked, "What other ones?"

"One of the other kidneys." His eyes took on a gleam that was terrifying. "I've saved them, you know, kept them on ice." He smiled. "They're just like new."

"Why?" Claire blurted out.

He sat on the mattress by her feet and smiled as if he was getting comfortable for a long visit. She cringed as his weight caused her body to tip toward him. His voice softened.

"I'm saving them for my mother."

It flowed out of him, like a purging. His words tumbling over each other, coming so fast some of them were intelligible. He talked about his mother's illness, her surgery, her hospital stay, the dispassionate nurses. His eyes gleamed with anger as he continued to rant. "Trying to take me out of her room, trying to hug me, telling me it was okay to cry. The bitches."

Then he said his father's name. His face hardened and his knuckles clenched. Claire needed to diffuse his anger before he turned it on her. "Where is your mother?"

He leapt off the bed so abruptly she had to brace herself as her body rolled back to the midline of the mattress. His cheeks flared crimson. He waved his arms and screamed, "No more. No more questions."

What now? Was her kidney to be added to his collection? She wrenched at her bindings. The scent of her blood mixed with the noxious odors of damp spaces and disinfectants as the rope ripped through her flesh.

Then that sweet smelling cloth pressed against her mouth. She tried not breathing but dizziness overcame her and she felt like a huge wave was dragging her into a dark abyss. A part of her brain heard him storm out of the room, slam the door and she wondered how long before he returned? Claire heard the metallic click of the lock turning just as the blackness swallowed her.

♥∂♥∂

It was a long time before Jefferson stopped shaking. Damn the bitch. He wanted to kill her right now but he needed more ketamine. The last full bottle had slipped out of his hands and shattered on the tile floor. The increased security at the hospital didn't help. He hadn't been able to get his hands on any more.

'You should have been more careful. Things are going wrong. You let one get away and now you don't even have enough drug to finish the job.'

Jefferson covered his ears. It didn't stop the voices. He didn't want to think about his mistakes. The voices kept taunting him.

'You clumsy fool. You broke the last bottle. Can't you hold onto anything? If you hadn't dropped the box, that teacher wouldn't have got away.'

The woman was still in the hospital. That stumped him. He still couldn't figure out why the drug hadn't worked. If he hadn't been hurrying to get more. If the box hadn't spilled. Like videotape on slow speed, he saw the box slip out of his fingers, the bottles twirl through the air, roll across the floor. He was fumbling to retrieve them, running to the shed, the empty shed. The mental movie cut to a blizzard of static. He clenched his fist and hit the closest object. The wooden doorframe splintered with the impact.

Could she identify him? He'd tried to see her. The fucking hospital. They were watching like hawks. Then that damn Wyshinski. Reporting him to the police. He knew the cops didn't believe his story. Could he risk going back for more ketamine? He just needed one more to complete his collection.

He'd used the last of his ketamine on Sherry. Jefferson smiled at the memory of her begging for her life. He'd enjoyed operating on her. It was his best prize so far. And now he would add the kidney of the beautiful Doctor Valincourt.

❧❧❧

Claire fought her way back to consciousness. Shadowy outlines slowly came into focus as her eyes adjusted to the dimness. She was in a garage, or large shed. Tall wooden cupboards stood against a far wall. A waist-high bench lined most of another wall. Centered above the bench was a two-foot high window, its wooden frame weathered to a dull grey. Sunlight strained through years of encrusted grime. The light cast an eerie quality to the assorted garden tools scattered across the bench's surface. The other wall was fifteen feet away, between it and the bed, stood a large stainless steel table. Claire shuddered at the thought of its use.

A shimmer of movement caught her attention. Claire looked up. A circular, stainless steel light hung above the bed, two feet in diameter, a heavy-duty chain secured it to a rafter ten feet above off floor. The lamp swung like a pendulum counting out the last moments of her life. Her heart slowed to match its rhythm.

A door creaked, footsteps tapped across the cement, Claire's heart quadrupled its rate. She thought she'd already reached her maximum terror point, but the smell of his sweat dispelled that theory. And his voice, his voice caused her to shudder uncontrollably.

"Hello, Claire, I'm back." His laugh grated like claws deboning a carcass. "I know you're happy to see me. But we have to wait. I need more ketamine. You don't want me to cut out your kidney without it, do you?"

Her heart beat faster, racing as if she'd just finished an intense workout at the gym. But now it had no warm-up and no cool down, just this constant accelerated pace. How much could her heart take?

He stroked her hair. "No. I didn't think so. You'll just have to wait. I'm going now. One bottle should be enough, shouldn't it, Claire?"

She nodded woodenly. Could she escape while he was gone? The damp cloth pressed over her face again. She struggled against the sweet smelling fumes.

Darkness came quickly.

CHAPTER 63

Surveillance continued on Powalski's apartment and store. He hadn't returned. Finally at three-fifteen they sighted his van heading south on Wellington Street. Was he heading home?

Rosko took the station stairs two at a time and raced to his car. Turning left onto Pine Street, he swerved around a blue Honda, hit the siren and sped through a yellow light at Dundas Street. He picked up the radio and called dispatch. "Get Wilson. Tell him where I'm heading." He pulled up behind the surveillance van, Thompson waited inside. Powalski had gone into the building.

Backup was on the way. Rosko wanted them to arrive before anyone went in. While he waited in an unmarked cruiser across from the shop, he sent Myers and Thompson to keep an eye on the back alley.

Would Powalski realize his apartment had been searched? They had been careful to leave everything in place except for the trophy box. Hopefully Powalski wouldn't go looking for it and bolt before backup arrived. Too bad they hadn't found a vial or two of ketamine. Where did he stash that?

They stationed a female officer in the neighbor's apartment. They told Mrs. Jensen she was there to watch for Powalski's return, but the officers' instructions were to keep Mrs. Jensen inside her apartment no matter what happened. They didn't want her warning Powalski of their search, or ending up in the line of fire when they arrested him.

The lights came on in the shop. It was three-thirty. Was he opening the store? Rosko waited for the "Closed" sign to be turned around. Where the hell was backup? He wanted to walk in and arrest the bastard right now. Logic and experience, his own and others, made him sit tight no matter how antsy he was. He picked up the radio. "Where backup? And where's Wilson?"

A female dispatcher reported, "Wilson's on his way. SWAT team should be there any minute."

When officers searched the basement they had discovered an old coal cellar. It had been used recently. An undercover officer, parading as homeless, guarded it. Rosko checked in with him. Nothing was happening from that quarter either.

But Rosko didn't have to worry about Powalski sneaking out the back. He'd just put the radio back into its holder when the store's front door flew open. Powalski jumped into his van, revved the engine, and screeched away from the curb. Rosko grated his car's starter and swerved onto the street after him. He ignored the horns honking in his wake. Traffic was bad and after several blocks, he lost sight of the van. Speeding down Gerrard Street, he had just crossed Dundas when he spotted Powalski's van. He eased his foot off the gas. Picking up the radio he had dispatch put him through to Wilson.

"I'm on the way. Which way's he heading?"

"We're going north on Gerrard."

"I'll cross at Main Street and head south."

"Good. I'll have dispatch keep this frequency open," Rosko said. "Thompson's behind me, but I don't want Powalski to see the cruiser. Myers is keeping up surveillance at the butcher shop in case he heads home."

Rosko concentrated on the van ahead. It was keeping to the speed limit. Obviously Powalski didn't want to attract attention. Rosko relaxed his grip on the steering wheel. A pick-up tried to pull in front of him. He pressed the gas pedal and cut it off. He couldn't afford to let anyone in, especially some souped-up truck that would obstruct his view, get between him and the van.

As he crossed Jarvis he spotted Wilson's car going through the intersection. He waved as his partner passed him, going south. In his rear view mirror he watched Wilson navigate a U-turn into the northbound traffic.

Day shifts at local factories were ending, increasing the traffic and making it difficult for Rosko to maintain a two-car spread. He saw Powalski turn west and followed. They wound through the downtown traffic making frequent stops and starts.

Leaving the radio on, Rosko kept the team updated. He hoped Powalski would stop soon. He was tired of this cat and mouse game but didn't dare pull him over in the middle of the city in case he was armed. They had enough victims one at a time without having a shoot-out and multiple people getting killed.

Another vehicle tried to pull in front. Rosko cut the car off. He hoped Powalski didn't hear the blare of the angry motorist's horn. The van was in his sights when the light turned amber. Powalski sped through it. The Honda behind him squeaked through on the tail end of it. The Volvo in front braked, Rosko screeched to a stop.

By the time the light turned green, Rosko had lost a lot of ground and the traffic wouldn't let him catch up. Ahead, Powalski made a left turn, then a quick right. He was winding through the town. Did he know he was being followed? Was this a wild goose chase?

A pickup forced its way between the two cars in front of him. The van was no longer visible. It took more than a minute before Rosko could maneuver past the car ahead, by then the van was no longer in sight. He backtracked and searched the surrounding streets.

Nothing. He'd lost him.

He picked up the radio and spoke to the dispatcher. Within seconds an all units bulletin for Powalski and his van blasted over the radio. If Powalski knew he was being followed, he might ditch his vehicle. He didn't have to wait long. Powalski's van was sighted leaving the hospital. Rosko gave the order to observe but not apprehend. He was on his way. Before he got there, the van was headed back down Gerrard Street.

"Wilson?"

"I'm here, Boss."

"Heading south. He might be going home."

"On my way."

Rosko caught sight of the van turning into the alley behind the shop. He parked his car just past the alley and got out. He watched Powalski exit the van carrying a small pouch. But instead of going into the back of the shop, Powalski headed farther down the alley. He slid through a wire fence. Where the hell was he going? Shit. I can't lose him again.

Rosko raced down the street and turned right. Lenny's white van sped past him with Powalski at the wheel.

He radioed Wilson. "He's trading vans. Son of a bitch. He just took his father's old van out of Lenny's parking lot. I don't like this. Is he planning another killing?"

"I'll be there in two minutes. Keep me posted."

Rosko jumped into his vehicle and sped after the white van. He was close behind when Powalski turned onto Gerrard Street and headed south. After a few miles Powalski put on the van's signals. Rosko radioed Wilson. "He's heading for the highway."

"Keep on his tail," said Wilson. "I'll get a roadblock arranged."

"There are too many turnoffs. We can't monitor him if he gets out of town."

Rosko stayed with him. He did fine until a transport cut in front of him. Then another one sped up beside him and blocked the other lane. He was boxed in.

He considered putting the portable siren on the car and forcing the transport trucks out of the way but that would alert Powalski. He didn't want to risk that. By the time he got free, the van was no longer in sight. The steering wheel vibrated from the direct hit it received from Rosko's fist. He sped down the highway for several miles. There was no white van visible.

Slowing the car, Rosko steered towards the shallow grass ditch separating the lanes. He heard and felt the ground scrape the undercarriage as it dipped into the valley then strained to make the incline. He gunned the engine, displacing grass and dirt. The car shot forward onto the other side of the highway. A car swerved out of his way. The driver gave him the finger. Rosko ignored it, focusing on the landscape ahead.

His right foot was to the floor as he topped the hill. He could see the road for miles ahead. Vehicles were visible in both directions. None was a white van. Rosko cursed. Hauling on the steering wheel, he turned the car toward town. It was then that he saw it, a side road branching off the highway. He floored it. Coming up to the exit, he swerved right. He had to tighten his hold on the steering wheel to keep the car on the pavement.

The road ran parallel to the highway for half a mile then turned right. Rosko followed until the pavement changed to gravel. Trees and a farmer's fields surrounded him. He slowed the car and picked up the radio. "Patch me through to Myers." When he was connected, Rosko demanded, "Have you got that computer going?"

"It's running," Myers answered.

"See if Powalski owns any other properties. Start in Alborough County."

"It's searching. By the way, there was a call for you, an old lady. She was adamant she speak to you. She's called a few times. Here's her number."

Rosko memorized the number. It wasn't familiar. He'd make the call while he waited for Myers's search. There was little chance of finding Powalski now. He punched the number into his cell phone. "Hello, this is Detective Rosko."

A shrill voice answered. "Well, about time. I've been calling you all day."

"Sorry, ma'am. What can I do for you?" He hoped his irritation didn't come through in his voice, he was concentrating on catching a serial killer, not chatting with gossipy old ladies.

"It's about Claire," said Mrs. Chegetto.

Rosko sat forward. "What about Claire?"

"Well, she didn't come home this morning."

"Maybe she's still at work."

"No, I called. She left this morning after her shift was done. But she hasn't come home."

A terrible sense of dread filled him. He tried to rationalize it away. She was still at the hospital, just not in the emergency department. Maybe she was assisting Mac with an autopsy.

"I'll see if I can find her, Mrs. Chegetto."

"You do that. And let me know as soon as you do. My old ticker can't take all this stress."

Rosko depressed the receiver and punched in the number of Grace Memorial. He wondered how much more stress his heart could take. When the switchboard answered, he asked for the emergency department. Doctor Valincourt left the hospital that morning after her shift. He asked to be transferred to Doctor MacFarlane.

Mac's cheery hello answered. "No. I haven't seen Claire for a few days. I went over to the emergency department to talk to her at seven-thirty. I just missed her. But it's odd. Her car is still in the parking lot. I can see it from my office window. I thought she was in a meeting, so I had her paged. She never answered."

Rosko rang off. Where was she? The similarities between Clare and the victims flashed in front of him. His throat felt like parchment. Did Powalski have her? Where were they? Rosko slumped into the seat. Should he stay here or head back to town? He'd never felt such helplessness. He flipped off the radio and dialed Wilson's cell. He picked up on the first ring.

"What's wrong with the radio?"

"Nothing," Rosko barked. "Listen." His voice echoed his desperation. "Claire seems to be missing. She didn't come home from work this morning. Nobody knows where she is. Mac's been paging her. She's not answering, but her car's still in the lot."

"I'll get an officer to check the hospital, and one to check her apartment. I'll call you as soon as I know something."

"Thanks, Wilson."

"We'll find her, boss."

Rosko flipped the radio back on and rolled the front window down. He got out of the car and paced. The gravel took the brunt of his frustration as it met the toe of his shoe. Finally the radio crackled.

"I found a parcel of land out by Delaware. It's five acres, has an old house and an outbuilding. It's registered to a Lillian Payne. She's in a nursing home." Myers paused. "But guess who her nephew is."

"Jefferson Powalski?"

"The one and only."

"Let's get out there. Have someone get us directions."

"I'll get a search warrant and meet you there."

"Get somebody else to get the damn warrant. He may have another victim."

With the surreal flashing of the police lamp, Rosko sped down Highbury Ave, toward the small community just south of Strathburn. He was halfway there. He should make it there in five minutes. He pressed his foot hard on the gas. Maybe three minutes.

CHAPTER 64

Claire's head felt like a hundred pound weight swathed in layers of fuzz. When she opened her eyes, pain shot up the back of her neck. This time conscious thought came quickly. She knew she was a prisoner and knew she had to escape before he returned. She struggled to get up. Nausea engulfed her. She closed her eyes and waited for it to pass. Finally, able to open her eyes, Claire peered around the room. She had to find a way out.

Against the back wall stood a metal shelving unit. Gallon-sized bottles filled its bottom shelf, quart and pint-sized bottles and various sized cans were on the shelves above. Even with her limited vision, she could see the skulls and cross bones denoting toxic contents.

It looked like an old farm shed. The odor of ammonia and formaldehyde permeated the air reminding her of the morgue. Blood and rotting flesh were present too. Her nausea returned.

Her wrists and ankles were still tied to the stainless steel bed. Claire yanked against the ties. They slashed into her skin. Blood oozed beneath the bindings. Bracing herself, Claire jerked her right arm. The nylon stretched, digging into her arm. She jerked again. The binding slid an inch along the metal rail. Her heart leapt. Could she rip the ties?

Claire focused on sliding the binding along the metal railing. It slid easily for three inches, then snagged. Was there a burr in the metal? She dragged the tie over and over the spot. Each time it caught, jumped free, then slid along the rail. Her arm tired quickly, and the searing pain in her wrist become unbearable, but Claire dragged the nylon across the same spot again and again. It felt like hours passed before she felt a slight give on the binding. Adrenaline surged and she worked with renewed vigor. There was a tearing sound and her wrist jerked free.

Claire twisted onto her side and worked at the ties on her left hand. Several knots secured the rope to the bed. Her struggling had tightened them. Her fingers tore at the tangled mess. Again it seemed forever before the knots loosened enough for her to slip her hand out. She rubbed the pain from her wrists then began on her feet. They took less time.

Struggling upright, she slipped her legs over the bed then let her legs slide to the floor. Her head swam and her legs buckled, she had to lean on the bed for several seconds.

How long before he came back? She glanced at her wrist. He'd taken her watch. She had no idea of the time or how long she'd been here.

Claire took one tentative step, and then another. The cement floor was cold on her bare feet. Where were her shoes? She still had her jeans and t-shirt on, but her running shoes were gone. She took a quick look around. They were there, just under the foot of the bed. She bent to dig them out, felt faint, and her knees buckled again. She grabbed the bed rail. Closing her eyes, she blindly dug for the shoes. One, then the other, she shoved her feet into them.

Now, for a way out.

At the far end of the shed, twenty-foot wide double sliding doors served as the major portion of the wall. A few feet away, stood another door, a single wooden door. Her heart leapt. A way out? With unsteady legs, Claire wobbled towards it. By the time she reached the door, she felt drained and had to lean on it for several seconds.

Then her flight instinct kicked in and adrenalin surged through her body. She had to get out, now. Grabbing the handle, she pulled. Her hands were soaked with sweat and lost their hold. She rubbed them on her jeans and pulled again. The door wouldn't move.

Locked.

She hobbled to the double doors. Seizing the long metal handle, she hauled on it. It moved two inches then clanged to a halt.

Claire froze. Did she hear something? Was he back? She listened for several seconds. Nothing. She tried the doors again. Something held them fast. Through a thin crack in the doors she saw the edge of something metal, a large padlock.

Her shoulders sagged. Trapped.

She fought to remain calm. Maybe she could get out a window? Would he hear the glass breaking? She glanced around the room. There were two windows. Metal bars had been attached to the exterior of both of them, so much for that idea. She surveyed the room then headed for the workbench.

Tools and hardware littered the work surface and shelves below. Her fingers shook as they rummaged through the objects. She needed a weapon. Grime on the window blocked light and created shadows making the search difficult. Her hand hit something hard. It clunked to the floor.

In the silence of the shed, the sound was deafening. Did he hear it? She inched her way along the workbench and peered out the closest window. Through the dirt she made out the back of an old farmhouse and a driveway. The driveway was empty. Claire sighed. He wasn't back yet.

She backtracked, searching the floor for the fallen object. Her foot found it. She bent to check it out. It was a screwdriver. Its heaviness gave her a sense of comfort. She ran her fingertip along its thick metal shaft. It was over a foot long. Her finger grazed against the sharp tip where a shard had broken off. Claire slid the metal shaft through a loop in her jeans. This was a start. What else could she find?

There were several power tools, saws, drills, but they were useless as weapons. At the end of the workbench, Claire found an assortment of garden tools leaning against the wall. She dug out a long handled shovel and leaned it against the bench. Then she pulled out a long handled three-tined rake. Its ends were razor sharp. She stood it beside the shovel.

The shelving unit was next. It contained bottles and cans, fertilizers and pesticides. The gallon containers on the bottom shelf would be too heavy to manage. Claire focused on the smaller containers on the higher shelves. She tried to read the labels. The shed was too dark. One by one Claire held them up to the window. The chemical names were long and parts of the words worn off. Some of the ingredients she recognized, others she didn't.

Picking up a dark brown bottle boasting a large black roach, one of the ingredients jumped out at her, Parathion. She knew about that one. It was a pesticide, extremely toxic. She'd looked after a farmer who'd accidentally spilled it on himself while spraying crops. A shudder ran through her. Carefully she put the bottle back on the shelf.

She searched through the upper shelves. Dust scattered everywhere. She needed a pair of gloves. There must be some here. She spotted them. As Claire reached for the heavy leather gloves she heard a loud rustling and froze. Her heart skipped a beat. Something rough rubbed against her fingers. Her hand recoiled. A large gray rat scurried along the back of the shelf and down behind the cupboard. Claire bolted backward. It was several seconds before she calmed enough to try again.

Her fingers trembled as she reached out and grasped the edge of the gloves. She inched them towards her. No further creatures emerged. Claire shook out the gloves, before carefully donning them. She reached for the brown bottle and placed it on the workbench.

Next to the shelving unit stood a large metal cupboard, the doors partially open. Something on one of the upper shelves caught her eye. Her breath turned to ice and lumped in her throat. There, in front of her, were several empty vials of ketamine.

She rummaged through the rest of the cupboard. Discarded needles, syringes, cotton balls, alcohol swabs, littered another shelf. There were bottles of Poviodine. Another shelf held green towels, some neatly folded, others bloody and stuffed into the space. Claire picked up one of the folded towels. One corner had the letters GMH surrounded by a woven circle, the Grace Memorial Hospital logo. She dropped the towel as if it was on fire.

He'd stolen them from the hospital.

Her terror escalated as she realized this mad man had been in her hospital, working beside her, working beside her friends, working beside her patients, a trusted employee. Would she ever be able to function without wondering if the person working beside her was friend or foe?

Stop. You don't have time for this.

She focused on the shelves. Taking a folded green towel, she wrapped it around the small brown bottle and placed it carefully into the left front pocket of her jeans. Part of the bottle protruded from the pocket. She would have to watch her step. Next she shoved a large syringe and needle into her front right pocket. What else?

A stainless steel cylinder held cleaning fluid. She tipped the container almost dropping it when she saw two scalpels soaking in the liquid. She upended the container. The gleaming blades clattered onto the counter. She couldn't leave them there. If they weren't in the cupboard, he wouldn't be able to use them against her. Taking another syringe, Claire twisted the needle off and shoved cotton balls into its base. She slipped the scalpel blades into the barrel, pushing their razor sharp points into cotton batting, then slid the syringe into her back pocket. She headed for the door.

As she passed the window, she glanced outside. It was still light, still no vehicle in the driveway. How much more time did she have?

On the opposite side of the room she saw the gleam of the long stainless steel table and the circular light above. Her breathing quickened as she thought of the table's use and the women who had been on it. Was she going to be next? She stumbled away.

The hum of an electrical appliance caught her attention. Claire turned towards the freezer. Oh, God. What did he keep in there? The kidneys? She had to see. Bracing herself, she placed both hands on the cold metal handle and pulled.

The door stuck. Claire pulled again, grunting with the effort. She felt the door lift slightly, then catch. It was locked. Where would he put the key? Most people kept it near the freezer. Claire ran her hand over the rough joists behind the freezer. Splinters of wood stabbed into her. On the third joist she felt a nail protruding from the wood. Her fingers curled around the small key. They shook as she inserted it into the lock and turned it. She pulled on the handle. Nothing happened. Grasping the handle with both hands, Claire pulled again. With a pop, the lid jerked open.

A tiny bulb cast an eerie glow on the interior. White, gallon-sized plastic containers lined its bottom. Claire counted, five of them. She picked up the nearest one. It was coated with ice and numbed her fingers. She pried off the lid. Her gasp was involuntary. A human kidney. She slammed the lid of the freezer shut. It was true. Even through closed eyes she could see the semicircular blood-stain on the bed of ice surrounding the organ. Her own blood felt as cold as the inside of the freezer.

Claire stumbled several times in her hurry to get back to the door. She yanked on the handle and prayed. Still locked. She listened for noises outside the shed. All she heard was the pounding of her heart and the hum of the freezer.

There was a small stool nearby. She needed to rest, needed to be ready. She placed the stool behind the door. Sitting down, she leaned against the shed wall. It was several minutes before her heart rate settled. The chloroform was still affecting her. She needed to gather her strength.

She looked at the freezer and shuddered. His trophies. And now he was planning to add another one to the collection. Well, damn him. Claire strode back to the freezer. She yanked the cord out of the outlet, opened the lid, and picked up the first container.

The sound of an engine jerked her back to her senses and she hurried back to the door. Her heart raced, a lump grew in her throat. Maybe someone had come to rescue her. She peered through the dirt-stained window.

The van pulled up beside the house. Claire hid behind the door. It wasn't long before she heard him coming towards the shed. With each footstep her heart rate accelerated. Would he hear the pounding when he opened the door?

She heard him fumble with the lock. The handle turned and the door swung open. Her mouth went dry. Each breath burned as it traveled her constricted throat. His dark form filled the doorway, blocking out the sun. He crossed the threshold and spoke.

"Claire."

His voice was soft, not much more than a whisper. "Claire, I'm back."

He entered the shed, passing where she hid, her body pressed into the wall behind the door. Only then did she remember the shovel still leaning against the workbench. How could she have been so stupid? There was no way to get it now. He was past the door and crossing toward the stainless steel bed, the empty bed. She had to make a run for it. Claire pulled the door open. Its rusty hinges squeaked. She glanced over her shoulder.

He hadn't noticed. His focus was on the freezer, the open-lidded freezer. He screamed when he saw the white plastic containers lined up in front of the freezer, their lids removed and the contents exposed to the heat of the day.

Claire ran out the open door.

After the dim shed, she squinted against the sun's glare. Her vision impaired, all she could see were the shed, a wooded area, and a driveway leading to the farmhouse. She bolted for the trees.

Her legs were wobbly and she stumbled several times before reaching the tree line. She kept running, deeper and deeper into the woods. The ground was damp and she skidded frequently. Once she tripped over a protruding root and landed on all fours. She scrambled to her feet and kept going. Her breath came in a series of rapid gulps.

Branches crashed behind her. She kept going. The sounds got closer. Something hard hit her right shoulder. The force knocked her to the ground. She flung out her arms to break her fall. The ground was solid. Sharp pain stabbed her shoulder and she felt the warm trickle of fluid down her arm. Blood.

Her shirt stuck to her arm as the bleeding increased. Then he was on top of her. Claire struggled. He shoved her into the ground. She twisted. His weight pinned her down. She tried to push him away, she tried to reach her back pocket, she tried to reach the screwdriver. He grabbed her arms and held them close to her body. He lay on top of her, panting, his sweat dripping on her exposed neck. Claire turned her face away from the foul odor of his breath.

Then his arms wrapped around her and he jerked her to her feet. With one arm he clamped her to his chest and pinned her arms to her sides. His other hand circled her throat. His fingers pressed into her windpipe. Claire fought to breathe.

Slowly, he dragged her back to the shed.

CHAPTER 65

Rosko made it to Delaware in record time. Backup was on the way. He needed to find Powalski's property. Myers called with the concession line and nearest crossroads but Rosko wasn't familiar with the area. He needed help.

"Dispatch?"

"Sir."

"Patch me through to the local sheriff. See if he knows where the hell this place is.

"I'm on it," she responded.

"How far away is back up?"

"Four units are on their way. Right now, they're about ten minutes outside of Delaware."

"Keep me posted."

Homes grew closer together as he approached the town core. Rosko disregarded the speed limit. A small gas station was on the right hand side of the road. He veered into the driveway. An attendant lumbered out of the store. Rosko snapped. "Do you know of a Jefferson Powalski? He's got a place somewhere around here."

"Nope."

Rosko tried to recall the name of his aunt. Payne. Lillian Payne. That was it.

"Do you know of a place owned by Paynes?"

"Lots of Paynes around here." The attendant answered in a slow drawl. Everything about the kid was slow.

"Lillian Payne."

"Oh, that one. Yeah. About five miles back the way you came, third concession, take a couple of rights, and then go to the end of the road."

The pavement squealed as Rosko stormed away from the station. A couple of revs of the siren kept the roadway clear. He made sure it was off before he made his first right turn. The old farmhouse lay at the end of a long dirt road. Farmer's fields, trees, isolated farmhouses were all he'd seen for miles.

Lots of privacy.

He cruised past the long driveway to the house leaving the car near the road, out of site. He went the rest of the way on foot.

Where the hell was backup? He couldn't wait. The bastard might have Claire. He prayed he wasn't already too late. Visions of Sherry's lifeless body flashed through his mind, then Claire's face superimposed the reporter's dead one. He shook the image away. He couldn't think of that now. He didn't know for sure if Powalski had Claire. He needed to concentrate on the job. He needed to arrest Powalski.

Rosko snapped the holster of his Glock then adjusted his Kevlar vest.

Keeping to the trees, he ran towards the farmhouse. He picked his way until he came to the back of the white van parked in the driveway. The license plate was a match and the hood still felt warm. He peered through the window. The van was empty. He circled the house. No activity there. Was that a noise from the shed? He slipped the Glock out of the holster, flipped off the safety, and headed toward the outbuilding.

CHAPTER 66

Claire screamed but only a strangled cry crossed her lips. Her chest hurt. Her throat burned, every breath scalded, every breath a struggle.

Powalski had kept pressure on her throat all the way back to the shed. Halfway back, her energy sapped. She'd stopped fighting. Like a limp Raggedy Ann, he'd dragged her back. Her shins thunked against the doorframe. She gasped as pain shot up her legs. The agony intensified as her feet bumped and banged with each step he took across the cement floor.

Yanking a fistful of her hair, he shoved her onto the bed. Claire struggled frantically. Her heart galloped like a thoroughbred in a derby. She couldn't let him tie her up. She knew she wouldn't escape again. She twisted away from his grip. Her hair tore from its roots. She yelped as a searing pain tore through her scalp. He slapped her face. Her head reeled and she felt the imprint of his hand on her cheek. He reached for a cord.

Claire felt his grip loosen and twisted sideways. Drawing up her knee, she rammed it between his thighs. His body curling into a fetal position, he grunted with pain. Releasing his hold, his hands shot to protect his precious jewels.

She was free.

Scrambling to her feet, she stood above him. The blow wouldn't incapacitate him for long. She gasped for a lungful of oxygen. She had to stop him. How? Her heart rate slowed to a trot as she thought of all the women he'd killed, thought of herself on that stainless steel table, refused to see her body on a slab in the morgue. Drawing the screwdriver out of the loop of her jeans, she raised it above her shoulder. Claire took a deep breath, brought her arm down in a wide arc and rammed it into the middle of his chest. Then she pulled down on the handle with all the strength she had left.

Blood erupted from his chest. She released her hold and stumbled backwards. The blade remained imbedded just below his left clavicle.

His face contorted in shock and pain. Bright blood spurted out of the wound. He pressed his hand over the site. It did little to stop the bleeding.

Claire stood fixed to a spot a safe distance away. Had she hit an artery? That would account for the way the blood was pouring out. She couldn't believe she'd stabbed him. She was a doctor; trained to save lives, not take them. But how many women had he watched bleed to death? Now, it was happening to him.

Pulling off his T-shirt, he bunched it into a ball and pressed it against the open wound. He winced as the screwdriver shifted. Blood stained the cloth within seconds. Anger raged in his pale eyes. He staggered after her. Despite the hand pressed over the wound, the blood continued to spew.

She heard a noise at the door, squeaking hinges. Sunlight streamed into the room, then a large silhouette filled the space. Rosko. Claire sighed in relief, relief that vanished in a second when she sensed Powalski behind her. Out of the corner of her eye, she saw his hands reaching. She lurched sideways. His fingers twisted into the strands of her hair. Her head jerked backward. She winced.

Powalski yanked her body against him until it formed a barricade between himself and Rosko's drawn gun. He twisted his hand again, wrapping a hank of brown hair around his wrist, pulling until it strained at the roots. She yelped. The sound distorted as he snapped her head back until it was cheek to cheek with his. The stubble on his face scraped her flesh, the scent of his sweat overpowering. She gagged.

"Let her go." Rosko stood just inside the shed door, his gun aimed at Powalski's head, his voice deadly calm.

"Drop the gun," Powalski shouted back.

"You can't get away. Within minutes, this place will be crawling with cops."

"Drop the gun, or I'll kill her."

Directives raced through Rosko's head, all the prescribed ways of dealing with the situation. Damned rules. All well and good until you were in the situation and emotion clouded the way. He made another attempt to reason with the man.

"Powalski, you can't get away. Give up before anything else happens. You're bleeding pretty good there. We need to get that thing out of your chest." Rosko paused. His voice took on a conversational tone. "Now, just let her go."

Powalski yanked Claire's head back. The blood oozing from his wound had eased, but the blade remained imbedded in his chest. Claire shifted to squint at her attacker.

His eyes flashed, raging with an edge of insanity. His fingers curled around the handle of the screwdriver. A cruel smile played at his mouth. With a quick wrench, he pulled the tool's blade out of his chest. Blood spurted from the wound. He paid no attention. Instead, he stared at the bloodied metal shaft. His lips contorted as he placed the jagged tip into the delicate curve of Claire's throat. She felt blood from the blade drip down her neck. She also felt as if every drop of her own blood had drained away.

"Drop the gun, Rosko."

Rosko placed the gun on the floor. "Let her go."

"Now, kick it over here."

Not taking his eyes off Powalski, Rosko kicked the gun with his right foot. It landed two feet away from the man.

Shielded by Claire, Powalski shuffled toward the gun. He used his foot to drag it closer then bent to pick it up. As one hand scooped the gun, the other relaxed slightly. Claire felt her hair slipping out of his hold and clutched at her chance. She wriggled and squirmed and twisted until his hold broke. She staggered backwards, turned, ran.

Behind her she heard sounds of a scuffle. She didn't look back until she was twenty feet away. Rosko had lunged for Powalski and both men were on the floor, struggling for the gun. There was a loud retort. The gun flew through the air. Blood dripped from a wound on the detective's left temple. He struggled to get up. He was on his knees, he went limp, then he was falling. His body crumpled in a heap on the cement floor. Claire stared at his lifeless body.

Hearing a thud, she turned. Powalski weaved towards her. He held the blood-covered screwdriver in his outstretched hand. Her eyes darted around the room. The shovel leaned against the workbench five feet away. She raced for it. Trembling fingers clenched the wooden handle.

Claire turned abruptly. Her grip tightened. Powalski was closing in. She raised the shovel above her shoulders. It made only a slight whoosh as it swung through the air.

The blade of the shovel hit him full on the top of the head. He staggered drunkenly to the ground, fell motionless at her feet. The shovel thudded to the floor. Unable to move, Claire stared at him.

His breathing was shallow, his color pale, and his body limp. Was he unconscious?

Cautiously Claire leaned over his body. Her fingers pressed at the base of his jawbone. The blood flow in his carotid artery felt weak and slow. She estimated the rate in the forties. He didn't respond to her touch. How long would he remain unconscious? Blood continued to ooze from the wound in his chest. She had no idea how much damage the screwdriver had done.

Across the room, lay the detective's slumped form. She needed to check him. What were his injuries? She was afraid to find out. Was he even alive? If he were, she needed to get them both of them out of here fast.

The threat of Powalski rousing and recapturing her forced her into action. His body blocked her way. Carefully, she stretched her right leg over him. Her left leg was still in the air when something brushed her pant leg. She looked down. Powalski's right hand shot up and grabbed her leg. His fingers clenched around her ankle. Claire tried to shake her leg free. His fingernails dug into her skin.

Claire closed her eyes, took a deep breath, and shot her foot upward. Her ankle flew out of his grasp. Her leg continued its upward path unbalancing her and she stumbled forward. Stretching her arms out in front of her, she broke her fall, then jumping to her feet, she looked behind her. Powalski was rolling onto his side, trying to gather his legs beneath him.

She had to stop him. Where was the shovel? She remembered dropping it and hearing it clatter to the floor. She glanced behind her. It lay several feet away. Could she reach it before he got up and came after her again? She ran, clutched the handle, swung it at him. It hit him on the shoulder, knocked him back to the ground. He tried to get up. Claire hit him again. Finally he lay still.

Would that stop him?

Claire looked around. What if he got up again? Where was the gun? She'd never used one before. Could she now? She stepped back and her hip hit the edge of the workbench. The bottle in her jean pocket began to slide out. Claire pushed it back into her pocket. Her hand remained on its neck. Could she use it? She didn't want to.

Powalski began to moan. He rolled slowly onto his back. Claire saw a cold gleam in his eyes. The corners of his lips turned up. "I'll get you Claire," he whispered.

Gasping, she leaned back against the workbench. What would it take to stop him? She looked at the shovel. It lay where she'd dropped it, a foot away from him. There was no way she could reach it. She saw the leather gloves. Her hands were slipping into them before she realized what she was doing. Then the pesticide bottle was in her hands and she was twisting the cap.

He was on his knees now. Claire watched in horror as he worked his way upright. He took a faltering step towards her. She tightened her grip on the bottle. He took another step. His body swayed. He reached out to grab her.

Claire closed her eyes. She remembered his hands on her mouth, his hands on her neck, his hands tightening until she could no longer breath. The cap was off the bottle. The liquid sprayed in a golden arc that hung like a rainbow in the air for several seconds before cascading over his face and upper torso. Glistening yellow fluid streamed down his body. He lunged at her. Her fingers clenched the bottle, she raised her hand and sprayed the final contents of the bottle at him. Some of the liquid landed in his open mouth, some landed on his chin, some on his neck. The rest trickled down through the V of his T-shirt.

He shivered as the cold fluid made contact with his skin. Still he came at her.

She shook the bottle, releasing the last few drops, then flung it at him. He put a hand out to intercept the bottle. The action unbalanced him, he staggered, then his body was tipping, swaying, falling to the ground. He lay still. With her foot, Claire pushed him over. He flopped onto his side.

Claire held her breath waiting for him to get up, come at her again. But he lay there, his eyes open, the whites glistening, the pupils dilated. Suddenly, he began to sputter and cough. Claire ran.

She had to check Rosko. Was he still alive? Bending over his unconscious body, she felt his neck for a pulse. Blood bounded through the artery. A loud sigh escaped her. The pulse was a bit slow, but it was strong and steady. Her fingers probed the wound at the left side of his temple. It was only a graze. She prayed he'd rouse soon. Could she drag his unconscious body out of the shed? She had to try.

Sliding her arms under his shoulders she began to lug him out of the shed. He was dead weight and it took her several seconds to move even a few inches. Claire glanced back at Powalski. He lay on his back, his arms clutching his chest. Between spasms of coughing, she heard a wheezing sound as he breathed in and out. Fluid was building up in his lungs. She tried to ignore the sound and concentrate on getting Rosko and herself to safety.

The detective's car had to be close by. If she got out of the shed, she could use his car phone to radio for help. She braced her feet and tugged again. The surface was uneven and Rosko moaned as Claire dragged him over the cement floor. She pulled harder, made it to the door. Rosko winced when she hauled him over the ragged wooded edges of the doorframe.

The glare of the sun hit her in the face, blinding her. She squinted but kept moving. Several feet from the shed, Claire positioned Rosko on his side and ran to find his car. The radio was on and they were calling for him. Claire depressed the button on the receiver and screamed into the handset. "Help us, please."

"Who is this?" a female dispatcher demanded.

"Claire Valincourt. Detective Rosko is here. He's been shot. I think it's just a graze, but we need an ambulance here, now. He's still unconscious."

"Help's on the way. I'll send an ambulance."

"Send two. Tell them there's been a Parathion poisoning." Claire spelled the word to the dispatcher.

"Got it. Stay on the line," the dispatcher told her.

"No. I have to get back to him."

Claire dropped the receiver and raced back to Rosko. He was still where she'd left him, but now conscious enough to attempt to move. He was trying to turn over. She rushed to him. His eyes opened slowly, but it took several seconds before the glazed look faded and he could focus. He shook his head when he recognized Claire.

"What happened?"

Claire quickly told him. Before she was finished he was trying to get up.

"No. Lie still. You're okay."

Rosko struggled to his knees. Claire put out a hand to restrain him but he was already struggling to his knees.

"Help's coming."

He shook his head. "Powalski, where is he? Have to check on him…"

"He shot you, but I think it just grazed the skin."

Rosko put his hand to the spot at his temple where blood continued a slow trickle.

"Does it hurt?"

Rosko nodded slowly as if the effort increased the pain.

"Stubborn and a hard head. I'll have to remember that."

"Stay here. I'm going to check on him."

"It's okay. He won't be killing any more women," Claire reassured him.

"What?"

She relayed the events following his shooting. Determined to see for himself, he let Claire help him get to his feet. Once upright, he was more stable and together they walked back to the shed.

Powalski lay on his side where he'd fallen. He held his chest and coughed spasmodically. His cheeks were flushed purple with the effort. Splotches of blood speckled the phlegm that spattered the floor beside him. Blood-tinged spittle oozed from the corner of his mouth. A similar red fluid trickled from his left nostril.

His clenched fist dug into his chest. Pain and terror reflected in his constricted facial muscles and clouded his constricted pupils. He tried to move but his muscles allowed him no more than a feeble effort. His head turned toward them. His lips moved but his words were jumbled.

Claire saw a slight twitch by his left eye. It happened again. The twitch moved to his right eye. His left check jerked. The twitching radiated to the right side of his face. His right arm jerked and his eyes rolled back in his head. The spasms spread to his other arm. Within seconds it radiated to both legs, then his body writhed as he went into a grand mal convulsion.

Rosko bent to touch him.

Claire grabbed his arm and pulled it back. "No. Don't. The insecticide is all over him. It leeches out to the skin. You can't touch him with your bare hands. It will get on your skin. We can't even get close to him. We could be overcome by the fumes from his body."

So they stood helplessly by and watched his body jerk violently several more times before going limp. He lay still for several seconds before his body suddenly lurched violently. He took one last ragged gasp then went still. His eyes grew dull, staring lifelessly out of their sockets.

Rosko and Claire stood silently, shoulders touching, as blood and spittle oozed out of the flaccid corners of Powalski's mouth. His motionless body took on a bluish tinge. Claire had taken an oath to help people, and tomorrow she could feel all the guilt she wanted for not rushing to make him comfortable in his last moments, but not now, not now. Tomorrow would be time enough for that.

Rosko's arm went around her shoulders and together they walked back to his car. The whine of sirens echoed through the evening sky. "Come on, Claire, let's go home."

About the Author

Award-winning author Bev Irwin lives in London, Ontario with three assorted cats and a collie-cross, named Tiff. Her three children have flown the coup. As a registered nurse, she likes to add a touch of medical to her romance and mystery novels. She also writes YA, children's and poetry. She prefers spending time in her garden, writing and reading to being in the kitchen. For her romance novels, she writes under the pen name of Kendra James.

Made in the USA
Charleston, SC
02 February 2013